Science Fiction

HARM'S WAY

COLIN GREENLAND

Other Avon Books by
Colin Greenland

TAKE BACK PLENTY

HARM'S WAY

WAY

COLIN GREENLAND

AVON BOOKS
A division of
The Hearst Corporation
1350 Avenue of the Americas
New York, New York 10019

Copyright © 1993 by Colin Greenland
Cover art by [illegible]
Published by arrangement with the author
Library of Congress Catalog Card Number: [illegible]
ISBN: [illegible]

All rights reserved, which includes the right to reproduce this book or portions thereof in any form whatsoever except as provided by the U.S. Copyright Law. For information address Avon Books.

First AvoNova Printing: [illegible]

AVONOVA TRADEMARK REG. U.S. PAT. OFF. AND IN OTHER COUNTRIES, MARCA REGISTRADA, HECHO EN U.S.A.

Printed in the U.S.A.

AVON BOOKS • NEW YORK

AVON BOOKS
A division of
The Hearst Corporation
1350 Avenue of the Americas
New York, New York 10019

ISBN: 0-380-76883-6

In Memoriam

ANGELA CARTER

Fireworker

Either for honor or for expectation of profit, or from that unconscious necessity by which a great people, like a great man, will do what is right, and must do it at the right time, whoever had the means to furnish a ship, and whoever had the talent to command one, laid their abilities together and went out to pioneer, and to conquer, and to take possession, in the name of the Queen of the Sea.

JAMES ANTHONY FROUDE
"England's Forgotten Worthies"

And this shall be my dream to-night:
I'll think the heaven of glorious spheres
Is rolling on its course of light
In endless bliss through endless years.

EMILY BRONTË
"How Clear She Shines"

So many worlds, so much to do,
So little done, such things to be.

ALFRED, LORD TENNYSON
In Memoriam A. H. H.

Contents

Rain. Rain on a foul, chill, smoky day at the thin end of November. It rains at a quarter of ten, sullen and steady as it has rained all morning. It rains as though it has never done anything but rain; as though it means never to do anything else ever again.

By Divine Order, it rains, and like the Mercy of Heaven, dropping on the Cathedral of St. Paul; the great gray dome of Sir Christopher's monument shines with rain. Below in the City, like the bounty of all the worlds, it rains, on the pinnacle of the Exchange where Urania stands, arms wide to gather it in. Water runs from her marble elbows. Down the spires of many a lesser church it courses, and cascades down the lofty windows of Garlick Hill where the telescopes stand idle. There will be nothing to view today: no stars; no ships, though the entire Fleet under full sail should pass by overhead; nothing but the rain, which abides no man his entertainments, and goes tumbling heartlessly on, down toward the little and low streets, that are all barnacled with cockeyed roofs and squinting casements. Evenhandedly it pours on both the cab that comes jolting into view and the beggars tagging along behind, a mixed gaggle of urchins elbowing with a tattered brood of Cæruleans, blue as forget-me-nots.

The cab stops by the corner. The alien beggars jump up on the mudguards and paw the door, squealing and whining for alms.

"*Get out of it!*" The cabman curses the whole pack in a growl. The urchins take this as a signal to jostle harder, with jeers and cuffs. "Holloa the Blue Boys!" they shout, and whistle, stretching with their filthy fingers the corners of their mouths.

Nothing happens. The door of the cab does not open. The cabman shoulders his whip and ignores them. He ignores everything. He sits hunched in his greatcoat, oblivious, impervious to the rain.

The rain pelts the cabman's hat. It pools in the upturned brim and streams down behind his back onto the roof of his cab; spills over onto the hindquarters of his long-suffering horse; trickles thence, as by a process of natural justice, down the necks of the struggling beggars; and sinks, like all things at last, into the mud.

Hunched under a single umbrella and holding an empty shopping basket between them, two women come splashing hastily around the corner. Though it is a filthy day, when none but dogs and desperate men would be out of doors, yet there are mouths to feed. The women take no notice of the cab as they go by, though one of them turns and shouts something angry and admonitory at one of the urchins.

No sooner have the women run past and disappeared into the rain than the cab door opens finally and a man leans out. He seems to be an ordinary human man, in a peacoat and muffler and so forth, though he has come out without his hat and wears his coat collar turned up against the vileness of the day. He takes out a couple of ha'pence and throws them back up the street, scattering the beggars, who run after them. Descending, he does not look up at his stoical charioteer but knocks with his knuckles on the side of the vehicle; and we see that neither has he any gloves. The cabman clicks his tongue and the cab jolts away along the street.

Reconvening around the erstwhile passenger in hope—for those who have nothing must always have hope—the beggars look up. Between the wings of the collar they see the white wedge of a man's face, a man of perhaps five-and-thirty years, clean-shaven. He is a short man with a broad head and brown curly hair. With his cab and his practiced handful of coppers, and a gold signet ring which the sharp eyes of the little blue men were quick to spot on his finger, he might almost be a gentleman; but his trousers are plain dun worsted and his boots are ungaitered and dull. For certain he is no one who belongs to these poor streets; nor does he look like one who might have business here—not a tradesman; not a bailiff's man; nor a policeman either. He looks very much like no one in particular. He may be some kind of sailor, in that coat. Hc has the sailor's air of being equal to all places, beneath this grim sky or any other. The way he thrusts his hands into his coat pockets and walks briskly off between the beggars, with his head up and heedless of mud and puddles, declares him for a man of purpose and one who will never in his life lose his way, even here in the lowest and most entwining entrails of the mother of cities.

A deep bell tolls the hour as he rounds the corner and enters the dismal back street from which the women came. A sign on the wall above his head reads: Turkey Passage. The visitor passes it without inspection. The rain continues.

The beggars have already dispersed, vanishing back into their murky dens. Perhaps the speed of their departure was not unconnected with the two tall, powerful silhouettes that have come hurrying through the rain, across the street and around the corner after the unparticular man. Two huge, high-shouldered figures they seem to be, in greatcoats and with what look like enormous Scotch bonnets on their heads. They move through the clinging mud with an easy lope that speaks of origins on a world of fiercer gravity than this. Whether the man knows he has acquired these menacing adherents, there is no way to tell. His back is most uncommunicative.

The two shadows sidle into deeper shadows in low adjoining doorways. Though the thoroughfare is so narrow, they are lost to view. Perhaps a keen ear might hear them breathing, harsh and deep as aged bulldogs. Or perhaps that is the hissing of the rain.

The unparticular man walks directly down Turkey Passage to a particular door, quite as though he had been there before. He knocks, and waits. While he stands there a rat runs over his boot. He kicks at it, and is rewarded by a shrill squeal. He does not smile. Nor does he look over his shoulder, at the deep shadows of the doorways behind him. He waits, and thinks of nothing at all.

A young girl, thin and pale with some twelve starveling city summers, cracks the door to look at him. She looks at him doubtfully. She does not know him, and it is early yet for customers.

"Molly," the man says in a low tone; and the doorkeeper stands back without a word to let him in.

As he crosses the threshold, the unparticular man gives the girl a single, searching look. A future apprentice in the trade, no doubt. Too old to concern him, her thin young face already grave with ancient cares. He dismisses her from his attention.

The hallway of the house is narrow and black as a coal mine. In the open door of the front room a man stands leaning against the wall. He does not greet the visitor, though he inspects him. He is a large hulk of a man like a hulk of timber. His sleeves are rolled up, and the arms crossed across his bulwark of a chest are blue with old tattoos. The grip of a bludgeon protrudes an inch from his belt.

The visitor is not offended. He likes things to be clear. He ignores the bully as he ignores the girl.

The hallway reeks of damp, and boiled vegetables. There is the thin, piteous sound of a baby crying in a room somewhere at the back of the premises.

"Take your coat sir?" says the girl.

The visitor does not respond. Perhaps he is a foreign gentleman, and understands no English.

The girl is supposed to take their hats, if they have 'em, and their coats, if they will, as a surety; but if they won't, there's an end of it. Moreover, she is supposed to quiz any customer she doesn't know to make sure he has money; but there is something about this one's very impassivity that checks her. She glances at the bully, but he does not move or speak.

"Upstairs at the front," the girl says. She leaves the hall while the caller starts to mount the stairs. He is a man, and of no more account than other men. The girl returns to her other chores; to the kitchen, and the crying child.

The door to Molly's room is ajar. She opens it to his knock. There she stands in the doorway, a grubby dressing gown of some worn shiny stuff in powder blue and pink pulled around her ample frame. She smiles at him as if she has known him for years. It is a smile of the lips and teeth that does not much concern the eyes. A bitter smell escapes from the room behind her, composite of powder and sea coal and gin, and the reek of tired, coarse flesh.

Molly's visitor spends a moment considering her, dispassionately, as if through the eyes of another man. Her figure is plump, bosomy: the motherly kind, who tends to men's woes. Her head of bright orange curls she owes to a bottle. Even at this hour her face is powdered and painted, her mouth a broad, succulent bow of carmine lipstick. Above it, her black-lined eyes are tired, creased at the corners by her life, though there is life in them yet. She looks like forty pretending to be twenty, is perhaps halfway in between, as far as the calendar is concerned. She does not look diseased.

The unparticular man makes an unconscious gesture, running the tip of his finger down his cheek.

"Come in, sir, don't stand out there in the cold."

Her voice. Her voice is melodious. That would have had a lot to do with it.

He reaches once again in his pocket and puts money on the table by the bed. He handles it vaguely, casually, as if it has no value to him, as if he has too much of it to give it any attention.

Molly Clare too is now wondering if perhaps he is a foreign gentleman. "Lord bless you, sir," she says. By the gratitude in her voice it is apparent to him he has given her plenty, not that it matters.

He glances around her boudoir. It is not as grim as its setting. There are even lace curtains at the narrow window, and a fussy green plant in a pot. A coal fire burns in a small grate. Between that and the bed stands a wicker chair, its arms and seat bowed from the weight of Molly's body. On the mantelpiece are a few knickknacks or ornaments—gifts, conceivably, from gratified patrons, for there are pieces that seem to be bronze and jade rather than the gimcrack and painted plaster one might expect in the room of such a woman. In fact, for all the foulness of its purpose, the whole room has a coziness to it that seems to set at naught the world of mud and rats and cold November rain.

Her bed is of iron, and her washbasin enamel. Her visitor sees that beneath the bed her chamber pot has a cloth over it. Meanwhile Molly has cast off her dressing gown and poured water, and has started washing under her arms and under her shift. She talks to him all the while, in cheerful, complimentary, automatic tones, like a barber. "I know you gentlemen like a girl fresh," she is saying. She has noticed his ring, plain gold with no insignia, and the buttons on his waistcoat, mica from one of the moons of Mars.

He is not listening to what she is saying, and neither is she. He undresses, putting his clothes on the chair. He has decided to have her, a small, secret gesture of defiance, because he was not told not to, and because the implied insult amuses him.

Molly is puzzled. Once, not long ago, it was different; but these days, in this room, there are none but common men, and two kinds only of them: those who are lustful and urgent, and those who are guilty and contemptuous. This one is neither. He remains distant as the stars. As much as he's paying, he says nothing of any special needs or fancies. His prick is hard, but his face is smooth, closed.

He seems like an inspector of women. Molly has heard of men who do that, who travel from port to port, sampling women of every race and kind, like collecting butterflies. Or it may be there is something on his mind. After they spend, some men like to confess to her, to pillow their heads on her soft breasts and tell her all their troubles. Not this one. He is as secret as the grave. She feels obscurely pleased, and kisses his chestnut curls.

He lies with his head on her shoulder, not objecting to the sweat of her stubbled armpit. "You are a good girl, Molly," he tells her, as familiar as you please, and she wonders if perhaps he has been before; but it does not do to let them know you don't remember them, so she lets it go, listening to the sound of the rain on the window, and wondering when the other girls will be back from the shops, and what they will bring for supper.

Her visitor sits up and swings his legs out of bed. He sits with his back to Molly, looking at her bits and pieces on the mantel. He picks one up. It is a photograph in a frame of dark green metal. It shows a woman with corkscrew ringlets, wearing a low-waisted dress, high-sided boots and a Toriodero cap and bolero. She stands against the corner of an Italianate loggia, with a shiny plain and a black sky beyond. There are other people in the background, but they are only incidental, he judges, because it was taken in a populous place. They seem to be ladies and gentlemen of quality, such a crowd as one might see on any night, leaving the opera or ballet.

Their figures are blurred with movement, and none of them is looking at the camera.

The woman is Molly Clare. She is holding a bouquet of white flowers with long, slack petals and smiling a bold smile. The picture is quite recent, no more than two or three years old. It has been curiously cropped, perhaps to fit into the frame: part of her left shoulder is missing.

"What's this picture, Molly?"

She lifts her head to look. "That? That's a holiday souvenir. That's me at the Sea of Tranquillity." She speaks proudly, rolling the long word off her tongue, enjoying the feel of saying it; though there is sadness too in her tone. "D'you know it?" she says.

He does not speak, and it is hard to tell from his uncommunicative back whether he does or not. He merely returns the picture to the mantelpiece, as if it has no interest for him. Molly is not offended. She is at ease now, he has paid for the rest of the day and all night too, if he fancies, for all he was so quick. He is reaching into his clothes on the bedside chair, she supposes for a cigar case. She thinks about a pot of tea.

When he turns back to her, he is holding something out toward her, something slim and black. She thinks it is a cigar and he is offering it to her, fancy that! And she starts to laugh, but stops at once because with his other hand he has taken hold of her hair, pulling her head sharply back. Out of the corner of her eye Molly sees the thing in his hand flash out a light too bright to look at. She hears a low sharp buzz and smells the tang of ozone. She gasps, her red lips framing words that will not come. She sees the damp place on the ceiling whose shape always reminds her of the head of a donkey braying. And then she sees no more.

The blade of his knife is made of light, cold buzzing light. It has poked a tiny slit in her neck, and cauterized the flesh on its way in, so there is very little blood. While Molly Clare's plump hand came up to the place and her tired eyes bulged with shock, trying to focus for the last time, the unparticular man saw a vigor, an anger in her gaze, as of a fighter taken off guard. As though she understood, but was not expecting it, not this morning, not suspecting him. Now, as those eyes fade and fall still, they seem to have filled with a strange exultation, almost with relief. The man is skilled at reading faces, the expressions that come and go in them; yet this expression he cannot interpret. He dismisses it, and lets go of her.

When he squeezes the hilt of the knife, the blade vanishes. He slips the device back into the pocket of his jacket where it hangs on the back of the chair, then retrieves his shirt and underthings, and puts them on. He feels chilly after his exertions. He takes the poker from the stand in the hearth and stirs up the tiny fire. There is a smell of warm wet wool in the room. Pulling on his trousers and settling the braces on his shoulders, the man steps over to the window and opens it. The frame is warped, and squeaks as he pushes it up. Rain splashes on the windowsill and spatters into the cozy room.

The unparticular man does not lean out of the window, but bends down to the gap and puts a whistle to his lips. He blows. No sound that human ears can hear comes from the little instrument; but a shadow stirs in the black mouth of a doorway on the other side of Turkey Passage.

Molly's visitor puts the whistle back in his pocket and closes the window. He makes a cursory search of the cupboards and drawers in her room, such as they are. He finds nothing but feminine fripperies, underclothes, sexual accoutrements, and articles of hygiene; no letters or papers. He seems to be looking for some particular thing, but without finding it. He looks beside the washbasin. Nothing. Now he takes Molly Clare's hands, one, then the other. He looks at her fingers, which are bare. She was a discreet woman. She would not have lasted so long had it been otherwise. Now she lies on the bed, staring fixedly at the ceiling. Since her soul has flown, an indefinable sadness has come into the room. The curly-headed man with the unparticular face sits beside her pulling on his stockings. He hears an indistinct thumping sound from downstairs.

While he fastens his muddied boots he looks again at the picture standing on the mantelpiece. He recognizes no one in it. He destroys it anyway, crumpling it as he pulls it out of the frame and throws it on the fire.

The stairs creak under a weighty tread. The door of Molly's room opens, and in comes one of the tall figures who followed her visitor up the street. His appearance is quite alarming. He is taller than the door, almost too tall for the room, and his head inside the oversize Scotch bonnet is shaped like the head of a hammer, with a large globular eye at each of the ends. His head continues down without the benefit of a neck into his chest, where his shirt has been cut away to accommodate two goitrous organs that continuously swell and flatten like bladders beside his mouth, which is oblong. His skin is a chalky grayish blue color, perhaps from poisoning by this alien air. With his greatcoat open, the smell of him is something between strong cheese and rotting leaves, overcoming the taint of burnt flesh that hangs in the room.

The hands of the intruder are like the paws of a mole, but their hard shiny skin is more like the carapace of a lobster. There is blood on these hands, red human blood. The newcomer gapes at the man sitting on the bed: a bovine, lugubrious expression. The man nods. His accomplice breathes hoarsely, but does not speak. He bends over the bed to attend to Molly with a knife of his own, a perfectly commonplace mild steel skewering knife, such as is used every day by every butcher in the land. There is a vile unnecessary thing to be done with the innards, for the sake of Scotland Yard.

Through the open door Molly's visitor can hear that the baby is no longer crying. Indeed, there is no sound at all from the rest of the house. The man goes downstairs while the brute is about his work, leaving the money on the table beside the bed. He finds another brute at the bottom of the stairs, with another knife. The tattooed bully of the house lies beside him on his back on the floor, his eyes stark and staring with fear he no longer feels, wherever he is. His little club never left his belt. The curly-headed man cocks an eyebrow; ponderously the brute nods. They are Hrad, from the planet Jupiter, or a moon of it. Pushing past, the visitor looks swiftly into the kitchen, and the rest of the rooms downstairs. His assistants have been thorough, in obedience to their instructions. None who lived here does so any longer.

The curly-headed man runs a finger down his face, his unparticular face, and steps out of the back door, pulling up the collar of his peacoat. A puddle reflects him an instant while he pauses, getting his bearings; then he is gone. In a minute more the Hrad have finished their work and leave too, crossing a malodorous yard and loping away along the maze of alleys.

It continues to rain, the foul, chill, smoky rain of old Earth.

1

A most exclusive spot

From the steps of the Aeyrie the visitor can see the ships that come and go from the Port. Today, among the nine o'clock departures we might have marked the frigate *Leventeia* with her Boston rig, and the fearsomely blackened *Criollo* of Aparicio Sarmiento, Admiral of the Argentine. One by one they climb, nosing into the hazy sky, while around and about flock the giant blue dragonflies of the region. With their metallic luster and glinting, faceted eyes these resemble masterpieces of ornamental crystalry, creations of Fabergé animated by clockwork. From this height you would not guess they are the size of eagles. Now they hover high over our heads; now, at the boom and clatter of the opening of the Aeyrie's great doors, they flicker and dart, vanishing away into the diamanté groves far below. Their wings blur like oval slivers of pale light.

The Aeyrie is a very private institution, and not easy of access. These portals of darkly gleaming local mahogany are removed from all but the men best qualified to reach them: those who come out of the sky; by means of the abstruse conductivity of space itself. For the Aeyrie is the Headquarters of the Most Worshipful Guild and Exalted Hierarchy of Pilots of the Aether. It is their college, their club, their Livery Hall. Here each man comes, first as a cadet reporting for training; then as a freeman, to check the postings and catch up on the news; and finally as a master of the craft, to relax between jaunts and quaff a bumper or two, to loosen his belt and collar and let the cares of his calling slide from his shoulders. In the saloon and in the private dining rooms he may entertain his fellows and associates; a good deal of business is done around the bar and on the veranda. The fair sex is not admitted, to the guild or to its sanctum: neither women nor conversations about women, though that old rule is dishonored daily.

Thus every pilot in the system has occasion to put in an appearance at the Aeyrie. Some of them practically live here. In the cool and spacious foyer, out of the sun, are generously proportioned ottomans where a member has only to sit and wait, and anyone he wants to see will eventually come strolling across the yellow carpet. That is where we find Captain Arthur Thrace of the *Unco Stratagem*, sitting and looking about him.

Today there is a larger group than usual of idlers, reading the papers and gossiping around the notice-boards. Last night Habbakuk of the Low North-West received the Master's Silver Medal, and there was much jollity in the commons. Mr. Habbakuk failed to finish his ale at one swallow and the Master's portrait was drenched with a soda siphon; even now the slaves are still cleaning up. The Master himself, Lord Lychworthy, twenty-eighth Earl of Io, was not present for the ceremony, which was performed by his emissary, Mr. Cox. His Lordship is rarely here, but Captain Thrace can see a good sample of the exalted and worshipful: Commodore Delauney having a word with the porter, no doubt asking him to keep an eye on his son; the Sarkar of New Borneo nodding respectfully as he passes the old hands, grim faced and gaunt, who occupy the best seats in the bar. It is obvious just from looking at them that these scarred old men know every inch of the flux; their very bones are hollow from the blowing of the solar wind.

Around them slump pale specimens in neckscarves, habitual inhabitants of the fug of the inner commons. Inert and uncommunicative, they lounge all day in low armchairs drinking scotch and soda, wearing their purple glasses but never seeing the sun. See where the Ophiq steward appears, ledger in his large fist, to confer with one of them in the matter of an outstanding account. And there, in the hallway by the stairs, did you catch that glimpse of a white satin cloak? It is a starman, on his way up to pray. The east wing of the Aeyrie contains a whole floor of meditation rooms, each with its single white chrysanthemum or small bowl of beaten brass. Starmen are ascetics to a man, devotees of the inner arcana of the mystery.

They are the pure-hearted knights of space, and disapprove of the lack of spiritual refinement in their lowlier brethren. It is his devotion to the physical world, the starmen believe, that keeps the subsolar pilot paddling in the shallows of space.

Yet that slender white-caped figure sailing lightly upstairs has more than he imagines in common with the japesters and sluggards here below. Both world-hoppers and starmen are Romantics. All pilots are Romantics. These men with their Canopan cigars or their zen contemplations, they will be all gone in three days' time. Look for them then beyond Ceres, out on the open way. Then you will see them in very truth, in full array upon the bridge of some six-master, then when they place the circlet of gold about their brows and open their mind's eye to the current of the flood—that is their purpose and their joy. To stand on deck, your foot braced on a spar, and look out in the hard glare of space at the sails, yards of sheer white-black nothing, gossamer-thin, spread out across leagues of nothing blacker yet—to see them spread and swell in the aether wind—to raise your hand and point the way of fresh tides and high streams where the ship can run—what greater glory has life to offer? There they go, the stars in their eyes, and in their ears the pure high song of the void. God speed them! Without them the worlds would scarcely turn—shops and larders could not be filled—the explorers of the great empires of Earth could not go forth to shake hands with their brothers under other suns.

Mr. Cox, Lord Lychworthy's emissary, is already aboard his master's yacht the *Unco Stratagem*, ready and waiting to leave. The pilot for the Earthbound run is late, as usual. That is why the captain has been obliged to come down in person to fetch him. And of course, he is nowhere to be found. He is not in the commons; nor in the garden; nor yet on the roof, where his kind like to gather. That is why Captain Thrace has fetched up here, on the ottoman nearest the door, on the very edge of the ottoman. One or two men nod civilly as they pass, seeing the crest on his uniform, but nobody else sits on his ottoman, though there is plenty of room. Captain Thrace is not a member of the Pilots' Guild.

Spotting a gentleman in need of service, the steward toddles up and stands directly in front of the captain. Their eyes are on a level. "Sir?" says the steward in his fluting voice.

"Oh. Ah," says Captain Thrace. He clears his throat. "I—ah, ahem—don't suppose you've seen Mr. Crii today, have you, steward?"

"What you suppose is true, sir," toots the steward. The captain flinches from the earnestness of his tone. He looks away, then back at him, doubtfully.

"Beauregard Crii," says the captain. "You do know him?"

"I do, sir." The steward remembers Mr. Crii perfectly, and his father. He remembers Mr. Habbakuk's father, and Lord Lychworthy's father, and all their fathers, for the talent runs that way, and the Ophiq are a race of marked longevity.

The steward is greatly vexed by the outrage done to the Master's portrait. He is afraid that this man, whom he knows by sight, will mention the incident to Mr. Cox, who will be obliged to report it to the Master himself. Clapping his huge hands he summons a page, and sends him about the halls to call for Mr. Crii.

Meanwhile Captain Thrace looks around the foyer, over the bald brown dome of the steward's head. He takes out a perpetuatum-stained handkerchief and blows his nose. The acidity of the air is annoying him. "I imagine he's not in yet," he says gruffly.

"To imagine is free," says the steward.

"What?" exclaims the captain.

"Truth is not to be denied, sir."

"Ah. Hm. H'mm-hm." The captain folds his hands and glumly considers the unreliability of angels. Mr. Crii, confound him, will turn up when it pleases him and not apologize for being late. It would no more occur to an angel to apologize for anything than it would to a cat.

The Ophiq, having no waist, cannot bow, but he gives his customary bob, and toots, "May I enquire after his Lordship's health, sir?" He asked the same question of Mr. Cox, of course, but he is helpless to convey his concern without alerting the captain to the state of the painting.

"What?" replies Thrace again, bewildered. "My health? Perfectly fine, h'rrumph, thank ye kindly."

The Ophiq goes light blue. "His Lordship's health," he says.

Captain Thrace realizes he means Lord Lychworthy. "How the devil would I know?" he says, irritably.

The steward is afraid of Lord Lychworthy. He is one of the most powerful men in the universe, and one of the most private. His father had a temper, as did his grandfather, but this one's displeasure is dangerous to incur. He disposes of inadequate staff as other men dispose of gnats. His relatives have a nasty knack of disappearing on odd jaunts to obscure corners of the solar system. With his snout the steward twitches the corner of a disheveled *Telegraph* into line.

Though he has no doubt of the time, Captain Thrace looks up once more at the array of clocks on the wall.

"Nine and thirty-nine, sir," says the steward; and now he tidies abandoned cups onto a tray.

"Thank you," says Captain Thrace stiffly. He continues craning his neck hopelessly around.

Hopefully, the steward pats the captain's boot with his big mitt. The captain jumps. "A pot of tea, sir?" suggests the steward.

"No. H'rrumph. No, thank you, steward." The cleaning slaves have brought a robot to help them. One of the wags is painting a comical face on it with ink. Gouts of steam puff uneasily from its joints.

The steward goes white and rolls the lips of his snout in distress. "A bacon sandwich?" he proposes.

"Nothing, thank you," says the captain, more forcefully than he intends. He is unhappy. Glances are being directed at him over newspapers.

Still the steward lingers. Now his warty hide is starting to blush a dingy yellow, like an unripe satsuma. "To breakfast is sound, sir," he points out.

The captain shuts his eyes. "Yes, humph, harrumph, thank you, I have already eaten," he says. How the devil else can he put it?

It isn't, thinks Captain Thrace, as the little man stumps away at last, that Ophiq are servile. Far from it: they tend to get in and run things while you aren't looking. It's simply their nature to console and advise. It's their way. They like to make each other feel comfortable, and everyone else too.

Captain Thrace is not comfortable. He is not a comfortable man. His job, for one thing, brings him little comfort. What it does bring him is sight and taint of more unpleasantness than he ever dreamed of in the Merchant. And he is never comfortable in the Aeyrie.

Arthur Thrace is not one of those spacemen who hate all pilots on principle. He's known some fine men among them, men he admires, with no nonsense about them. You can't tar them all with the same brush. But since no one can sail far without one, they have become a law unto themselves, especially since the present Master came in. They give themselves airs—seem to think they own the aether, some of them. Those chaps over there in the corner, smoking a hookah and telling lewd stories with their hands. And now here comes one, a Frenchman with a body slave, a dark-eyed little Martian boy in a suit of silk, on the end of a lead. Captain Thrace averts his eyes. The Aeyrie is not for the likes of him.

Captain Thrace looks once more at the clocks. The pressure of time is suddenly palpable to him, like the pressure of this poisonous brew of an atmosphere. Then the page returns, shaking his head. "Tch'ah!" snorts the captain loudly, occasioning a rustle of newspapers. Unable to sit still a moment longer he takes up his cap and puts it on, pulling the visor down over the peak and fastening it at the back. With a curt, impatient nod to the steward, he marches through the saloon and out on the veranda.

Outside fierce sunlight blazes down, flooding every corner of the veranda, but revealing no sign of Mr. Crii. Captain Thrace strides past tables, empty and occupied alike, to the railing, which is made of foot-thick bamboo the color of honey and rises four feet from the deck. The captain braces his arms on it and stands frowning down into the jungle.

The morning haze has dispersed. From up here on the plateau it is like looking down upon a vast confusion of shaggy green lace and spiders' webs. From the narrow ledges of the pearl-colored cliff calendulas straggle and spill, frothing around the spires of *campanilea* that break the cobweb canopy. Their spindles of white florescence look as if they had been carved just this minute, out of wet white soap. Beyond, ten thousand pedestals of red onyx sweep down to the winking turquoise river, bearing urn flowers, majolica cradles, encrustations of giant periwinkle and false amethyst. Giant fawn tulips lie open to the penetrating sun, their throats glistening yellow-white like the meat of a banana.

To Captain Thrace, of course, at this moment everything is purple: purple trees, purple crystals, purple tulips. The beauty of the prospect, which made Rossetti weep, is lost to him through the metallic glass of the visor that shields his eyes from the bruising, razing glare. None but the Pilots would choose to congregate here, high in the Venusian Andes.

The air, pure and fine at this altitude, smells corrosively of arsenical gases and salts of molybdenum; it can inflame the lungs of a novice in minutes. The captain's trade has turned his membranes to leather, yet he feels his nostrils prickle. From this world it was, he reflects, that fifty years ago the Fever came which stormed through the civilized capitals of Earth. He snuffles in his handkerchief.

At that moment the captain hears the sound of his own name. He is being hailed. Wiping his nose, he turns himself about, and there at a table not ten yards distant, his back to the celestial view, sits a guild member he knew in the old days. "Dixon!" he cries and, stowing his handkerchief, goes toward him along the railing.

Capless, perspiring in the sun, Captain Dixon grins up at his old shipmate. "What brings you here?" he asks, in a jovial tone.

"Looking for my pilot," grumbles Captain Thrace.

"Inbound?" asks the other. "You've missed the tide."

Captain Thrace is well aware of that. He thinks of Mr. Cox, the sarcastic rebukes that will be visited upon him when he gets back up: as though it were *his* fault. He bangs his hands on the railing, grunts: "H'rr*umph*," and spits violently out over the shimmering jungle.

Dixon casts an idle eye around the company on the veranda. An Indian waiter walks along the line of crippled veterans in their bath-chairs. Montmorency of the Procyon Corridor, his elbows on the table, stares through his visor at a blob of translucent jelly swimming in a glass tank. There is a chessboard on the table between them. "Who's your man?" asks Dixon.

"Mr. Crii," says Thrace.

"Ah." Dixon pulls a face, a mournful smirk. "The Albatross of the Asteroids," he says unkindly. Beneath the table he kicks the vacant chair. "Sit down, old man," he says. "Have a cup of tea."

Without waiting for Thrace to reply, he signals a waiter for more hot water and a second cup. Gloomily Captain Thrace accepts the unwanted invitation and takes the seat. Across his companion's shoulder he can see a section of the jeweled valley. If he had a telescope, he could follow the shrouded course of the turquoise river that meanders away beneath the lacy greenery. A flock of dragonflies rises up, alarmed by something. Dixon is saying: "You fly for the Master now, I see."

"For the Master's man," says Thrace. He knows that Dixon knew that perfectly well. "On the *Unco Stratagem*," he says; and recalls that Dixon, like many freemen these days, runs his own boat, the *Lory*, a tidy brig. He envies him slightly.

"Congratulations," says Dixon smoothly, swirling the tea around in the pot. "I expect they keep you pretty busy, eh?"

Captain Thrace overlooks the insinuating tone. He is used to people fishing for unsavory gossip. His duties may have altered over the years, but he is proud of his commission and loyal to the last. In any case, even in the seclusion of his estates on Io, Lord Lychworthy hears all, and is swift to deal with anything that smacks of disaffection. He has spies. This man might even be one. "H'rmm," Thrace rumbles, and answers stoutly: "Mr. Cox is bound for London, to give the House his Lordship's opinion on the Ganymede Secession." He fishes a pillbox from his waistcoat pocket and takes out a Nitrox pastille.

Suddenly a pair of angels fly up from beneath the veranda and land with a thump on the rail. They squat there, unnervingly, grooming themselves in the vicious light. Their movements are bestial and strange. In broken French they call for the steward, their hoarse, moaning voices tuneless as the voices of the deaf. They have caught a bird on the wing: it hangs, limp and broken-necked, from a horny fist.

The pair are seven feet tall if they are an inch. They wear white kilts of woven leather, without insignia; their chests are bare beneath the vast collarbone, the thickened shoulders that power those huge white outgrowths, so like a swan's. Their faces have something feline about them, more like a panther than a man. Unprotected, the yellow eyes blink lazily. There are several in the guild, and Venus agrees with them: they look sleeker here than in their native habitat, the bloom of their feathers more lustrous, their taut skin brown as any tanner's.

The steward bustles up, looking blotchy and pained. The angels are demanding to have their catch roasted and brought to them. Their palate is unsuited to the consonants of human speech: they stretch their jaws as though to free the alien sounds from their larynxes.

One of the angels catches sight of Captain Thrace. He dips one wing slightly, and smiles. Thrace knows it for a smile, this baring of carnivorous teeth, the thick, sensual lips drawn up and back. He puts away his pillbox and rises from the table, wiping his hands on one another.

"Mr. Crii."

2

In which I introduce myself

Dear Sir or Madam, whoever you are—permit me to introduce myself. My name is Sophie Farthing. That was the name I used to hear when I was a little girl: the name shouted out by my papa, who was but is no more, whenever he needed food or drink or an audience for his groans.

There, that much is right, at any rate—to begin there, on the High Haven, and recall my life in the house of my papa, and try to tell you it all in order, setting forth everything as it came upon me. Yet even to decide so little I have sat until the ink has dried in the nib of my pen, and I must huff on it to make it flow again. I, who have written so much news, so many greetings and wishes and pleas on behalf of others—ask me for my own story, and I sit staring at the paper.

For nothing ever happened to me on High Haven. I did nothing there but sweep and sew and wash and fetch and carry and *drudge*. I was nobody, and I knew nobody, save Percy the cat and Kappi. When ladies and gentlemen of quality came by me in the street, riding down through Jericho to the Prince

Edward Dock, I went aside, like a good girl, and did not stand gawking but hurried on about my business. Nobody greeted me, for I was nobody's daughter. A tar-mucker's apprentice could push in front of me at the cistern, and tread on my toe, and the women would do nothing but tut and pass remarks, as if it was my fault for being in the way.

Papa, now: he was your man for stories. "The *Nègre Baguido Bago* went by last night," he would tell me, "with her bare yards like the bones of a skellington, and all her rigging in tatters. I saw Lady Archimand herself, Sophie," he would say, while I sat shivering at his knee. "Sitting right on deck, she was, with her fishing line out, fishing for stars! You remember Lady Archimand, Sophie. The one with the cobwebs all over her suit."

Do you know the High Haven, Dear Reader? When you look up from Lambeth Bridge, on a clear night in autumn, to watch some great ship go by, I know you have sometimes seen a glint of light—there, north by northwest when the Moon is waning. That fleck of polished tin, that is High Haven, the flying island, where the men labor in the shipyards and the women of the sail shed cut and sew the precious cloth that bellies in the winds of space. My papa was Mr. Jacob Farthing, night watchman of the Eastern Dock, and our house was the night watchman's cottage on St. Radigund's Wharf, in between a timber merchant's office and a warehouse full of beans and grain.

You think High Haven is a dreary place; a place of trade and confusion, of nuisance and noise. You have only seen the docks, where you have quarreled with some slow official, been given a wrong quay number or discovered your luggage has gone by mistake to the Moon. It is not all like that. The Haven has its share of gentry, like anywhere else, in their glass-roofed houses on Hanover Heights.

"You stay away from there, Sophie! They see you there, they'll call a constable!"

"Why?" I said.

Papa leaned forward in his chair as if to give me a clip around the ear, and I shrank back. "You do as you're told, my girl!" he shouted.

So I stayed in my poor corner; and I think it was indeed the meanest corner in the whole Haven. The cottage was dark, and always dirty. It was hard to keep anything clean there, you may imagine, with the water always to fetch, and bits of dirty straw drifting in from the wharf. And Papa was not able to help me. When he was not asleep he would sit in his chair, talking: giving me orders, warning me of the dangers of the worlds, complaining of his hard life, while I toiled at the stove, making our poor meals out of scraps and scrapings.

Some of Papa's tales were grand. When I was little he used to tell me about the blind harbormaster who could read the flux as well as any pilot, and name each ship by her bow wave; or about the golden caravel of Don Caldero, with her Hottentot bos'n who whistled up the starwind on his pipes. I believed him then. I understood nothing of the power of the black gum I had to fetch, once a week, in a screw of paper from the apothecary. Papa sucked it up in spoonfuls of gin— in a minute he would be describing the gryphons of Uranus for me. "Their beaks can shear plate steel! Their feet char the ground where they walk!" And I would cower on the rug and hug his shins, sure at any moment the fearsome beasts would come walking through the wall. Oh, Papa told me stories— so many stories—but never the one that mattered: never the truth. Never, until the last.

Papa and his stories were all I knew, then, of ships and travel, and all I wished to know. I hated waking up to see a ship that had docked by night, like a dark tower over the cottage. I hated all ships. It was a ship had taken away my mama. When I had to go out I would always keep my face turned down; and then how I dreaded any errand that took me over the Jericho Bridge, where space lies beneath the gaps in the roadway, like a deep black lake brimming with silver stars.

Benny Stropes and his gang would always be about too, brawling in the gutter or clambering out beneath the piers with one another's shoes. If they caught me they would try to steal my bonnet. I used to squeeze through the railings and creep along under the stairs—but Benny's little brother Tib, always at his elbow, would see me and give a piercing yell. Then they would all shout—"Sophie's a bastard! Sophie's a bastard!" Then I would run, and they would run after, throwing things. They were boys, and could do what they liked. They had no cares, as I had. Boys have no care for anything, except for their esteem in each other's eyes. "Wharf rats," Papa called them, and bade me take no notice of them—though they would chase him too, if ever they caught him about by daylight. How miserable I let them make me.

I should have counted my blessings, you say—Dear Reader, you are right. Unlike others, I had a roof over my head, a father living, beans in the pot. There was a wage coming in, if Papa had not lost it on the way home. Being young, and un-Christian, sometimes I forgot to be grateful.

It was not until later that I was to hear about the consolations of religion. I had never seen a Bible; Papa would not have one in the house. Bibles were for the Methodists, and the Salvation Army who kept the Kingdom Hall on Marley Street and every Sunday came marching about the docks with their bugles and tambourines. Papa had an oath for them and every ha'penny fools gave them. *Mors est certa*, his text was, and mortal peril wherever you went in the whole wide universe.

I have seen pictures of the gods of the Hindoo, with their thousand hands and a sword in every hand. I think it was one of them that ruled me, when I was a little girl. I had a thousand pricking fears. Oh, I was afraid not only of Benny Stropes, but of everything and everyone—the gruff wharfingers chewing their tobacco—the clerk that winked at me from the window of the timber merchant's—the ne'er-do-wells lounging in the door of the *Cormorant*, making comments on all who passed by—the port women, with their hair yellow as custard and their faces white as floating ice. Every other poor child in High Haven was out as soon as he could walk. You only had to look out of the window to see them, girls as well as boys, in patched old suits and helmets spotted with pitch, scrambling among the ratlines of the harbor boats. But you know that I did not make a habit of looking out of the window.

The only time I ever set foot on a ship was when I had to go with the parish outing over to Mare Sanctorum, the Sea of Saints. I knew I should fall overboard unnoticed and go spinning off into the dark. Sailors often found the bodies of little children, Papa had said, abandoned in orbit, frozen cold. I was sick from fear and lightness, and had to spend the whole day strapped in a hammock. Would you believe it? Would any one of you believe that, now? What a dormouse you will think me. One day I shall have a ship of my own, and call her the

Golden Dormouse, and she shall take me wherever I choose.

Papa, you know, had never been a sailor; never sailed even to the Moon. What had ships brought him, he would say, but bad luck and harm? Yet he had a tattoo on his arm, like a sailor. A woman with wings, it was—an angel, only with a nightdress on. When Papa flexed his muscles he could make her flap her wings. Below her feet there was a scroll, and her name written on it, Estelle.

Benny Stropes and his gang followed me down from St. George Street and cornered me in the alley behind the Customs and Excise. "Why ain't you got no mother, Sophie Farthing?" Kipper Morgan asked me, with a sneer.

I pressed myself against the wall, trying to squeeze myself flat. "My mother's an angel," I said.

They smirked and crowed. "Ow, Sophie's ma's an *angel*!"

"Where is she, then?" Kipper wanted to know.

"She's dead," I said.

Boys always know better. They all crowded in on me. "Your pappy never married no angel, Sophie Farthing," said Benny Stropes. Little Tib was picking his nose with glee. "If he married an angel," Benny pronounced, "he'd be dead, not her."

My voice was tight in my windpipe. "What do you mean?"

The gang nudged each other—this was fine sport—as Benny thrust his grinning face into my face. "She'd've had him!" Benny said. "She'd've *had* him and *had* him and *had* him till his brains ran out of his ears!"

I didn't understand. My head was full of their filth, and I was desperate to get away from them. I lashed out with my foot and caught Benny Stropes on the kneecap. He howled in pain and surprise and toppled over, crashing on top of Tib. I made a dash between them and tore down the alley into Toomey Street, and hid in the smelly cavern behind the water pipes until they went away.

Why indeed could I not have a real mama, instead of just a picture? How had Benny come by Mrs. Stropes? I knew nothing of birth, though Papa told me much about death. She would have been my mama, his Estelle, but she went down in the wreck of the *Hippolyta*. "The finest woman that ever lived," Papa would state, his poor face so sour and grim. "They say she is with God." He banged his fist on the arm of his chair. "Then I say God is a thief and a bully—and no gentleman . . ."

It was when things were blackest Papa would speak of her. He drank till he sweated and shivered, then he cursed me because I was not her. Or he wept, and commanded me to pay attention and repeat his words back to him, as though between us we might conjure her into being, and rescue her at last.

Estelle was not an angel when she lived, but a human woman who came of a good family. She was beautiful and sweet-tempered. She had long, fair hair, pretty hands, and nimble feet. She was modest, and knew when to hold her tongue—unlike his miserable wretch of a daughter, who was idle and deceitful and did nothing all day but ask questions to spite him and try his patience.

Oh, I think he did not truly hate me—but Papa had grown bitter and ill with the years, and there was no one else but us two. Even the cat shunned him. When it went hard with him, Papa would come stumbling from his bed at teatime, and Percy would flee the room at once, while Papa stood there swaying on his feet, cursing me for an imp and claiming I had stolen his poppy juice. He would shout at me to bring it at once, and I would, fumbling with the gin bottle and the spoon, and get a cuff about the head for my pains. Then he slumped in his corner by the hearth, casting black looks at me, while I had to fetch his tea and fill his lantern and shine his boots, quick as I could, and try every way there was to get him out the door and off to work.

I was saved when Kappi knocked to call for him, which he did more and more. Kappi would be on his way to bed, dog-tired, poor creature, because our days are longer than theirs, not natural to him. Still he would make time to come by our door and coax and cajole my father out to the watchman's tower. When at last he left, I would wash the dishes, then crawl to my own cold bed and lie there alone, while the shadows of the evening sailings went up across the wall.

"Kappi," I said, "what do they do, up in Hanover?"

Kappi rubbed his cap and shook his heavy head. "Great business, not to be disturbed by the small," he said. "Wise of the daughter to obey the father."

Kappi, will you read my story? It was you, you know, induced me to write it. I know you will read it, and blush mauve as lavender to find yourself in it, which you will deplore and say you do not deserve, though you are the noblest creature in the book. Certainly you did not deserve the shameful lot they gave you in High Haven, to make you sweep the streets and bridges—and light the lamps, teetering on the top of a wooden ladder! Was there ever a creature less suited by nature to his work? Kappi, you should have been a teacher, as you were to me; not a plodder of the streets, a struggler with shovels and brushes, a scavenger of refuse and dung. But you were the wrong size, I suppose, for philosophy, and the wrong shape.

Sometimes I think the universe is a gigantic jigsaw puzzle, and we are all the pieces, all jumbled up and out of our fit places; and however we voyage, veering and tacking all our lives, the puzzle will never be done.

Kappi is an Ophiq, the only one of his kind on High Haven. When I was seven, Kappi was eighty-two of his own years. He knew all the stars and named them for me, over and over, while Percy wound in and out of his little legs. "Which one do you come from, Kappi?" I asked, sitting on his barrow and gazing up into the black sky.

He spoke then in his own tongue, a name like water running over stones. "No, Kappi, no!" I cried, and I slapped him in my frustration, though his tough hide hurt my hand.

"To seek the brightness," he said, after his manner. "There," he said, and pointed with his snout.

The Ophiq is a pachydermatous biped, it says in *Strake's Register*, from Arcturus IV, a heavy world. There is an engraved picture, and it is Kappi to the life: four feet tall, and shaped like a bell. Kappi was our only visitor—a perfect associate for Papa, despite their working different ends of the clock. It was like Papa to choose company he could lord it over: the humble and lonely who would not oppose or offend him. There sat I at the table, cleaning Papa's boots with a rag, while Kappi, taking off his ancient hat, sat on the rug like a second child, carefully holding a mug of tea and listening to Papa's conversation.

Rumors were afoot again about the station the Dutch were planning to build, or perhaps it was the Austrians, to be connected to High Haven with a railway running between them.

Papa was against it. He was against most things. "The engines will run off the rails. It happens every day down below." He struggled in his chair, as though the very cushions were conspiring against his comfort, and pulled his blankets tighter. A coal clinked, settling in the stove, and reminded him of another theme. "Railways bring nothing but filth and pollution," he maintained. "While you sleep, cinders creep into your lungs. You wake up coughing up black."

"To breathe without ease is pain, very much," said Kappi, no doubt thinking of his own world, far away. I wish I could write his voice for you—you must imagine how he coos, soft and high like a pigeon, always sounding so sympathetic.

"Oh, you'll be all right, you're not so much in the air as I am," said Papa to his guest, ungraciously and not very logically. "You're closer to the ground."

Kappi took no offense but turned brown with solemnity and said to me: "Fortune to us small ones, Miss Sophie, not to suffer like Mr. Farthing."

Papa ignored me when he talked to Kappi, and ignored Kappi when Kappi talked to me, and that was that. That was how it was. But Kappi never ignored me.

"Have you ever seen a railway engine, Kappi?"

"To say true, Miss Sophie," he fluted. "In London, at the Hamp-stead Harbor, engines to come and go in all directions!"

"Did they blow up?"

"Don't talk poppycock, girl," growled Papa, though I had learnt this from him, that railway engines were always exploding and killing everyone for miles around.

Kappi pouched the lips of his snout, as he did when he was thinking about something. These lectures gave him great difficulty. He was too polite to contradict Papa, even in private to me, afterward, when Papa had forgotten all about whatever it was. "If danger flies, a virtue to be small," he concluded.

"Here, Papa," I said, giving him his boots, for I was tired of cleaning them; and fetching my ABC, I sat down beside Kappi on the floor. Kappi was teaching me to read and write—none too soon, for I was already ten years old. Kappi it was who taught me to spell my own proper name, which is Sophrona, and not Sophia as everyone always thinks—but that was not yet, we were only recently embarked on the alphabet, and had got no farther in our journey than C.

"The Cat sat on the Mat," I read. There was a picture of it, looking much like our own Percy, who was curled up asleep beside the hearth, as far as he could get from Papa's chair.

"Good, Miss Sophie," said Kappi.

I was already turning over the page to find out what the Cat did next—woke up, perhaps, and went looking for his tea—but the Cat was not there, only a Dog worrying a bone, and opposite him an Empress in her Ermines, balancing on top of a globe of the Earth like a circus seal on a ball. "Where's the Cat?" I asked.

Kappi regarded me soberly with one eye at a time. He had gone a sort of sandy yellow. "To read is to discover, Miss Sophie," he said, hopefully—so on we went. We reached I the Ink, where I squirmed and complained there was still no news of the Cat. My teacher hinted we might find it further on, at M the Mouse perhaps. And when we finally achieved that enormous distance, limping and fatigued from wanderings off in all directions, only to discover M was a Martian, stiff and proud in his great sunbonnet, I was cross. "M isn't for Mouse," I said.

"Yes," said Kappi. "To watch the pencil." And taking it in his paw he wrote, with infinite pains and great delicacy, the word MOUSE.

One letter might do for two words, then—or even three. I pushed back through the pages of our book. "Look, Kappi: Mat is M too."

Thus was I schooled in the letters of our tongue, by a poor patient creature who did not own it. Papa permitted it, though reading made you weak, he said, in the powers of eyesight and memory. For a girl, he could allow the case, since our powers were slight by nature and needed artificial aids; and reading could occupy me when I had nothing useful to do. For all his great fund of knowledge, Papa understood nothing of letters, no more than were in his own name and mine, and Estelle on his arm. Semaphore he could read, and the lights of ships in the offing, the red and green lanterns winking amid the stars. In any event, if he needed something read, there was always Kappi.

"Most good, Miss Sophie," hooted Kappi at my announce-ment, satisfaction blossoming in orange blotches through the yellow. He pulled his street sweeper's pouch around in front of his big belly and started digging in it. He had brought me something. A present. A reward.

It was a foreign coin, for my collection.

Papa disliked Kappi's giving us anything. "I suppose we are beggars now," he would grumble, "taking charity from a dustman"—so I kept my treasures out of sight, in a mustard tin: my League of Hope pin—my crested brass button off a sailor's uniform—precious things, that had sifted down from higher realms to turn up among the dust in Kappi's shovel. Doubtfully he would offer them: "This you may consider is to keep, Miss Sophie." How purple he turned, at first, when I accepted them from his great mitt! Discarded ferry tokens— a commemorative thimble from the Calliope Landing, with a chip out of it—and a curious ring I had had so long I could not remember a time when I had not. It was made of golden-colored metal, but never seemed to go dull or green like the button, and it had a little oval of crystal engraved with an emblem of a compass arrow and a human eye. I have it still. It is on my finger as I write.

Papa said the pictures on my ring were a kind of writing, which showed it was Chinese. When he said that, Kappi went green and doubtful, and he said perhaps Mr. Farthing was thinking of Ancient Egypt—at which Papa made a fuss. He always made a fuss when he saw me playing with my ring, and told me to put it away; but I thought it was pretty. "Did you give it to me, Kappi?" I asked.

Kappi said, "No, Miss Sophie—"

Then Papa interrupted, commanding me to tie his boot-laces for him. "Don Caldero came back from Betelgeuse, you know," he said, as I struggled with the knot. "No one could make out his colors in the glass but I." I ignored him. His sto-ries had come around again and again, each time more bald and ragged, while Kappi and I were beyond the ABC now, into books which did have stories about cats, and about cat-erpillars and camels and Cinderellas, none of which was ever to be seen in the Haven.

I think the first whole book we read was Mr. Defoe's *Robinson Crusoe*. It was full of surprises. I knew the blue

patches beneath the white shrouds of Earth were seas, like the
seas of the Moon—but were they full of *water*? That made my
eyes wide—and Mr. Defoe's ships sat in the water, and did not
rise up and fly away but even fell down into it—this was a
powerful novelty to me, scarcely to be believed. I sank down
under the flood of Mr. Defoe's marvels like Mr. Crusoe's ship
under the sea—and I kept returning to the book as he to the
wreck, to prize some other astonishing thing from it. How I
wished I could live like Robinson Crusoe, on an island with
no other soul there but me—and Kappi to be my slave, like
Mr. Crusoe's Man Friday.

It is a childish thing, I believe, wanting a slave. To be
followed around and looked after everywhere and have your
food and drink brought by someone who you pay not a penny
wage for it—what is that but the state of childhood? But this
is by the by. Time was passing, and I had begun not to be
a child any longer; and my father was coming to approve of
my reading as a profitable accomplishment. "It will stand you
in good stead, Sophie," he said, "when the time comes. There
will be a good position for you as a secretary or apprentice to
a scribe. Or even a teacher in your turn, think of that!"

He spoke so highly of teaching who had never let me have
any but his own, not even what the old wives taught at the
sail shed. I said nothing, but in my heart I knew, and I am
sure Kappi knew, that this notion of a position for Sophie was
nothing but another opium dream. My position was to look
after him, and keep his house. Low and cramped as it was,
there were always chores to be done. No matter how hard I
worked nothing was ever clean or decent.

Perhaps I did not work hard. Perhaps I sat for hours and
twisted my hair between my fingers, or scraped out the grain
of the table with my fingernail. Sometimes, for sure, when the
wharf had grown still and the kitchen was shining with moonlight, I would stand bolt upright shuddering with the scrubbing
board in my hand, gripped by a sudden panic. I was fifteen
and folk looked at me in the street with pity. If my mother
had lived, I would think, things would be different. And then
I would weep into the sink, and curse the *Hippolyta*, in words
I had learned from my papa.

One morning I stepped out as usual, on my way to market.
A pair of blackened pigeons fluttered up out of the road, and

I wondered how they could manage in the poor, thin air that
was all we got down at the Eastern Docks. I looked out and
saw the shadows of the ferries sailing back and forth across
the blue face of Earth like shuttles across a loom. There was
some kind of grand yacht berthed nearby, a three-master yellow as butter that had got in by mistake with all our luggers
and tramps. I thought she was Cinderella's coach among all
those scaly hulls. But I was not interested in ships. I turned
away quickly up Toomey Street, following the cries to the
greengrocer's stall.

As I stood there, crushed among the crowd, trying to find
a small cabbage neither yellow nor worm-eaten, I saw behind
the next stall, selling cheap crocks and Brummagem ware,
Benny Stropes's crony Kipper Morgan, and his brother Lew.
Kipper had a scarlet kerchief around his neck and a cloth cap
jammed down over his bristly red hair. They were talking
about the yacht I had seen on my way. Lew said her name,
the *Unco Stratagem*—she belonged to the lord of some guild
or other. "I saw her master," Lew said to a gaggle of customers. "Proper peeved, he looked."

"What's she doing down on East Dock?" someone asked.

"Prince Edward's full," said Lew, laughing. It amused him
that such a man should be inconvenienced. "Proper peeved!"
he said again. "What do you say, Sophie?"

The *Unco Stratagem*—it was not a name I knew. Papa had
never mentioned her. I hunched over the vegetables. "I don't
know," I said, mumbling. "I don't know who you're talking
about."

"Why, Mr. Cox, the envoy," Lew said. "You should look
out for him, Sophie—what a sight he is. Long, curly brown
hair, and a crimson coat with gold all over everywhere."

Seeing my discomfort, Kipper Morgan moved up the stall
toward me like a fox after a chicken. "And a firm jaw, Lew,
wouldn't you say?" said Kipper. "Ow yes, a very firm jaw!"
He sniggered. There was some joke here he was enjoying
keeping from me. I felt my face grow warm, and hated him
for it.

I had to get served at once, I couldn't stand to be near
them a moment longer. As I seized a cabbage I heard Kipper's brother muttering to him about me. " . . . if she'd put a
good frock on and do something with that hair . . ."

I turned hotly and saw—not the grinning boys, but myself, reflected in one of the shiny plated trays on their stall. My face, red and sullen, shone back at me like a baleful moon. What "thing" was it Lew meant, that I should do with my hair—my hair black as space, straight as string, hanging in a raw fringe across my broad forehead? When I was a child, Papa used to cut it short all over like a powder monkey. Now, whenever it got in my eyes and down my neck, I chopped it off myself in ten seconds with a pair of shears.

In all truth I'd never devoted a single minute of my life to concern for my appearance. We had no mirror at home; nor had I ever wished for one. I knew what I looked like. My eyes were big, my forehead broad, my nose round as a mushroom. My mouth was fixed in a permanent scowl. Beauty was something other girls had, like mothers.

"The gentleman is an inspector," I said, "sent by the King of Switzerland."

People began to stare at me.

"They are going to knock down this whole marketplace and build a dock for railway ships," I went on, wildly. "He told Papa all about it."

Kipper guffawed. "They'll be having him to tea next, Lew!"

I threw my cabbage back on the greengrocer's stall. It hit the other cabbages and tumbled to the ground, and thence went rolling and bouncing across the street—while I fled with the sound of their laughter at my heels.

At home Papa was in bed, asleep. I went to my room. A good frock! I had no good frocks. I had a dingy gray smock that had used to be black, and a dingy black one that had used to be brown. The only pretty thing I had was my ring with the carved crystal. I got it from the tin and put it on, but my hands were red and worn from housework. The ring made them look no better. Downstairs, the stove had gone out and I had to riddle and lay and start it all again. I knelt down at the cold hearth. Until a tear splashed into the coal scuttle, I did not know that I was crying.

That evening Papa rose as usual. He came from the bedroom and sat at the table. He looked haggard, his face like candle wax. In a good light you could see the veins through his skin. The opium was to be bought two or three times weekly now. His eyes were always red, though they were sharp as

ever. When I set his soup before him he saw the ring on my
finger.

The sight of it had never ceased to agitate him. He said:
"What do you think you're doing with that on?"

At once my ears grew hot, and I was cross and bothered.
Could no man ever speak to me but I must shrink like a salted
snail? I made no answer.

"I don't like you wearing it," he said. "You'll lose it." His
voice that had once seemed to bruise my ears was now small
and peevish, full of fright at the slightest thing. I did not want
to sit there in the room with him while he slurped his soup
and tore the bread apart with his palsied fingers.

I put the pot back on the stove. "Your boots are clean,
Papa, and your lantern is on the shelf by the door, where it
always is."

"Sophie! Where are you going?"

"To bed." There was nowhere else for me to go. The night
was Papa's domain, dangerous, lit by the twin lanterns of his
eyes. Papa had told me, when I was still an infant on his lap,
how the Haven needed him to watch at night, for brigands
would come a-crawling through the docks, all to steal young
maidens away. In bed I remembered how I had used to clasp
myself to him for protection, twining my childish hands in his
beard. My fingers remembered its softness; and my nose the
smell of his maroon flannel waistcoat.

I tossed and turned, but sleep came no nearer. At last I heard
Papa go out, banging the door behind him. I got up and put
on my clothes, and tied my bonnet strings under my chin.

Outside, it was quite dark. The blind night face of Earth
hung close, immense. I thought it was a great black hole
where something had eaten up all the stars, and it would soon
be swallowing us. Kappi had been around already, lighting
the lamps. They hissed softly, casting dim pools on the black
brick walls.

I walked quickly down our row to the footbridge, and across
it to the dirty brick apron that fronts the dock, heading away
from the watchtower. As the thin air of the edge blew about I
could hear bursts of accordion music from the bar of the *Cormorant*, and excited voices raised in mirth and argument.

At the railings I stood, looking out at the thick web of haw-
sers that crossed each other this way and that way and every

way, and I studied my discontent. If every evening was so
weary, how long would it take me to get my whole life lived?

I gripped the rail, uneasy in the low gravity, breathing deeply and trying to calm myself. There was a constant restless
breeze, stirring the dust and dry rubbish that Kappi always
left behind him, no matter how he swept. The nearness of
space sucked a little swirl of grit flying out past my cheek
and away into the deep.

Before me, riding high at all angles, a harbor full of silent
black boats hung suspended from their giant hooks. Far beyond
and beneath, the Milky Way lay like a reef of broken light.
I stared at the familiar scene, feeling angry and stupid and
unhappy. I cursed myself, and I cursed my papa—I would
rather sail away on a ship this minute, I told the night fiercely, than go home to him.

My eyes were watering. I blinked—something golden I could
see, gleaming faintly in the light from Papa's tower. It was the
ship of the high lord's man: the *Unco Stratagem*, the Morgan
boys had called her. They said her masts were yellow as barley sugar, and there was stained glass in the fo'c'sle. I turned
my back on her amongst her uncouth companions, and walked
on toward Prince Edward Dock. I was going to walk to the
statue and back, and then home to bed and hope to sleep.

No sooner had I thus made up my mind than a gentleman
seemed to rise up out of the bricks at my feet.

3

Showing how I began
my journey

First there was a tricorn hat—then after the hat came long
curls of dark hair, with a narrow face between. I could not
see his face. I could see his coat, a heavy, rich one, just as
Lew Morgan had said—and then one of his boots came up, a

high top boot with the leg of his breeches gathered into it. He was not a very tall gentleman, once he was full-grown, but I started backward as he came up the last step and struck me with a flap of his coat.

"Your pardon, ma'am," he muttered, not looking at me as he swept me aside.

"Granted, sir, I'm sure," I said loudly, covering my fright.

But now I had spoken he stopped in his course and turned to look at me.

He was no brigand, not with all that gold braid. He must be someone very important. Feeling something more was called for, I made him a clumsy curtsy and said the first thing that came into my addled head. "They say there will be a storm in the crossing, sir," I said. "There often is, when the passage is so close."

He struck a pose with his cane, leaning forward on it. "Then hurry home to your bed, child," he said. It was the voice of a gentleman he had, though it sounded strange. He spoke most precisely and carefully, like a gentleman holding a fork in his mouth.

His face was still hard to see. It was quite black at the bottom; I supposed he had a full beard. I realized I was staring at him, which was rude.

"I'm not a child, sir!" I said.

He straightened his back. The gaslight across the way shone over his shoulder. It shone on white lace sleeves that came flouncing lightly down over leather gloves. It lit the rings that he wore, on top of the gloves, gold and silver, and one with a ruby like a big black currant.

"I see," said the envoy. His tone was different now, not so filled with contempt and impatience. It sounded as though something had caught his fancy. Still he didn't move his head, nor his feet; but put one hand to his chin, and I heard his rings tap on metal. It must be a respirator then, of course.

"You come on your own initiative, do you," he said, "not inviting me to sample the charms of another?"

I didn't know what he was talking about.

No more did I know what I was doing standing there talking to him. I thought I should be gone at once, but his word *inviting* was sounding in my head, and my mouth had a will of its own.

"They said I should ask you to tea, sir. And I would, gladly, you would be most welcome, sir—but my father is not well. It aggravates him to have visitors. And our parlor is no place for a gentleman such as yourself, sir." I felt full of bubbles, ready to burst out laughing at the very idea. I wondered if this was what they called hysteria.

My victim was himself amused. No, I could not say amused, but he was puzzled, and game for the puzzle. "Are you drunk, girl?" he said.

"No, sir!"

"Mad, then."

"Neither, sir," I said, though I thought perhaps I was, saying whatever came into my head, like any lunatic. I seized control of my tongue, before I should get myself into trouble, as Papa was always warning me, and I curtsied again. "I wish you a safe passage, Mr. Cox, sir," I said. "And good night!"

Now I was on my toes to flee, but he had a reply for me.

"You have the advantage of me, girl," he said.

I said nothing. I would not betray myself that far. Yet he was stepping towards me.

"I beg your pardon, sir," I said, trying to duck past him. "The storm, sir, remember! Good night to you."

"Wait," he said; and in a trice he had me by the arm. I protested, but he gripped my wrist and lifted my hand, and bent his head over it. For one moment I thought he was about to kiss it. But of course he was looking at my crystal ring; and his whole frame had become stiff and very still.

"Where did you come by this ring?" he asked me. His voice was quite calm and light now, as though it were a matter of the most casual interest.

"It's mine, sir," I said. "I've had it all my life. Since before I can remember, sir."

"You're lying, child. I think you stole it, hm?"

"No sir. Ask my father, if you do not believe me."

I saw the gaslight gleam on the knob of his stick as he lifted it, and I flinched. "Who is your father?" he asked, rapidly, squeezing my fingers.

I didn't want to tell him.

"Who?" he asked, gripping me tighter.

I didn't want to tell him, but I wanted him to let me go. I

tried for a lie, but no lie came. So I said my father's name, with some dignity—he was a constable after all, more or less. "Jacob Farthing, sir, if you please. The East Dock watchman. Ask anyone; they know him."

That was true; for though my father had no acquaintance, yet he was known—everyone on the east side that was up early or late coming home, they knew him, that chalk-faced man who walked in the middle of the road, muttering to himself, and held up his lantern to stare at them as they passed. They knew his walk, and his way.

My captor was not listening to me. I thought he had not heard a word I had said. "Come over here, child," he said, in a voice that was used to being obeyed, and he stepped over to the lamp, pulling me with him.

Under the lamp he put his stick under his arm and held my head in both his hands, tilting my face to the poor light of the gas. He studied me closely; and I studied him meanwhile.

He was a man of forty years, I suppose. He smelled of snuff and pepper. His head was narrow and long, like a hound's; his skin was fair, his curls a wig, dark brown with some red in it. His eyes were deep set either side of a long nose that curved up a bit at the end—I thought they were clever eyes. His upper lip was thin, and shaven clean. He was wearing no respirator—his jaw was made of iron.

I almost cried out to see it, the dull gray metal chin with its hundred dents and million scratches. The sides of it curved back beneath the long curls of his wig. His lips and cheeks were ridged with old red scars where the metal went under them. I marveled then at his speaking so distinctly; and I began to guess the power of his will.

I said again to him: "I'm not a child."

He looked furious with me, as though my impertinence was but a poor return for his curiosity. I saw his nostrils flare, then narrow with self-control. I supposed he must know all about that, and about pain. Here was a man most determined to overcome all difficulties.

"Oh, but I see you are," he said flatly. He seemed to be speaking to himself, or for the benefit of someone else, as Papa sometimes did—someone who was not there. "That's

precisely what you are," he said, and now he was speaking
to me again: "Miss—Farthing."

I heard a gust of the music from the accordion, the banging
of a distant door on Half-Moon Street, a crowd of people
calling one to another. There were women laughing harsh
and high.

He gave no sign that he heard them.

"Tell me of your mother," he said.

"She is dead, sir."

He disregarded this. "Well?" he said.

"Her name was Miss Estelle Crosby," I said.

"Was it indeed," said the gentleman.

"She went down with the *Hippolyta*," I said—and then,
because he did not seem to be impressed yet: "Mama is an
angel."

Unexpectedly he laughed. It was a noise of derision, short
and harsh as the bark of a dog. I could see his teeth, the upper
ones all crooked and stained black, the lower ones chiseled out
of iron. I remember supposing Mr. Cox didn't like to laugh;
he laughed as if it hurt him to.

He looked me in the eye. "An angel! Is that what they call
them here?" he said, drily. "And on the *Hippolyta*! An inven-
tive man, your pappy, by God."

He let me go, with a flourish of Callisto lace. I rubbed my
wrist where he had hurt me.

"Go your ways, lassie," he said quite gently.

He drew a white lawn kerchief from the sleeve of his coat
and flapped it at me as though I were a gnat; but he was merely
shaking it open. "Tell no one we have had this little chat," he
said—and now he took a little horn box from a pocket in his
waistcoat and opened it up. "I shan't expect to have the pleasure of meeting you again," he told me, pouring snuff from the
box into the crook between his finger and thumb.

One thing only had penetrated my stupid brain. "You knew
my mother," I said.

"Home to bed, girl," he said, more forcefully. Mr. Cox
sniffed noisily, throwing the snuff up his nostrils and baring
his teeth. "The storm!" he said mockingly. "Remember!"

I stood my ground, though my feet would have run. I knew
I had been lucky. I had been forward, and played the fool, and
been forgiven. I should have run home, as he told me.

I wanted to get away from him; but I didn't want to let him go.

I understood suddenly that he was nervous too. I had frightened him somehow, and he was doing his best to conceal it. I had to know why.

I thrust my hand at him. "Will you not tell me about my ring, sir?" I said, in a high voice like a sweet little maid who knows she is a sweet little maid and trusts that everything will follow.

He took the hand I gave him and looked at my ring again, shaking his head slowly from side to side. I was sure he was thinking of a lie. He would tell me my ring was worthless paste, he had been toying with me merely.

That was how they found us, then, with his hand holding mine.

There were four or five of them, coming down from Half-Moon Street in a line, bareheaded, with brightly printed scarves loose around their shoulders. "Evening, your worship," they called. "Are you looking for a nice girl?"

It was the port women, that all despised so, and the menfolk glanced at sidelong. Their hair was yellow as sherbet and their mouths were red.

The tall one called Rita reached us first. She seized my hand and pulled it out of his, thrusting me around behind her. I protested but she ignored me completely. She pushed herself between him and me, shoving me with her hard hip. "You come with me, your lordship, I'll see you get your buckles polished."

"Leave him be, Rita," called one of the others. "Can't you see the gentleman prefers 'em small and dark like me?" She gaped a vacant smile, dimpling at him. Her teeth were all out.

The women crowded in between the envoy and me, jostling Rita. They stank of armpits, gin, sweet violets, and black lead. I realized they were protecting their trade. In their wake they had brought a couple of young men, who now leaned on the wall, watching like punters at a fight.

I thought it might even be a fight, in a moment more. Rita's first contestant, taking advantage of Mr. Cox's small height, reached up to wind her finger in his curls and tried to plant a kiss on his cheek, above the iron. I would not swear she did not step on Rita's toe to do it.

Mr. Cox flung up his arms, stepping backward with a curse and shaking them from him as if they were inquisitive dogs. He raised his stick. "Away with ye, ye daughters of corruption!" he said. "I know your foulness." He brushed his sleeves in loathing. "Faugh, you stink to high Saturn. Be off, or I'll have the law upon ye!"

Affronted, they began to jeer and mock him, all good companions now they knew the color of his mind. "Leave our children alone, then, you cradle-jumper!" shouted the small dark one, although she was probably no older than I, and she came and grabbed my hand. Everyone was grabbing my hand tonight. "We'll take you home, chicken," Rita announced. "You'll be all right with us."

Like fine ladies they summoned their men and gathered a little procession around me. I thought for a second Mr. Cox would forbid it, but he let us go. I looked back once and saw him watching us walk away, his old-fashioned hat like the pointed head of some overgrown insect waiting beneath the light.

I wished they had waited until he'd said something about my ring. But I was glad to be going home, and relieved somebody had decided to take me. The women were protecting me indeed, if only from my own folly. I was surprised to find they knew who I was—I had never spoken to any of them, nor knew any of their names but Rita; everyone knew her. They all knew me, though, and where I lived. As we walked they wanted to know if the man had "laid a finger on me," or said anything improper. I hardly knew what they meant, truth to tell, and answered in one word and two.

At home at last in the silent cottage I fell back into bed, but I could not sleep. My brain was in a fever about Mr. Cox. Who was this proud gentleman with his antique wig and his horn snuffbox, his iron jaw? A complete stranger from a world abroad—yet he knew my mama. Why did he say she was not on the *Hippolyta*? Obviously he had mistaken me for someone else. Not for the first time I thought I could see Mama, hovering over me where I lay, and feel the breath of her wings on my clammy forehead.

Next day I told Kappi about my adventure, and he was sure it was all a dreadful misunderstanding. I should be grateful, he said, to the women, for bringing me safe home.

I thought of them, with their tight skirts and their hard faces. "Why did he say they were disgusting?" I asked.

Kappi went lavender blue. "They are to take money for what belongs to love," he said. "To clean the man who has lain down with one, never is possible."

I was horrified. Kappi patted my hand consolingly. "This is not to trouble Mr. Farthing with," he advised me.

But I was too curious, and told Papa when he woke up that afternoon. As soon as he came in the room I told him, I had met a man who knew Mama.

Papa leaned on the table where I was sitting. His red eyes peered down at me as if from a great distance. "What are you talking about, girl?"

I reached out and took hold of his sleeve. I had completely forgotten our upset last night. "Papa! He knew Mama! Listen, Papa: he said she was not on the ship."

I wanted to say: Perhaps she is not dead. But I had dared too much already.

"Hold your tongue, child!" Papa said, and he clasped his arm, where the picture was. "Your mother is an angel," he moaned.

"He said no."

Papa swore an oath then, and struck out at me. I drew back, scraping the legs of my chair on the floorboards. My hands fell to my lap; and I felt the ring in my pocket. I understood now what I had always suspected: it was Mama's ring.

I knew better than to say Mr. Cox had looked at the ring, but I kept hold of it. "Who is he, Papa? Was he a friend of mama's?"

Papa pointed a shaking finger at me. "You stay away from him!"

My eyes had begun to water as if the blow had truly landed. "I only want to talk to him," I said.

Mind you, I had no idea how I was ever to do such a thing. He was a fine gentleman of high degree. I had never spoken to any such before. He had told me not to trouble him again. I didn't know what he might do if I did.

Papa sank into his chair. "Where's my tea?" He picked up the teapot and wrestled furiously with its lid. "Can't you even make the tea? You've no business to go about bothering gentlemen," he said, rambling now, tiring. "Your mother's

dead and gone and you'll show some respect for her memory."
Papa waved his arm, almost sweeping the teapot to perdition.
"You're not to go down the dock," he finished.

Now they had both told me. Papa was shivering, though,
I saw. Papa was afraid. His life was always full of fear; but
this time it was no bogey, born of poppy juice. Papa knew
Mr. Cox, I was sure of it; or knew what he was, or what he
knew—*something* he knew, I could tell. Papa was afraid, and
I, for a wonder, was not—but Dear Reader, I hated him that
morning. Had he nothing to give me but fear?

"Go to bed, Papa," I said, getting up from the table.

His eyes widened. "You stay put, Sophie Farthing!" he
whinnied. "You keep out of harm's way!"

"I'll bring your tea up," I said, and went past him to fill
the kettle. He looked exhausted. His powers were slight, and
anger at the end of a long night consumed them. Still he had
a punch to throw.

"You'll not go out of this house today," he said.

He went and locked both the doors. Then he went to bed
and took the key with him.

I was furious, and all the more determined.

I made his tea and put the whole of a three-day screw of
opium in it.

I looked in later to see if he was asleep. He lay like a baby,
with the covers pulled up to his chin. But I was the baby,
for all he could tell. "Sophie!" he cried. "Come and sit here,
Sophie, here on the bed. I've been thinking about the gryphon, the one Lord Hamilcar bagged on Miranda. Did I ever tell
you? I saw them unloading it, in chains. Longer than four men,
it was, all fur and feathers . . . There was a man there, with a
camera. . . ."

"There's some tea left, Papa," I told him. "Drink up. That's
the way."

"The beast was all wet from the ice they kept it in. Bits
of it were already falling off. You couldn't get near for the
smell . . ."

Eventually his eyes rolled up in his head, and closed. He
muttered to himself for a long time. Then he fell to snoring,
loud and slow.

I took the key from where he'd put it, under his pillow.
Then I put my bonnet and clogs on and out I went.

I knew there were no gryphons; not even on Miranda.

Sunlight was blazing fierce and full on the wharf. Beyond our Haven, space was so black it looked almost green. Dazzled, I had to screw up my eyes, and I almost fell over Kappi the Ophiq. He was in the road, sweeping. "Miss Sophie!" he cried, looking up at me, scanning my face with both eyes rolling. You could see him blushing red and purple. He was trying to keep it in, like someone trying not to hiccough, but I knew he was not there by chance. Somehow he had sensed our trouble and come.

Here is *Strake's Register of Sapient Extraterrestrials, with Notes on their Character, Disposition, Customs, &c.* In here it says the Ophiq are curious, and diplomatic, and obstinate. In character they are phlegmatic. Though all their physiological and nervous reactions are clearly visible in the changing colorations of their hides, they are modest creatures, and go clothed in human society for decency's sake. They have a developed moral faculty, and make good companions for children, whom they befriend with ease . . . But Kappi had not come to help me.

"To leave the house is dangerous, Sophie, with the father ill inside," hooted Kappi.

I pointed across the docks. "Kappi, there's a man who knew Mama. She wasn't on that ship. He said so!"

"Sophie, to forget the dead is most wise!"

He put his broom in my way. I looked down at him. I hated his horrible hat, his permanent reek of cigar butts and old orange peel. I realized how much taller than he I had grown without noticing it.

Most of all I hated his knowing. Papa had told him, whatever it was, and he was keeping it from me too.

"He's asleep," I said. "You mustn't wake him." Then I jumped over his broom and hurried on without a backward glance. My clogs echoed on the footbridge and down Half-Moon Street.

Along the docks I ran, looking here, there, and everywhere. Where were the masts of golden barley sugar?—Nowhere. The *Unco Stratagem* was nowhere to be seen. Why, Mr. Cox must have prevailed, and had them find a place for her on the Prince Edward after all. I ran on, one thought only in mind: to find that envoy of mystery, and demand to know what he knew, though he have me clapped in irons for it.

On the Prince Edward Dock there were men everywhere—sailors shouting, passengers in throngs, greeting and being greeted, porters pushing barrows piled high with baggage. In and out I ran between them and along the dockside. I ran and ran—the jetties seemed to stretch out forever into space—grimy and gray the high hulks loomed above me, hanging stiffly on their hooks, all tilted at strange angles. I was lost amid a forest of masts bare and black as frozen trees, that seemed to sway and beckon me into the black gulf of stars beyond. I broke into a sweat. I swallowed, and tasted sick in it.

Behind me—was that a shout? Was someone shouting at me? Was it Papa? To all sides the boats seemed to be multiplying. I gasped aloud, feeling the hulls closing together and crushing me. Not looking where I was going I struck my foot against one of the huge chains that hung up from the quayside, great thick links like the rungs of a ladder up to a bright forecastle. Here! Here she was at last—this must be her, with her planks agleam with fresh varnish, velvet curtains at her portholes!

Without another thought I climbed her chain, swaying as I felt my weight begin to go, leaving the air behind me like a fallen cloak.

I almost fell onto the deck of the yellow yacht. My heart pounded and I was starting to choke—I had to find my way below at once. There was a hatch. I went down it.

It was dark on board. I waited, stock-still, and listened. There was nothing stirring. Which way to go? I could not make up my mind. I went a few feet this way, then back that. The darkness closed around me like a fist and all my courage flew away out of my breast.

Hide. I had to hide. In a panic I jumped back up through the hatch and onto the deck. I saw the lifeboats, sealed with tarpaulins. I ran over and wriggled my way into one and knelt there, panting. I was dizzy now, my ears were hurting. Suddenly I knew I was going to be sick, and I was, in a corner of the boat. I crawled to the farthest seat and lay there curled up in a ball. I shook. My thousand-armed god came back and took possession of me.

I knew then I was nothing but a child, and a very foolish one. I was afraid of the ship, of the sailors, of Mr. Cox. I was afraid of Papa's waking up and coming after me—and of Papa's not waking up and never coming after me. I lay there in the lifeboat and shook. My head was pounding like a mason's hammer; I was sure I was going to die.

I fainted then, and lay I know not how long in a swoon.

I dreamed a dream of a creature whose hide was like a carpet, tufted, coarse, and brown. I was sitting on its back. It was very big—as big as the whole High Haven—and very hot. I could feel it under me, breathing. Here and there across its back, clumps of trees grew. Small children in clothes that were very fine, but all pale colors, came out of nowhere and stood under the trees, watching me. One of them clutched a hoop and stick, another a kite.

I understood, in my dream, that it was my duty to help these children, and many other people, adults too, though they were not to be seen. They could not control the giant beast; yet I could.

I dug my heels and fingers into its thick pelt, and shouted, but no sound came out. I looked for the head, but it was too far away to see. I *thought* at the beast. I willed it to move.

Then there came a crack like two rafts splitting apart—and to either side of me, blotting out the stars, the creature opened its wings.

I woke. I knew at once the noise had been real. A sharp voice shouted somewhere near at hand, then fell silent. My head was still throbbing and I lay there stunned, confused by the power of my dream. I took a deep breath. The whole lifeboat smelled of my puke. There was nothing to hear now but a soft creaking of timbers. Someone had come aboard, I was sure of it. It must be Mr. Cox, and Papa with him, coming to drag me home for punishment. Shakily I got to my feet, remembering how light I was up here.

There was a doorway at the stern of the lifeboat, with a curtain of thick rubber across it. With some difficulty I pushed through it and found a short collapsible tunnel of canvas and wood that went below deck. My legs felt funny, and my arms. They would not stay down, but kept floating into the air. My head ached; I wondered if I had a fever. I clung weakly to the side of the tunnel, unwilling to leave my refuge. Somewhere a brass bell clanged, startling me.

Slowly, fearfully, I managed to creep aboard, and found myself in the gangway again. It was not so dark now. I could see the shape of a porthole nearby, though it was hard to see out of it, for the stern of the lifeboat was in the way. There was a name painted on the lifeboat, I saw: the name of the ship herself, as the custom is, in letters of black and gold. The *Halcyon Dorothy*.

The *Halcyon Dorothy*. Not the *Unco Stratagem*.

In my confusion I had come aboard the wrong boat! I had to get off at once. I leaned to one side of the porthole, looking to see if there was anyone watching on the dock.

The dock wasn't there.

4

The Nightingale of the Spaceways

I shouted aloud. I jerked my head away and threw up my arm in front of my face, not wanting to see what I saw. My head kept going and hit the bulkhead with a bump.

A voice called out: "Who's there?"

There were doors farther along the gangway. One had light under it. The voice was coming from behind that door. It was a lady's voice, and sounded cross. "Who is that?" she said.

I gazed again through the porthole, longing to have been wrong the first time. Still there was nothing out there—no docks; no ships; no High Haven. I was taken aback. That is what the sailors say, you know, taken aback, when the currents of the starwind turn suddenly about and catch you contrary and stop you in your tracks. Well, you could say I was taken aback—and I did spin all the way around on my toes; yet nothing that I knew could I see, on any side. Only the fearful black cold of the deep came washing back over me—I had not meant to go into space! I pressed my knuckles to my mouth and gave a little moan.

"I know you're there," the lady called. "Come in here," she said. "I want to see you."

I sniffed, and swallowed.

"Come along," she said.

I went reluctantly over to the door where the light was, my legs feeling as though I was wading through treacle. I grasped the doorframe and stood holding on to it, my head pounding fiercely with a pain that gnawed at my skull. I worked the latch and opened the cabin door, and hung there in the doorway blinking stupidly.

The light came from a gimballed lantern overhead, but it could not get around very well inside the cabin because of all the furniture and clutter. Most of the room was filled with a four-poster, well bolstered with feather beds and coverlets and straps that looked in need of a wash. Night-things and underclothes were strewn shamelessly about, on the bed, on the bureau, on the tea table, some of them spilling down onto the floor, where they lay about haplessly.

There were unwashed teacups and glasses everywhere, and too many magazines stuffed in a magazine rack, where their pages fluttered, weak as the ghosts of birds. Against the inboard wall was a black iron stove, putting out quite a bit of heat, with a squat kettle on it steaming gently. In front of the stove was a fire screen decorated with scraps and scorched brown varnish, and in front of that, a human lady sitting in an armchair. The lady was looking at me. She was not smiling. She was screwing up her nose. "You smell," she said.

I thought she looked like a parrot. She had big brown eyes like gobstoppers with big purple circles painted around them—her nose was beaky, and on her chin you could have balanced a wineglass. It didn't make her look any less like a parrot that she had a pink feather boa like a crest nodding over her head. She was wearing a huge, pink dressing gown and tight leggings spotted like a leopard. The slippers on her feet were satin, and they were pink too. She was a tall lady, and not young.

She did not sound like a parrot, her voice was strong and full. "Have you just been sick?" she said, in disgust.

Dumb, I nodded.

"Clean yourself up, can't you? Well, can't you?"

I wiped my face on my sleeve.

"Oh for goodness sake, come here."

As soon as I came within reach she grabbed me by the arm and started wiping my face with her handkerchief, which stank of eau de cologne. What with that, and the heat and fume of the stove, I was starting to feel sick again.

It was not very clean, her handkerchief. It was not very clean anywhere on board the *Halcyon Dorothy*.

You do get filthy, in space. People never mention that, somehow. Perhaps it seems too obvious to mention. Pitch, rust, wood that sweats beads of sticky black—sometimes it starts to pit, and if you don't catch it, turns to sponge. Strange molds grow on your clothes. Everything seems to rot and perish. It must be that, I decided, that had made me so ill.

The parrot lady wiped my front. She shook my arm. "Stand up, girl, do," she said. "Are you still feeling groggy?"

I nodded, and then she helped me up onto the bed. I sat on the edge, holding on, and looked around while she closed the door. There were withered flowers and pieces of printed paper stuck all over the walls.

The lady moved easily to the stove, which she opened, and threw in her soiled handkerchief as though it were any old rag. "Who are you?" she demanded. "What are you doing on my boat?"

I said my name, but that was all. "Are you from the High Haven?" she asked. I nodded.

She cocked her head, considering me. Below my feet, a petticoat slipped out from under the bed, silently, and crept purposefully across the carpet like a cruising jellyfish.

"Are you running away from home?" my hostess asked. I could not speak. "Good God," she said, "you're not in the family way, are you? You look a bit young for that."

I didn't know what it was, but I knew I wasn't in it. "No, ma'am," I said. "I think I'm in harm's way, ma'am."

"Do you know who I am?" she asked. I shook my head. "I am Evadne Halshaw," she informed me, rather grandly; and she waved her arm at the wall, as if it would explain.

I looked, and saw that the pieces of paper stuck all around the walls of the cabin were yellowed postcards,

letters, playbills, tickets, etchings, photographs, cuttings
from newspapers, posters—"Sonder's Cleft Pump Rooms
TONIGHT * * * ONE NIGHT ONLY," they said. "The
Nightingale of the Spaceways EVADNE HALSHAW. 'Her
renditions never fail to thrill'—*The Mercury Dispatch*. 'Peer-
less tones'—*The Operatic Gazette*." The Galileo Hippodrome,
I saw, proudly welcomed Miss EVADNE HALSHAW,
with the Mare Ignis Orchestra, conductor Sir Bedivere
Stokes.

I said, "I thought this was the *Unco Stratagem*."

"The what?"

"The envoy's ship."

"What envoy?"

"Mr. Cox!" I said, as if that would explain everything.

Miss Halshaw and I stared at each other, both, I suppose,
equally baffled. The petticoat slid slowly past, around the corner of the bed, spiraling gracefully out of sight.

"It's not, is it?" I said, tearfully. "Where are we? I've got
to go home!"

"Impossible," said Miss Halshaw, like someone in a bad
dream. "Stop sniveling, girl. Sit up properly, if you won't lie
down. Fold your hands in your lap. Gracious, girl, did your
mother teach you nothing?"

I gulped. "No, ma'am," I said.

Well may you smile now at the picture my younger self
must have made, perched on that mountain of bedclothes in my
grubby dress, my swollen eyes peering miserably from under
my ragged black fringe, my mouth like the slot in a bulkhead
screw. But Miss Halshaw gave me some perpetuatum and a cup
of strong tea with milk and sugar, and she told me to account
for myself—and once I had begun to speak I could not stop,
but let the whole wretched story come tumbling out.

I told her about my papa, and how he hated me to remind
him of Mama. I told her about Mr. Cox, and his iron jaw.
I told her how with a word he contradicted everything Papa
had ever told me. I told her how Papa had tried to keep me
from him, and how Kappi had tried too, and who Kappi was.
I told her everything I have told you, and Miss Halshaw sat
and listened. She said nothing but: "Well, fancy that!" and
"Goodness me." She said: "I can't give you brandy because
you're not old enough, but you shall have a brandy snap."

And she gave me one, though it took some finding, and was rather stale.

Miss Halshaw said, "She was from High Haven, your mama?"

"I don't know, ma'am," I said. Mr. Cox's attitude had confused me. "She lived up by Hanover there," I said, doubtfully.

It was plain Miss Halshaw knew no part of the Haven: never went ashore when they docked there. "Why don't you go and ask for her family?" she said.

"They're fine ladies and gentlemen up there," I said. "The Lord Mayor lives in Hanover Way."

"Well then?"

"I couldn't talk to them," I said, aghast.

"You're talking to me, aren't you?"

"But I didn't mean to!" I exclaimed—then I ducked my head—"Oh, I beg your pardon, ma'am," I said, and felt very foolish.

I must work my passage, I decided. It was my only hope.

I looked about me. "Would you like me to tidy your cabin, ma'am?" I asked.

"Whatever for?" said Miss Halshaw, her eyes bulging. "No," she said. "Now come along, my dear. We must show you to Tobias."

As I climbed down from the bed I saw the petticoat again. It had finally come to rest, wound around and around the legs of a music stand. And there we left it, Miss Halshaw leading the way forward, with me wobbling after. It was not until I had to move that I truly felt the ship was in motion, and it took all I could do to move myself in the right way at all; and while I was thinking about that I discovered that my headache had almost gone away, without my noticing.

"You feel lighter in space, you know, Miss Farthing," Miss Halshaw told me as we went up the companionway to the bridge, "because there is not so much under your feet, do you see, to weigh you down." She said it with assurance, in the sort of voice that meant someone had once told her that it was so, and she had made a point of remembering it. I was not sure I did see, but I could hardly care. I thought it was like walking in a dream, where you miss your step but float gently on to where you were going anyway. And I was wondering, *Who is Tobias?*

Ahead of me Miss Halshaw was saying: "Did you know we have a stowaway, darling?"

The man at the wheel turned from the stars and looked instead at me, hard. Around his strange eyes, tanned flesh crinkled. "Tobias," said Miss Halshaw, "this is Miss Sophie Farthing. Sophie, I hope I may call you Sophie—this is Captain Tobias Estranguaro."

Captain Estranguaro was an elderly faun. He flexed his eyebrows and bared his back teeth. They have a very vulgar grin, fauns. I took a step backward, into Miss Halshaw's open hand.

"Toby is my captain, my manager, my agent, my friend," she said, firmly. "My pilot too, you know."

You used to see them sometimes on the wharf, fauns, off ships from Nippur and Caraway. They wore slashed britches and things sewn on the shoulders of their coats: foxes' claws, cowrie shells, things like that. They would go trotting along, very fast, and once one jumped up and ran along our windowsill, leering in at me through the glass. They were a menace to women, or so Papa said. I didn't know. To me everything was a menace, in those days.

Captain Estranguaro was amazingly wrinkled, like all of them. Sparse brown wool was starting to turn gray on his head and hooves. He definitely smelled goaty, though I didn't know then that was what it was, I'd never seen a goat to smell. He wasn't wearing faun garb, though. His trousers were plain drill, each leg tapered neatly and fastened at the side with a button. Above he had on a navy blue blazer with plain brass buttons—over a boiled shirt of white linen—with a gay red-and-white striped cravat at the throat. There was a battered space officer's cap squeezed in between the stumps of his horns. His horns had been filed off, years before. I thought they looked horrible, like mutilations; I couldn't stop staring at them. I don't know how anyone could bring himself to do that. I didn't know then they have to, if they want to be civilized, on Nippur and Caraway.

"Sophie joined us at the Haven, Toby," said Miss Halshaw. I could hear the music in her voice, now she was talking to her usual audience. "By mistake. She says she was following Mr. Cox, only she got a bit lost."

I looked past the captain's muscular shoulder, out through the domed glass, and I wondered how anyone could tell where we were, and where we were going. Space robs you of every direction except down; and that one's none too certain.

Captain Estranguaro spoke. "Mr. Cox is going to Jupiter, wasn't he," he said. His voice sounded lazy and congested, and pleased with itself. "It was wrote in the newspaper."

"Who is he?" I asked him. I was amazed to hear myself talking to a faun. "Who is Mr. Cox?"

"He does work for some lord or other," said Captain Estranguaro. "He represents the Pilots' Guild, isn't he, Mr. Cox," he mused; while overhead the sailors climbed and a sail flapped in a long slow curl, and I thought I could see, far off, a tiny red pip among the white stars. I wondered if it might be Mars, and if that was where the yacht was going; and I felt excited and frightened both together.

"He has a house—" Captain Estranguaro said.

Miss Halshaw had begun to speak at the same moment. "Miss Farthing has just been telling me her extraordinary story, my darling. Mr. Cox knew Miss Farthing's mama."

Captain Estranguaro turned his grin on her. "Is it extraordinary, dear Evadne?"

"Miss Farthing," explained Miss Halshaw, "didn't."

"Oh, can we go to Jupiter, Miss Halshaw?" I asked. "Please?"

"Quite out of the question, Sophie, I fear," said Miss Halshaw. "Toby and I are off to Adonis. I have an engagement for the season. Do you know Adonis, Sophie? But of course you don't."

Captain Estranguaro lowered his waxy green eyelids. "We can take you to the Moon, won't we," he said to me. He swung the wheel and I felt the ship shift beneath my feet, her timbers flexing with the tide. Her head came around, and in a moment I saw the Moon appear below us, on the right, to starboard I should say, and much closer than I would have guessed.

"Oh yes, Toby, how nice," Miss Halshaw said, with relish. "We can put her off there. What a shame we can't stop. Sophie's been to the Moon, haven't you, Sophie?"

A shadow must have crossed my face when she reminded me of it, for she went on: "It's not all saints and salt baths, you know. Why, you haven't even seen the marshmallow gardens! Or the ice glissades at Mandragora Park!" Miss Halshaw rested her hands on the beading of the dome and looked out of a triangular pane, wiping it with her fingertip. "Oh, yes, you'll like the Moon."

"I was thinking of the Registry, wasn't I," said the captain, his voice like the flat blare of a brass bugle.

"Of course!" Miss Halshaw clapped her hands. "What a good idea, Toby, you are clever. The Registry of Births and Deaths, Sophie," she explained to me. "In Crisium. They'll be able to tell you about your mother. They've got everyone written down there, every single subject of the British crown. Fancy that! You're a British subject, aren't you? Well, there you are, then."

"Captain Ester—" I attempted. "Captain Esteran—"

"You call me Toby, young lady." He grinned again, his eyes never leaving mine. "They all do, don't we."

"Only how will I get home, then?" I said, feebly. I supposed I should have to go home, since I couldn't go to Jupiter.

"The ferry," said Miss Halshaw, as if it was obvious, and I suppose it was. She spoke as one accustomed to having the machinery of all the worlds available to her—that was quite a new idea to me. "They'll tell you at the Registry where you go to get it. When you're ready, you can just pop back home." Miss Halshaw laid her hand lightly on my wrist, commanding my attention. "But if there's time, do go and have a look at Mandragora Park, my dear, it is so marvelous I can't tell you."

"But Miss Halshaw," I said, "I haven't got any money!"

Captain Estranguaro looked at me archly. He batted his bottle green eyelids. "You must persuade someone else to let you ride for nothing, don't you?" he said. I didn't know whether he was rebuking me or teasing me; or whether perhaps he simply meant what he said. I think I merely stood there looking glum.

The captain came stalking rapidly across the deck toward me, his hooves shockingly loud on the planking. I noticed that the wood was covered in little triangular dents. He came and stood so close to me I pulled back from the reek of him.

"A pretty young girl like you will have *no* difficulty, will she," he said slowly, "persuading."

I stared at the muscles that moved at the corners of his eyes—their eyes are like green olives and their eyelids turn up at the corners, and there he stood, six inches away, squinting into my face and smiling as if he'd just swallowed the honey spoon.

"Fiddlesticks," said Miss Halshaw, and hit the captain on the nose with a chart rule. "Oh, take no notice of him, Miss Farthing, he's shameless." She took my hand and pulled me toward the stairs. She was as bad as Rita and her friends for pulling me around. "Now come along, Sophie," she commanded me, "let's get out of the way. Ladies are not welcome on the bridge, you know." And so nothing more was said for that time about money, or persuasion.

In Miss Halshaw's cabin we drank more tea, while overhead the sailors ran about, taking in canvas. Miss Halshaw said she had to practice. She said, "Normally I allow no one to watch me practice, but on this occasion—" and she preened herself like the great rosy bird she resembled. "I shall introduce you," she said, "to some of my favorite material." I remembered that her renditions never failed to thrill—I wasn't quite sure what a rendition was, so I waited to see if I felt thrilled; but if I ever did it was hard to tell. I wished Kappi had been there, to explain it to me.

All of a sudden Miss Halshaw declared that was enough singing—now she had decided she must tell my fortune, at once, and she made me look among the jumble for a pack of playing cards. I found them in the pocket of her dressing gown. "There's a young man," Miss Halshaw said, laying them out on the bottom of the tea tray for want of any clear space in the room. "He is hiding his face. He is standing on the ground," she said, in a very imposing voice, "or on a rock. Good gracious." She looked me in the eye, the corners of her mouth turned down. "He has a sword."

"I don't know any young men," I said. I didn't quite understand what we were supposed to be doing. "I've never stood on ground, either."

Miss Halshaw turned up a heart. "Oh my goodness gracious me. A kiss. He's going to kiss you, Sophie."

I felt myself begin to go red as the card in her hand. "I've never—"

"Never mind," she said, and quickly scooped up the cards all together in a heap. I thought I caught a look of wary distaste on her face, as though she'd seen something that

offended her. She pouted at me. "Just you be careful who
you kiss when you do, my dear, that's all. Make sure he's not
wearing a sword, first." Then she gave a giggle and ducked her
head, patting the air with the tips of her fingers, as though she
were ashamed of herself for something.

My headache had come back, slightly. I had begun to feel
shut in in the hot, stuffy cabin. I did not want to sit there—
I wanted to go and look at the Moon. Eventually I plucked
up courage and asked. Miss Halshaw said of course, which
was very strange to me, I was not used to getting my own
way without an argument. She took me into the saloon, which
was all in darkness. I could dimly see a piano there, and a
couch, where Miss Halshaw sank, directing me to draw the
curtains. When I did I saw also a great number of potted
plants, and a brass telescope on a stand—but the brass was
sticky with verdigris, and the plants had large black spots on
their leaves.

Miss Halshaw gave the upholstery a distasteful pat, releas-
ing slow spouts of dust from the rotted silk. "One tries so
hard to keep the starlight out," she said, "but what's the use?
It draws the goodness out of everything."

In the map rooms at the Aeyrie where the deep space charts
hang in ranks, smelling of starch and ink, the clerks mark the
places where the Black Suns are supposed to be. The starmen
say those suck everything up like giant mouths. The young
daredevils scoff: they believe there is no such thing; yet the
instructors speak about the alchemists and astrologers of old,
the Chinese with their Dragon Sun that eats its own tail and—
what then? Turns inside out; like as not. That would be a sight
to see. It would be worth traveling some way to see a sight
like that.

What do I think, you ask?

I? I think there may be anything out there. Anything.

I ran the glass out along the rigging, to look at the sailors at
their work. They were perfectly ordinary young human men,
the ones I could see. After Captain Estranguaro, I own I was
rather disappointed.

Then I looked away up at the Moon. It was huge now, and
hung tipped over us like the lid must over beetles in a biscuit
jar. I was convinced we would be washed up on that shore,
and smashed into a thousand pieces. It was dark there, with

the Earth behind our shoulder, and I could make out nothing until Miss Halshaw sat by me and pointed out the faint little fingerprints of light that were cities and harbors. She was full of commendations—everything was all so charming and pretty on the Moon.

After that we seemed to hang a long time in space without drawing any closer, though Miss Halshaw said Captain Estranguaro would be most intent and busy. I imagined him putting on the gold circlet that pilots wear, pulling it over his poor ruined horns, while his eyes rolled up in his head. Then suddenly I saw the bos'n signal—the lookout had sighted the platform we were aiming for—and now we were slipping sideways, inch by inch, sliding toward it.

Miss Halshaw was at the telescope. "Oh, look, Sophie, there's a balloon in," she said. "You might catch it. Oh come on, Toby, do hurry up." But the *Halcyon Dorothy* seemed to linger—it was an age broadsiding the raft, and by the time we had the orbits married the waiting balloon had long departed.

While the yacht hove to, ready to drop into her berth, Miss Halshaw got up and left me sitting there in the saloon. I sat and watched the bellows men dart effortlessly here and there like tumblers at a circus, catching the lines the sailors threw and signaling one to another with their hands and feet.

Miss Halshaw reappeared with a thick coat and a glass helmet in her arms. "I hope this will fit," she said. "Stand up, Sophie, please." Bemused, I did, and she helped me on with those unfamiliar things. "The coat you can keep, it's ages old," she said, trying not very successfully to fold back the cuffs, and looking doubtfully at the hem that trailed on the floor.

"Oh please, ma'am, I can't," I said, feeling shy and awkward again suddenly.

"Nonsense, child," she said. "You can't go out there without a coat on"; and she popped the helmet over my head, continuing to talk to me. "We must take great care," I thought I heard her say, through the glass, and she rapped on the top of the helmet with her rings.

I took the helmet off. "I'm already in your debt, ma'am," I said miserably.

She pursed her lips. "You can bring the helmet back, if you like," she said.

"But you're going to Adonis," I reminded her.

"Goodness gracious, Sophie, Adonis isn't the other side of the Sun, you know."

"Yes it is," said Captain Estranguaro, who came jauntily in, rubbing his hands.

"Oh be quiet, Toby, Miss Farthing knows what I mean." Miss Halshaw took my hand in both of hers. "I mean we'll be back, dear, in a year or so. We're always having to go to High Haven, aren't we, Toby?" she said airily.

"We come and take you to a concert," he suggested.

"You're so kind, both of you," I kept saying. "I don't know how I can ever thank you."

That was when I found the purse in the pocket of the coat.

"That should see you home, isn't it," said Captain Estranguaro, waving his hand at it as though he detested money, and was only too glad to be rid of the nasty stuff.

"There might be enough for a sandwich and a dish of ice cream at the rink," said Miss Halshaw.

And Reader, I began to cry.

5

An apologetic clerk

Many ships wait at the high platforms, that are too large or too busy or too grand to put down on the Moon—that day I remember a troopship called the *Lars Porsena*, and some dinghies and suchlike, and a little black wherry all hung about with nets and bundles, by name the *Arvyst Gos*. Now the dockers strove at their wheels: the whitewashed side of the platform loomed; and the *Halcyon Dorothy* settled gracefully onto her hook, wallowing like some great yellow hippopotamus. They secured lines, and made all fast—and there we were, ready to go ashore.

Miss Halshaw was staying aboard, as was her custom: for the sake of her throat, she said. She made me take a Nitrox pastille, and put some more in my pocket for later. "I hope they have good news for you at the Registry," she said. "Just imagine: perhaps your mother was a Martian princess, living there in secret! Oh Sophie, what a splendid tale that would be!" And thus she continued; but I did not want her to speak of my mama, so I put on the helmet, lifted the skirt of my coat, and stepped out along the gangplank.

It was quite a small platform, uncovered, scant of gravity, and without any air at all to breathe. Suited travelers were gathered at the stanchions, while on board the ships faces looked from every porthole, watching to see who passed— sneaking a forbidden cigarette—one picking his teeth with a nail end.

Captain Estranguaro took me to the ticket office and paid my fare down: a single, unaccompanied; then we waited, a little apart from the human passengers, the captain being for- eign. Around us were coats and helmets and respirators of every shape and kind. Everyone was reading newspapers and checking watches, or gazing over the railing at the great dun Moon spread so broad beneath, looking for the first sign of the ascending balloon. I wanted to go and look, but I was feeling rather light and insecure.

I touched my helmet to Captain Estranguaro's. "Where does he live?" I asked him. "Mr. Cox, I mean?"

"He has a house in London Town," I heard him say. "Per- haps Cox goes home, while they fit for Jupiter," he said. The captain's green eyes twitched and his wizened face looked very strange, so close to mine; and I wondered whether he was telling me the truth in all this. I began to feel very lost and small out there, floating so many miles above the Moon. My helmet filled with the sound of my own breathing.

At last the aether balloon arrived, swelling up through its dock, to rise above us like some vast canary-colored pudding. The car followed, crammed with departing passengers, and then the lightermen swam forward, holding up their placards. The footbridge was swung into place and out they all came: the fine ladies and gentlemen first, with their personal attend- ants—and next, a bustle of clerks and scribes, carrying their

portfolios and writing desks—and then a tumbling company
of soldiers, plainly the worse for drink—and last of all the
foreigners, people from Corregio and Tethys and who knows
where. One person, I remember, looked like a hairy black
Labrador, though it was the size of a bear and walked upright,
in boots.

Boarding, I was glad the captain was with me, knowing at
any moment I should step too high or stumble over my coat
and go spinning away into space, so excited and unsteady did
I feel. He escorted me to a seat on the benches, and when I
was settled he fastened my belt, though I thought his hands
lingered rather too long over it. Then he took my hand and
kissed it. How warm and vigorous his lips felt. I was startled. "Always happy, don't we," he drawled, gently, "to help
a damsel in distress."

Then he left, pausing and slipping the conductor, I suppose,
half a crown to keep an eye on me, before tripping back across
the bridge. I watched him go, but I could not see if he was
carrying a sword anywhere about his person. It would have
had to be a small one.

Many of the passengers that had boarded the balloon seemed
to be in holiday mood, joking and talking together loudly.
Another unaccompanied woman sat next to me, a solitary
little Cærulean, and quite lost she did look without her family. Behind was a young gentleman bringing a cluster of the
intelligent sponges that come from Strachan's World. They
took a great fancy to an elderly citizen in a silk hat, and kept
climbing up the back of his seat to hang upon him, nestling
against his neck and humming softly. The gentleman was rigid with rage; and their escort, very smart in pin-striped trousers
and morning coat, was continually apologizing—but I have to
say that people were laughing, and so was I.

The conductor didn't laugh. He was a fat, melancholy, black
man in a pale green uniform who worked the gas, pushing his
levers of brass back and forth as we fell out of the dark into
the dark. He came over with his hat in his hands, and in
a soft, high voice he asked the young gentleman to restrain
his party.

Across the car people had begun to sing; but I sat silent on
the hard slats, nursing Miss Halshaw's helmet in my lap. There
was a stove in the car, but I think we were all quite cold. The

blue Cærulean was shivering. She looked anxiously into my face, then shyly offered me a crystallized worm from a paper bag that she had. I shook my head and buried my nose in my new coat. It smelled of mothballs and lily of the valley.

In a while I began to be bored with the ride, and wondered how long I had been away from home, and whether Papa was still asleep. With the dose I had given him in anger I supposed he might have slept through the beginning of his shift, and the end of it too. I had no idea how long I'd spent on board the *Halcyon Dorothy*. Then a hooter sounded, making me jump and almost drop the helmet. Thin clouds were whirling past us—then part of a ring of mountains, with distant buildings high among them. Then more buildings, closer, rushing by in a jumble, and we were down, jolting on the springs of our seats. People fell against each other and exclaimed at the indignity.

Traveling, I had decided, was easy. There was nothing to it. Now it was the thought of actually being somewhere that began to be alarming. I hated the Moon, I remembered; but this time I would keep my chin up—I was determined, I would carry out Captain Estranguaro's instructions; Miss Halshaw's too, I thought, why not? Not the least of the gifts of that remarkable pair had been to remind me there were other things to see, other places in the universe than the night watchman's cottage on St. Radigund's Wharf, whatever the night watchman himself might say against it.

"Is this Crisium?" I asked the Cærulean, but she merely yipped and scratched her muzzle, and scurried away with the departing throng. The conductor was holding the door open, supervising. I came up alongside him, and asked: "Please, sir, is this Crisium?"

For answer he did no more than point with his finger to the lights away across the harbor.

"How do I get to the Birth Registry?" I persisted.

"Trams at the pier gate, miss," he said, in his high, sad voice. Despite the captain's half crown, I saw he did not mean to leave his station by so much as a step of the foot. His eyes were dull and he held on to the brass handle of the sliding gate as though the man had become a part of the machine.

The balloon had landed in the middle of a flat plain of dust. It was too dark to see how far it stretched. Two barefoot little boys were rushing toward the balloon in great sliding strides, with flat pieces of wood strapped to their feet and torches held over their heads. They unrolled strips of coconut matting and laid them down for us to walk our way to the pier, rolling them up behind us and laying them down again before us as we proceed. It was some way.

At the pierhead the sponges were being penned up in a fish tank with netting over the top. They looked unhappy, skulking in a heap all up one end. The other passengers were climbing into pretty, fur-lined cars pulled by young men on tricycles. I had no idea how much money Miss Halshaw had given me, or how far it would go. I set out to walk along the pier, as quickly as I could, though I was heavy again now, more so than I had ever been. I started to look out for the trams.

They have paved the shore of the Sea of Crises with dull gray slabs of slate. At the pier gate the women gather before dawn, bringing bags full of the mysterious vile creatures the menfolk have caught during the night, out in the deep dust where big ships cannot go. I knew I had seen them before, in nightmares, those huge centipedes without eyes—warty logs—round-shaped creatures that are nothing but teeth. A woman hailed me, pointing into her sack and grinning, rubbing her stomach. Had she pulled up something good to eat? It looked innocent enough, a big white gourd that was soft and crumbly inside. But when she dug out a handful and thrust it at me, tossing her head and grunting, champing her jaw, I saw how the thing tried to slither away beneath her arm. I picked up my coat and hurried by her.

There came a tram, clattering up behind me—I turned and saw its lamps like glowing dandelion clocks, soft balls of light in the dusty darkness. I waved and shouted, and the driver stared at me from his unprotected platform, like an owl in his woolly scarf and huge goggles. With a hiss of steam he braked his craft and gestured me to jump aboard. "I want to go to the Registry!" I shouted, my voice echoing around the plaza. I don't know if he could hear me. With a gloomy sweep of his arm, he repeated the gesture, sweeping me aboard. I sorted a coin from the purse, and he took it without a word or sign. I thought he might be the balloon conductor's brother.

The tram car was curiously empty. There was a sharp smell of spirits coming off two men in quilted jackets who were asleep in their seat, one's head on the other's shoulder, his hand splayed around a yellow bottle that was propped on his fat stomach. I took a seat farther down the car. Behind me a man in uniform was berating another man in the same uniform, in a foreign language. His words washed over me and mingled with the snores of the sleeping men; and I thought of how Papa breathed in his sleep, that it had seemed to fill the house and wrap me about where I sat, shirking my duties.

I remembered the story of Mr. Crusoe, and how much he repented disobeying his papa, when the seas of Earth rose to swallow him up. I was glad this accidental journey of mine would be over soon. I should go back to Papa with the truth about Mama, and see how he liked that story. Yet even as I resolved so, I looked out of the window and saw that we were driving along the promenade—and out to sea the black shade of a schooner was going up toward the stars, yellow lights on her masts and in all her windows. I flinched and looked away. I was not, after all, looking forward to the ferry home: in no hurry to be so ill again. Instead I tried to puzzle out a card above the seats, that showed our route.

The tram swayed and climbed a hill into a region of narrow crescent streets, then across a viaduct into a gaslit circus that was laid out in the shape of a kidney. The buildings were more grand than any in the Haven, built of a stone that was black as coal, each like a palace with twenty pointed turrets and two hundred windows. In the middle was a ten-foot statue of a man in a top hat, pointing up into the black sky.

A hand fell on my shoulder. I turned and saw the silent man leaning toward me. "This is your stop," he said, in English. I think it was the only thing he had said. I thanked him kindly. He nodded, glum, settling down to the rest of the harangue. The first man had not stopped talking all the while.

I got off the tram in a cloud of steam and watched it rattle away. There was a kind of snow on the pavements here, or thick frost. It was melting in a puddle where the tram had stood. I was glad of Miss Halshaw's coat, and I wondered why anyone would choose to visit a place so cold and dusty, let alone come and live here.

The air was thin and cold, and there was not another soul about. I walked along the railings until I came to a brass plaque on a gatepost that glinted in the starlight. H. M. Registry of Births, Deaths, and Marriages. Enquiries, it said, and there was a carved hand that pointed around the corner.

I followed the sign, looking up at the building. I could see a tower, and leading to it a bridge of milky white stone that had a dim glow to it. White shapes were darting all around the upper stories, zipping here and there at great speed. One of them swooped into the street in front of me and I thought I heard it squeak. It was a bat, though it was as white as a fish.

I tried the great door of the Registry, but it was locked. Nights are long on the Moon, and it was barely dawn. The Registry would be closed for hours yet. The handle fell back against the wood with a dull boom, like the death knock of my hopes and energies; exhausted, I sank down in the porch. There wasn't a seat, so I sat on the cold tiled floor.

Dear Reader, I sat there on the hard tiles, and gave way to misery. I wished I'd never come. I thought of my papa, still snoring, no doubt, or else up and cursing me, stumbling around looking for his poppy juice. I thought about Miss Halshaw and Captain Estranguaro. I don't think I understood then quite how lucky I'd been to end up on their yacht rather than another. Not all travelers would have been so kind. Yet now I was away from them, I began to wonder what in the worlds I had been doing to allow them to abandon me here, hungry, weary, and alone. In that dark hour I was sure it was a terrible mistake. Mr. Cox had taken me for someone else, another who wore such a ring. Mama had been a beautiful and virtuous woman from the Hanover district, and she had died in a famous and horrible wreck. No Register would be able to tell me any different.

Wretched and uncomfortable, somehow I must have managed to fall asleep, for the next thing I knew the Earth was up, like a sunlit slice of blue and silver apple, and there was a charwoman leaning over me. She was for sending me away, but I insisted I had come all the way from High Haven on important business, and then she did grudgingly unlock and let me come inside with her. She took me across a courtyard to a waiting room, where she lit a gas fire and left me alone. There were copies of *Arms and Armigers* and the *Illustrated London News* on the table, a large clock, and an even larger

picture of Her Majesty the Queen on the wall. I sat in a chair
and tried to doze. Strange lights and visions danced continually about in my head.

At half past eight, a young clerk put his head around the
door. His hair was neat and black and gleaming with oil. "Hul-
lo!" he said in a very brisk way, and he favored me with an
approving smile. I stood up, though he prayed me not to, and
I told him I had come to enquire about my mother; and I gave
him my full name, Sophrona Farthing.

"That's a very unusual Christian name, miss, if I may be so
bold," he said. He put the palms of his hands together, joined
at the fingertips. "It's Terence, isn't it, if I'm not mistaken?"

"No," I said, puzzled. "Sophrona."

"Quite," he said, rubbing his hands, and I thought he swallowed a smirk as he bowed. "Would you be so kind as to
follow me, please, Miss Farthing?" He attended me with as
many manners as if I'd been a young lady of quality, though I
must have looked a sight in my outsize coat and loudly clack-
ing clogs, carting that clumsy helmet with me everywhere I
went. The clerk wore a black suit with a high stiff collar, and
shoes as shiny black as his hair. They squeaked.

The corridors of the Registry of Births are arched high, too
high to see the ceiling without ricking your neck. There was
the sound of a heavy door slamming somewhere, a sound like
the clap of doom. I had had but little sleep, and that of the
poorest, thinnest kind. I was confused by the corridors, the
stairs, the men in high collars and boys in buckled shoes
streaming ceaselessly up and down with scrolls and ledgers
and thick-pleated parchments. I barely knew how to respond
to the civilities of my guide. Among the dark rafters the white
bats flitted silently by.

The clerk took me underground, along another corridor, and
into a small cubicle, where I sat and waited again. When he
came back he was holding a slip of paper in the palm of his
hand. He held it in front of him and he looked down at it,
then over it at me. "We have no record of an Estelle Farthing,
miss," he said. "Not on High Haven. Not ever."

I didn't understand. I waited for him to tell me what was
on the paper.

"The maiden name was Crosby, you said, miss."

"Yes," I said.

"And the Christian name Estelle. You are sure of that."

"Yes," I said.

He looked at his paper again. "Residing in Hanover Heights."

I held up my chin. "Of course," I said.

The clerk looked at his paper again, as if in a last hope to make it come out different. Then he admitted there was an Estelle Crosby, yes. And she was listed among the passengers of the pleasure cruiser *Hippolyta* when it hit the beacon rock and broke up, leaving no survivors.

"A Miss Estelle Crosby," he said, awkwardly. "No record of marriage." He seemed quite uncomfortable, and paused, as if waiting for me to say something. When I did not, he said, "No issue."

Then he looked me in the eye again. "I have checked, miss," he said, apologizing in a very gentle way, as if he had done me some awful injury quite unintended. He showed me the piece of paper. Neat pencil marks swam before my eyes like tadpoles—names, dates, parents. And at the bottom: "n.i."

I didn't understand. I was dumbfounded. I didn't know what to do. I heard a voice in my head saying, Mr. Cox was right. He was right.

"I'm sorry if it's bad news, miss," said the clerk.

I thought to reach inside my coat then, into my pocket, and I took out my ring, and showed him that. "This was my mother's," I said.

He looked at it, at the sign of the eye and the arrow. "Why, that's the pilots'," he said. "The Pilots' Guild, miss: you see the sign? That's one of theirs, that sign." I was hardly hearing him. His face, his hands, his trim little finger pointing to my ring: I could hardly see them. An awful black shame was rising up before me, nameless, formless, blocking out the light.

"I've never seen such a ring," the clerk went on. "And a fine one it is, if I may venture an opinion. Would you be so kind as to lend me that ring for a moment, miss, to show to my superior? I shall take the greatest care of it, I do assure you." He spoke gladly, as if by complimenting me on my ring he could make amends for the wrong I had made him do me; and he held out his hand.

I did not want him to take my ring—nor did I want him to leave me alone again. I put the ring on my finger and stood up, gathering the folds of my coat around me. "I'll show him myself," I said, resolutely, "if you please."

"To be sure, miss. This way, miss. After you."

The apologetic clerk's superior was a thin gentleman with an even higher collar. His forehead was high too, and quite bald. He sat in an office of his own, in a heavy chair behind a heavy desk, and stared at my person and the ring on my hand. He did not offer me a seat—I could see he was not accustomed to entertaining grimy-faced little girls in his office— and when his junior told him about Miss Crosby and showed his significant little slip of paper, I began to be aware that he regarded my whole tale as nothing less than a ruse, a device by which I thought to come into their mighty establishment for some wicked purposes of my own. A red flush began to well up from out of his collar, reaching to his hairless ears, and he brushed aside the rest of my introduction. "Where did you get that ring?" he asked. He did not call me "miss," or indeed anything at all. He stretched out his hand across the desk. "Let me see it."

But now I was wary, and pressed my hand flat on my breast, and held the end of the ring finger in my other hand, to keep them from taking my ring off.

"It has a sign of the pilots on it, sir!" said my clerk, growing excited. "The eye and arrow, sir, don't you know—"

The senior clerk made a peremptory gesture. "Take it from her," he ordered.

But I clung to it, and the junior clerk apologized to me, and to his superior, and was in a torment that he could no way come about to do what he was bid, or placate either of us. "It is a very fine ring, sir!" he exclaimed, chewing his lips.

Then it was inevitable—like Mr. Cox on the dockside, the senior clerk accused me of stealing the ring. And when I still denied it, and refused to give it up, he grew irate, and the red tide washed up over the bulwarks of his ears and suffused his whole countenance. "It's perfectly clear you have stolen the ring," he proclaimed, "and that coat you're wearing too, I'll be bound. Henderson, go and fetch the porter. Fetch a constable!" he cried.

"Yes sir!" cried the clerk, who had been gazing from him to me and back again, wide-eyed and openmouthed—delighted to be given a command he could actually carry out, he rushed from the room. I heard his shiny black shoes go tapping away down the hall.

I snatched up my helmet and ran out too.

The senior clerk was too slow, too dignified, too trapped by his own heavy furniture, to catch me. As I darted into the hall I heard him bellow. "Henderson! Henderson!"

Henderson had gone one way; I went the other. Kilting up my coat, I ran on, around a corner, almost colliding with a young gentleman wheeling a trolley heaped with documents. With a spiteful sweep of my arm, I struck them with my helmet and knocked the whole tottering pile into the air and onto the floor, while I ran on by. Behind me papers spiraled like flying bats and shouting echoed faintly in the great arched corridors. Dodging a boy encumbered with two enormous books, one under each arm, I found myself at the bottom of an ill-lit iron spiral stair and set off up it. Cursing my weight, my heavy clothes, my noisy clogs, I climbed. A constable would send me home, if he didn't lock me up. They would take Mama's ring away and I should never get it back. I dived from the stair at random into the corridors. Faces appeared at doors, startled to see me run by. Fingers pointed at me.

I whirled into a hall where the walls were hung with monstrous white antlers and stuffed dead pike from out of the deep sea. Ahead of me I could see the flat white glare of sunlight! I jumped a flight of steps, squeezed past an ornamental bust, and almost ran straight into a messenger in buckled shoes, heading at me from the right. I ducked and swerved for the doors, and the messenger went crashing into the elderly porter who had at that moment been striving to intercept me from the left. I bounded out into the street, my lungs heaving in the skimpy air.

I was at another side of the building, looking down a street of fashionable shops. Not for the first time in my life, I fled for safety into the crowd. In and out of the strolling throng I ran until I could run no farther, then set myself to walk as quickly as I could, downhill. My heart was beating fit to burst, and my legs ached from my unaccustomed weight. Overhead, the merry ships went sauntering across the dusty sky. I risked a glance over my shoulder, but saw no one following me. I felt conspicuous, and angry, and afraid. I kept moving, heading for the harbor below.

In the arcades I saw ladies in expensive clothes stoop and peer through shop windows. In the lamplit interiors, younger women sat, and walked, and turned about, modeling the latest Paris gowns. I have been there since, by chance: turned a corner and found myself unexpectedly in that district where I ran in terror as a young girl. One woman, dressed perhaps in a costume of tweed, stands and looks through a pane of glass at another, dressed in an evening gown of ice blue tulle. What those women seem to want is to be each other. The one on the outside has money, but no contentment; while the one on the inside has no money, and no contentment either, but would rather be free and at large in Paris, or Constantinople, or anywhere but sitting in that window all day.

In the cafés I saw gentlemen I would recognize now as the officers of trade and their associates. They sit at tables carved from moonrock and drink brandy and mineral waters with a dish of the marshmallow of the day. Then they put on their hats and take a cab to a meeting where they raise the harbor duties and condemn the traffic in Jovian drugs. All I knew then was that they had monocles and fierce mustaches and vast expanses of waistcoat and there would not be one among them who would help me. I hurried on, into the cold breeze and the dust that drifts in from the sea.

When at length I came back into the region of the pier gate, I turned aside into the back streets, to seek out a public house. I did not like public houses then—indeed, I knew none, having done no more than glance into the public bar of the *Cormorant* as I passed its doors—but I knew how the men I must find liked to gather there, turning their hard-earned silver into pipes of baccy and jugs of beer. There was one, across the street—I forget the name on its signboard, the *Mermaid* or the *Harbor Tap*—I took off my ring, held on tight to my purse and my helmet, and in I went.

Inside it was dark, but not unpleasantly so: there was a coal fire blazing and a cheerful glow of lanterns on the glass and pewter and brasswork, and on the faces of the customers. The locals sat in the public, feeding babies and playing dominoes; but the ship captains and officers were collected in the private room, a dozen or more of them at tables round about. When I told them what I wanted, they tried to direct me to the ferry— "But I have no money," I said, feeling the hard edges of the coins in Miss Halshaw's purse within my pocket. And I told them I would work my passage.

"What can you do?" they asked. I could see they were already amused at my presumption, and the uncomely figure I presented.

"I can read and write," I boldly said; and they chuckled. Then I felt myself go red and stubbornly I went on: "And look after a gentleman, and do everything he requires."

Then they laughed aloud, and one said: "Promises, promises!" And I grew bothered, not understanding their jest.

Then a man in the corner held up his pipe in his hand, and he spoke to me, not unkindly. "Could you write a letter for me, girl? A letter to my missus?"

I said I could, and I pushed between their broad backs at the tables and went to speak to him alone.

He was a man of middle years, with red hair and a sweaty face with as many warts and moles as there are currants in a bun. "Can you make it fair," he said, "with sweet words and so?"

Sweet words had not been plentiful in my short life, but I had come too far to hesitate there. "Indeed I can, sir," I said. "Nothing easier," I claimed.

The captain, whose name was Mr. Allardyce, bought me my breakfast, and while I ate I plainly told him that I had come from the High Haven looking for my fortune; but I did not say anything to him about clerks or constables. I saw some constables in the harbor when we left to find his ship, but they were not looking for me.

Like Mr. Crusoe, I was to regret my voyage—not then, no, but later I cried vain tears and lamented aloud that I hadn't followed Miss Halshaw's instructions and caught the Haven ferry. But on that day in the harbor of Crisium, I turned my back upon the Haven and upon Papa, with his whining and his jealousy; and I set my face toward Earth: to London.

6

An unremarkable face

The assassin wakes suddenly. He is woken by someone gently singing a line of Verdi, in a bass voice.

"Va, pensiero, sull' ali dorate . . ."

On the moon called Dread, it is not yet day. Still the young man feels he has slept long enough; he feels tranquil and refreshed. He has passed the night in a guest suite at his college, the Ancient and Circumspect Order of Assassins. He slept alone, as he always has.

The room where he lies is high-ceilinged and rather plain. It is light enough to make out that the walls are whitewashed plaster, above a dado of deep brown oak, from Earth, which the young man has never yet had occasion to visit. A slender crucifix of black wood hangs on one wall, and on another a painting of the rings of Austriga IV.

Down the hall the voice sings the same line of Verdi again. It is the senior house's man, preparing the morning tea.

The assassin sits up in bed and rubs his face. He has momentarily forgotten the man's name. Names are such slippery things, so easily revised and displaced.

The assassin gets out of bed and opens the curtains. Outside the window he sees a spiked iron rod running along the top of a white wall. Beyond is a sky the color of fresh meat.

The name of the moon is Dread, and it is not a popular place, generally, because of the air, which is like trying to breathe broken glass; and because of the college.

The assassin gets back into bed. He is content with the place. His father is recently dead, and he never knew his mother; so if he thinks of anywhere as home, it is this institution. Now he is in practice he does not stay anywhere for very long.

He is human, and nineteen years old.

The manservant is human too, but elderly. He enters with a tall glass of hot water in a stand of chased silver. In the water are four or five bright yellow berries and a small, stiff, bright green leaf. Automatically the assassin checks the color and the vapor, sniffing it subtly; looking, without even thinking about it, for poisons. The servant smiles to himself. He knows what the young master is doing.

Such youth is not unusual in the order. Many of the finest practitioners have been young. They do their best work before thirty, it is said, as mathematicians do; before the personality becomes too fixed. It is possible to grow old in the trade, though no insurer would write you a policy. Downstairs, here in the senior house, live several professors who practice very rarely, but spend their time teaching, debating, and giving advice to visiting policemen. The existence and influence of the order, illegal on every civilized world, are admitted by none. The college is not marked on any map.

"You leave us again today, *signore*," says the manservant, as he whips up a mug of soap.

"With the tide," says the youth, staring at him. He drinks his tea.

"Today it is that you go to take up your post," says the man, pushing back the boy's long hair.

The assassin watches him, watches the movements of his face and body, as if the man were a subject. (*Subject*, they say, not *victim*, which is vulgar.) The youth means no harm by his scrutiny. It is the only way he knows to look at someone.

"Your father's post and his before him," says the man complacently.

"Do you wish me luck?" the young man asks him.

"No, *signore*," the man says with a smile. It is a ritual exchange, a pleasantry of the order whose members boast that they never leave anything to chance.

"How is the weather?" asks the youth.

Vile as ever, the man says. The steward has not put it up on the board yet, but the weather today is certain to be vile.

Shaven, the assassin feels his cheeks. Only here, he thinks, would he allow another's hand to shave him. He refuses breakfast and dismisses the man. He dresses in his traveling clothes, which are the only clothes he has with him, and he puts his boots on; then he goes down to be fitted with a face.

The world is not yet up, but the sun is rising. It shines in a ground floor window and up the stairs, gilding the edges of the banisters. The youth walks down into sunlight. His boots are india rubber and felt, soundless on the stairs. Some junior boys on their way to a garotte class fall silent as they see him coming down, pressing back against the wall to let him pass. The prefect in charge of them greets him respectfully.

The master of masks stands in the middle of his laboratory, surrounded by his charges. Eyeless, they gape at him from their glass bowls. The air smells of saline solution. The master is wearing his black leather apron and gauntlets. He stands with his hands on his hips. "I could give you the face your father wore," he says.

This is not at all what the young man wants. "No, Federico," he says. "Give me the face of no one."

The master of masks looks around the ancient room, looks at all the faces. He is insulted, and amused by the insult. He spreads his hands. "How can I do that, *signore*? Every man here was someone once. When you take them out, they are someone again."

The youth shows no inclination to choose. He folds his arms. "You know what I mean, Federico," he says. "An everyday face. The face of a man you pass in the street without noticing." He flexes his beautiful fingers, tapping them on his bicep.

The master shrugs. He walks to a bowl where a face floats, hollow, white as wax. With its open mouth and wide eye sockets it looks shocked to find itself there. "This is the face of an adulterer," the master says. "He was caught hurrying to get home before his wife." He smiles the ghost of a smile, the merest curl of a lip. "Is it common enough for you, eh, an adulterer?"

The assassin glances at it. He frowns. "No," he says, thinking: guilt attracts the inquisitive as jam draws wasps. He holds up his hand, specifying. "A face you might see every day of your life yet be unable to recall. Please, Federico, let me have that face."

The master goes along the table. He stops at the next bowl. The face that swims here is older and fatter. Its cheeks are slack, and blank of time's traces as an unborn babe's. The skin is so clear the veins of the alien lining show through it.

Federico makes a small flourish of demonstration. "Here is the face for you, *signore*. This face. This, *signore*," he says, "is the face of a gentleman's butler, whom the gentleman has completely ignored for years." The mask master smiles. "His master no longer sees him. He does not know that the man who stands at his shoulder when he is eating has lost his face."

The assassin goes over. He cocks his head and touches his jaw. "No," he says. "Not that either." For he knows that people in public places look at the servants of the great, in envy or in pity. He cups his elbow in his hand and says: "Give me a face, Federico, that is beneath notice. And quickly, Federico, hm? The boat is waiting, but the tide will not."

The mask master shakes his head. He glances around his stock as if thinking this is a tall order. "I cannot satisfy you, *signore*," he says. "We have no such faces. Unless—unless it be this one," he says, glumly; and he points at the face in the next bowl along.

"This is the face of an undertaker," he says. "No one ever looks at them."

"That face, Federico?"

"This exact same face, *signore*."

The face hangs tipped toward him, staring at the floor. Its cheeks are long and blue, as blue as the deep sockets of the eyes.

The assassin chuckles, without much mirth. He taps the glass bowl with his knuckle, as though to attract the face's attention. With his other hand he slaps the master lightly on the arm. "A good joke, Federico," he says. "An undertaker, eh?"

He turns, nodding his head, surveying the ranks of faces suspended in their bowls of arcane liquor. He points at random. "I'll take that one," he says. "Whose was that? No, don't tell me, I don't want to know. The less I know, the lighter I shall travel."

He sits up in the adjustable chair. Federico puts a bib around his neck and tilts him backward. Now the chosen face lies upon his own, inert and wet. The lining, an alien slime mold from beyond Betelgeuse, requires a moment or two to warm up. It feels cold, salty—rather like a jellyfish, in fact, and it stings a trifle too, though the tea the young man drank takes the worst of that away. The process is not unpleasant for him; he has learned to enjoy it. Since boyhood he has borne more faces than he can count.

He asks again about the weather in prospect. The tide will be strong, Federico says. Then he falls silent. He smooths the mask into place, coaxing the lining along with a brush dipped in spirits of wine. The young man lies back with his eyes shut and thinks about his new master, the man who will now command and keep him. He knows him well, the man who employed his father. While his new face is creeping about, nestling into his nostrils and sealing itself moistly up behind his lips, he imagines his master in certain characteristic poses: seated, in full regalia, at a state function; toying with a scorpion at the point of a poniard; sprawling with a bumper of port before the hearth of his hot and solitary mansion. The youth permits himself a moment of reluctance to go out there and serve him.

The times have changed much from what they were. The situation of a retainer is now not thought quite as desirable as it once was. Gentlemen have a greater regard for the law than they did in the wilder days of the last century, and though they inherit your services, they fail to employ you properly—yet they will not let you go. They keep you kicking your heels on some godforsaken asteroid, without commissions, and without liberty. The careers of some notable practitioners have dwindled in this way, until they have become merely ornamental, like a rack of swords hung up in a dining hall.

The young man would far rather go on as he has been, free-lance; but there is a place for him, and a family tradition to uphold. Obviously there are advantages to being in service. It will be nice never to have to go cold or hungry. In any case, the young man is confident that his master will have work for him. His father was always occupied, right up until the day he died.

This is not to say that these young arms will be permanently steeped in gore, as the illustrated magazines like us to imagine. Most of a practitioner's time is spent making a study of his subject, watching him, reading up on him. He has to know him perfectly before he can dispatch him. He must be utterly reliable and entirely invisible. There is never a relic, unless the commission requires one.

"There we are, *signore*." Federico dries the young man with a towel, and unties the bib. The youth touches his new face. It feels more or less like his own, though the cheek he fingers is numb. Soon enough the drink will wear off, and the alien protoplasm settle down, and then he will be able to forget he is wearing it; and no one else will ever be able to tell.

He thanks Federico, and tips him ten soldi. He walks on down the hall to the cloakroom, where the attendant bows and hands him the cloak and helmet he indicates. "A pleasant journey, *signore*,". the old man says. The young assassin does not reply. He pulls on gloves that adhere to his hands like a second skin.

He stands a moment looking out through the lead glass across the scoured, porous plain, at the vast pink blot of Mars now shouldering into the sky, stirring up the aether wind. The boat will be waiting at the mountaintop. He really ought to hurry, so they can catch the tide at the turn; but he is dawdling, loath to take up the reins of his new life. It was his father's cruiser, and now it is his, and it will wait for him, tide or no tide.

The young man catches sight of his reflection in the cloakroom mirror, and thoughtfully he runs the tip of his finger down his cheek again. He wonders how long it will take him this time, before he learns to recognize himself.

7

I take up lodgings at Lambeth

On Earth, on a pitch-black evening in October, in the middle of the street, I saw a man dancing. He was twenty feet up in the air. I remember he had a white nightshirt on and a necklace of lions' teeth, and the wind blew sparks around him out of the bonfire while he swayed and wobbled, jumping from foot to foot. The gravity is so strong there, I knew he was in the greatest peril, and my heart was in my mouth.

When I think of Earth, I think of that man, Jack Spivey, and of the glorious journey he made, from one side of the street to the other. I wish I had a rope like him on this trek, to keep me straight, for a current of words is trickier than any tide, blows hot and cold and sweeps away your pen to where it will. No—I must not write of Mr. Spivey yet, but tell you about him only when I get to him; and I must say something first of how I fell to Earth.

We went up from Crisium in a small balloon. It had an open basket: I remember leaning over the rim, watching the black spires sinking, seeing a tram rattling along the promenade. I was feeling very pleased with myself and not afraid at all.

Captain Allardyce touched his helmet to mine. "Mandragora," he said, and pointed. I looked down and saw a silver park. I could see statues of animals, stood as if they were drinking from the frozen lake. There was a curved bridge of white stone, and some Pierrots having a picnic. I waved to them, in the best of spirits, as we sailed away, out above the pockmarked plain of the giant crater. A lone, lost moon gull tried to follow us up, but we left it far behind.

The *Appleby Bull* was a four-winged clipper laden with bales of fluorspar. We crossed slowly to Earth under full canvas because we sat so heavy in the flux. The straw floated about and got into everything, even the food. I was set to help the cook, whose name was Bleen. He was a foulmouthed old spacer with a cork leg, which had been many times mended with tar and brown paper. When it grew too hot in the tiny galley he would take it off and scratch his pink stump, not caring a scrap what I might think of it.

I stayed in the galley for the whole crossing, while I got my own space legs under me. My good mood did not endure. I wasn't sick, but my head did ache; and sometimes my Hindoo demon was at me again, pricking me with his swords. I had fearful dreams about a fast, fierce river. After the Registry, and until we had passed the Haven, I was sure the captain and the cook and the bos'n would all pounce upon me at once and laugh, telling me they had tricked me and were taking me home after all. Sometimes I think I hoped they would.

Earth was getting bigger by the hour. It grew and grew until I did not think it could grow any bigger; but it kept on growing. I had not realized there would be so much of it. Soon it was everywhere I looked. I thought of Mr. Cox, with his metal smile, and shivered. Even if he was there, I should never find him. I should not know where to begin. What did I know of the Mother of All Worlds? Nothing but Her cargoes, that passed through High Haven in tribute from all Her children—Her laborers, who came up to carpenter and weld—Her gentry-folk, who hurried to and fro at the Prince Edward Dock with handkerchiefs pressed to their noses. My own mother was on the Haven, if anywhere, for Papa had certainly never been anywhere else. I began to realize I had made a mistake.

I thought about the apologetic clerk. I was not registered. I did not know what that meant, but I was ashamed, and would keep it to myself. Of course it was not Mama's ring I had, as I'd been so ready to believe. There were no women in the Pilots' Guild, even I knew that. The ring must have been one of Kappi's presents after all, dropped in the street by some carousing subaltern.

I hated Papa for hiding me away, and I wished him at the other side of the universe. What did I need with a papa, or a mama either? I could let Mr. Cox go: good riddance to him too. For I was a sailor now, and thought myself a great traveler. By the time the *Bull* started to descend over the Atlantic Ocean, I was regretting the end of my journey, and had begun to plan my next. I should go to Adonis, and drink brandy with Miss Halshaw; and then in a day or two I should be off, skipping over Pluto, and away to Godfrey's Star, to see the Jewel Worlds. The ship rolled, and I banged my elbow. Rubbing it, I crept to the porthole and peeked out.

We were much lower now than I had ever been, and the Earth was a dazzling white carpet of cloud beneath our keel. The British Isles were under there somewhere, Mr. Bleen said. I could see nothing, neither sea nor land, but only a corner of the landing sailing up to meet us. It was bright with red and green and colors I had never seen on the dark wharves of the Haven—and I was amazed to see how many vessels there were in the roads, scores of them, tacking daintily in and out like fish in a tank. I could not stop staring.

While the men ran around overhead and the *Bull* bumped against the fenders, the cook bade me take a sugar sack and fill it with dates and hard oat tack. He too seemed to understand that my great voyage had only just begun. When I said good-bye, he held my cheeks between his hard hands. "Good-bye now, you little weasel," he said, "God damn your eyes." Then he took me up on deck and gave me back into the charge of the captain.

The ship had slung her hook and floated at ease. The unloading had begun and there was shore leave for the crew. I stood by while Captain Allardyce thanked each man, saying a word to this one and that as he gave him his pay. Then he and the mate and the pilot took me into another private balloon, which bore us down into the air. We seemed to take a long time falling.

The cloud beneath us was like a vat of porridge, with little black dots upon it as if someone had scattered a handful of cloves. I asked the captain, "What are those, sir?"

"Those are the kites, Sophie," he said, "watching the weather."

"They've got 'em all at full stretch today," said the pilot, lighting a pipe of tobacco.

I felt so ignorant. I knew what a kite was, I had read of them in a book—but how could a kite watch anything? These were complicated box-shaped kites made out of black and yellow sailcloth—they were very large, I realized as we crept down upon them—and when we finally passed below one, I saw the man that hung from it, buckled and strapped into a wooden frame, with goggles upon his face and a long colorful scarf around his neck. The kite-man saluted us, and then with flags and binoculars he and the mates of his watch signaled to each other.

"High cover one-twenty," observed the pilot in an offhand tone, reading the signs, and silently we sank into the woolly white region of cloud. It was nothing like the faint, dusty blossom I had passed through the night I landed on the Moon. It was all made of water, the captain told me— I scarcely knew whether to believe it. It looked nothing like water, which would slop happily about in the buckets as you carried it home from the cistern, but never ventured to blossom and hang in the air in that vague and uncooperative manner.

When we were through the cloud, I saw something more marvelous yet. "Land!" I cried, "Land ho!"—and the gentlemen laughed. It was more land than I had ever seen, more than I could see, in either direction. The Moon was nothing to it. Here they had hills and fields and woods, and tiny cows in the valleys and tiny windmills turning and everything everywhere green and growing.

But what was this, swelling up to swallow us, this shapeless face of gray and black behind its veil of yellow smoke? Could this be London? Why, this London that was the wonder of the world—she was nothing but High Haven grown gigantic! She was nothing but chimney pots and dirt, and steeples stabbing up at us like unsheared bolts—I knew in another minute they would burst our balloon and make us fall out of the sky. The roofs of London—there were more roofs than there were stars in the heavens. In the whole universe there could not be people enough to live under them. Her streets were only ordinary streets indeed, but there were so many of them, that seemed to scramble off in all directions, and all crawling with traffic like a dog with fleas—Oh Reader, how can I explain? Though the hills and fields of Britain were vast to me, and the Earth herself more vast; yet London seemed vaster than all.

The captain saluted her, then took off his cap. He said to me, "What do you think of her, then, little girl?"

I know I should have said that I marveled, thinking of all she had done in the worlds, of how far she had stretched forth her mighty civilizing hand. My heart should have swelled to enter the capital city of the glorious Empire. Hanging there in her sky surrounded by her skycraft rising and falling, I could see her noble buildings; her broad thoroughfares; the busy traffic on her waters—I could see her parks and her lavender fields. Yet I was an ignorant child, with my borrowed helmet in one clammy hand and my sack of sweetmeats in the other, and my mind was running on what Mr. Hans Christian Andersen wrote in one of his stories. You remember: the porcelain doll, who is too stiff to get down from the shelf, asks the rat, who has traveled; and the rat says, "London! Ah, that is rats' Heaven!"

So I did not answer the captain: but I was thinking of the rats, that lived in all the drains and under the floors and in the walls and in the cellars and wharves and warehouses of

London, and I thought what a scurrying and a squeaking and
a gnawing of them there must be, and Hampstead beneath us
grew all muddled with Hamelin in my mind, so as her towers
swelled ceremoniously to receive us, I could see this was a
palace, a dozen palaces, heaped with the spoil of a hundred
worlds. Was this where the Queen lived? Or only rats?

And it is a palace indeed, Hampstead Harbor. Its coffers
lay open to me, full of riches, heaped in glory. Yet I was
aghast. You could have buried the whole Eastern Dock in its
sand and coal heaps, and lost St. Radigund's Wharf for good
and ever.

There were ships everywhere, ships of all sizes. I saw
freighters and cutters, and a hundred battered brigs—was the
Unco Stratagem there? I never would have seen her. I saw a
huge windjammer, on blocks, her stern in a great corset of
scaffolding. The captain pointed out to me two of the gigantic
steam tugs they would need when it came to putting her back
aloft, where she belonged. Beyond, disappearing now down
behind the roofs of the hangars, were gasholders like cruets of
gray iron. We scattered a flock of pigeons wheeling up around
us, while on the ground three young men in blue uniforms ran
toward us pushing a wooden staircase on wheels.

Though the sun was shrouded, I had never been so hot.
And buffeted, winded, drowned by noise! Echoing shouts and
whistles, squeals of scraped metal, the battering slow roar of a
railway engine starting to roll, and under everything, booming
through the palace vaults, shaking the very ground, an unseen
steam hammer pounding away without pause or mercy.

I could not hear myself think; I did not know where to look.
Beneath the roof of vaulted glass, black girders and bridges
crossed and recrossed like the web of a giant iron spider: a
maze of darkness, blind corners and hidden drops. But then,
from some high unseen skylight not entirely caked in grime,
a sudden shaft of sun shone through and lit on a metal cradle stowed beneath a gantry, its ribs and davits picked out in
bright scarlet paint. Even the manufacturer's brass nameplate
winked with polish. Pigeons flew out of the darkness into the
sun, across the landing field to perch on the sills of a high
brick wall full of windows. The windows were narrow and
arched, picked out in bricks of two colors. Above, behind a
parapet, swags of bright red flowers and thick skeins of ivy

spilled out of ornamental urns. Below, starving urchins huddled on the pavement.

A crowd of passengers were waiting for a balloon. The
gentry had seats, and servants with sunshades. There was a
tall African in white robes, with the bearing of a prince and
a company of fauns and shambling giants around him: Hrad,
I thought, but by then I had lost sight of them in the crowd.
I saw families with all their household goods tied in a wheel-
barrow, shipping out to the colonies. They looked anxious
and tired, and were having difficulties making account of
themselves to the gentlemen with brass buttons who were
going among them with calipers, charts, and sheaves of official paper. There were scurrying porters and conductors and
an ice-cream man with a tin cart. I saw a lady and gentleman saying good-bye to their son, who was standing very
erect and white, perspiring in a stiff new uniform of green
khaki. To one side stood a girl weeping silently into a tiny
handkerchief, with an old nurse comforting her—his fiancée,
I supposed. She looked no older than me.

Through the atrium the captain strode and I plodded after
him, heavier than I had ever been. A sentry saluted and opened
an iron gate for us, and Captain Allardyce led me straight out
through the great arch with the blue mosaic and curly gold letters on it spelling ARRIVALS, out under the yellow-gray sky,
pierced now with a wound of sunny blue. I was painfully hot
in my space coat, and breathing hard, and my poor luggage
weighed on my hands like lead. My nostrils were filled with
an astonishing stench of malt vinegar and perishing rubber, of
sweat and dung and smoke.

Down Spaniards Road more people than I had seen in the
whole of my life were walking, running, riding. There were
men, women, children of every hue and kind, jostling shoulder
to shoulder. Still the din continued. Cries of hot potatoes and
sweet rosemary were all mixed up in my ears with shouting
newsboys and squalling infants. The mud had dried to a crust
in the heat, but in the shadows of the tilting houses it was wet
and mired with filth. Coattails flapping, the captain swerved to
go around an enormous puddle which suddenly yawned at our
feet. Slithering back from it, I scurried to follow, and immediately walked into him, banging my nose painfully against his
back, for he had been stopped short by a blockage in the

crowd. It was one of the Lizard-Men, standing motionless in the middle of the way, basking in the sunshine. "Hi, there, you!" cried a red-faced old man in tricorn hat and buckled shoes, and he battered the stranger's back mercilessly with his knobbed staff. "Get along there, can't you?" The captain explained to me that indeed he probably couldn't, since our sun is apt to make them forgetful and slow to stir. "They go quite stupid, in the end," the captain said loudly, "and lose the civilized parts of their brains."

That may be so. I cannot swear that it is not—but writing it down here, I think of what many people say about angels, that they are beasts without sense and only mimic human ways, as apes do. Which is very ignorant, or flat slander. I have never yet been among the civilized angels of the Martian Orient, but in the Canyon de Saint Charles I might have Rachel and Gaston beside me for an hour and more, picking their way through a story in a scrap of newspaper—why, even Thérèse, in her humor, could tell you what she had been doing that day—But none of that was yet, and I was trying to keep everything in order for you, and move in a straight line—oh, I wish a book were like a letter, and could contain everything just where you think of it, and no one would take offense.

There were no angels in Spaniards Road, but I saw purple faces and brown; fine ladies with their slaves trotting alongside; a tall creature in a frilled shirt with the face of a stork—alien? human?—he was gone before one could tell. Here was a huddle of old men with black skullcaps and long white beards; there a proud young dandy with curled whiskers, eyeglasses on a ribbon, rosettes on his cherry-colored shoes, dragging a fierce little dog on a lead.

My head was turning like a spinning top—suddenly there was a huge four-legged creature careering straight toward me up the road, powerful shoulders higher than my head. I glimpsed complicated headgear, straps of leather and rings of brass, huge black shields hanging to either side of its long face as though it were the basilisk, which kills you with its stare. I threw myself at Captain Allardyce, shrieking, "What is it?" It was a cab horse, driven by a gaunt Corregian.

"Watch your step there, girl!" the captain cried roughly, and chivied me unceremoniously onward. Beneath the statue of Dædalus Triumphans sat a beggar in the tattered rig of a space legionary, with hideous red- and black-encrusted bandages on his feet. "Only a ruffler," said Captain Allardyce, directing me firmly past. "A sham. They put on the agony with the uniform." But I was still staring in horror and wondering how he could tell, for there were cripples and beggars everywhere, playing the spoons and jigging about for attention, or sitting dejectedly in doorways. That was when I saw the first rat, running over a sprawled leg. I held on to my few poor coins and knew that I would be sitting there amongst them soon.

On we went, past women in threadbare shawls and men in shabby hats with the nap wearing off; soldiers and soothsayers and sellers of pies—

Enough. In a word—there is hubbub at the heart of the Empire. That is no news. Dear Sir or Madam, I beg your pardon for filling these pages with the noise and dirt of it. What care you about the crowd? Either you are of it, and know already more about it than you could wish—or you are apart from it and above it, and wish to know nothing.

We crossed over the bustling river by Waterloo Bridge, and found our way by winding streets to the captain's lodgings, Mrs. Rodney's in Lambeth Walk, where the market is. I was tired and bewildered. I stood in a dark kitchen looking at the flagstones. A tall, muscular woman in an apron told me to put down my things, then sit at the table with her and the captain. She put a cup of tea in front of me, and shouted out of the kitchen door to someone called Johnny to go and borrow ink and paper from the bookmaker's.

"Poor thing," she said, when the captain told her of my circumstances; and she reached out and stroked the hair on my head. Startled, I recoiled, staring as warily at her as Percy at any boy with a stick. She gave me a smile. "Drink your tea, then," she said. Her voice was rough, and her face was red and chapped as the bare brick wall; but she smiled.

Revived by the tea, which was the color of tar with the treacle in it, I wrote another letter home for the captain. I wrote it very carefully. He lived in Ys, the British quarter. His wife was a Martian, he said: her name was Amreeh, and she worked in the mortuary, mixing tinctures for the Ministers of Decay. He told her we were come safe to Earth with our cargo, and what price he expected it to fetch—then he scratched his head and mopped his brow, and with much cudgeling of his brain

devised to tell her he was well, and indeed he hoped she was
the same—then he said, dictating: " 'London is hot and nasty.
I wish I were with you, my dear, but that cannot be yet for a
time as you know.' And there you may draw to a close, Sophie
girl, and put, 'My best wishes to your mother and father and
all your sisters.' " Feeling very satisfied with myself for the
good job I made of it, though I still had to guess how some of
the words went, I said I wondered if "kindest thoughts" might
not be better than "best wishes," and he was pleased. Then he
told me to end it with, May the Emperor live forever. "You
have to put that, there," he said, nodding his great red poll.

I wondered what it would be like to be married. I was
sure it was horrible, to have someone there watching you
all the time, sleeping in your bed. But what if you were
apart, like Captain and Mrs. Allardyce? It did not seem to
make him happy. I snatched a look at Mrs. Rodney, who
had got up and gone to scrub potatoes in a bowl, and wondered what to make of her, and what Mr. Rodney would
be like. Then I learnt I was to share a bed myself, with
their daughter Gertie, which sounded almost as bad as being
married.

Gertie had the face of a bulldog. She was no more keen on
the arrangement than I. "They asked me and I said no, but here
you are anyway," she said, when she had brought me up to the
little room under the eaves. "This is *my* pillow. Everything on
this side of the room is mine, all right?"

I stood in the doorway, panting from the climb upstairs.
"I'm not staying long," I said, scowling. "Only a few days."

"Good," said Gertie, who was a year and a half younger
than I, though I felt like a proper child next to her. She put
her hands on her hips now and gave me a suspicious look and
said, "Board and lodging is by the week anyhow."

I nodded carelessly, as if I were always making these arrange-
ments, and went downstairs. I was weary through and through.
I had no money except what was in Miss Halshaw's purse, but
now was the time when I had to give it up, and right sorry
I was to do so. In Papa's house I had learned early to hang
on to every penny that came in. Any labor I might do was to
be counted worth the money it saved. Mrs. Rodney, though I
could not suspect she was a wealthy woman, made no sign
of being worried by my indigent state. "There'll be plenty

for you to do, Sophie," she said. "It won't be all letter writing, I can't say that. But it'll be useful having another pair
of hands." She put her head on one side and looked pleased
with me, as if I were the one that was doing her a good turn.
I couldn't fathom her at all. "It'll be nice not to have to go up
the street every time I need something read. Gertie knows how
to read, don't you, Gert?" she said, turning to her daughter,
who was standing against the door, thumping it idly with her
heel. "Only sometimes the words go all slippery," explained
her mother, "and she can't get them to lie straight nohow."

Captain Allardyce seemed well pleased with his letter. He
could read it, he said, on account of knowing what it said; but
it would have taken him a month to write so long and substan-
tial a letter. He would take it to the post tomorrow on his way
to Hampstead. He had to go back up first thing, he said, to
see to the loading—the *Bull* was bound for Mercury, to trade
pickled herring for their twilight fruit, which she would then
take to the Moon.

I said to him: "Sir? Where does Mr. Cox live?"

I had told Mr. Bleen about my acquaintance with Mr. Cox,
and he had told Captain Allardyce. The captain laughed and
patted the table, twice. "You'll have to go and ask them up
at the House of Lords," he said.

"Where is it?" I asked.

"He's pulling your leg, darling," said Mrs. Rodney. "That's
not a place little girls can go," she said, and she chuckled, as
if she had made up her mind I was the queerest creature she
had ever seen.

I said: "I suppose I can always ask a policeman anyway."

The captain wished me the best of British luck, and he went
out, to the pub, the Hope and Anchor, where Mr. Rodney
worked. I understood I was not to follow, but I trailed out
into the street after him and stood on the doorstep, looking
up and down the market. Perhaps the pilot lord's envoy might
come strolling down to buy a pound of chitlings.

Gertie and Johnny, her little brother, were out there, with
a crowd of other children gathering. They were all staring at
me and whispering. When they saw me looking, one of them
picked up a bit of dried mud and threw it at me. Stung, I ran
back inside. I was right: Earth was no different from High
Haven.

Mrs. Rodney said there would be no more work for me that day, and sent me to bed, to rest after my long journey. I went and lay there alone, tired and dejected indeed, but could not sleep. I looked in my sack and found there was a knife in it, hidden among the food. It was a paring knife: one that belonged in the galley of the *Appleby Bull*. The cook must have stolen it for me. I knew its cold black shape, sharp-pointed as the tooth of some hideous iron creature; and very frightened it made me to see it there. I lay in Gertie's bed, feeling lonelier than I ever had in my lonely life, and stunned by the great, loud, indifferent Earth. I felt like a fly squashed upon its pavements. I fed myself dates, and wept very quietly, and when Gertie came up to call me to supper I pretended to be asleep.

Next day Mrs. Rodney let me sleep in. I didn't wake when Gertie got up—or when Captain Allardyce went out—no one roused me until Johnny came running upstairs to say the mate of the *Bull* had arrived with a letter to be read.

He was sitting in the kitchen. His hair was wet, it was raining. I read his letter to him while I ate breakfast, which Mrs. Rodney made for me specially. The mate's letter was from his wife, in service in Northumberland. He had not seen her for three years, he said. In her letter she said many things of a very personal nature, and very strange indeed I felt speaking them to him, though he thought it no shame, but only smiled at me. I read boldly, and with great confidence, even when I wasn't truly sure. And Mrs. Rodney turned and stood with her back to the sink, listening to me read and smiling at me.

As soon as the mate had gone, I ran out in the street and jigged around, heavy as I was, with my head thrown back and my mouth wide open. I'd never seen rain before; it was water and it fell out of the sky! A raindrop hit me in the eye and I blinked madly, laughing in surprise. Gertie and Johnny were watching me from the window. Now they knew I was quite mad.

Mrs. Rodney came and called me in. She sat me down and explained patiently to me what chores Gertie had to do every day, and how I must do the same. There was my bed and board to earn, she said: that was my immediate future settled—but I could not wait, not when the man I had come to visit might sail away at any moment; so as soon as I had done the first task set me, out I slipped again into the rain.

They had said I must not dare go near the House of Lords; but I knew Captain Estranguaro had said Mr. Cox was a most important man in the Pilots' Guild—so I thought I should go there. I was soaked to the skin long before I found their offices in Whitehall, and all that happened there was that a big policeman told me to be off. I couldn't even get as far as the door. I wanted to show the policeman my ring, but I knew he would lock me up. Crestfallen, I turned and trudged home, my feet aching with their unaccustomed load. I hadn't got halfway before my shoes started to fall apart. "Whatever were you thinking of, Sophie!" said Mrs. Rodney, setting her teeth at the state of me. She made sure to keep me busy after that, and never let me out of her sight unless it was to play with Gertie, who would permit my company if she was very bored. It was as bad as being at home. "Oh Sophie, be patient," said Mrs. Rodney, and she gathered me with one arm and gave me a hug as if she thought I was her daughter. "Mr. Rodney might have some news for you soon."

Mr. Rodney was the cellarman at the Hope and Anchor. Without telling me, he had asked the landlord, Mr. Mountjoy—and Mr. Mountjoy had asked a postman who came in there to drink—and one day the postman came back in with the news that the gentleman they were inquiring after had a house in Kensington. Mr. Rodney brought me the address, written down on a piece of paper. I thanked him with great joy and went out to sit on the doorstep and read it over again.

"Let me see," said Gertie, though in truth she had no patience with letters or numbers, so I told her what my paper said and asked her where Kensington was. She pressed her lips tight shut and shook her head vigorously—she was having nothing to do with it; she went off with her friends, Abigail and the rest of them—but Johnny piped up then and said he'd take me there. The other boys sneered at him for taking a girl to look after; but when they heard where we were going, where the rich lived in tall houses with gardens and trees, then they all wanted to come, and we all went running off in a pack together. Mr. Cox's house had a huge wall all the way around, with trees above that—you couldn't even see it from the road. I remember not wanting to go in the gate, but Danny Corby and the other bold ones pushed me through, and came with me partway up the drive; though when the house came in sight, frowning at us under its eaves, my escort deserted me and ran back to hide behind the gateposts, and let me walk up to the door alone.

A footman in a powdered wig and white stockings answered the bell. He took one look at my shabby clothes, my disintegrating shoes, and told me to clear off. I said, "I have an urgent message for Mr. Cox." It was the only thing I could think of. He informed me with a sniff that Mr. Cox was on the way to Io and not expected home any time soon. When I wouldn't leave my message, he shut the door.

"Best thing too," said Mr. Rodney at tea. "You can't just go looking for a gentleman like Mr. Cox, Sophie," he said, in a voice that meant what he was explaining to me was a law of nature. "Have some common sense, girl, do." Stemming my outburst of justifications and questions, he waved his fork in the direction of Kensington. "What you'll have to do is write him a letter," he said.

"That's all they meant when they found out his address for you, you silly child," said Mrs. Rodney, frightened what retribution I might bring down on us all for my abuse of such privileged information.

A letter to Mr. Cox. It was obvious. That didn't mean I could do it. What was I to say? "I'll tell him Papa sent me," I said.

"You'll do no such thing, telling fibs, whatever next," Mrs. Rodney scolded me.

"She's always telling fibs, Ma," said Gertie.

"You be quiet, girl," said her father. "Just present your compliments, and apologize for bothering him, and tell him you would be much obliged if he could direct you to where your mother is living now."

"Tell him you'll be very much obliged," concurred Mrs. Rodney, nodding; but when I got to my feet she raised her voice. "Where are you going? There's the water to fetch, and all the washing to do."

"Write it tonight and look it over in the morning," Mr. Rodney suggested. "Make sure there's no mistakes or nothing."

If I had thought it would be difficult before, their advice made it impossible. Half a dozen times I began, and made the

paper foul with crossing out, imagining Mr. Cox's fearsome
face and changing my mind how to say it; and I put it away
till later.

Even Gertie was awed by my recklessness in bearding a
footman. "Weren't you scared, Sophie?" she asked me that
night in bed. Of course I was. I was afraid of him, and terrified of his master, who had already told me not to bother him
again. Indeed I was afraid—but fear was normal—my whole
childhood had been a state of constant fear, and where had that
got me?—To Lambeth Walk, apparently, "just across from the
Archbishop," as Mr. Rodney liked to put it. There seemed to
be no escape. I, who had thought myself the great explorer,
had only tumbled from one cage into another. But this cage
was warm, and there was laughter in it, and sometimes a song;
and though I was sorry to find there was housework to do even
in London Town, I had to stay sharp to make sure Gertie didn't
leave me all the worst jobs.

At first, they were glad of me in the kitchen. Gertie was
no use, she went at everything in a rush and spoiled it, then
flew into a temper. Mrs. Rodney was pleased to see I knew a
ladle from a dish-mop. She had a paring knife already, so I
did not tell her about mine that Mr. Bleen had given me, but
let her roll my sleeves up and—for the first time in my life—
tie an apron around my middle. Alas, it was not long before
she discovered that, for all my experience, I had not a jot of
training, and that my system of cooking was entirely Papa's
invention and my own. "Who told you to do that?" cried Mrs.
Rodney in dismay, seeing me making the tea with the water
we'd boiled the potatoes in. Her patience was short, the back
of her hand hard. "Go out and play, you stupid girl."

Outside I found Johnny and his friends, playing at hopscotch. Gertie had joined in, because she was good at it. They
couldn't believe I didn't know how. "Don't you play hopscotch on High Haven?" they cried. I was sure Benny Stropes
did, and all of them—but they would never have asked me to
join in. If Gertie could play, she told them all loudly, I could
too. So then it was hopscotch—and hide-and-seek—and crick-
et, with three crooked stumps chalked on the wall at the back
of the grocer's. Every once in a while I would look up and
catch sight of the High Haven glinting like an iron snowflake
in the west, and feel guilt snatch at my careless heart. There

was another letter I owed, that I could never write. Captain Allardyce, who had gone long since, had promised to leave word at the high landing with some ship calling at the Haven, to tell Papa I was alive and well, but not to say where. That would have to do for him.

As for Mr. Cox, there was no rush to write to him: he would not be home for ages. When I hurried by the market, traders would wink at me and toss me a bruised apple, for nothing. "Where's that fine gentleman of yours, young Sophie?" they would say. "When's he going to come to take you away with him on his yacht?" I thought of the Morgan boys, and tossed my head, and thought how it would have amazed them to discover everyone in London knew my name now.

It was October, as I said, the night a man walked on a rope from one side of the street to the other. He was a local man, Jack Spivey, though known from Stamford Hill to Battersea; from Exeter to Edinburgh, even: wherever the circus played. I think the whole of Lambeth had turned out to see him. He cried, "Come one, come all!" and pulled a burning stick out of the fire and waved it in the air. Johnny and Gertie and I were all right up front, and as close as we could get to the fire, because we were cold.

Mr. Spivey had on a nightshirt that was caught up at the waist in a big knot, with velvet slippers on his feet and long tight trews black as the London sky. He did not look cold at all. He was wearing a big broad hat, and all admired his necklace of lions' teeth that glinted with the flames. He tossed his flaming stick to a crony of his, who caught it. Everyone clapped, then put their hands back in their pockets.

When the drum rolled he twirled his waxed mustache and struck a pose, pointing up at the length of tarred rope that stretched across the road from the cobbler's to Mrs. Rodney's. It was our window, Gertie's and mine, where the rope was tied. Dinner at Mrs. Rodney's was free for him tonight, if he could walk it.

"He'll never do it, will he, Gertie?" little Betty Pride asked, and Gertie laughed. "I can't look!" she cried. "Tell us if he falls off, Johnny! Tell you what, Bets, if he falls off, Sophie'll catch him, won't you, Soph?" and she punched me in the arm.

I said, "Shut up, Gertie," and then they all sniggered. All

the girls were in love with Mr. Spivey, but I was the one who got teased about it. I was fifteen, and my heart was ignorant as a beetroot. Mr. Spivey was up on the rope now, balancing in his velvet slippers. The breast of his nightshirt glowed in the firelight. Mr. Spivey was like a god, so quick and brave, though we saw his wife and children every day, in the Walk. They never had any money. "Lord bless you, mum," Mr. Spivey would say, sitting them down at our table that night. I only spoke to him the once, that night at dinner, to ask him did he know Miss Halshaw. He didn't. I couldn't speak again, but only sit and look at his wonderful mustache. He was the most dashing man I had ever seen.

I remember how he set off on his epic walk. He ran the first three steps, his arms swaying in a slow, rhythmic flail. He paused, balanced, one knee fitted behind the other, his hips turned toward us.

His trews were very tight. And Gertie was looking, whatever she pretended. She nudged me hard. "How do you like that view, Sophie?" she said, and they snorted with laughter again.

I pretended I hadn't heard, but my cheeks flamed. Abigail Cook put her hands on our shoulders and jumped up, cheering. "There he goes!"

Now Mr. Spivey was halfway, the rope slanting up behind him and before. He wobbled. He began to sway. Everybody gasped, and someone laughed. "He's off!" Dan Corby announced; but he wasn't. He was jumping up and down, bouncing on the rope, doing a little dance. The boys started to clap in time, and whistle between their teeth. We stood in our little huddle, marveling.

He did the rest in a sprint. It had been easy for him all along. There were cheers and whistles louder than Guy Fawkes Night when he finished, and he turned and waved and doffed his big hat to us; and just as he ducked his head and went in at our bedroom window a cloud of bats from the church came whirling over the rooftops, confused by the heat of the fire. I looked up and saw the Moon peering down at us through the chimneys, as if she wanted to know what was going on. In the night half you could see a city twinkling like a glimmer of the faintest silvery dew. I wondered if it was Crisium. I remembered its icy windows, the lines of them all glittering in the black walls. I realized I had not thought of Mama for a long time; or Mr. Cox. Perhaps he was home by now. I must start my letter to him at once, I resolved, and waste no more time.

Poor Mr. Spivey died the following spring, somewhere in the west country: lost his footing and fell while trying to wheel a barrow across a gorge. The circus and the Walk chipped in and had a proper funeral for him, with a gentleman in black gloves going before the procession from street to street, bowing at the stations of his life: his father's house; his school; the spots where he had performed his first feats of balance.

I remember the day they buried Jack Spivey: it was the same day that Abigail Cook told us there was a star-schooner come home. "She's been everywhere, they say, away out in the deep." And when we went to look, she had my name.

8

Several benefactors

I took another clean sheet of paper out of my writing desk, and dipped my nib. I put no address or date, but wrote directly:

Dear Papa,

I am still alive, and quite well too I should say, though I had a cold last week, caught from some children where I am staying. I hope you are as well as you can be, I am sorry for you there all on your own. I know Kappi is helping. I'm sure Mrs. Stropes and Mrs. O'Riley would help if you would let them.

I sucked the end of my pen. I was sure of no such thing. They had never been kind to me, the neighbor women of the dock, though they helped each other and looked after each other's children and old folk as neighbors do. Papa, they thought, gave himself airs and brought all his woes on his own head; and me they pitied, folding their arms and smiling grimly to one another while I passed.

I looked out of the window of the loft. Mr. Rodney was down there in the yard behind the pub, mending a barrel, with Johnny helping. Johnny was holding the nails, flinching every time the hammer hit, but holding on. I sighed and dipped my pen again.

> *I have today seen a grand schooner in: Lord and Lady Plumstone, home from their Galactic Passage. Sixteen years they have been traveling. No one has ever seen a ship so rotten black*

There was no point in putting that. Papa would certainly have seen a dozen, fifty, and all far worse. I struggled on:

> *Her hull is all flaking, like ash. People have been pulling bits off her for souvenirs.*
> *She is called the* Sophrona. *You can still read it on the prow where they had it painted, in letters of gold. The Plumstones are from Halifax and have mines in the Asteroids. I suppose you know that. I suppose they left from High Haven, Papa, and you saw them go.*
> *A woman was here today who asked me about Mama. She seemed to think her name was*

I broke off there, sure I should have said nothing about my visitor, and not knowing how to go on now I had started. Of course the letter joined all the others inside my desk, at the bottom. I could not have finished it for all the pearls of Neptune. I sat in my office and thought of Gertie that morning, pointing to the bits of gold paint that were left on the prow of the worn-out ship. "Sophie, does that say your name?"

"Sophrona," I said. It felt funny, saying it. It didn't sound like my name. I never said it. No one had ever called me it. I thought somebody ought to, one day.

She was a grand ship still, for all the black frost had eaten. Her masts seemed to touch the clouds, and her shrouds were

crammed with colored bunting flying gaily in the wind. I am
sure she felt she was still racing through the sky. Sunlight
flashed on her brass, on the lacquered trunks the porters were
still bringing off, on the blue and yellow uniforms of the crew.
The ballad singers were all out with their accordions, singing
her brave voyage, and the broadsheet men were busy. Somebody set up a cheer, Hip, hip, and we girls all cried Hurrah!
with the best of them. Fickle hearts that we were, poor Mr.
Spivey was quite forgotten.

Some of their livestock had survived. They brought it ashore
now: cages of ducks, one scrawny goat, and then some things
from foreign worlds, Diomed turtles, and three big creatures
that looked like squashed ponies with the legs of giant spiders. We all squealed to see them, and clutched at one another,
hiding our eyes.

Mr. Mountjoy's nephew Albert was laughing at us. He was
there working, selling cigarettes to the gentry and filling mugs
of ale from a barrel. A young gentleman in a silk hat was whistling to a paperboy, who ran around as fast as his legs would
carry him. All the boys were there, fetching and carrying, running errands. They touched their caps and spat on their palms
and rubbed them on their backsides before holding them out
for their pay. Norrie Clamp was at the young gentleman now,
trying to sell him a nosegay from her tray. Three pickpockets
stood leaning against a corner, watching everything, watching
the policeman who was watching them.

"I've got to go," I said.

"Don't, Sophie," all the others said, and they made to detain
me; but I too had my work to do, so off I ran to the Hope, with
the cry of the paperboy in my ears. "Fears for the health of the
Emperor of Mars!" he cried. "Read all about it!"

To get out of helping Mrs. Rodney, I often went with her
husband now to the Hope and Anchor, where there was always
a penny to be made. Mr. Rodney was already there today, and
Mr. Mountjoy saw me come in, and he shouted at me: "What
time do you call this, Sophie Farthing?" I didn't answer, but
made myself busy running around collecting empty pots and
taking them out to Mrs. Mountjoy in the scullery, who dipped
them a fistful at a time in her tub of gray water.

Everything in the Hope and Anchor was gray. The clothes
of the customers were gray and their hair was gray and their

faces too. Every night they all came shuffling in and sat in their usual places. They knew where they belonged. The women brought their babies with them, and indeed I think they were gray too. They were thin and sick, certainly, and whined and grizzled until their mothers would calm them by giving them rags dipped in gin. The urchins would steal in and set up camp under the tables. They were ill, as urchins always must be, with running noses, and the ringworm, and rat bites on their legs—and they would start squabbling and fighting, until Mr. Mountjoy came striding from behind the bar to turn them all out into the street. "Be off home with you!" he would roar; but they were orphans, some of them, and had no homes. Wherever there are sailors, I think, there are orphans.

When word got about that I could read, the customers began to bring me letters from their menfolk, who were spacemen and sailors and soldiers. They had kin who were settlers on Caraway, and Dusk, and St. Malo. A woman once brought in a letter from her brother in New Bermuda, in the Centaur, posted thirty-seven years before. And foreigners came too sometimes, human ones, and beseechingly held out halfpence to me, and pieces of paper that were yellow and soft with folding: letters in Martian French and tongues I could not even recognize; Arab script, one of them was, that looks like a string of Christmas holly. Those I had to send away, over to Fleet, where the real scribes are. The rest I read, and helped them write replies, if they wanted; and for a while, at least, whenever one spoke to me, I asked: "Have you heard of Mr. Cox, that is the Pilots' envoy?"

They had not. They were too humble in the Hope and Anchor to know anything of so high a gentleman, though they were all most interested in the ways of the great and mighty, and discussed them frequently and at length. Today their talk was of the Plumstones, and their *Sophrona*. When they asked me I said I had seen her too, and yes, she was a beauty. They did not think anything about her name, because they did not know, and I did not tell them. Later on some of her crew came in and there was a strange, clumsy, sad welcome for them, with much exclamation and recollection on both sides. All the men were deck crew, haggard, the skin of their hands and faces gnawed with the lupus of space; but no one mentioned that at all. "You all look so young," folk kept telling them, and told them about Mr. Spivey, and many others known locally who had passed on.

One man sat on a barrel in the corner with a face as long as a wet weekend, his kit bag on the floor beside him. He had found that his wife had moved away while he was in space. He had not known. A couple of our regulars stayed with him and bought him his drinks. His shipmates were already drunk, and telling tales of distant worlds of wonder, such as I used to hear from Papa—here was one world that was plated with rainbows—here was another, where armored creatures like stag beetles tall as trees did battle amid burning rocks. The sailors told in tones of awe how through a glass they had seen the Center, where the suns melt down and whirl together. Then they laughed, and told a coarse story about a pilot.

I was at the bar, putting out the clean pots, when Mrs. Baxter from the chandler's came up with a woman in a drab blue dress with her sleeves rolled up. "Here she is, Ginny," Mrs. Baxter said, sitting herself on a stool in front of me. "This is her."

The drunken sailors were shouting: "Ginny! Ginny!" But the woman ignored them and leaned on the bar. She said to me: "Are you the girl from High Haven?"

She was a big, rawboned woman with an impatient face. You could see she was another spacehand by her pigtail, and by the scars that spiraled up her arms. She was chewing tobacco with teeth that were all stained brown and crooked. She chewed as if her life depended on it; as if tobacco was the very fuel that drove her along.

I said I was that girl. She said: "What's your name?"

I made up my mind to say, and did. "Sophrona Farthing," I said.

Mrs. Baxter exclaimed; yet her friend seemed not to be surprised. She only said: "What's your pa's name?"

I put more pots on the shelf. "Jacob Farthing," I said.

"What about your ma?" she said then. "What was her name?"

Uneasy, I tossed my hair back out of my eyes. I didn't know Mrs. Baxter very well. I didn't know why she had brought the woman to me. Not for a letter, I was sure of that. I thought I heard invisible angel wings beating away from me in the beer-soaked air.

"I don't know," I said. "He never said."

Mrs. Baxter tutted for the shame of it. But the big woman nodded, as if it too was no more than she expected. She spat a jet of brown juice into the sawdust. Her eyes never for an instant left my face. I was glad we had the bar between us.

"Not Rose, was it?" she suggested. "Mrs. Rose?"

A cold wind started to blow in my heart. Desperately I wanted that big woman to go away, back to her ship, back to the black void and leave me alone. I said: "What do you know of my mother?"

"Nothing, could be," she said.

Still she stared. Now I was truly frightened. I knew whatever she was going to say next would be something terrible. But she didn't say anything, just stood there and chewed her fuming quid. I caught Mrs. Baxter's eye and I could see she was starting to wonder whether being so long in space had turned the woman's wits. It does, sometimes. You stare into nothing long enough, it will swallow you whole, suck the soul out of you between one blink and the next. Perfectly good men go out and cling to the mast tops and won't come down.

I dried my hands. I said to the woman: "Who might you be, then?" Quite boldly it came out, considering.

"Ginny Wigram," she said—then she turned without another word and left. She pushed through the bar, waving away her shipmates' cries of appeal and scorn, and she walked straight out of the door. I was left with Mrs. Baxter, who said to me: "Is that really your name? Sophrona?"

I nodded. I was watching the shape of Ginny Wigram through the yellow window, disappearing. I said: "Who is Mrs. Rose?"

Mrs. Baxter raised her eyebrows, stuck out her bottom lip, and shook her head.

"And who's she?" I asked, still looking at the dark and empty window, meaning Ginny Wigram. I felt relieved and disappointed, both together, now she had gone.

"She's one of them, off that ship what's got your name," said Mrs. Baxter, and she jerked her head to the side. "Don't you know the Wigrams, up here, number sixty-three?" she said, opening her handbag. "She'll be back. Pour us a gin, ducks, I've been on me feet since breakfast."

So I did, and after that sneaked away upstairs to my scribe's office. I took out paper, and wrote as I have told you already.

My office was in the loft of the Hope and Anchor. You might have mistaken it, at first sight, for a lumber room, a glory hole. It was indeed a low shadowy region under the eaves, filled with overflowing boxes, defeated furniture, solitary boots, crippled candlesticks, and crates and crates of empty bottles covered in dust. In wet weather the roof leaked, so I had an old bucket set under it. I did have a notion to improve the luxury of my quarters by rigging some device of a funnel and a system of pipes which would catch the rainwater and pour it into the bottles one by one, for I was always forgetting to empty the bucket—and there were hundreds of bottles—but when the day was fair, why, no scribe ever had a finer office!

My writing desk was a big, flat cigar box that Mr. Rodney had found me, with a lid to keep the mice out. In Johnny's cast-off clogs and Miss Halshaw's coat I would sit on my stool that had once been a chair, with my writing desk on my knees, and write all their letters for them, whoever came, and seal them with wax from the necks of whiskey bottles, that I heated at the candle on the point of my knife. I would not use my ring for the seal, not wanting to get wax on it; so I kept that hidden still and showed it to no one, not even Gertie. It was no wedding ring; I had made sure of that by Mrs. Rodney's ring and the rings of all the wives who came in the Hope, all the ones who hadn't pawned their rings.

The schoolteacher, who never came in to the Hope to drink, had been in to see for himself the little scribe from High Haven. He tried to coax me to school—how tempted I was—but I said I had my living to earn. One day, on another world, I would be a teacher myself, of course, with the strangest class, you may think, that ever wrestled with their ABC—yes, Kappi, I was—but of that, as Mr. Crusoe says, in its place.

No teacher had I to teach me how to write a letter: only the folk who came and told me what they wanted me to say. You will know, Sir, Madam, that there are rules and formalities, the art of correspondence, such as proper scribes follow—appellation before reflection, reflection before comment—we had none of that. Our letters were humbler, and had to make their way across the great gulf without such dignifications. Some were business, but most were personal, and all they were to say was, Here I am; or, I keep my promise; or merely, God Bless. Letters to say, Remember me.

The young men's were funny. They always wanted "darling" and "sweetheart" all through, like the words confectioners put all through their sticks of peppermint rock—but once they were married they never thought of it, unless there had been some quarrel. Their wives wrote about money, about the housekeeping and problems with thc landlord; but somehow, without mentioning it, their letters were full of love. I thought so at least—the men didn't seem to notice—except the ones who hadn't been married long, and they were bashful, and seemed to see love everywhere. I thought of poor Jack Spivey in his coffin and I knew my poor heart was broken, and I should never, never love again.

"Miss Sophrona Rose," I said to my own reflection in a crate of bottles; then I sighed, and abandoned my letter to Papa, and went back down into the bar. There was a celebration going on, half wake, half homecoming: Mr. Cook the kiteman had brought his fiddle, and the Battersea bricklayers, who could smell a party across five parishes, were there with their squeeze-box, their banjo and spoons. Old Gorch the ratcatcher was drunk and dancing with a woman who had come in collecting for the Mission to Spacemen. Mr. Cook played on, deep into the night, and Mrs. Cook sang. She sang:

At Mr. Wisty's wedding she was nowhere to be seen
Though the bridegroom searched the village up and down
Mr. Wisty looked for Dodie from the duckpond to the green
But Dodie and the duke were outward bound!

The sailors from the *Sophrona* sang loudest of all, and tickled the whores that sat on their knees.

Mrs. Baxter had said Ginny Wigram would be back, and she was. She was waiting outside when Mr. Rodney and I got there next morning. There was fog off the river, a real London Particular, but I knew it was her by her shape.

She stood there like a knife fighter waiting for her hour, not moving as we came up, except her jaw, eternally chewing. Mr. Rodney she ignored altogether. To me she said, "You're to come with me, Sophie."

My heart leapt. But Mr. Rodney took me by the hand and stepped in front of me. "Just a minute, Ginny Wigram," he said.

She looked levelly at him, though still speaking to me. "I've had a word with the guv'nor and he says you're to come."

I pulled my hand from Mr. Rodney's, taking no notice of his disapproval. "Where are we going, Ginny?" I asked.

She squirted stinking bacca juice from her mouth into the road. "Miss Wigram to you," she said. I supposed I had somehow earned her displeasure. I thought she was a strange creature, so self-possessed, and I was determined to be more like her.

"I'll be in later," I told Mr. Rodney. "You can leave the pots if you like."

He frowned a dark frown. "You be careful, Sophie!" he warned me. Miss Wigram had already left, so I gasped him the barest of good-byes and hurried after her into the fog. There were halos around the gas lamps and all the bricks were glistening. Cabs loomed and vanished like ships in the clouds, the sounds of their hoofbeats ringing mysteriously from the invisible walls. Striding along a yard ahead, Miss Wigram would say nothing, not even acknowledging my company, but chewed us both all the way to the Elephant and Castle, where the men stood smoking in the bookie's, waiting for their fortunes to arrive. They watched us come, they watched us go. We turned a corner. On the wall above the corner shop I saw a tin advert for Simpkins's Soap, and under it a sign: Corunna Street.

Miss Wigram spat her quid in the gutter and knocked at number fifty-eight. It was a narrow old house, leaning right over the street. There was yellowed lace at the parlor window, and a stuffed magpie in a brass cage. An old woman in black opened the door.

All Miss Wigram said was: "Is she awake?"

The woman looked sour, as if our arrival was a chore to her. I was not introduced, or even remarked upon. The old woman took us upstairs, saying to Miss Wigram: "I told her you'd been"; and on the top landing she knocked on a door.

"Visitors for you, Mrs. Rose," she said, opening it. "I suppose you'll be wanting tea now."

"Who is it, Mrs. Peggley? I can't see!" The room was even smaller than I had expected, partitioned off, to pack in more lodgers, I suppose. The room was half-filled by the bed where a small woman sat in a ribboned cap, reaching for a pair of eyeglasses. Her voice was old. She was not my mama. I knew that in an instant. I wondered if she could be my grandmama. Her face was wan, very pasty, as if she never left her bed.

Mrs. Rose worked the wires of her spectacles behind her ears. "Is it you, Ginny Wigram? When Mrs. Peggley said, I could hardly believe. Of course I would have been there, but, there it is. My sciatics." Her voice was high, gasping, as though it hurt each time to break off a fragment of thought and utter it. Her window was closed against the fog, and the air in the room was very stale and dusty.

Miss Wigram squeezed by the bed to her side. "Hello, Mrs. Rose," she said, loudly but without much warmth. "We're back."

"Safe and sound. Praise the Lord!" Mrs. Rose reached up as if to touch Miss Wigram's cheek, but did not complete the gesture. "You look so well, Ginny," she said. "So young. While I—Well, of course. Naturally." She was already looking past Miss Wigram to me. I could see her, trying to work out the riddle of my presence. "And this is your—"

"This is Miss Farthing," Miss Wigram said. "From Lambeth."

"My dear," said Mrs. Rose. "Enchanted." And she held out her hand to me. It was thin as a bundle of sticks, and wrapped in a black net glove with no fingers to it. "So very kind," said Mrs. Rose. The spectacles made her eyes look like two green fish swimming in bowls.

"Miss Farthing. Beg you will forgive the condition. Charmed to be acquainted. Charmed . . ." Eagerly her fingers squeezed mine, then dropped to pick at the threads of the coverlet. "So little company these days. Not like the old days, I can tell you! Such great ones then, oh great ladies, and gentlemen . . . But there, foolish to—" She gazed at me like a navigator gazing into a great abyss. "You were not there," she said, cautiously, "were you? With Miss Wigram? With our blessed Lord and Lady Plumstone?"

I looked at Miss Wigram for help or explanation, but she wasn't giving either. She had taken the only chair and was leaning her head on the wall, watching.

"Do you know Mr. Cox?" I asked Mrs. Rose. "Mr. Cox of the Pilots' Guild?"

She looked vaguely at me, as if the fog had got into the room and obscured my face. "So little company," she told me. "All my friends," she said, and she laid her hand on a worn black Bible which lay beside her pillow.

I wondered whether that meant all her friends were dead, and whether there were stories about them in the Bible. I thought of Papa, then, who had no friends, and no Bible either, and I had left him all alone. "I am sorry, ma'am," I said.

Mrs. Rose seemed pleased with this reply. "Thank you, my dear. I'd receive you properly, only my sciatics, you know." I said I knew. She beamed at me, triumphant in her disablement. "Perhaps Miss Wigram has told you," she said, and gestured in her direction; but she did not say what it was Miss Wigram might have told, and indeed she had told me nothing, as you know.

"Mrs. Rose used to work for Lady Plumstone," said Miss Wigram then. Her voice sounded harsh in those stuffy, muffled quarters.

Mrs. Rose's eyes skittered behind their glass walls and she spoke even more rapidly. "My benefactor Lady Plumstone, most generous, praise the Lord." She indicated her tiny dingy room, the uncleaned grate where a thimbleful of coal was burning sulkily. "Most generous, Miss Farthing, but perhaps you've had the honor?"

I started to speak. "No, I—"

But Mrs. Rose interrupted. She was not going to listen to me. She had something to show me, a bookmark from her Bible. "Their lordships. My benefactors. In person."

It was a dim, brown photograph of a married couple of high estate. To one side was the lady, sitting down, but her dress was so large you couldn't see the chair. To the other stood her husband, his hat upon his head, his right hand tucked into his waistcoat, his mustache stiffly waxed and perfectly enormous. Behind and between them on the wall you could see a large painting of a star-schooner.

Mrs. Rose pressed her fingertips to the photograph, as though to get closer to her benefactors. "I thank the Lord Jesus," she said fervently. "But of course you know. Like Miss Wigram, I too was proud to serve," she said. "Fortunate indeed."

My head felt thick and full of feathers. I had hardly understood a word since we came in the room, and I didn't know what to say. I was sure I was there by mistake, some crazed idea of Ginny Wigram's.

I pointed to the painting in the photograph. "The *Sophrona*," I said.

"So beautiful! Across the Milky Way! Praise the Lord!"

"That's my name," I said.

"What is, dear?"

"Sophrona, ma'am," I said. I was determined it would *be* my name when I said it; but still it didn't sound right.

"Miss Farthing comes from High Haven," Miss Wigram added, pointedly.

Mrs. Rose gave a gasp and clutched at her coverlet. Pale as she was, she now grew paler still, and gazed at me in as much dismay as if I had been some frightful monster instead of a little girl in a big coat. "She?" she cried, in a quavering voice. "Is it she? This one? Oh my heart! Oh my sin!"

Weakly she tried to pull the sheet up in front of her like a shield. "Oh forgive me in Jesus name in Christian charity!" she cried.

I saw Miss Wigram's eyes glint. She looked pleased with herself, as if she had done a satisfying duty.

I took Mrs. Rose's hand between mine. "Forgive you, ma'am? What for? What have you done?"

"Scarce weaned! Walked away and left you crying! Oh, please, Miss Farthing—"

There was a knock at the door.

"Here's your tea, Mrs. Rose," said Mrs. Peggley.

"Oh, tea, tea!" cried Mrs. Rose. "Oh, praise the Lord!"

We drank tea. My hands lifted the cup to my mouth, and my mouth drank the tea; but I swear I knew nothing of it.

So this withered powdered creature was my mother after all, and she had abandoned me. She was my father's shame, never to be mentioned; and I had been her ruin. Yet she was not looking at me like a mother at a daughter lost and found. She was looking at me as if I were a horrid dream. She had snatched her hand out of mine. I did not know what to say to her. I wanted to run away home at once.

Miss Wigram put more sugar in her tea and stirred it. The spoon clinked inside the cup.

"Mrs. Rose," I began.

"Beautiful," she said, interrupting me as soon as I spoke. Her lips quivered. "Beautiful ship." She stroked her photograph. "I was hired," she said. "For that great voyage."

Her voice was sad. She was speaking of loss and defeat; of shame. She took off her spectacles.

I sat like a cat that has seen a bird about to land.

"Hard. So hard," said Mrs. Rose. A tear fell from her eye and plopped on the bedclothes.

I helped her find her handkerchief. She crumpled it to her breast. "Mrs. Rose," I said, as boldly as I dared. "I never knew my mother. I don't know who she was, Mrs. Rose."

She nodded sorrowfully, her shrunken bosom lifting as she rallied. "Sit down, Miss Farthing," she said. "Sit here, on the bed. Some more tea, Miss Wigram, so very. Miss Wigram, my witness. Charity rejoiceth not in iniquity," Mrs. Rose said rapidly, "but rejoiceth in the truth."

She slipped her picture back inside her Bible so it could not betray her again. Then she straightened the coverlet once more and addressed herself to me.

"I did not always live here," Mrs. Rose said. "Over in St. Paul's. I knew her, only to speak to, you know. Neighbors. They called her Molly Clare." She waved her hand, as if sweeping something away from her. "A wicked trade, Miss Farthing," she said, sternly; "but—" she begged to remind me, "—Christian charity."

I saw Miss Wigram frown. It was plain that it didn't sound like the story she had been expecting.

"One morning, there she was, I was in the middle of packing. With a basket, she lifted it up and put it down on the kitchen table. There was a baby in it! I said, Bless her, though to them they are a curse, Miss Farthing, you know. She said, I know you are going on that ship, and I know High Haven is your first port of call. It is, Mrs. Clare, I said, I knew

she was no man's wife being every man's wife as they say,
but no reason not to say Mrs. out of charity, Miss Farthing,
out of Christian charity. She said for God's sake, Mrs. Rose,
take her."

Mrs. Rose drank a mouthful of tea.

"Take my daughter, she said, for the love of Jesus, and
give her to the man who keeps the night watch at the East
Dock."

Mrs. Rose recited that as if she had said it over to herself
a thousand times since. She looked from me to Miss Wigram
and back again.

"I did it," she confessed. "Hid you in my cabin. Fed you a
banana mashed in milk."

"Then her ladyship found out," said Miss Wigram.

Mrs. Rose's face crumpled. "Her ladyship! An hour before
we docked. A mere hour!" she lamented. "But ah, deceit, Miss
Farthing, the snare that catches the snarer!"

I did not know what to think. I thought of Old Gorch going
down into the cellar of the Hope and Anchor with his jingling
sack of traps.

"High Haven, everyone else went ashore," said Mrs. Rose.
"I put a cloth over you, you didn't like that! Oh dear. Asked
a constable the way." Her lips worked as she recollected. "A
wharf. Named after a saint."

"Radigund," I said.

"Praise the Lord!" she said. "I knocked, but no answer,
naturally, being daylight, you see. Well, I couldn't stay. I did
write a note. God has blessed me with a little education, you
see, Miss Farthing."

Miss Wigram spoke up. "Miss Farthing reads and writes
for everyone at the Hope and Anchor." She spoke as if she
thought she owed me something. Her bacca pouch was in her
hand, and she was stroking the lip of it with her great brown
thumb.

"You started to cry," said Mrs. Rose to me, dabbing her
own eye again. "I took fright, not wishing to disturb. Ran
away," she said, her mouth shaking with remorse. "A cat
in the window, I saw it watching. Pleasant for a child, a
cat about the place." Her voice went quavering up into a
squeak and she buried her mouth in her handkerchief once
more.

So now I knew how Papa must hate me: his accidental child, unmeant, unwanted. Something cast away that had drifted back to his doorstep with the tide.

I breathed in hard, squeezing my nostrils shut. I said: "And what was my name?"

"She gave you none," said Mrs. Rose. "No name, no history, the harder to be found." She smiled then, proudly. "I named you myself," she said. "For the ship." Her fingers started to stray toward the Bible again, seeking her picture. "The finest ship in all the worlds. I left him a note of it, the name."

I felt my eyes water. "And a ring," I said.

"A crystal ring," she recalled. "Hers. You pulled it off her finger while she was kissing you good-bye. Let her take it, she said, for all the comfort it brings. She sounded bitter, oh, bitter and sad, and you were crying so!"

I bowed my head.

Miss Wigram said to her in a low voice: "Could she not have kept the child?" You could tell it was all new to her, she had not known about Molly Clare, had never heard of her before. Nor was she disbelieving, for the old lady's sorrow was not to be denied.

Mrs. Rose answered, but speaking to me still, as if I were the one who had asked. "It broke her heart to send you away, though it would have been your death too. The wages of sin," she said. "I will repay, saith the Lord. But judge not, that ye be not judged," she chided herself, quickly, and laughed a laugh of fright. "What do you think? Before the year was out she was dead. Murdered."

I cried out, a small, quiet cry.

"Murdered by a maniac," said Mrs. Rose, in a hush as though she feared the murderer might be listening to us that minute, out on the landing. "She and her whole household. It was in the newspaper. Lord Jesus forgive their mighty, mighty sins."

I was thunderstruck. I do not know why they say that: thunderstruck. There was no loud noise, no storm; nothing save a great bleak calm and emptiness in my heart.

I sat there dumb. Mrs. Rose and Miss Wigram spoke over my head. Mrs. Rose was remembering High Haven. "Streets all different heights and sizes, joined up by bridges of iron.

Buildings all piled up anyhow, one on another's back. Earth
like a big blue marble rolling up the sky. Praise the Lord. Like
a marble!" She spoke proudly. She had been to the brink of
the infinite sea, and that was enough.

"Lady Plumstone dismissed her," said Miss Wigram. "From
the *Sophrona*, before we sailed."

"Not fit," said Mrs. Rose herself quickly, as if that went
without saying. "My sciatics, you know, Miss Farthing."

For some reason that it was that pierced me at last, and I
began to weep in earnest; and I embraced that good woman,
my unknown nurse and savior. Dear Reader, you must forgive
my stupidity; I was a stranger yet to the ways of Earth. Not
until that moment did I understand that like Miss Wigram,
Lady Plumstone, too, had thought the baby Mrs. Rose's own.
And thus it was Mrs. Rose had come so low.

My tears alarmed and flustered the poor old lady, and she
rushed to calm me. "Unfortunate subject, oh dear," she said,
and thrust something into my hand. "Here, Miss Farthing."

It was a wooden matchbox. It was empty. I stared at her
numbly.

"Keep one always by me," said Mrs. Rose, "for the spiders
and the woodlice. They crawl up on the bed and I rescue
them." She pointed up at the fogbound window. "I make Mrs.
Peggley tip them out. Earth down there somewhere," she said
confidently, and laughed, as if she had embarrassed herself.
Then she put her spectacles on and stared at me anxiously.

I asked Miss Wigram to take me home. As we left Mrs.
Rose asked how was my father. I said he was not well, but
that I was writing him a letter. And went downstairs feeling
like a ghost.

9

A capital city

In Ys the little sun comes up, and all the sky at once turns a hard, sour yellow. High on the pinnacle of the Black Well the *kiiri* are the first to see it. Sluggishly they rouse, creeping out from where they nest, among the high carvings of twisted bodies and tangled limbs: from under tentacled arms and marble intestines they emerge, treading on one another, pecking the ticks from one another's scaly wings. It almost looks as though the carvings themselves have come to life. They are something like crows, *kiiri*, though they are the size of condors. They bare their teeth and stretch their necks, holding their throats out to the cold dawn wind that blows in from the canyons, into the veins of the city.

To the *kiiri* the incipient day reveals itself in a hundred creaks and whispers, a thousand smokes and stenches. They taste breakfasts, sacrifices, sewers. Launching themselves high on silent, gliding errands, the *kiiri* quarter the city, monitoring the slow currents of life that stir below, beginning to trickle now into the streets. There goes a Well Woman with a pitcher, carrying water to the Seneschal of Morning. As she passes the blind beggar slumped at the corner, she will pause to fill his cup. As long as she continues to do so, every morning, the *kiiri* are not interested in the beggar, or the water maiden. They fly down again, some of them, and perch up under the Gate of the Seventeen Adversaries, fouling its tiles with their pestilential dung. They watch as the travelers who have camped outside the city all night begin to come in; and the Corregi from the Gah Sheraa, bringing their austriches to trade. The travelers and the tribeswomen are nothing either to the *kiiri*.

On, then, beyond the Grand Canal, where the humans are already stoking up their infernal dredger, to the Juarouq Quarter. Here the *kiiri* circle, calling one to another in their creaking, high-pitched voices, clustering in the branches of the giant spindly purple cacti that line the streets. The streets are narrow and zigzag, as if the very buildings must huddle close for warmth. Here there is no one to see but peasants trudging to the canal with bundles of washing, or with barrows to the harbor market. A fat barber in a green dress signals impatiently to his dawdling customers, tumbling both hands and flapping his ears. Everyone falls silent and turns to stare as a French patrol passes, keeping close order. The *kiiri*, too, come slipping down through the air to inspect the French patrol, for it is followed by a lizard-drawn wagon full of slaves, some of whom seem far from well.

The French were the first to reach Mars and send news back, all Britannia's embassies having made straight for Ys and disappeared without trace. After that none but the poorest and most desperate would go: prospectors from France and Spain, who landed in the barren south, far away from any cities. They it was who discovered the remains of the gigantic forests that once darkened the face of the planet, long, long ago, before the Noachian Age. Trade sprang up when it became known that though the cities of the equator were barbarous, and of perilous might, yet they knew nothing of coal. The French built the splendid space harbor at Ys for the first royal visit, and now there is a flourishing native market, exporting diamonds, importing fruit. Ys, the biggest city in the world, sprawls contentedly over the buried Lake Ventre, husbanding her waters.

The French have planted palms along the Grand Canal, from the embassy to the Imperial Palace. There they make their *promenade*, officials and their wives sauntering to and fro in the midmorning, when the racing moons stir the fine, cold air until it bubbles like champagne, and it is thought salubrious enough to walk abroad. The *promenade* excites much local attention and emulation. Here a pair of native ladies amble by in crinolines, parasols held stiffly over their shoulders. A native man in a cap salutes a Frenchman in a top hat, and is allowed to perform a small service, perhaps to brush with a whisk broom the all-pervasive dust from the coat of the Frenchman's lady. For this he will receive a small brass coin in fee. The Martian slaves who scrub the pavement in front of the embassy look on, uncomprehending.

Along the façade of the embassy the *kiiri* look down, comprehending everything, everything that needs to be comprehended. For example, over there, behind the latrines, there is a dead human in the bulrushes. He has been there a week, undiscovered by slave or dog, ripening slowly in the cold air. That is what the *kiiri* are interested in.

Humans are numerous in Ys now, and a great many of them seem to be dying. It is regrettable, how many of them die. Yet can one wonder at it? It is a foreign world on which they dwell, and they are unfamiliar with her dangers. Their children fall in the canals, and their servants succumb to mysterious diseases. The isolated outposts of S. Etienne and Roche du Cobra were both suddenly overwhelmed by sandstorms, each time a whole fort at once and no one left to tell the tale. Their standards have been sent home by royal pinnace, to hang on the walls of Notre Dame. The Emperor sent a message of sympathy on behalf of his people.

Though the day is now well advanced, in the imperial bedchamber it is still and always night, with lamps always burning. Braziers too, filling the hazy air with heat, and the smoke of healthful resins. In his sickbed the Emperor of All Mars dreams of an importunate messenger with long bony fingers, and wakes, a chill on his ancient brow. He summons his steward, with stimulants and sweet ointment, and his women.

The signal is given, that the eyes of His Imperial Majesty have opened to gaze upon another day. In a moment a mournful horn sounds from the palace roof, and outside on the Grand Canal the dredger begins its dreadful clatter and chug. The steward bows and says: "Your Orient Splendor, High Priest Keegheeta is waiting out in the pavilion." The Emperor grunts and folds his eyelids. He will let him wait, while he entertains this more welcome company. The women climb into the Emperor's bed. One of them says she saw Friar Lambert's mule earlier, tethered in the cactus garden. The Emperor smiles, his temples swelling. It amuses him to think what will happen if the two men have to wait in the pavilion together, how polite they will be to each other. Seeing the Emperor smile, the women smile too.

In fact the friar is nowhere near the guest pavilion. He is at the stablehouse, christening a baby born to one of the bird-grooms, one of his converts. He blesses the leathery brown bundle, happy to be gathering another small soul into the universal fold. The mother takes communion, wincing and smacking her lips at the unaccustomed taste of wine.

That ceremony done, the friar takes his leave and rides up to the harbor market, where the sellers of sweetmeats tempt him with the local white snakes which they drag wriggling from buckets and boil alive in sizzling oil. Friar Lambert passes them by and passes, too, the slave stalls, where the Ophiq, the rainbow folk, huddle together in their cage, green with fear. How bright that green glows in this dusty orange light! Friar Lambert blesses them also, in the name of the Father, the Son, and the Holy Spirit. He goes to collect an order of medicines and the post for the mission, the Sisters of Lamentation at S. Sébastien, in the high desert.

Friar Lambert has had news from S. Sébastien. There, at the bottom of a dry well, S. Juliade has appeared to an errant novice. Mother Lachrymata sent the friar a messenger, a native boy, begging him to come and advise her. That was several weeks ago. In this cold and gritty season, the desert is an uninviting destination. In any case, Friar Lambert could feel no urgency to answer the reverend mother's plea, though he did pray for her, and for the poor bewildered novice, that she might learn to see the pure light of truth.

It is not that the holy father doubts the young girl's vision. Visions are plentiful in the desert, high and low: so much so that Cardinal D'Aubray no longer sends anyone to investigate reports of miraculous visitors, stigmata, apparitions of the Blessed Virgin. Friar Lambert knows the cardinal would condemn all such giddy fancies without exception, but his hands have been tied by Rome herself. In the confusion over early reports of mountain cities populated by angels, the entire planet was blessed by the Holy Father.

Mighty and mysterious are the works of the Lord, the Worlds He hath made with His Hand. Friar Lambert has met and spoken with the K'mecki, the tribe that follows its hallucinating cartographers through the desert from waterhole to waterhole. And didn't he himself once, whipping his mule up the slopes of Mont Royal, for an instant see something—a vast brown figure shouldering up out of the valley below, a gigantic man, of human form? Yet even while the friar gasped and drew rein, crossing himself, it was gone.

Indeed, indeed, thinks Friar Lambert as he rides in at the gateway of S. Sébastien: Mars is a planet of dreams, its alien air full of things to puzzle poor, ignorant sinners. He hears the sisters' confessions, and examines the wretched trembling novice with half an ear, because it is his duty, but there is no sense to be got from her. As far as she knows, she really has seen S. Juliade. The question is, does S. Juliade herself know anything about it? It is a hard question, too hard for a humble pastoral brother. All Friar Lambert can do is pray with her, and give her her penance, and then take luncheon with Mother Lachrymata and the sisters. They enjoy the grapes he has brought from the market.

From S. Sébastien the friar rides on up the line to Coin Brut, to hear the silver miners confess their dreary sins of fornication with native prostitutes, to correct their misunderstandings about Hell.

Many of the miners are Peruvians, with superstitions of their own to mingle with the natives'. They have put up a shrine to the Devil in the mine, to appease him. They call him the Uncle, for fear of uttering his true name. "If God is up in Heaven," they explain, "the Uncle must be under the ground."

Wearily Friar Lambert reminds them of the Holy Father's edict. They nod, and cross themselves, and thank him; but it makes no difference. To them, Hell itself is clearly located on this cold, foreign planet where they toil in darkness alongside angels with amputated wings. Beneath the South Pole, the miners believe, the souls of the damned are stacked seven hundred deep in caverns of black ice. At confession they swear they have heard them, groaning and wheezing and whispering blasphemous temptations, deep underground.

Meanwhile, down at the palace, the Emperor of All the Martians is occupied with theological enquiries of his own. He has admitted the High Priest at last, and takes water with him.

"Their God is not like ours, Keegheeta. He is far away, up above the sky somewhere, where their ships come from."

The High Priest bows stiffly in his giant headdress, his voluminous skirts. He finds the imperial bedchamber too hot, its atmosphere sickly and stifling. "The Imperial Wisdom reaches beyond the stars," he murmurs.

The priest regrets these strange notions the Emperor has begun to entertain, learnt from the foreigners. The Emperor, for example, believes there are still giant crocodiles, just as there were in the days of his great-great-great-great-great-grandfather. The same giant crocodiles, in fact. The Emperor believes they continue, somehow, in a place beyond mortal ken, an existence after life. He believes he will see the giant crocodiles, and his great-great-great-great-great-grandfather too, very soon. High Priest Keegheeta, on the other hand, considers that his sovereign has already lived for an enormous number of years; so many that his skin is crumpled, his mind spotted with darkness.

The Emperor's lips move again, effortfully. "The Cardinal was here again, with his acolytes," he recalls. "He spoke of giving me absolution," he says; and the High Priest flexes his claws with indignation, while the women coo and wipe the imperial brow with scented kerchiefs. "What is a 'sacrament,' Keegheeta, do you know?"

The High Priest gives his cup to a slave and lays his hand on his chest. "Sire," he rumbles, "will you hear my counsel?"

"You have always been the most considerate of servants, Keegheeta," croaks the Emperor of All Mars.

"O most receptive of masters," the priest says, "again I urge: by no means let them persuade you. This sacrament is a despicable crumb of bread, which they eat, and a mouthful of wine."

The Emperor strokes the hair of his cupbearer. "The wine, at least, Keegheeta," he suggests, slowly. Wine has been a most acceptable part of the Terran tribute, wine and coal, of course. But the High Priest is saying no, even the wine is tainted, by something called "transubstantiation": "With their misshapen mouths, they change the wine into blood . . ." The man is like a buzzing fly in the chamber. Wrapped in his bedclothes, the Emperor stares into the luscious black eyes of a concubine. They are soothing, those eyes. He wishes the High Priest would go away. He thinks he could fall asleep now, looking into those eyes.

" . . . the blood and the body of their Jésus Christ."

The Emperor catches the name, the one Cardinal D'Aubray says so often. "That is their God."

"Yes, Majesty."

The art of royalty, on Mars as on any world, is getting the gist of things. It is an art the Emperor can still summon, even on days when the brain in his head feels like rotten slime.

"They think they eat their God."

"Your Magnificence is the most concise of commentators."

The Emperor's ear flaps twitch closed. Wearily, contemptuously, he whispers: " . . . disgusting . . ."

"Our stomachs rebel," says the High Priest readily. "Their stink is in our nostrils." And he makes a ritual gesture, holding his scarf across his face. The women stir, disturbed: the scent of the gums smoldering on the precious coals is rich and fragrant, but barely masks the stench of the canal, not to mention the stink of the Emperor.

The High Priest is unaware of his offense. Ears spread with irritation, he is launched upon his favorite subject. "They defile the sacred city with their machines."

Outside the narrow windows, the dredger toils on. It has been toiling in the canal all week, amid loud din and clouds of steam. The pelicans have abandoned their ancestral nests in the Emperor's Pool and vanished into the canyons.

The High Priest's tone becomes whining and fierce. " . . . vermin on the face of our noble planet . . ."

"Have they stolen your women?" the Emperor pipes.

The priest steps back, bridling his anger. "My compliments on your companions," he says carefully, "O most virile of potentates."

"Juicy, aren't they?" the Emperor agrees. "Would you like one?"

The priest sways his head in distaste. "Alas, sire: my vow . . ."

The Emperor seems to be sliding down sideways among his pillows. He looks terrible, but his eyes are still bright. What is it they put in his water? "No, tell me, Keegheeta," he insists. "Which one do you like best?"

The priest takes a deep breath. "Most jocular of patrons," he says, smoothly, "they are all so lovely there is not a sword's breadth of advantage between them."

The Emperor clutches the sheets in mock alarm. "Do you want to take them all?"

The women squeak and flutter, covering their breasts. The priest is writhing now. He attempts a smile, and a jest of his own. "The Well Maidens would be most annoyed . . ."

The Emperor's voice creaks in the smoky room. "If you won't take a woman, Keegheeta, I expect you will take a tub of coal as usual. I remember how cold it is in your chambers."

The High Priest bows, hissing deferentially. The dredger thuds and thuds. The Emperor does not care. It reminds him of a sharp spring day, some years ago: a grand parade, the endless ranks of human ships passing overhead, their brasswork glinting and all their guns firing loudly in salute. The signing of the Olympus Treaty, between Mars and the League of All Worlds. The Emperor rode in the new imperial balloon the King of France had given him. He is fond of his balloon. He knows he will never ride in it again.

"Their machines," he points out, "carry them in their tall black hats from world to world. Our own people are learning the secret paths of the sky sea. One day, Keegheeta, we shall learn all their secrets. Then we shall have worlds of our own to plunder. Rich and juicy worlds!"

The priest hisses. "You yourself will lead us to their fountains, O most gloriously scarred of veterans."

"Nonsense, Keegheeta, I can't get out of bed."

The High Priest ventures one last rally. "Then give the word, sire, and let your warriors destroy them and seize their ships. Our pilots are the best in the galaxy!"

"Long and far may they journey, Keegheeta," exhorts the Emperor of All the Martians, "hand in hand with our Terran brothers. Now we shall rest. I expect the steward will have your coal ready for you. I treasure your advice like a flagon of fine Bordeaux. May the sun shine on your departure."

The High Priest spreads his skirts and bends his forehead low. "Most durable of monarchs!"

"Exhausting man," is all the Emperor will say, after the priest has gone. It was their habitual argument. Both men detest the pale intruders, but their tribute is rich, and they keep the winged folk down. What matter if they do steal women from the desert villages? The humans are welcome to them, they are only peasants, ugly creatures in dirty, drab clothes. Sometimes, these days, the Emperor thinks he dislikes all his people. All those clamoring voices, those grabbing hands. He is not sorry to be leaving them soon. His women smile and stroke his eyelids, and rearrange his pillows for the thousandth time.

High Priest Keegheeta walks down the private stairway from the imperial apartments. *Kiiri* rise up from the roof and wheel over his head, screeching, but he takes no notice. He is displeased with himself for having once more lost his patience in the presence of the Emperor. He summons his slaves, who carry him and the tub of coal for which he came along streets crowded now with lizards and donkeys. The little white snakes flee from their hurrying feet. The embankment road is blocked by idlers leaning on the parapet, watching the dredging. The priest detests that boat. They say it works ten times as fast as a gang of slaves. Certainly it creates twenty times more noise and nuisance. He commands the curtains of his palanquin to be lowered.

Later, in the evening, the Emperor's son Ariak comes to visit his father. He, too, is preoccupied. He is thinking of changing his name, to Henri Ariak, and he wishes to leave telling his father as late as possible. His Majesty was angry enough when he saw Ariak wearing the fashionable "top hat," and this announcement will make him very angry indeed. Ariak decides once again not to mention it. Instead he speaks of the latest meteors, far up near the northern ice, which make the French miners rub their hands and speak of "gifts from Heaven"; and he mentions that he saw Friar Lambert this morning, near the stables. Ariak encourages the friar, intrigued by this man who sets such value on the lives of slaves, the sick, women, and children. He allows his servants to give the perplexing Terran old clothes and leftover food, just to see what he will do with them.

"I thought he came to see me," wheezes the Emperor. "Or was that a dream? Somebody came." The day seems endless to him; as if the stream of time itself has silted up, like the canal.

"I should like to see the bridge at T'reegnava again. This summer, Ariak, let us make a passage through the kingdoms." The Emperor thinks of the spa cities on the Grand Canal; the

red and golden valleys; the plains where the water runs shining and cold and straight from horizon to empty horizon, for
hundreds on hundreds of miles.

His son stares at him, keeping his ears very steady. He
inclines his head and says: "A splendid plan, O Indomitable
Overseer."

On the pinnacle of the Black Well, the *kiiri* crawl all over
each other. Inside they are rehearsing for the ceremony. The
screaming has begun.

10

In which I change my dress

In the great library in Westminster I sat on a tall chair with
a leather cushion and looked up and around in wonder and
delight. I had never been in a library before. I decided to stay
there forever, surrounded by elderly ladies translating Virgil
and earnest gentlemen whose enormous beards grew all tangled up with the pages of their Commentaries on the Gospel.
I should need no other sustenance, but read every book on the
shelves, starting with the *Encyclopædia Cælestiana* and Mr.
Shandy's Life and Mr. Lamb's Tales and *Paradise Lost* with
its wonderful pictures of worlds full of devils and angels. But
first I had to turn the stiff, rough pages that lay before me,
which had pictures of devils enough. Here THE ST. KIT'S
CREEPER was depicted for me, with his fearsome scowl and
his ragged cloak; here GENTLEMAN JACK O'NORBURY,
menacing a swooning lady with a dripping dagger.

They were old newspapers, the library gentleman had
informed me, and police gazettes, of fifteen and twenty years
ago. They were full of speeches made by Commissioners of
Parliament, and these drawings of Trials by Law and Shocking
Events. I turned another page gray with tiny print, and caught

my breath. Here it was. FOUL MURDER IN ST. PAUL'S: MASSACRE AT HOUSE OF DEPRAVITY. A picture of a house, with a fat policeman standing in front of it; another of a room where dead women lay at all angles across a bed with big black holes in their fronts. THE PITIABLE VICTIMS. One of them had a little girl slumped beside her in an attitude of despair, with her throat cut; another seemed to point with her lifeless hand to an infant in its cradle.

My eyes swam. I could look no longer at the pictures, and hurried to the words. Alas, there was nothing in them for me, nor anything at all but Horror and Gore. The women were described as "poor wretches," and vaguely it was said that they were "of the worst kind": as though they had deserved to die. Mama was not named, nor anyone else in the house, not even the man who in another picture lay all bent and broken at the bottom of a staircase, like the old man in the nursery rhyme who wouldn't pray. Infants were among the slain; injuries were fearsome. An inspector of police declared it was clearly the work of a madman, and spoke darkly of "brain fever and loathsome diseases."

I turned to the vast beard and shoulder in the chair next to mine. "Please, sir," I said. "What does 'depravity' mean?"

Everyone around the table, and I think everyone in the room, frowned at me and made a sharp hissing noise. A pretty lady sitting opposite me put her finger to her lips. Hotly, feeling the corners of my mouth turn down, I sank again into the wilderness of the page. Again I looked at all the dead women. I could not even tell which one she was.

Mrs. Rose shuddered when I told her about the loathsome diseases. She blessed herself and assured me quickly Mama had not been one of that sort. In fact she had had some fine gentleman callers: "One took her to the Moon, they say!" Did he have an iron jaw? Mrs. Rose thought no one had been particular about the jaw. She did not think anyone had ever seen the gentleman, only the carriage, with the blinds down.

I tried to cheer Mrs. Rose, taking her jam tarts and little flowers, which you find growing everywhere there, between the paving stones; but we did not become friends. Miss Farthing, she continued to call me, though I asked her to say Sophrona, "the name you yourself gave me, Mrs. Rose." How could I ever make it my own if none would call me by it? Yet she could not manage it. "Miss Farthing, what a pleasure!" she would cry when I entered the room, and then clasp her hands together in fright and shrink back on her pillow as if she had done me a great offense.

Poor Mrs. Rose. I was a walking reproach to her. I reminded her of Mama when I opened my mouth, and of Lady Plumstone when I didn't. What she knew of the one was rumors and scraps, and none of it fit to be repeated to an innocent maid. "Such lovely red hair," she said. "Not like yours at all. Oh dear. Oh bless us." And instead she would tell me about the other, who was such a great lady, and then she would stop suddenly and ask me a question about High Haven. Then I would fall glum, reproached in my turn, and Mrs. Rose would start to talk rapidly about Lady Plumstone and Lord Jesus, Lord Jesus and Lady Plumstone. Sometimes, I knew, she believed they were man and wife.

Dear Reader, how can I tell you how sad it was to see her there, dwindled to that cramped, damp cell, a woman who had once been chosen to walk among the stars? I could not lose hold of the memory that it was my life that had blighted hers; I had brought only poison and shame everywhere I'd been—Mama had not loved me—everything was hopeless. Even Gertie ceased to taunt me when I came home in that mood, and watched me with a wary eye.

I was ashamed of Papa, and of myself for existing, but I must confess I was never ashamed of Mama. I did not mind that she hired out her body like a dinghy. Papa had had nothing but contempt for them, the painted women of Half-Moon Street who worked the ferries, riding up and down with the tide. Now I knew how the bitterness had come into his life, wrapped around what one of those women had sent back to him like a rejected gift, delivered in a basket to his door. I wondered how many of them he had had in consolation for his beautiful Estelle. One too many, at least.

Mr. and Mrs. Rodney remembered the Turkey Passage Massacre. Already Mrs. Rodney had begun to look at me differently, as if I were marked with it, like a crimson stain upon my face. "Poor Sophie," she said. "You mustn't think about it, child"—though it was obvious she could think of nothing else from that day on. Soon all the neighbors did too. "Can't you remember her at all?" Betty and Abigail wanted to know.

"No," I said. It was a lie. She was in my mind at every moment, rising up from the bed like a fish from a slab, with all her wounds upon her; only I never could see her face. I would see her from behind in the street, among the crowd, and run out of my way, dropping packages and jostling passers-by to catch her—calling out once, "Molly! Mrs. Clare!" until the red head turned and showed me the face of a young lady of fashion. Murdered by a maniac; while I lay squalling in Papa's impatient arms. Why had she sent me away? Mrs. Rose told me not to ask, and talked about someone called Baby Moses Bulrushes and a Good Shepherd who saved little lambs. I confess I paid scant attention. I had a poor opinion of any savior who would only do half of a job.

Miss Wigram did not come with me to visit Mrs. Rose, though she continued to come in the Hope and Anchor. She did not speak to me, but nor I think did she speak about me, for no gossip spread. I would catch her looking at me with a face of scorn, and I knew that was because star-sailors must have stone hearts and feel no pity. I wonder now, did she think I blamed her for spoiling this haven I had found, with her bad news and unwelcome history?

Then came the day I was mopping the floor when Abigail Cook came to the door and said: "Papa says, the *Uncle Stravagant*'s in the offing."

"The *Unco Stratagem*," I said.

Abigail nodded, gazing into my face, hopping from one foot to the other. "She'll be docking this afternoon, he says."

For a moment I wondered why she was telling me. I had promised Mr. and Mrs. Rodney, and Mr. and Mrs. Mountjoy, that I would stop pursuing Mr. Cox, and I had. I had stopped thinking of him altogether—though I do remember one day wondering if there was a Mrs. Cox. I supposed he was too hideous for anyone to marry. Still, Mama had taken his fancy enough that he had given her a ring. "Let her," Mama had said when I took it from her hand, "for all the comfort it brings." I wondered what promises he had given with that ring, that she had turned so against him.

I stood the mop in the corner and called out to Mrs. Rodney, "I'm just going up the road with Abigail"; and before she could answer I was out of the door and away up Juxon Street with Abigail close behind me.

It took us a long time to get there. Abigail and I were still
in the thick of the crowd on Hampstead Hill when I saw a
smart coach coming down towards us, drawn by a gleaming
pair. On the box of the coach it had painted the pilots' coat
of arms; and I saw part of it was the sign on my ring, the eye
and arrow.

I shouted to Abigail and struck out through the crowd into
the road, dodging the hooves to get closer to the approaching
coach. There, through the window: it was his chin, his long
brown wig; a flash of gold braid on his shoulder. Straight
at the spinning wheels I ran, shouting out at the top of my
voice: "Mr. Cox! Mr. Cox! Remember Molly! Remember
Molly Clare!"

But my voice was swallowed up in the hubbub of the traffic and the street, and the coachman cracked his whip over our
heads. "Way, there, give way!" he cried in a voice like brass,
and they swept on by. I stood on the bridge and clenched my
fists as Mr. Cox sailed on down the hill; but my brow was
damp and my stomach was empty, and a strange relief broke
over me like a sea wave. He had not seen me, or heard me.
He could do me no harm.

Abigail was frightened. "Was that him?" she shouted, grabbing me by the arm as if I would try to throw myself under an
omnibus. "I hope you're happy now, Sophie," she said, panting, then her eyes widened further still. "Look out—Peelers!"
A band of constables was coming, moving idlers and dawdlers
out of the road. Some of the constables were Hrad, I saw,
swinging their long arms and twisting their leaden heads to
study the crowd.

Hrad do well on both sides of the law, on all worlds civilized and savage, wherever there is rough work to be done.
The demolition gang pulling houses down in Black Prince
Road, they were Hrad too, many of them. The Hope was
always full of them in their greatcoats and heavy boots, their
huge fists clattering on the table as they shoved the dominoes
about. They drank great quantities of ginger beer, sucking
wetly at their mugs and laughing at one another in their
wheezy voices. They would have their horrible pets with them,
the ice-weasels, that eat all the sawdust off the floor and
then they always vomit just where you're going to put your
foot down.

"We'll come another day, Abbie," I said, craning after the vanished coach like Columbus on Neptune, "when there aren't so many people."

"Come *on!*" she said, hauling at me by the sleeve.

When I told Gertie in bed that night, I made myself a brave adventurer indeed, and quite the bold hero. She said, "You're mad, Sophie Farthing. He'll have you locked up."

"What for?" I said. "I haven't done anything."

"Mr. Cox is a great high gentleman!" she said, as though I was to blame.

"He's no higher than you," I said. Gertie was growing, and so was I at last, I believed.

"Don't be stupid. You can't just walk up and start talking to him."

I would not reveal to Gertie my qualms for all the spice on Caraway. "I did before," I said.

"And he sent you about your business pretty sharp."

I put my hands on my chest. I was sure I was growing there too, even if you couldn't quite feel it yet. "He won't even know who I am," I said.

I hadn't thought of that until I said it. It was true. No longer was I the wide-eyed waif that had stopped him in his tracks beneath the gaslight. In fact, he wouldn't recognize me at all. He would remember my ring. Aye, he would remember that; he would accuse me of stealing it and call a constable. I turned over hard, drawing my knees up, and pretended Gertie was not there, that she did not exist, so that she could not see my wretchedness. How I wished Mr. Cox had never come back to Earth to trouble me with his iron face.

On that tide of hidden misery I swept out into the ocean of sleep, and dreamt that I was back at home with Papa, who wanted me to bathe his arm and dress it too, for it was bleeding. And when I looked at it, I saw the blood was coming from under his tattoo; and wipe as I might, it would not stop, but rained down all over my skirt while Papa shouted and shouted at me.

Then I saw that the whole room was red with blood, that it was all over the carpet and smeared up the walls, and on a lot of mirrors that seemed to be hanging there. And a figure stood up in front of me, a woman bleeding from the head and bosom who wailed, "Depravity!" while the bells of St. Paul's made a din in the room.

I woke up with a great start and found myself clutching at Gertie and feeling I had wet myself, and my belly hurt. In fear I began to complain aloud, which brought Mrs. Rodney into the room with a candle.

Gertie pushed me, as though I had woken her up on purpose to annoy her. "She's started, Ma," I heard her say.

Mrs. Rodney pulled back the bedclothes and I wailed to see my shift stained with blood. So I had been murdered indeed!

But Mrs. Rodney hugged me and told me softly not to be so silly. She managed me, while water was warming, and we cleaned the worst up. I sat in the kitchen, with a hot drink. "I saw Mama," I said, hugging myself in the blanket she had wrapped around me. "She was walking around. She spoke to me."

"Oh now Sophie dear," clucked that good wife of Lambeth, her hand to her breast, "you mustn't fright yourself so! Why, you know very well your poor mama is at rest in St. Saviour's Churchyard, sleeping quiet in the ground. Now get you back to bed, poppet, and get some rest." But before I did, Mrs. Rodney told me of what it is that all women do, under the Moon, and how to count the days and tell when to keep rag by me. I understood now what Gertie had been making such a mystery of, saying I'd "know soon enough."

When fine weather came I moved my scribe's office out to temporary premises in the park. Courting couples strolled up and down and nursemaids pushed perambulators while bold brown sparrows darted after crumbs. One morning as I sat there on my bench in the sun, trying to teach Betty Pride her letters, who should I see come riding up the path on a white horse but the Nightingale of the Spaceways, Miss Evadne Halshaw in person! And Captain Tobias Estranguaro, of course, trotting along beside.

"Good gracious, Toby, it's that girl!" Miss Halshaw cried, quite loud enough for me to hear. I am sure she is accustomed to being loud, and no one in her life has ever told her to be quiet. She was dressed quite outworldishly again, in thick felted bags and a loose, full blouse of Madras cotton. She wore neither cap nor bonnet, and her hair was bleached and curled up in a tall dome on top of her head, and there were rings in her ears like a gypsy.

Captain Estranguaro was wearing a boxing trainer's suit, cut down to size, with cowrie shells sewn down the left arm. He carried carrots for the horse. He made a leg, insofar as they can, and a bow. Betty cowered beside me.

"Good morning, Miss Farthing," Captain Estranguaro called in his rich, reedy voice. "Such a pleasure to see you again, isn't it?"

Miss Halshaw drew rein and looked down at me in triumph. "She was in the cards, Toby, you remember! Jack of Spades, a dark young man or woman. But Sophie, my dear, what are you doing on Earth? Have you run away from that dreadful father of yours?"

I told her I had, and the handsome radiance of her approval shone round about me. I stood up, remembering my manners, and introduced her to Betty and Betty to her. Miss Halshaw held down her hand. She was wearing gloves of bleached kid, white as snow, and Betty took the hand doubtfully, by the fingertips. "Miss Farthing and I met on the way to Adonis," Miss Halshaw explained. "Since then we have been to Menelaus, where all the trees are blue, extraordinary, and what was the other place, Toby? Toby?"

Captain Estranguaro came forward. He was sweating hard, you could smell him above the horse. "What place, my lady?" he said, though all the time he was looking at Betty. I sat down next to her quickly.

"Where the stage manager wouldn't let you in and I had to speak to him?"

"New Sebastopol," said the captain, and Betty muffled a scream as he hopped up onto the arm of the bench beside us. "Blake's Chain," he said. He perched there on his dusty hooves, stinking, preening his mustache at us.

They had been everywhere, every apple on the tree of civilization, said Miss Halshaw. Now they were home, thank goodness: "I shall be performing at Stackpole's Theater, in Waterloo, I expect you know it," she said. "Work, work, work. Never mind. Cassandra's pleased to see me, aren't you, Cass?" she said, and patted the neck of her mount.

The horse leaned its enormous nose at us and snorted loudly. Poor Betty didn't know which way to move, a horse one side, a faun the other. I closed my book, while the captain gave Cassandra a carrot. We would get no more work done today, I could see that, though meeting Miss Halshaw and Captain Estranguaro was surely much more educational than any poor teaching of mine. "I'll get your things now, Miss Halshaw," I said. "I only live over there."

Miss Halshaw frowned. "Things, Sophie? What things?"

"Your coat and your helmet," I reminded her, getting to my feet. At once Betty picked up her piece of paper and clutched it to her, getting up too. If I was going, so was she.

Miss Halshaw flapped her hand at me. "Oh that terrible coat," she said, "you can keep that."

I sat down, then got up again. "I'll fetch the helmet, though," I said. "It won't take a minute, truly." I was eager to get rid of it, now I'd decided I was never going home, never leaving Earth again.

"For heavens' sake sit still, child," said Miss Halshaw. "You make a soul quite giddy. Toby. Toby, your handkerchief. You're dribbling, you disgusting thing."

I asked Miss Halshaw what it was like, on Adonis. "Oh, I don't know," she said. "They're all the same, aren't they, those little places. When a ship is due from London the word soon gets around. They buy all the sheet music before one even sets foot ashore, practically. And of course they can't wait to hear the latest gossip, I have to remember every little thing or everyone complains so." She smiled proudly. "Then there is a dinner at the Town Hall, with all the local bigwigs, and their wives all quiz me about the new modes as if I were a *couturier*." She gave a little, very deep laugh. "I make it up, half the time, don't I, Tobias?"

I knew no figure of fashion could ever be more splendid than this airy Amazon, Miss Evadne Halshaw, magnificent in cream and gold astride her white horse. "Why don't you come to the theater?" she said. "Come to the matinée on Friday; bring the helmet; bring your friend. Toby, leave Miss Farthing's friend alone."

In his Register Mr. Strake compares the fauns of Nippur and Caraway. The fauns of Nippur he calls the proper, or woodland faun. They browse in herds, showing a particular fondness for honeycombs and ivy. They are shy as the fauns of ancient Greece and barely sentient, though the Franciscans have tamed them and taught them to kneel, and sing hymns, and weep when a crucifix is shown.

The fauns of Caraway, the "false" fauns, are in fact far more numerous. They are fauns of the plain, who live in leather tepees and hunt on foot, in packs. With their bare hands they pull down the yellow buffalo. Not so meek as their distant cousins on Nippur, they adapt well to what Mr. Strake calls "the lower reaches and outskirts of civilization: *viz.* the circus; the gambling den; the cattle range." Captain Estranguaro, I imagine, comes from Caraway.

Hopping down from the arm of the bench where he had been running the fingers of both hands back and forth across his broad chest while slowly advancing his face nearer and ever nearer to Betty Pride's neck, Captain Estranguaro bowed deeply. From some unseen pocket he produced two tickets to Stackpole's Theater, and gave them to us with an elegant flourish.

The Rodneys were impressed with our complimentary tickets. Gertie was jealous; she tried to make Betty give her hers. Then she realized there would not be tightrope walkers or fire-eaters or ladies on horseback. "Who wants to go and hear some old hag screeching?" she said.

Betty and I didn't care. We showed everyone the posters plastered up on the walls alongside FYNNINGTON'S MOST DELICIOUS & CELEBRATED BLANCMANGE and SOLV-ALL *Lightning Lubricator*. "Stackpole's Theater, that says," Betty told them. "That's where we're going, Sophie and me." I got out Miss Halshaw's helmet from under the bed and dusted and polished it. Then I sat with it a little while on my lap, and where my thoughts were then I know not and could not tell you.

Friday came, and Betty and I went to the matinée at Stackpole's Theater. It was warm inside; the air was thick with cigar smoke and the seats were covered with itchy stuff. A gentleman in gray played the piano while Miss Halshaw sang "Come into the Garden, Maud" and "Britannia, Pearl of Terra" and a great many songs from the Italian opera, and Betty and I pinched each other to stay awake. Afterward we clapped for a long time, then a boy came and led us into the strange world of Backstage, where the air smells of canvas, carpentry and liniment, and people carry strange furniture around.

In her dressing room Miss Halshaw reclined on a faded couch in her enormous pink dressing gown with the quilting leaking out of it. There was the scorched brown screen from the *Halcyon Dorothy*, with the satin dress Miss Halshaw had worn on stage draped over it. Captain Estranguaro was drinking brandy and adding up figures in a long black book. Miss Halshaw was eating an orange, tearing it apart with her fingers, making a right mess of it. "Come in, girls!" she said, and asked whether we liked the show. We both said yes, very much, and she preened, calling us "dears," and insisted on feeding us bits of orange.

Even her apologies were remarkably grand. "The matinée audience is never as distinguished as the evening," she said, while she directed me to put the space helmet in a handy hatbox. "Commodore Mears of the Pilots' Guild was here on Tuesday, you know, with all his daughters."

Now you are aware, for I have told you, that I had decided to let well alone. Poor Mama was sleeping peacefully, I had learnt to say, under the grass. Of course mention of the Guild still made me curious, and I wanted to know— but Want must be my Master, as Mrs. Rodney was always saying. The Lord Pilot's man was a frightful gentleman; a gentleman with men about him armed with pistols and horse-whips, who could flick me away like a gnat. I had made a new life here. Let Mama sleep on, forever buried in his breast.

Still there could be no harm in asking.

"Do you know Mr. Cox, Miss Halshaw?" I said.

"Is he the one with that hideous chin?" said Miss Halshaw, lifting her own. "I should not like him to kiss me, and I don't care who knows it." Captain Estranguaro chuckled throatily, and Betty squeaked.

"Could you please give him a letter," I said, "and not tell him who it's from?" I had remembered an old plan, you see, to write to Mr. Cox without signing my name, but to seal it with his own ring.

"Goodness gracious, Sophie," she said. "I don't *know* the gentleman. We've never been introduced."

I said: "But you're famous!" which made Betty murmur in horror, "Sophie!" and tug my sleeve.

The Polyhymnia of the Planets looked at me down her grand, great nose. "You must commit your letter to the Royal Mail," she said, "if you can afford the stamp. What do you want of Mr. Cox in any case?"

She had plainly forgotten our conversation on the *Halcyon Dorothy*. I suppose she met a great many people and had a thousand things upon her mind. I said: "He knows who killed my mama."

There was an odd sort of pause, then, while they all sat very still and stared at me. "Well," Miss Halshaw said, recovering first, "if he does, he'll hardly tell you, my dear, will he?" She looked vaguely at her faithful companion for confirmation. "No, Sophie: you must go more secretly to work." I thought of the cottage on High Haven, where I had sometimes been very secret indeed, trying not to let Papa know I was reading a book when I should have been washing his clothes.

"She must be quick, isn't it?" said Captain Estranguaro. He picked up the *Times* and began leafing through it with great energy, rattling the pages. He showed me a small paragraph, a list of sailings. It said the *Unco Stratagem* was to depart the next day, back to Io.

The world seemed to shift around beneath me, like St. Radigund's when a big ship used to nudge the wharf and set the crocks swinging, bashing into one another on their hooks. I said: "I must get on that ship."

Betty Pride screwed up her nose. "You're a girl," she said.

I was about to say, So was Ginny Wigram a girl once, though she was born on board ship, and her family were all sailors and always had been. But Miss Halshaw spoke first. "That's easily taken care of," she said, jovially. "Come here, Sophie, come," and she snapped her fingers. I got up and went to her, and she turned me about and took hold of my hair and held it back behind my neck. "You see?" she said, triumph in her voice.

I did not; nor, I could tell, did Betty. But things started to happen very quickly then. "Toby, you'd better leave us," Miss Halshaw commanded. "Go over to the chophouse, why don't you, and see what they've got on. Sophie Farthing's fairy godmother is about to cast her magic spell."

Captain Estranguaro rubbed his hands and bustled out, chuckling wheezily. We could hear his hooves rapping loudly down the hall. Betty and I simply stared at each other.

Miss Halshaw was looking at both of us, looking rapidly from one to the other, at first expectantly and then excitedly. "Well," she said, with some impatience, "have you never been to the pantomime?"

I shook my head. I did not know what a pantomime was. Betty had never seen one either. Miss Halshaw sighed. "What do parents think of these days?" She told me to go and stand in front of the dressing mirror, to put my hair back behind my ears, and tuck my skirt between my knees. "You see?" she cried. "You see?" And with that she swept out of the room, only to come back moments later, saying, "There's no time to waste!" There was a gray-haired lady with her. This, Miss Halshaw said, was Mrs. Curwen, the wardrobe mistress. She was carrying a small sailor suit on a hanger. It had rings at the neck and cuffs, and straps at the knees for a bellows. Mrs. Curwen held it up against my front. It looked as if it would fit me.

Miss Halshaw took the suit from her and hung it on the screen beside her own dress. Mrs. Curwen objected. "I couldn't let her have it, ma'am," she murmured to Miss Halshaw. "Not without permission from Mr. Stackpole."

"Mrs. Curwen," said Miss Halshaw grandly. "Leave Mr. Stackpole to me." Then she put her hand behind my neck and lifted up my lank black hair. "The shears, Mrs. Curwen."

"Sophie, no!" said Betty Pride, but I ignored her. I stood on a sheet of Captain Estranguaro's newspaper in front of the hearth and let the wardrobe mistress cut my hair short all over, just as Papa used to do.

Meanwhile Miss Halshaw was pacing up and down, saying, "Let's see now, you have traveled, but not worked a ship—you are an orphan, from Earth, you must not know High Haven, you see, you must never even mention it." She took down the suit again and fiddled with the trim. She said: "If you're a foreigner, of course, then you wouldn't have to speak very much at all. But perhaps he wouldn't hire a foreigner."

"It's all right," I said, blowing falling hair out of my eyes.

Miss Halshaw cruised on, like a lofty schooner in her disintegrating dressing gown. "And your name is—"

"Don't tell me," I said. "I'll make my own name up."

Betty Pride clenched her fists and squeezed her knuckles into her mouth. Her eyes above her hands were very bright.

Evadne Halshaw's own eyes bulged in their sockets. "Darling," she said to me, her hand on my shoulder, "you mustn't improvise, you're far too inexperienced." She pressed her other hand to her bosom. "You can't just make things up as you go along!"

Suddenly the whole room seemed to go red, like the room in my dream. The room was red, with a dark spot right in front of my eyes, where I could see nothing at all. I heard myself. I was shouting.

"Don't tell me what to do!" I shouted. "You're all the same, Papa and Mr. and Mrs. Rodney and Mr. Cox too! Even Kappi tells me what to do! I shall call myself what I like and say what I like, and tell Mr. Cox what I please," I told them, and I started taking my clothes off as I spoke. I could see them again now, the two old women and the little girl. They were staring at me as if I had two heads. I cared not a feather for them, or their stares. My head was hot and I felt enormously strong. "Did you not know," I said, extremely loudly, "that my mother let me do what I please, and go where I will, too, to the devil for all she cares, for she cast me out like Baby Bulrush. Not that I care," I told them fiercely. "Why should I care for that? She was a whore and had no time to look after a little child. She was busy going to the Moon with fine gentlemen. Let her keep her Moon; I have a boat to catch," I told them straight, like any traveler meeting with local hindrance; and I thrust my hands out to take the suit.

Betty gave a little chirp of excitement. Miss Halshaw looked at me, her eyebrows raised, between amazement and amusement. Then she started to applaud, and Betty too, and then the wardrobe mistress joined in, and shouted "Bravo, miss!" while Miss Halshaw clapped me on the shoulder and put her head on one side like a parrot. "Steady, old girl," she said. Then she sat back and called out directions and encouragement while Mrs. Curwen helped me on with the suit.

When I was dressed in it Miss Halshaw clasped her hands and inspected me. She looked at me with one eye, then with the other. "It needs a cap, darling," she said. "Is there a cap, Curwen? Oh, well. Get yourself a cap, Sophie."

"Yes, Sophie," Betty echoed, in her hushed little voice. "A cap would help."

I thought it had grown very cold in the room suddenly, and felt a shiver run through me.

Miss Halshaw snapped her fingers and pointed to the hatbox. "There," she said. "There." Betty jumped up and got the helmet. She held it out to me, but Miss Halshaw took it from her and put it back over my head.

She said something then, I saw her lips move, but I couldn't hear, so I lifted the helmet. What she was saying, proudly, was: "Break a leg, darling." That was worrying. But I put the helmet on again and stood in front of the mirror. I was the complete sailor.

When they saw my haircut, Gertie jeered and Johnny laughed, and so did their father. I told them I had had it cut because I was going home. Mrs. Rodney cried out and said no, but Mr. Rodney said, Let her go. I knew I was eating more than I earned. The prospect of a new lodger and a proper rent made Mrs. Rodney pause and think again. She asked me when. "At the end of the week," I said. Then there was a clamor indeed.

I felt very calm. I sat there like a hedgehog and ate my tea. I did not tell them anything else. I did not want them to know how soon I really was going. No sooner had I found safe anchorage than I was cutting myself adrift again. I wanted to slip silently away without questions and difficulties, without good-byes.

I do not like to say good-bye. Sometimes now, when the flux is out and the vessel will not run, my head starts to ache again, the way it used to when I was a girl; and I feel as if my head were the heavens, torn by a mariner's hook. I imagine tracing the long wake of all my journeys from world to world, arc upon arc across black space like a chain of invisible rainbows. Then it is that my life seems to have been all good-byes: all going away and leaving, and never an arrival.

Next morning I rose by candlelight to put on my jacket and trews, and tied a faded kerchief around my neck. Gertie lay and watched me. She said: "I'm going to call Papa."

I was eager and impatient to be gone. I said, "Don't, Gertie."
She lay there solemn as a judge. She said, "I'm going to
call." She opened her mouth wide, but she only pretended to
shout. "I'm going to tell them you're going. I'll tell them
you're going dressed up as a boy," she said.

I leaned over her bed and crossed my eyes, which I knew
she hated. "You can tell them I went off dressed up as a donkey, if you like, Gertie Rodney, just don't tell them till I'm
gone."

Gertie stuffed her arm in her mouth and started to giggle.
After a moment, that started me off. We sizzled like bacon and
thumped each other on the arm. Then we went very quiet and
I sat and stared down at her. I said, "You can have the whole
bed now."

"Only till someone else comes," she said.

After that we seemed to have nothing more to say to each
other. Gertie actually turned over and closed her eyes. I took
up my old sugar sack, but there was nothing I wanted to put
in it. I did not know what a sailor boy should have, and I
could not take any of the things the Rodneys had given me.
I took the helmet and that was all.

I knew Gertie hadn't gone back to sleep, but I knew she
wanted me to pretend she had, and I wanted to pretend she
had too, so I crept out of the room on tiptoe, and downstairs
to the front door. When I opened it the cold day swept in
around me. The dark street stank of the river, of black clay
and mud. The air blew damp on my cheeks and in my lungs.
Where I was going, there was no air to blow. I closed the
door behind me and started walking. At once I stopped and
turned. "Good-bye, Mr. Rodney!" I called. "Good-bye, Mrs.
Rodney! I'll write when I get to—" To where? Where would
I get to? I broke off, dismayed, with nothing to say.

I turned back to the street, and walked on my way. My
stomach was hollow, but I could have eaten nothing more in
that house. I felt ashamed of scurrying away with a lie, and
under false colors too. Whenever I passed anyone I knew all
my dissembling must be transparent, obvious as a mummer at
Halloween.

By the time I got to the balloon station a kind of day had
dawned, very weak and somber. All around the cabs sat with
their lamps still burning, waiting for custom from the early

landings. Carters and draymen waited for cargoes arriving, for the warehouses in Holloway and Kentish Town. Porters and watchmen hung around the shelters, smoking and drinking tea. A dull fog clung everywhere between the gas lamps, and all the faces were like shadows, like half-lit masks. I was glad of it.

In the departure hall there were letter racks stuffed with uncollected post, a tea trolley with a steaming urn, and a whole forest of spindly palms leaning out of jars. Bleary travelers sat on couches, guarding mounds of luggage. One was an elderly Lizard with a cough. He was wearing a coat with an Astrakhan collar, and a very complicated respirator. He kept coughing, then looking at his watch. I wondered if he was timing the progress of his disease.

I went up to the ticket window and said to the man, "How much is it to the high platform, please?"

He said, "Which one, son?"

Son! He called me son! I felt like laughing out loud. "The one where the *Unco Stratagem* is," I said.

"Platform seven," he said. "Return?"

"One way," I said, and I gave him the right money. I had enough left for a cup of tea and a sausage in a bun. And when I had finished that, the bell rang and we all moved forward to the gates.

By the time I got on board the car was almost full. A foreign gentleman, very wide, was having trouble squeezing himself and his lady into a whole row of seats. Two elderly humans were protesting at the smell and demanding pomanders. Across the car sat a turbaned Arab with three black slaves, their bodies oiled and shining. Through the window, with field glasses, he watched the ground suspiciously, as if waiting for it to betray him, cursing in a low monotonous mutter all the while. I sat beside an old gentleman in an overcoat, who nodded good morning to me. "Good morning, sir," I said gruffly, touching my forehead, and I slipped a Nitrox pastille into my mouth. My heart was beating like a drum.

We lifted off, Hampstead shrinking beneath us, pulling the clouds over her head. The kites were up, flying their limit, but in a moment we could see water, and the gentleman beside me said it was the English Channel. You could see Mr. Brunel's bridge for a long time, winking in the sun like a necklace, or more like the spine of an enormous fish.

The bubble of our balloon went bobbing up out of daylight, out of the atmosphere, and soared on into the aether. I remember looking upward and seeing the air boiling off in swimming silver shards, like wriggling schools of whitebait in the indigo dark.

When we came to the platform I watched the dockers hooking us on, how they moved and how they swam, and tried to understand everything they did, and the order of everything. I wondered if there would be a book on board, that would tell me how it all went. Then I put my helmet on and buttoned my coat, and I remember thinking, *This coat used to be too long for me.*

I had already spotted the *Unco Stratagem* with her coat of yellow varnish and her stained-glass window. Her figurehead was the bust of a unicorn, freshly painted in white and gold; her masts had been sanded down and the carved tips of the spritsail booms painted and waxed. There seemed as much rigging on her as a star galleon, and all of it tarred and taut as woodwork. There were men on the platform by her, sliding boxes through the void, and one leaning at an angle on a bollard sucking a cold tobacco pipe. The bos'n, that had to be. I strode lightly from the balloon and went straight up and saluted him. I put my helmet to his and said: "Does his worship need a cabin boy, sir?"

The man spoke around his pipe. "No," he said.

I said: "I can keep all neat, sir. And do everything as a gentleman requires. I am quick, sir."

"Then be quick off home," he growled, and broke our contact, waving me away with the back of his hand and baring his teeth on the pipestem. They were long and straight, his teeth, and the color of shoe leather.

I knew not what to do or say. I looked around. There was a shelter, where a man in a gabardine was bending over with his back to me, and some crewmen were talking to a man in a greasy black coat. I knocked on the door, but none of them heard me. I turned and wallowed back to the bos'n, and ducking him an awkward weightless bow I said: "Beg pardon, sir, but I must see the master, please, sir."

The bos'n grimaced and opened the door, gripping my shoulder painfully and pushing me inside. There was an air pump in there, hissing loudly. The bos'n opened his helmet and raised his voice. "Mr. Cox, sir? Young gentleman to see you."

The man in the gabardine stood up and turned around. I saw the jaw. The wig. The eyes.

"Wants to know do you need a cabin boy," said the bos'n coldly.

Mr. Cox glanced at me. I saluted him, and held my breath. He said: "What's your name, lad?"

"Ben, sir," I said. "Ben Rodney."

He looked steadily at me. To the bos'n he said: "What can he do, Mr. Gilbert?"

"Sing his own praises, sir."

"Can ye do that, Ben?" said Mr. Cox. I had forgotten how soft his voice was, and how fair.

I saluted again. "Yes sir!" I said.

"That's an idle thing to do, isn't it," he said, turning from me, not waiting for an answer. "Ye'll not be idle again, Ben Rodney. Get aboard now."

I stood and stared at the back of his gabardine coat. I looked at the bos'n; I looked at the magnificent yacht. "Yes, sir! Thank you, sir!" I cried. My heart was beating fit to burst; I was altogether jubilant. They were bound for Jupiter: I would be near Mr. Cox for weeks to come. I would find out everything there was to know. Congratulating myself on the shrewdness of my plan, I flung myself aboard the *Unco Stratagem*.

11

Into the Asteroid Sea

Mr. Cox's cabin was the best aboard, naturally. It was right aft, and the whole width of the *Unco Stratagem*. He had bookshelves all around the top of the walls, a table and a desk with hundreds of drawers, and three brown leather chairs with brass-buckled belts. He had a proper bed; he even had a settee, carpentered to fit in between the counterstays. There was the theater, that stood on a table of its own behind the door; a telescope, and a wig stand; a carved bust of Mercator that belonged to the guild, and oh, a dozen paintings. One was a picture of two dead pheasants, I remember, and another one a fanciful German picture of the mountains of Io, with capricorns grazing. All these wonderful things were mine to dust.

The largest painting was of something called a seraglio. There were five women, human, I think, and one shaggy black man all lounging around a cistern in a walled courtyard. One of the women had on a flimsy dress of white and red and gold. She had a hat of brass on her head and she was resting one hand on a spindly hookah. Another woman was wearing only a skirt and sandals. She sat nearest us, on the edge of the cistern, with her back to the artist. "Don't you truly admire that back, young Ben?" Mr. Cox asked me once. "Don't ye wish she could just—turn around?"

When the going was smooth, Mr. Cox might spend the morning hours working at the table. There he would sit, winding a pipe cleaner around the neck of a clothes pin, pulling it tight. Meanwhile I would be at the porthole with my duster. I would wipe the glass, rubbing it very hard, and then I would cling there looking out. How many times I did stare out, during the weeks of that voyage, always hoping to guess our whereabouts. Ahead or astern, there was never anything but emptiness and distant stars. I thought, *There are no whereabouts in space.*

"What do you see, Ben?" Mr. Cox said. He knew at once whenever I stopped work.

The ship hung in the midst of the ocean of everything. Everything seemed very dark and lonely. The Milky Way was blotted and skewed by the thick glass, the white stars all run together, like a spatter of curds on a black velvet tablecloth.

Prudently I started my wiping again at once. "Nothing, sir," I said.

"Nothing?" said Mr. Cox quizzically, as he drew out a length of cotton. "All those suns?" he said. "All those worlds?" He wound the cotton around the neck of the pin and snapped it on the edge of his chin. "All those little—lives," he said.

He looked not at me, but down at his work. "What do you say, now, Ben?" he went on. "Do aliens have souls?" He asked it like a question in philosophy. "Do they have—immortal souls?"

Mr. Cox talked to me often in this way, taking advantage of my presence to air his opinions and exercise his voice. He was rather like Papa in that, except that Papa was always seeking to quarrel. Mr. Cox would not have permitted insubordination in the smallest degree. In any case, I knew he was teasing me with his elevated ideas and fancy expressions.

I kept wiping the porthole. My duster was already filthy, but there was no end to the dirt. Though the men toiled with wax and rag, everything aboard was always dirty, furry with it. Streaks of brown grease would appear suddenly, oozing out of the woodwork.

Mr. Cox made the quiet little clicking noise he always made when he was satisfied with something he'd done. I went and started dusting behind him where he sat at the table, and took a peek. The clothespin in his vise was getting a coat of navy cotton. He was winding it tightly around, from under the pipe cleaner arms down the length of the body.

"They have minds—" Mr. Cox went on, while he worked. "Some of them . . . Aye, I grant you that, Ben," he said, as if it had been my contention. "I grant you that . . . for what it's worth," he said. He reached the fork of the legs and tied the cotton off. "Look at us," he said. "You and me, Ben; all our busy race. Even we have minds," he said, reaching for a floating glue pot. "And we're no more than—apes in breeches . . ."

Mr. Cox's pin had breeches too: he had painted its legs dark blue to make them. He had cut the legs off short, and finished them with little black rims, for boots.

"Maybe one day we shall meet an alien race as far above us as we are above—virgules. Who will toy with us," he proposed lightly, "the way we toy with them." He had put a dab of glue on a disk of bamboo, and now he set it across the feet of his pin. It already had a painted face and cap. Mr. Cox had made another constable.

Whether it be a suitable occupation for a gentleman, this making of puppets, I do not know. I only know the days are long, in space; and he was very good at it. He did it as he did everything, neatly and quietly, and most precisely.

I had given dusting up as a bad job. I said, "My friend Jim Brady had some once."

"Virgules, Ben?" asked Mr. Cox.

"Yes, sir. He kept them in a jam jar, sir."

"What did he give them to eat?"

"Oatmeal, sir, and dandelion leaves. Sir, I've finished," I said, touching my cap.

"Very well, Ben. You may go."

While I inched past the theater to the door, Mr. Cox suddenly swiveled in his chair and fixed me with his shrewd steady brown eyes. "Have you communicated my invitation to the others, Ben?"

"Not yet, sir."

"Be about it, lad. And don't forget the pilot." There was a smile in those eyes. I knew he must be looking forward to the show. "Seven tonight, directly after supper."

Mr. Cox took out his pocket watch, which showed the time at Greenwich and at the house on Io, and having consulted it, he set to winding it up. His hands could never rest, and nor could he. As I left the cabin he was rising out of his chair to go and set his new constable with the others, who were waiting in their stiff line for their entrance. Now, I knew, he would occupy himself with his papers, his records and dispatches, the business of the Pilots' Guild. He would never do that while I was in his presence, nor did he ever speak of it, being the secrets of his craft and its fellowship. I used to wonder what he would say if he knew I had a guild ring on a bootlace in my bosom; or a bosom to keep it in. It was my great good fortune that my bosom was not the sort to stretch the front of a shirt.

You too will wonder, I daresay, how I could be such a spy, and keep from speaking out to him straight about the house in Turkey Passage and the Massacre. How could I bear to hold my tongue, that had always been so free? Free from thought, some have said.

In fact that part was easy, the keeping quiet. I had seen how Mr. Cox dealt with a topsail man who had spoken out of turn; I had fetched salt for the man's wounds with my own hands. Anyhow, I already knew he was guilty. The ring proved it.

All I had to do was bide my time and wait for the moment when Mr. Cox's own tongue would slip free. I knew from the *Police Gazette* that the Truth will always Out: that guilt itself would force a confession from that shuttered mouth. Meanwhile it was as well governed as his ship; locked up tight as his desk.

Below decks, the *Unco Stratagem* is just as fancy as she is above. She is all carved, with faces in the corners, fringes of playing-card shapes and wreaths of leaves. Along the companionway there are odd animal heads on bosses with padded rings in their mouths, ready to give you a swing. Going along, hand over hand, to do Mr. Lismoyle's cabin, I was thinking, I expect, about virgules. Do you know them? They look like little almond kernels, smaller than your little fingernail, and they are beautiful shiny colors, vermilion or blue. They come from Mercury, whole colonies a mile wide and more swarm on the cliffs. Men go down on ropes and scrape them off the rock, then bring them back and sell them to pet shops.

Jim Brady I had invented, to be sure. It was Abigail who had had the virgules, Abigail Cook. She took me up to her room to see them. We sat and watched them crawl around in the jar, making their bright, swirling patterns. They looked like Paisley jam.

Kappi once told me the Ophiq believe the patterns mean something. They think they are messages the virgules are sending to each other, or to us. Telling us their dreams, or the name of their sun. Cries of distress, it could be. Abigail's virgules died. They all do, after a while. Most of them die on the voyage, which is why the harvesters take so many, they say.

Mr. Lismoyle was studying hard as usual, for his exam, his head bent over Rossington's Tables of Tides, Occlusions, and Fluxes. His cabin always smelt of perpetuatum and black Jamaican coffee. Stealthily I took the empty coffee flask from the air beside him, and retrieved some wandering pencils.

"Morning, sir," I said. Mr. Lismoyle grunted.

I made a good cabin boy. I wore the monkey jacket they gave me, and a cap, which I jammed down tight and never took off. I slung my hammock in the water room, nearby the officers' cabins, and had a hook for my things there. Sometimes, when the ship was tacking to contrary, I would wake to find my coat and my helmet bobbing and tumbling slowly across the deck head above me.

I was quite at home in space now, though my head ached sometimes still, when the going got heavy and the flux ran hard and high, and cold fire spat and crackled in the rigging. Then it was that I would shiver, and sigh, and curse my folly at leaving the Rodneys. I wrote letters to them, calling them "Papa" and "Mama," and asking after "brother Johnny." Many were the times on that voyage I wished I'd taken more notice of Johnny, and how he went about. I hadn't ever thought much of little boys in Lambeth, none of the girls did. All boys ever did was kick stones and climb lampposts and call names and get into fights, preferably in the gutter. Johnny's unexpected brother Ben was not that sort of boy, though. He was very dutiful and quiet as a mouse and probably a bit stupid.

True it was, as Miss Halshaw had reminded me, I knew nothing about how to sail a ship; but I surely did know how to fettle for men, and between them the officers worked me hard. Mr. Crane had me up late making bumpers in the mess, then I would be up early ironing the Captain's stockings. Not that I could tell one day from the next, it was all night to me, the whole voyage a single night that went on and on without end while I hurried from cabin to mess and back, fetching water and laundry, dried sausage and rum. I cleaned shoes and retied queues, waxing them until they stood out stiff as a bird's tail. "Boy!" Mr. Crane would shout, and there I would be, ready to brush his periwig.

The *Unco Stratagem* shipped thirty-seven men, four officers, midshipman, and cook. Also, because she was a livery vessel of the guild, a scribe and two halberdiers, who berthed with the men and took their turn on watch. The men were like sailors anywhere, thickset and hard as nails, or lean and nimble. Their faces were brown, tanned thick, their skin crazed by the poisonous light. They had pits in their heads and limbs where cankers had been dug out. Strange accidents happen where things can have bulk without weight. Blocks run backward and sliding spars smash ribs in a blur of silent violence. There was more than one pair of legs buckled by spacer's crab, that makes your bones shrink and bend, and two fingers were missing from Jacky Pace's right hand. That did not stop him, whenever he saw me, trying to teach me how to tie knots.

I made Mr. Lismoyle's bunk and checked everything was
properly lashed down before I left the cabin. I told him:
"Tonight at seven, sir, Mr. Cox says, for the *Highwayman.*"

Mr. Lismoyle cursed and pretended to chuck his Rossington's at my head. "I've got to *work*, you imp." It was all he
ever said. He waved a pen at me as though I had brought him
another problem to solve. "Ask Crane. Ask the pilot."

"I will, sir."

"Have you seen him yet, Ben?"

"No, sir." I straightened the ends of a knot.

He gave me a glance, reminding me to be particularly
respectful with the gentleman, as with a senior officer. "You
mind your p's and q's."

The pilot was from Mars, I had heard Mr. Gilbert mention,
and spoke French. Now that he was on board I knew we must
be entering the Sea of Asteroids. I thought perhaps he might
be on deck, and went to the air-hatch to look around outside.
I put on a helmet and coat and buttoned myself up securely,
trying to remember the proper hand signals to salute a pilot
and give him a message from the master.

The instant I was outside, the semaphore was out of my
brain, and I was dazzled and breathless once again in a naked
prospect of stars. To every side, above, beneath, they loomed,
shining their high cold shine. Robinson Crusoe was amazed
when he lifted up his candle and found himself in a cave of
a hundred thousand jewels. What would he have thought of
outer space?

There was no one on deck but Mungo McGowan, swabbing
in the distance, so I dallied there, gawking. Our weight was
so slight I was able to stand on my toes and spin around and
around like a ballerina, my head flung back on my shoulders.
All around, the sails stretched dimly away, enormous squares
of blackness blanking out the stars. I remembered the women
who worked in the sail sheds of High Haven, sewing and shap-
ing that ingenious cloth that, rigged and tuned, swells to the
aether wind. None of them had ever seen this sight. I gazed
at the vast acres of gauze, trying to see how it bellied, how it
curled and slowly, slowly, flapped: could I not catch a glimpse
of the aether itself, the invisible flood in whose bosom we
sailed? I closed my eyes. I was sure I could feel it tweaking
the legs of my breeches, plucking at my sleeve.

The aether flux blows between the stars. It is a strange mineral magnetism that seems to polarize the very blood of men. It will show itself to this man and this, from father to son, human or foreigner; but never to anyone else. The Guild tests for the talent; provides training and discipline. They name a moon of Saturn and a season and expect you to plot the approach and the declination, and give the tides to the nearest fathom. They do not care what vision a pilot sees when he puts on the diadem of his calling. A twinkling flow of ghostly silver water, I used to imagine, like the dew on cobwebs.

On the orders of the evening watch, Mr. Crane was down for officer on duty, and with Mr. Lismoyle studying, that left an audience of three for Mr. Cox's show: the captain, the pilot, and me. I could see the captain on the bridge, with the mate, so I hurried back in and went to tell him. I had to wait, floating to attention, hoping he would hurry up because it was cold.

It was cold, on that ship—my hands were always cold. It was forbidden to wear deck gloves inboard. Mr. Simmonds was wearing his mittens without fingers that I envied so much. I never learnt to knit, I suppose because Gertie said it was boring. Mr. Gilbert could knit. I asked him once, would he knit me some mittens, and he told me to take myself off, and sharpish.

Captain Thrace would not be cold, I thought. His skin was like bark. He nodded gravely and cleared his throat when I gave him Mr. Cox's message. I knew it embarrassed him, so I took advantage of the moment to ask would he give me a look through his telescope. He would always let me look at passing ships, ever since Earth, when I'd asked to see a frigate called the *Santa Emilia* that was a little white speck off the lee quarter. Really I'd wanted to watch High Haven sinking over Java like a tiny cluttered tea tray. There was a strange-shaped ship now, above the larboard quarter. I thought she looked like something you might find in a Christmas cracker.

"Have you got her, Ben?" the captain asked, helping me aim the glass. "H'rrmph. What do you think she is, then?" She was the flagship of the Japanese emperor, they told me: the *Fragrant Chrysanthemum*.

"Permission to ask a question, sir?" I said, as the captain took the telescope back, and when he said yes I said: "Why are ships always 'she,' sir? And planets too?"

The mate grinned, but kept his eye on the binnacle. I could see he was listening for the answer. The captain was making strangled hawking noises in his throat, but in a while he managed to say: "Ships I can tell you about, Ben. Planets, I can't imagine, I'm sure, h'rmm. You'll have to ask the men, won't he, Mr. Simmonds? But ships, now." He was speaking very slowly and rather seriously. "What it is, you see, is this: ships are flighty, and they're unpredictable, humph, harrumph; and they need a firm hand on the rudder to keep 'em on course."

The mate started chuckling at that, and the captain too. I felt myself starting to blush.

I say I was used to looking after men; but I never grew used to being with them. I knew what men were like, to be sure, from the pub, and my brief service on the *Appleby Bull*, bound for Earth. But then, ah, I was a small girl among men. Now I was a small boy, and lived as one of them: sat at mess crammed in with three dozen big strong men, no closer quarters imaginable. I had to keep unbuckling and springing up to help serve at the captain's table, so I was always seated on the end, crushed against the beam. I remember trying not to stare at the bos'n's chest, where his brass pipe hung almost hidden by wild black hair.

I owned to fourteen years, though I'm sure they took me for younger. I had taught myself to smuggle my monthly rags out when I threw out the leftovers and visit the head only in the dead of first watch. The men thought me a queer fish, I know, but there was no sport in bullying a boy who was so meek, who was never in the way, and who spent so much time with the officers. It would shock me, some of the things they'd say in my hearing, though; and please me too, to think I was fooling them, to think I had something of theirs they didn't know they'd given me.

I stopped on the bridge a while and watched the tiny ship, the *Fragrant Chrysanthemum*, with her sails of folded paper. The captain and Mr. Simmonds were busy again, and I wondered how long they'd let me hang around idling there without dismissing me. But being Ben and very obedient, I did not like to chance it, and dutifully asked after the pilot.

"In his cabin," said Mr. Simmonds, and grinned. "How's your French, Benny boy?"

Beyond the Asteroid Ocean, Jupiter floated in three-quarter-phase, marbled amber and bronze, her majestic face sliced by the slim silver blade of her ring. Our captain looked through the glass into the asteroid shoals, looked at the clock, hemmed, drummed his fingers on the rail. "Let's have him up here, Ben. Ask him if he'd be so kind, h'm, h'rrmm."

The *Unco Stratagem* was lying to on a soft tide and the gravity was poor. My feet were light on the companion ladder as I ventured down to the bottom deck.

Outside the pilot's cabin I stopped, uncertain. The door was closed, and there was not a sound from within. But there was a strange smell in the air, a powerful, violent smell. It made me think of Percy. Did the *monsieur* keep cats? He must have a dozen of them in there. I doubled my fist and rapped on the door. The ship creaked and the lantern swung on its gimbals, sending misshapen shadows swarming up the wall. I knocked again and pressed my ear to the panel. All I could hear was my own heart beating quick and high.

I called: "Sir?"

I heard a man's voice reply, harsh and slow. "*E-entrez . . .*"

Obviously that was not really necessary. What I had to deliver could be done from out here.

"It's only me, sir," I said. "Ben, sir, the cabin boy."

"*E-e-entrez*," came the voice again.

I took a deep breath and opened the door.

The stink came out and swallowed me. It was a smell like cats, as I say, but there were feathers in it too, and dung. There was sweat and boredom, and sand, and a thousand other things I couldn't tell you; I am sure no one could.

He levered himself up on his forearms, claws scrabbling on the bare wood, and fixed me with his yellow eye.

"*Be-e-en,*" he moaned, and gaped at me. "*Mon copaaaain!*"

I took a step back. It was a smile, I knew it was. Still it was not a nice smile for a young girl to see, smiling up at her off the floor like that.

I ducked my head and touched my cap. "Yes, sir!" I said. "Ben Rodney, sir! At your service!"

The Martian put his head back between his wings. There was something crawling on his throat.

"*Suis Beaur'gar' Crii-i,*" he announced. "*A-a-a-ancha-anté!*"

The *Unco Stratagem* is a trim ship and a tight, but what she is not is spacious. Between decks is not much headroom, even Mr. Simmonds had to duck. How Mr. Crii managed I could never see. Mr. Crii is seven feet tall and twice that in span, wingtip to wingtip. He kept his wings folded when he went about; but in the privacy of his cabin he liked to spread.

Civilized as he was, he would have neither lamps nor furniture in his cabin. He could sleep on any perch, in gravity or out. He lay now on his mat like a sphinx, on his shins and forearms, with his wings raised, pressed tight up against the deck head. They seemed to fill the cabin. His chest was mighty and sleek, and his shoulders were enormous. I thought he was the size of a horse, not knowing then how brawny they get in the wild.

Mr. Crii crouched there smiling in his stink. I could see the moss he was chewing, a wet mess turning inside his mouth. He stared at me, hooding his eyes like a hunting bird. I knew he could see right through my clothes.

I hung there upright as a soldier and said: "Mr. Cox's compliments, sir, and you are invited to a performance of *The Hunted Highwayman* in Mr. Cox's cabin at seven o'clock tonight. And the captain asks, will you please come now, sir, to the bridge."

Mr. Crii looked up at me as if he understood not a word and didn't even care. As he arched his back, raising his chest from the floor, his wings scraped roughly across the deck head. He was wearing a white leather kilt, nothing else.

His nostrils flared, and he closed his mouth with a snap. It was not me he was looking at. I knew with those golden eyes he could see right through the universe.

"To the bridge," he repeated. "Be-en."

"Yes, sir!" I said, greatly relieved he had taken my meaning, and I held the door wide. He folded his wings, got up off the floor and came skimming out with barely an inch to spare, making me recoil again as he swept past me and onto the companion ladder. "*Allez,*" he said, tossing his head. "Be-e-ennn!"

"Yes, sir!"

Why was he taking me with him to the bridge? I had no idea. I was terrified of him. He was like no man I had ever seen anywhere; yet not properly a man at all, of course.

"The angels of Mars," it says in *Strake's Register*, "are creatures of pure instinct, innocent of all principles, unacquainted with shame. Though shaped and provided in all like men, yet they live on cliffs, like gulls." And so he puts them firmly under avians. "Strake's Defense!" the wags call in the Aeyrie commons, when they look likely to lose an argument with an angel, or a rubber of whist. "Birdbrain! Birdbrain!" they cry, and perch on the backs of the chairs hooting and whistling until one of them falls off and hits his head on the fire irons.

Mr. Strake wrote his book before the Martian Orient was opened up, when Mars still belonged to the shoveling miners and the Bright Arc with their rosaries. In Lambeth they still thought as he did, though, and in High Haven too. Except Kappi, of course. I remember Kappi got quite worked up about angels once when I asked him. "Mad to take an angel from the sky!" he piped, rippling white with horror and distaste. "Wicked to pluck his wings! To send him down underground!"

The crew knew Mr. Crii of old, and all remained wary of him. Angels, they said, were trouble; though Jacky Pace said he knew a sailor who had an angel for his doxy, and kept her in a cave. The crew would all chortle at that, making eyes and elbowing each other just like little Benny Stropes and his cronies. "Lucky bleeder!" they chorused. Women who lay down with angel men, on the other hand, were despised. I wondered how any woman could. Beauregard Crii did not make my heart beat faster. He threatened to stop it altogether, and that with the slightest look.

And here I first saw him—in his glory, I nearly said, but I should more properly say at his duty, on the bridge of the *Unco Stratagem.*

She was moving slow, sails feathered, floating gingerly through the eternal dark. Mr. Simmonds was at the helm now, and Mr. Lismoyle had replaced the captain.

"'*Sseyez*. Sit 'o-own," said Mr. Crii to me. He made me sit on the deck, while he crouched down in front of me in the same manner as before. He couldn't see where we were going from down there, but that didn't seem to matter.

"Ben," Mr. Lismoyle said. He was holding out the gold circlet for me to fetch.

"*Non*," said Mr. Crii, staring into my face. He looked like a swan guarding something. I was convinced if I did the wrong thing he would fly at me. "Lismo-oyle," he said.

"Sir," said Mr. Lismoyle, who hated deferring to him, let alone having his orders countermanded. He brought the circlet himself, carrying it carefully in both hands, and lowered it onto Mr. Crii's head.

The angel's gaze never left me, but already I could see he was gone from behind his eyes, gone away into the flux where ordinary people could never go. The gold hoop around his brow drew back the curtains of his mind and let him see the aether tide, rolling and boiling away ahead where we could see nothing but flying rocks and blackness.

Mr. Lismoyle stroked his little mustache. "What are you doing here, boy?"

"I don't know, sir," I said. "He told me to come. Mr. Crii, sir."

Mr. Crii took a great breath suddenly. The sinews of his neck stood out like whipcord and he shook his head like a swimmer surfacing from a dive. His eyes were still wide open, still apparently fixed on me.

Mr. Lismoyle hung close by me with his hands behind his back, watching Mr. Crii, waiting for the order. "Steady as she goes, Mr. Simmonds," he said.

"I thought he was going to eat me when I opened the door, sir," I said.

"Snap your head right off with one bite, Ben," agreed Mr. Lismoyle.

We had drifted all the way up to the St. Agnes light and almost over it before Mr. Crii spoke. He growled, "Lee heelm."

"Lee helm," Mr. Lismoyle called, with some relief, and Mr. Simmonds swung the wheel. Through the glass canopy I saw the pale sails sway and catch the light, beginning to fill.

As the ship turned I suddenly shivered, and felt myself break into a sweat, though it was as cold as ever on the bridge. Strange sensations went flitting through me, as if I had fallen asleep for a moment and dipped my head in a fountain of dreams. Was something wrong with our pilot?

"Sir?" I said in alarm. "Mr. Crii, sir?"

"Don't disturb him, Ben!" said Mr. Lismoyle sharply.

Mr. Crii crouched there without speaking as the ship bore away. He would be there for hours. I did not know why he had brought me with him. I had work to do, ropes to splice and brightwork to polish. I eased up off the deck, and when that made no impression on him, slipped quietly away.

At supper the men spoke of an enormous octopus one of them had sighted, drifting silently past in space like a gray balloon. They were all quite ready to believe it. In a minute there was someone else who had seen it; they all had. "Just like a rock it looked," said Mr. Chalk. "Gray, and all over crusty. Till I saw its arms move." The scribe would draw a picture, for the log.

The officers kept their own counsel. When I was pouring the port at the captain's table, Mr. Crane said to me: "Do you never take that cap off, young Ben?"

I said nothing, but squeezed the flagon carefully.

Mr. Crane said, "Not even in church?"

I shook my head. "Never been to church, sir," I said, pitching my voice low as I always did when they were all listening.

Captain Thrace was peeling a Venusian pearly apple. "Our young man here was asking me earlier, h-hr'rm, why all planets are *she*'s."

I was glad of the change of subject. "Venus was a lady, sir," I said, thinking of the pictures Kappi had shown me in Ovid. "But Jupiter and Mars were gentlemen."

Captain Thrace sat back. "Well, anyone?" he said. "Care to enlighten him?"

Mr. Lismoyle cocked an eye at me while I filled his cup, and pursed his lips, but nothing did he say. Mr. Crane was blotting his mouth with his napkin. "Planets are full of mystery, Ben," he announced. "No two are alike. Their mountains are beautiful, and their caverns are deep and secret." *Oho*, said someone.

Mr. Cox was drinking. He put down his cup, and spoke to Mr. Crane. "It's heavenly bodies you're talking of now, is it?" They all chortled then.

I bowed my head, not saying anything more than thank you, sir, and went as soon as I could back to my seat. I was red with bashfulness, and tickled too, by the way their minds went. I knew of the figures Mungo McGowan would whittle out of wood and pass around secretly from hand to hand. No puppets of Mr. Cox's ever provoked such whoops and chuckles. The whole crew's ideas about the female sex were strange, and not very complimentary. There was a difference between women, who were fickle purveyors of merriment and dole, and wives, who were misery through and through, a burden and a scourge to all mankind. I did not mind. Mama and I were safe among their illusions.

Clearing supper took longer than usual, so I was late, and had to run to Mr. Cox's show. From the portholes I saw we were making good speed through the Sisters of Rhea now, and all the yards were full. There among the starboard shrouds was Fillmore, like a peanut a mile long; and further off, that was Calliope, where Sir Marmaduke Carmichael had his estate, his palace built of steel. I thumped on the door of Mr. Cox's cabin and found the others were already there, Captain Thrace on the settee and Mr. Crii on the floor. The theater was pulled out to face the settee, and Mr. Cox was busy behind it. "Sorry, sir," I gasped, out of breath, and sat down beside Captain Thrace.

The theater was very splendid. It was crimson and gold and stood as tall as me. The scenery was painted on real canvas, and rolled up and down on dowels that you turned at the side. The curtains were thin velvet hung top and bottom on tiny chains. "My whigmaleerie," Mr. Cox called it, meaning a trinket or fancy thing. "Douse the light, would you, Ben?" And when I did so a large glass bulb he had inside the back of the theater glowed dim and yellow, like an ember that flickers but never burns out. That device was something of Lord Lychworthy's, Mr. Lismoyle told me; but the theater was Mr. Cox's own.

He worked it all himself, doing all the voices and the noises of the wind, the hunting horns and so on, and rushing all the characters about. He would have had one of the men to play the mouth organ for him, but they despised him and always had other duties. "Let him drill holes in his chin and whistle through 'em," Pete Chalk said when I mentioned it once.

Mr. Cox had several plays besides *The Hunted Highwayman*. Another one was called *Grigori's Revenge* and told an

old story from Russia. But they were all the same. Someone thought their beloved had betrayed them, and there was
a duel. The clothespin puppets swung their darning needle
swords with a will.

Beside me on the settee Captain Thrace sat stony-faced
through the whole thing. He was only there at Mr. Cox's
whim, and plainly thought it a childish pastime. Certainly he
endured the shows without enjoyment, snorting softly now and
then with irritation.

Mr. Crii was absolutely enthralled. He turned round to us,
pointing at the stage. "Little men-n-n!" he hummed, as if it
was the funniest joke. I nodded to him, and watched the play,
and loved it, for I was not yet past a child myself.

But that night our entertainment was interrupted. Craig Trott
came knocking at the door. "Terr'n vessel, sir, flying 'grave
news.' "

Mr. Cox stood still as a statue for once, with the villain in
one hand and the huntsman in the other. "What sort of vessel?" he said.

"For'n frigate, sir."

The theater party broke up and ran to the bridge. Fillmore
had grown very much larger, the men had started taking in
canvas for the turn. Mr. Gilbert was whistling "Captain on
the bridge." We all watched the ship that hung Earthward, her
sails shimmering in the frozen sunlight.

"French, to judge by the yards," said Captain Thrace, looking through his telescope.

"Topgallant royal set," said Mr. Crane, looking through his,
"and sprysails aloft and alow."

"Canvas for a fast run," the captain observed. "Harrumph."

Everyone looked at Mr. Cox.

He had Craig Trott haul out signal flags acknowledging, and
then the message followed. She was the *Jeanne Lehameau*,
French frigate of the line, recalled to Ys. His Excellent Majesty the Emperor of Mars was dead.

I looked around for Mr. Crii and saw he was up the mizzen-
mast, his great wings spread to the night. Then Mr. Crane was
ringing the bell and shouting: "All hands on deck! All hands
on deck!" And Captain Thrace was giving orders. "Spritsails
and moonsails, all square!" he commanded. "I want a fast
make and a fast turnaround!" He sounded very severe.

Mr. Simmonds worked the semaphore to relay the orders to the crew. Prepare to go about, he signaled. Haul her close. Lay mainsails to the mast.

Confused, I hung back. The Emperor of Mars had died and now everyone was rushing around. What had it to do with us? Mr. Crii was the only Martian aboard that I knew of.

Craig Trott came dashing past me to the flag lockers. "Where are we going, Craig?" I asked him.

"To Mars, Ben."

"What for?"

"To pay our last respects."

12

The Devil to pay

Papa had never had anything good to say of Mars. Martians, he said, live in holes in the ground. I remember Kappi going lavender with embarrassment and saying, "To except the great palaces"; and Papa replying that they wouldn't have palaces at all if we, which was to say the human race, had not shown them how to build them. The Martians were cannibals, he said, even the Orientals. "And the desert tribes are completely savage. Let them once catch sight of a human man alone, they chase after him, out across the desert. They can run for a hundred miles without getting tired. And when they catch you, Sophie, they rip your belly open and tear out your liver and lights, while you're still alive to feel it. Oh yes. That's the first part they eat, the liver. Then they string you up over a slow fire and have themselves a party."

Mars looked like a joke—like a ball of orange brick that someone had carved and hung in space to lampoon the poor old Earth. They had even given her two little tumbling moons, to cap the jest. The orders were that we would not put in at any platform, but dodge the moons and set down straight, in the hills of the Red Planet. From out here, she looked not so much red as tawny, and mottled with great powdery clouds of dirty yellow. Mr. Lismoyle said they were dust storms, raging in the desert. He pointed out the canals, faint as thread from a spindle. Then the planet spun sickeningly beneath us as the Coriolis force gripped our vessel and began to suck us down like a matchstick whirling down a plughole. With pennant and ensign flailing we went swooping into the atmosphere.

I took off my helmet and straightened my cap. Now I could hear the men singing at the halyards.

Our captain is a bully man
Hi, boys, hi
He drinks his grog from a watering can
All down the Gulf of Mer-cur-eye!

Mr. Simmonds had two men scrubbing the last of the scale off the decks with salt and four aloft with scrapers cleaning the lines. The guild scribe had already repainted the ship's name in gilt on the transom, and in mourning she had the Union Jack at half-mast and a black crepe bow on the horn of her figurehead. Through the glass I saw Mr. Crii on the bridge, upright, crowned, calling out the last fine vectors.

As the sails came down and we flew lower and lower the signs of civilization appeared, square shapes of buildings clustered in the valleys, more and more canals like a ragged green net stretched around the globe, and ships on the canals like black spots from a pen. We were coming in from the south, across the frigid plains. Ys lies in a deep equatorial valley; she is a maze of rosy sandstone with here and there a trace of dusty green. It looked not like the great majestic muddle of London, but all straight lines, little boxes fretted with narrow lines, lines of tiles as straight as if someone had drawn them with the points of a fork. We passed over the outskirts, the pink brick streets of pointed houses, the cactus trees along the canal, coming lower and lower until the city was all we could see, with the vast obsidian pile towering over it, looking for all the worlds like the hilt of a sword someone had thrust into the breast of the city.

"What's that, sir?" I asked, pointing.

"That's the cathedral, Ben," Mr. Lismoyle said. "The Black Well."

"Is that where they'll bury the King, sir?"

"His Imperial Magnificence, Ben. Yes, there's a hole waiting for him there." Mr. Lismoyle's face was grim. "That's a foul place, Ben, a filthy place."

I stared suspiciously at the tower far below. It was a monstrous thing, too tall, too thin, with no symmetry to its lines. As we passed over it I thought I saw things crawling on it. How would their Emperor sleep under such a horrid roof?

"Just be grateful you won't be there to see, Ben."

At the port many great ships were gathered. There was *H. M. S. Bravo*, that had brought Lord Cymbeline of Callisto— a fan-mast caravel called the *Hippocampe*, that belonged to the Comte de Perles—a galleon called the *Santa Veronica*, full of half the churchmen of Rome—and over there came in dignified and slow the ancient spaceship *Sweet Peg o' Richmond*, sweeping her venerable foresail over the sands of Mars. "Peg! Sweet Peg!" cried the men, and we all gave her three cheers. It was there I saw my first angel flock too. Slowly they circled, high in the air, scattering every time a ship came by.

Mr. Crii paid no attention to the docking but moodily sat and cracked walnuts with his fingers. I had assumed it was in some way for his sake that we were here, but Mr. Lismoyle said he would not be going to the funeral. No one would, except Mr. Cox, who often had to represent the absent Lord of the Pilots on such occasions. Mr. Crii was going home, his duty done.

Mr. Crii perched up on the taffrail and shook out his enormous wings. He flexed them, then beat them vigorously up and down. He was from the east, far beyond these sheltering canyons, and had a long way to go. I tried to duck away from the gritty wind he made with his flapping, but he saw me and called me to him. I was to rub his mighty shoulders and ease the joints. The stink and heat of him enveloped me. It was like trying to groom an eagle the size of a cab horse.

I stepped back from Mr. Crii as the captain came to speak with him and give him his fee. The angel did not turn again or say any farewell to me or any others, but took to the air and rose steeply and swiftly as though in delight at leaving the ship behind. I saw some of the circling flock fly toward him, as if to greet or detain him, but they veered off early and let him go. Then he was a streak of white dwindling in the desert sky. I smiled, glad to have seen him at last in the air, where he belonged. I liked him far better there than face-to-face. When I turned my attention back to the deck everyone looked larger suddenly.

It was winter in those latitudes. The air was sharp: it smelt dry and smoky with a tang in it, like rust. I wore my ancient coat and my cap, and left my helmet on its hook. The mate had said the men would look after me, help me find lodgings. I had had a sudden dizzy thought, that I should change my dress again and disappear into the streets of another city—I should become a Martian, and all my threadbare history fall in rags from me like a fading dream. Then a sudden hand fell on my shoulder. It was Mr. Cox. "You come with us, Ben," he said.

I touched the peak of my cap and followed.

The port offices were besieged with incoming visitors. No one in authority could be found, and junior men were running around shouting at each other. The crowd kept swaying excitably this way and that, starting after every uniform they saw. At the office of the guild things were no better—there was no carriage to be had, others having already arrived and taken them all. The local man could not make himself understood. He kept saluting and saying some bit of French over and over again until Mr. Crane started to curse. He strode to the door and disappeared out into the throng. Soon he could be heard shouting too. All the while someone was peevishly and continually hitting a bell.

Mr. Cox stamped his cane on the tiles. "Fetch a cab, Ben, for goodness' sake," he said, gesturing me outside.

On light feet I ran through stalls of a market. Everything was a great confusion of sand-shoes and smoking meats and clay bowls of stringy vegetables wound into balls. I cried out, seeing Ophiq in a cage. They were not even whistling, but sat there slumped in sick shades of violet and green. I stopped, to try to reach them through the bars; but Mr. Cox was coming, impatiently waving me on.

There were Martians everywhere I looked: strolling along between the stalls, pushing barrows, or standing talking together, flapping their ears and waving their elbows about. I thought they did not look much like the Martian from my ABC, armed with his pick and bucket, the Martian Mines our Gold. They were all different. There were tall ones, short ones, ones in divided skirts with blankets around their shoulders and others in top hats or crinolines. They looked most strange in human garb, as if nothing fit them properly.

You could not have told, I'm sure, that their king had recently died, for all the black stuff on show. No one seemed grieved particularly—indeed, some of them seemed quite excited; but most looked simply careworn, like people everywhere. I thought they looked hard-pressed, as if they were carrying invisible heavy weights; but perhaps that was just as Mr. Strake says, the character of the race.

Mr. Cox said nothing as we climbed at last into the cab. He was cross because he had to hire one, because it was expensive, and because of the nuisance and confusion. He liked everything just so, Mr. Cox. I took the seat facing him, and he noticed my eyes were wet. "Stop your weeping, lad," he told me. "You may save your tears for the funeral." He assumed I was sad about the Emperor; but the Emperor was nothing to me. I was weeping for the Ophiq.

The driver whipped up the lizards and off we went, down the road into the city. The way was crowded, and we were beset by beggars, who rose up out of the dust and pleaded for alms in piteous voices, stretching their thin hands through the windows of the cab until Mr. Cox bade the driver strike about him with his lash and clear the way. We rode freely then, for a while, and I began to look at everything in a daze of wonderment.

I saw palm trees everywhere like great molting brooms, their crowns splitting and shedding all over the street. I saw a hundred-foot wall with the shape of a gigantic beetle made on it in tiles. I saw huge cacti with scaly creatures slithering around in their branches, spreading wings like the wings of giant bats and dropping down to snatch something filthy and dripping from the refuse that lay everywhere banked against the walls of the buildings.

In the city the streets were dark and narrow and choked with traffic. There were French noblemen in *barouches*, and Martian ones in swaying litters, and all among them carts loaded high with huge black toadstools, wet and stinking.

We passed big birds with four legs and long necks, with
Martian women riding on their backs. They were herding a
gaggle of barefoot children, cracking whips over their scab-
by heads. Pedestrians of all species pushed into the roadway,
eating things and staring at everyone riding by.

In a while Mr. Cox seemed to recover his good humor.
"You see them, Ben?" he asked me, pointing with his finger.
I thought he was pointing at a lizard tethered there, that was
nosing a dead rat among the offal. Then I noticed the men:
lean, dark red men, tall as Mr. Crii, with dust all over their
faces and their hair caked up in spikes. Back-to-back they
stood, staring at nothing in particular. They were all chewing. As we passed I got a glimpse of the women, who were
all sitting on the ground around their feet, facing outwards,
with their knees up. "D'ye know who they are?"

"No, sir."

"That's the K'mecki," Mr. Cox said. "The wild Martians,
that roam up and down the canyon lands. Their pilots have led
them here," he said, facetiously, taking out his handkerchief.
"When they arrived on the streets of Ys with their mystical
maps and their moss-doctors, then the High Kingdom knew
their Master was doomed."

Spreading his kerchief on his knee, Mr. Cox took some
snuff. That was only more dead leaves, I thought, no different from the moss the Martians chewed. But I held my peace
and watched him snort and snuffle, and thought to take another lozenge for myself.

In the distance, the funeral procession was trailing slowly
by. There were children singing, concubines wailing, beasts
and captives in cages carried on poles, slaves bearing flares
that smoked and sputtered in the gloomy streets. At upper
windows women stood wailing, while the men blew their
mournful horns. "K'mecki are bad luck," Mr. Cox said. "I
don't suppose they'll be allowed at the service. Nor angels
either, I'll be bound."

I looked at myself then, at my shabby clothes, and I wondered why he had claimed me to take to the funeral, as his
only attendant. Obviously he meant to broaden my education;
like Captain Thrace showing me passing ships and telling me
their names. I was not sure I wanted to go. I had no place at
a state occasion. I was no one.

I *was* no one then, you know, Dear Reader, unless it was Ben Rodney. Sophie Farthing was dead and gone. Sophie Farthing had been very lucky to last as long as she had, on her inheritance.

I know I had it in mind I might be Sophrona one day, when I was finally out of Ben's shoes. I thought I might take my mother's name and become Sophrona Clare. A Farthing I would nevermore be; I renounced that inheritance. I had no father—or rather sometimes I thought I had a thousand fathers, I was the daughter of every man who trod the pavements of St. Paul's. How could she ever have known for sure?

Why I should celebrate Mama, who had renounced me, I could not tell. Whatever she knew, I still knew nothing. I had found out nothing from listening to Mr. Cox, nor had I ever been likely to. All my suspicions had been groundless. Every time I filched his cabin keys and searched his desk with its thousand tiny drawers, nothing did I find but papers covered with numbers, strange runes and symbols, all in code. Not even a lock of her hair.

We had joined the funeral procession, following behind a heaving litter decorated with black plumes. Already the Black Well was towering over us, like a mad, melted black bottle stretching down from the sky. It was more the shape of something that had spilled over and solidified than something built with hands, and it was made of a stone that glistened like wax. The walls were all blistered and carbuncled with carvings, cut up and down and plumbed with strange pipes. There were no windows that I could see. Inside was the deepest well on the planet, Mr. Cox told me. I did not feel much like going in to see it.

"Mr. Lismoyle said it was a cathedral," I said.

Mr. Cox smiled his stiff, chiseled smile. "The Martians," he said, "have their own ideas about God."

I remembered God. Mrs. Rose had talked about Him. I have to say I found it all rather odd. The more questions I had asked her, the less I understood. Seeing that horrible spire with all the giant crow-things wriggling around on it, I was sure she had made a mistake.

Nevertheless, I had to grant them this, those people who prayed to a God of Love: someone or something there was, that was protecting me. I had put myself time and again

into the way of harm. Many were the reasons for which I
should have died long before, or been thrown into a dungeon. Yet people had taken care of me—Mrs. Rose herself;
Papa; Miss Halshaw and Captain Estranguaro; Mr. and Mrs.
Rodney. Even a high powerful gentleman like Mr. Cox felt
moved to take me under his wing, without even knowing who
I was. That, I suppose, is what folk mean by Providence; folk
like Mrs. Rose, and the starmen.

The Knights Brethren of the Starways believe (so far as anyone can understand) that the flux itself is alive; that it is the
blood of some divine being. *Their* God is vast and thin, and
stretches throughout Creation. They have a creed like alche-
my, full of symbols turning into each other. The Great Bull
steers the Ship toward the World. On the Ship grows a Tree.
On the World sits the Eagle Crowned in Gold. They gather
in the cloisters, talking of cups and wands.

Fudge to all that! Give us something you can steer by—so
say the rank and file. They have no head for philosophy, the
men who prop up the bar at the Aeyrie, and no stomach for
the Sacred Quest for the Edge, where the stars run out. In
the six directions pilots, fine pilots, go out, more of them
every year, bound to seek the Edge or die trying. None has
ever been heard of again. I say it is a stupid shame, but who
am I? In my life, I too have done some things that were less
than wise.

"Stay close to me now, Ben," Mr. Cox bade me as he
climbed the steps, touching his hat and nodding to various
gentlemen who greeted him. The crowd was as thick as ever.
Everyone had come to see the foreign dignitaries. There was
Cardinal D'Aubray, getting out of a closed litter, and a white-
whiskered *maréchal* escorting an old Martian lady. There were
the strangest people I had ever seen: ambassadors from the
League of All Worlds, all shapes, and all in the most elabo-
rate mourning. A black-draped tank of methane-breathers was
being steered along the hallway, blocking the passage with its
size and slowness. The black stone was clammy beneath our
feet. There were huge urns of spiky rushes everywhere, and
from Earth and from Venus, those huge garish flowers that
the Martians love.

Tall, half-naked ushers with long hooked poles watched
over us all as we shuffled along. Mr. Cox tried to command

some attention, brandishing his own stick; but they took not a scrap of notice. Suddenly the crowd in front of us was clearing, and I could see between the parting people that we had come into the vast Chamber of the Well itself—that we were high up in it, high among seats that ran in rings all the way around the chamber and went down and down and down in tiers beneath us. Startled, I looked down over ten thousand heads, right into the mouth of the Well.

It makes you catch your breath, to look down and see such a sight beneath you. After you've looked at it, it's hard to look away.

It was like clinging to the inside wall of a volcano full of ink, and black as space. Around the rim of the lustrous black lake beneath pillars of yellow gas flamed up, dancing above their dim reflections, lighting the distant faces on the far side of the chamber like a bank of pebbles on a night of fog. The seats were so low, the slope so steep, that even on that light world I felt my knees buckle and looked for something to hold on to.

Mr. Cox took my arm and steered me firmly into an unmarked row, next to some human gentlemen with splendid beards and starched white collars. First they looked up at Mr. Cox, and at his jaw, and then their eyes slid across me and away, without even a "good-day."

Mr. Cox took off his tricorn and sat with it in his lap.

"Take your cap off, Ben," he said.

"In a minute, sir."

Far beneath us a rock platform hung out over the water like a broad stone tongue. There were more braziers there, glowing with fire, and a big statue of some kind set up at the back, a huge unidentifiable shape. It seemed to be something that was wrapped around or coiled up in itself in some way, but what it was supposed to be, it was too dark to see.

Mr. Cox seemed to be able to see something, nevertheless. I was aware of him on the bench beside me, catching his breath suddenly and becoming very still. I looked around and saw that he was looking not into the dark and smoky pit, but up into the tiers behind and above us—looking fixedly as if he had caught sight of someone or something unexpected.

"Can you see the Prince, sir?" I asked. One of the gentlemen who had spoken on the stairs had said the Prince of Wales was there, to lay a wreath on behalf of Queen Jessica.

Mr. Cox did not reply.

I stared at the platform again, waiting for my eyes to adjust to the dark. There were tiny figures down there, priests, I supposed, in enormous padded robes that made them look like bags of balloons—acolytes stoking the braziers—guards with long goads of black iron standing in front of the idol, as if they were guarding it from something.

"It looks just like Whigmaleerie Theater, sir," I whispered.

"Whist now, laddie."

I said no more, though I had been about to point out that he had been wrong: there were plenty of angels there after all. They were lying on the platform, near the edge. I thought they were naked. I thought they were angels because of their shoulders, and the ragged red places on their backs where their wings had been chopped off. It was hard to make out because there were so many of them, all lying in a heap. They lay without moving, as if they were asleep.

And this was the funeral service of the Emperor of Mars.

There was a lot of soft chanting and sighing first of all. Women played on pipes. That went on for a long time. Farther down the tiers the Martians were all continually swaying backward and forward, and from side to side, rocking just as humans do in grief. No one in the seats where we were rocked. People shifted in their seats and muttered to one another, and tried to smother coughs. Far below, the acolytes were heaping forkfuls of moss on the braziers. The smoke came creeping up to us, washing over all the heads like a river over pebbles— now I could smell it, bitter and confusing. It made my head feel like a lump of lard, heavy and thick and soft. I rubbed my eyes and wriggled on the hard seat.

Next, from everywhere around, a great groan went up. The priests had formed two lines, facing one another, and now the heart of the funeral procession began filing between them. The acolytes threw salts on the fires, making them blaze up, so that all could see. In came slaves hauling ropes; officials swinging flails; concubines in chains, howling; and under a tilting canopy the Emperor, stiff and preoccupied on his bier. I thought of my mama as they had drawn her in the newspaper, lying

on her bed of death, and I felt sweat break out in my palms.
Behind the Emperor came his son, Prince Henri, in a plain
white shift torn ragged at the knees; and when the crowd saw
him the lamentation redoubled.

The high priest stepped forward then and shouted, and
his voice came wavering and floating up the funnel of the
Well like the cry of a stricken bird. Then the prince replied,
in a strong voice like a man that sells beefs at the market, but rich and moist with grief. Then the priest yodeled
again, and all the attendants shook their flails. Now the prince
laid his hands on the canopy and drew it from the bier,
exposing his poor father to all eyes, and the wailing from
the Martian ranks grew louder and louder until it seemed to
swell up and batter my face like a living thing. The slaves
took up the poles of the bier again, and pulling and lifting
they hoisted it up on top of the heap of angels, clambering
on the bodies to guide the cumbersome thing into place. Then
they stepped down, from shoulder to leg, making much ceremony of leave-taking, and filed off the platform to either
side.

The angels lay at the tip of the stone tongue, and the idol
squatted at its root. It was still impossible to make out anything about it as it lay on the shelf of its shadowy shrine,
a heap of carven coils like some tangle of fat gray rope.
Between the idol and the sacrifice stood nothing but the high
priest, between two lines of braziers thickly smoking. The rest
of the attendants stood behind the braziers, lining the sides of
the platform.

Now the high priest faced the altar and lifted his arms and
gave a great harsh cry. At once the acolytes stepped forward
with bowls of water, and quickly and vigorously they doused
the braziers.

Now the wailing turned back into a chant, rhythmic and
urgent. Flails on rock clashed out the rhythm; bells clanked
and gongs dinned. Two by two, the guards with the iron goads
ran up and jabbed the idol with them, shouting mightily as if
it had offended them. And I felt again the presence of Mr.
Cox beside me, his limbs and body rigid with disgust and
loathing.

Then it was that that dark idol, that monstrous huddled
shape, loosened its coils and began to move.

I stood up in my seat and put both hands to my head and screamed at the top of my voice. I felt Mr. Cox pluck at my coat: "Sit down, Ben!"

My scream had been nothing, lost in the uproar of acclaim as the vast thing woke from its vaporous sleep and slithered down from its shelf with a rasping, sucking, resentful hiss. Where its gray flesh caught glints of flame it glistened like wet india rubber. It reared up and rearranged its limbs and flopped back down on its belly again. It writhed toward the high priest.

I bit my knuckles, tasting bile in my mouth and feeling a cold sweat start on my forehead. I knew I must be whimpering, but I could not hear my own voice.

The priest strode to one side, blowing on a mighty horn, and the guards with the goads and the men with the gongs and bells came forward and closed in behind the huge creature, driving it before them. Like the bole of a wet tree, uprooted and threshing—like a great slimy gray glove with too many fingers, it rose up again and fell upon the angels and engulfed them, climbing upon them, pushing them before it. Bodies slipped, limbs flopped. The Emperor began to rock unsteadily on his perch.

The noise went on and on as if it would never stop. The creature plowed on, shoving at the heap of angels. The bodies nearest the edge tumbled over, and fell splashing into the water. A high desperate squealing seemed to rise up and be heard amid the hellish music, and for an instant I knew the angels were writhing, screaming, they were alive—and then with a great seesaw the bier tipped, the Emperor slid from his last bed and disappeared into the heaving mass of angel bodies. Outflanked, outnumbered by trumpets, the beast gave a final wallow and pushed the whole heap over—and with a hissing roar and an enormous sickening splash, followed them into the waters of the buried lake, engulfing everyone and everything before it in its hideous arms.

Then from above, around, below, the representatives of all worlds and nations stood and cast their hail of wreaths, spinning down into the water.

And the funeral was done.

Throughout Mr. Cox had sat with his beringed hands resting on the knob of his cane, as if he were made of iron entirely and not just his face. And so, I'm ashamed to say, did Ben Rodney sit, after his feeble attempt to protest, still as his master. He sat and watched, to the bitter end.

People always say such things: to do something *to the bitter end*, or make *heavy weather* of something—someone is *on the wrong tack*; something has *gone by the board*—I never knew what those sayings meant, until I learned they are things sailors say. They say there is *the devil to pay*, and that means to stuff the bottom seam of the boat with tattered rope and pitch. What the devil gains from that, I confess I know not.

Perhaps we had all breathed too much smoke. Certainly I was the only one who had made a fuss. In the darkness I saw many bow their heads and cover their eyes, and I heard some stifled oaths; but gentlemen do not create a disturbance in the church of another species. So I, too, sat like a lifeless thing, and I said to myself, That was He. That was God.

The chanting was going on, but by now everyone in the foreigners' seats had begun to rise. Knots of people muttering and softly exclaiming to one another were starting the slow surge toward the exits.

The water in the well still slopped, lapping heavily against the stage; and still I sat like a stone, and as cold as one too.

"Ben? Ben. Come on wi' ye now."

Mr. Cox's manner was brisk. He seemed almost nervous, as though he thought God might be back up soon for His pudding. He jammed his hat on his head and tossed back his chestnut curls and held up his cane like a mace. "Way there!" I heard him say. "Way for the Guild! Guild business, I say! Stand aside!" And I followed behind, stumbling, my head at a reel.

Mr. Cox forced our way into the crowd beneath the arch, past a gentleman supporting a pale lady who was clutching a handkerchief to her mouth. He was murmuring to her, trying to calm her feelings. "Not a thing," he assured her. "They don't feel a thing. They give them a draught first, you see."

"But the poor prince, you know," said the lady tearfully. "How terrible for him."

"Brutes," someone growled. "No other word for it." But he spoke softly, not to be overheard.

With people in the passage, hurrying past—and people in the aisles, pressing us from behind—we became wedged in the arch, all of us jammed there together. I pulled my head in and shut my eyes. Somebody trod on my toes and I almost screamed then; as if my discomfort counted for anything. I was a stupid thing, and not fit to be abroad. All I could think was, That was He. Papa was right.

Mr. Cox reached back between the heaving bodies and seized the sleeve of my coat. "This way, Ben. Hurry now." How could I hurry? But then the jam broke, and we spilled into the passage and down the steps, all bumping and slipping and apologizing, and fetched up in a corner of the entrance hall. There the crowd started to ease, regrouping, dispersing, and a yellow-faced whiskery gentleman doffed a fine silk hat and ushering forward a stout lady and gentleman, greeted Mr. Cox with great civility: "Cox, my word, I might have known you'd be here somewhere. How are you doing, old man? I believe you know the Apjohns, Mr. and Mrs. Apjohn of Helion Villa?"

Now it may be that Mr. Cox was never the most sociable of men; but he had a public position to maintain, and he could be light and easy of tongue when he chose—and you might have thought he would welcome a moment to get his breath back and restore the shattered veneer of polite society with a little civilized conversation—but instead he astonished me by lowering his head, merely grunting something unintelligible, and rushing on by, dragging me yet by the arm.

"Sir," I complained, "you're hurting me." He took no notice of me, no more than of his startled associates, but pulled me across the hall to a flight of stone steps, which we promptly began to descend at a pace that might have been dangerous on a heavier world. I supposed he knew of some easier way out—indeed I hoped he did, for I was longing for some fresh air. But the steps were followed by more steps, and more. He seemed to be taking us deeper, far from the crowd, into the bowels of the building.

Down, down, past a place like a stable, where fat, sleepy-looking lizards lay in straw behind wooden rails. When they smelled us passing they reared their heads and began to whine. But we did not want them. Down again, deeper into darkness, down where sand had drifted deep in the corners of the stairs. Breathing hard, I could smell the lizards; and then a whiff of the black water, coming nearer. I could feel the rings on Mr. Cox's fingers, digging into my arm.

Far under the ground, below the floor of the valley of Ys, we slowed our pace. Mr. Cox peered into a low, lightless corridor.

"Will we go back to the ship now, sir?" I ventured. "Would you like me to call a cab?"

My voice echoed flatly from the tons of stone above our heads.

Mr. Cox did not answer, but called out aloud, in Martian, a sharp, cracking word.

Somewhere, scurrying footsteps answered. A light appeared along the corridor, growing stronger, a torch being carried from an unseen side passage. Mr. Cox hustled me along to meet it.

The torch was being carried by a Martian man. He wore a quilted robe and gold paint on his ears and forehead. I supposed he was some kind of priest. Mr. Cox hailed him at once, speaking Martian to him fluently, lifting my hand high.

The Martian curled his ears and spoke, a single, croaking syllable. He lifted his torch and looked at me.

The light of the torch spread through the darkness behind him. There I saw a barred gate, and through it a low chamber full of shadows. In the shadows I could see figures lying. Their eyes glinted in the blackness.

From the thick folds of his robe the priest drew a strange curved key. He opened the gate and led us into the chamber. In a spasm of presentiment I started to struggle; but with an unexpected shove and a quiet curse Mr. Cox thrust me inside. I turned, but he shut the gate and stood with his back to it.

In dread, I looked around. I could see no other door, nor any chimney. The air smelled stale, full of piss and sickness. The chamber was broad enough that the far corners were still in darkness, but everywhere I looked were people lying about in attitudes of exhaustion and defeat. They were young women, criminals, I supposed, or prisoners taken in some battle, some dashing raid. They were dirty and stank, as if they had been captive some time. They did not speak, not even to utter a moan, and seemed not to have the strength to get up, but stared at Mr. Cox, and at me, their eyes sad and incurious. I saw one then who had her back to us. I saw the ragged nubs, the dull shine of caked blood. We were standing in the gray God's larder.

Mr. Cox turned to me. He pushed back his heavy coat, the gold braid gleaming in the torchlight. He stood with his fists on his hips, tapping his toe impatiently on the dusty floor.

"This is your own fault," he said, and he spoke it not as to a servant or a child; but as one adult trying to excuse himself to another. "Time's up, I fear," he said.

I stared at him in horror, swallowing hard. I hoped he could not see me tremble there in the dark.

Boldly I spoke up. "Never mind, sir, I'll find myself another passage. There's always gentlemen like yourself on the look-out for a trusty boy . . ."

My words put him in a temper. His hand shot out and snatched the cap from my head, and flung it into the deepest shadow.

"Ye wee ninny," said Mr. Cox, shaking his cane at me. "Why the blazes couldn't ye stay where ye were set?"

I felt the cold weight of the ring that lay beneath my shirt, between my breasts. My master knew me; of course he knew me. He had known all along I was not Ben Rodney of Lambeth, but Sophie Farthing of St. Radigund's Wharf, High Haven. Now for some reason he had tired of the joke, and of me.

The cold breath of Mars touched me to the bone. "Because you killed my mother," I said.

The Pilots' emissary gave an angry sigh, and I heard the clank of his mouth as it shut. "Not I, lassie," he assured me crisply. "If I'd done the job I'd have finished it, believe you me." He was hauling out his pocket watch, looking at it as he spoke. "That reminds me," he said. "There was a ring, was there not."

Then the horrible thought rose up in me, surging up into my head in a vile writhing form like the gray God in the Well. I could not keep it down any longer, and my eyes filled with tears. "Your ring!" I shouted. I swallowed hard, and my voice shook. "Your ring, Father!"

That perplexed him. He smiled an incredulous smile of bone and iron, his face like a jack-o'-lantern in the flickering light. "I—?" he said, making a mock bow; and he laughed a high, whinnying laugh. "Now that is rich, lass!" he declared. "That's really rich!"

Suddenly all my terror welled up, buoying me up like an empty boat. I lunged at him, but the Martian grabbed me expertly by the waist. I fought, but he kicked my feet from under me and wrenched my arm until I screamed. The angels mewed feebly, shifting in their irons.

Mr. Cox sobered instantly, snapping his fingers at me. "The ring, if you please!"

"I haven't got it!"

He put his head back.

"I pawned it," I said. "I took it to Frankie Snow's pawnshop in Vauxhall. He gave me two half-crowns and I spent them on hot chestnuts and sausages!"

We stared at each other a moment, foreign creatures locked in fury. Then, losing patience with me, Mr. Cox touched his hat to the priest, spun around and left the dungeon.

I could hear his bootheels racing away upstairs.

13

Regarding life on Mars

Life on Mars is unkind. You learn that, soon or late.

In the town of Toussous, on the fringe of the Ulsvar Desert, there lives an old spaceman called Pierron, who took a Martian to wife. In the middle of the afternoon I used to see him emerge from his shack and prop himself on the doorpost, his eyes full of dreams. There he would stand, rubbing his arms and calling home his half-breed children. His wife, he said, has told him there is a storm coming; but where is she now? She was behind him a moment ago. Pierron turns and looks around the inside of the shack. She is not there. He cannot tell where she is. At last he remembers he has no wife. She died,

of some sudden, mysterious disease, years before. The grocer
told me. She had the sniffles one day, and the next she died.

Every few days the poor man must go through this misery.
In his dreams his wife is more real than the cold orange daylight, more real than the iron sand and the wind. Once again
she comes home from the canal with her jug of water, her
mantle over her head and her black eyes full of warning—and
Pierron stumbles to the door, seized by a sense of urgency,
and cries out to the empty street. His children run home then
and gather around him, put their arms around him, their ears
twitching with dismay. "They can smell your memories," the
grocer says.

They have learnt to believe Pierron's warnings, his neighbors
in Toussous. When Pierron says storm, they bar their shutters
and stuff the cracks of the doors with torn sackcloth, and the
cloth the Martians weave out of dried cactus. The sky may
yet be clear and bright, but at two o'clock it will grow very
dark very quickly—a heavy wind comes up, blustering—the
town lights its lamps and settles down to drink itself to sleep.
Once as I was arriving, hurrying Alexis on with my heels, I
heard a young man singing:

Tu m'as appris a t'aimer
Mais voilà que tu t'es envolée
L'élu est mon frère—
Que mon sort est amer.

Inside the store, there was nothing to hear but the storm. I sat
there, on the flour bin, listening to the waves of sand beating
against the roof and walls. "It sounds like rain," I said.

The grocer pulled his mustaches. "No rain out here," he
said, as if he thought I didn't know. It has never rained there,
the natives say, not beyond Svaufvaast. No rain since the first
man stood up out of the dunes and history began.

The storm continued, and the darkness. In the office next to
the staging post the company clerks lit the lamps. Then they
returned to their desks to drag their unwilling pens to and fro,
their gaze always turning and returning to the native slaves
who wait squatting in the corner, so motionless, so slender.
The slaves chew moss. So do their masters. The hours are
long here and empty. People grow strange. You start to know

things, like this about the clerks and the slaves, though you do not know how you can possibly know them.

Life on Mars wears you down. After a while the heavy red sand that creeps into the folds of your clothes and the creases of your body finds its way into your brain, into your very sleep, rubbing you away and making you its own. You know what was natural and reasonable in Toulons or Towcester—but they are fifty million miles away, and you are on the shores of a cold desert of rust where dead women walk and leave no footprints.

Sometimes, after a storm, some of the Earthmen cover their faces and ride out into the Ulsvar to look for angels. It is a good time to catch them, if you can find one exhausted by the wind. Sport, it is called; the companies turn a blind eye on it, and they are the only law down here, for all the Emperor's edict. The Church scolds—Father Matthieu denounces it from the pulpit and every head nods, gravely—yet nothing changes. When one of the flock is taken by marauders Brother Jude will mourn with them and pray for justice. On his rocky pulpit I would hear him croaking out: "*A moi la vengeance! A moi la rétribution, dit le Seigneur!*"; while all around his congregation would flap their wings and circle angrily, squawking together in their own harsh tongue.

But here I am with everything all backward again, telling you about Toussous and Brother Jude and Canyon de S. Charles before I have even got myself out of Ys, and mortal danger. You would think, would you not, that writing this would get easier the farther I go; but no. There are interruptions. Lectures, always lectures. Magnetism, logic, the Ptolemaic Legacy. Council meetings too, I hate them, and they hate my being there, which makes me determined to be. Now where did I inconsiderately leave myself? In the dungeon of the Black Well, I see, pinioned by a Martian priest, shrinking from the stink of his breath and his fierce babble in my ear. "Mr. Cox!" I shouted, as the turnkeys fixed the shackle on my leg. "Come back here! You can't leave me here like this!"

But they kicked me, and took up the torches, and utter darkness fell. The chamber smelled of sickness and ruin and despair. There were maimed angels all around me, but I could not see them; nor could I reach them. I pleaded with them, begging for help, asking what was to happen to us; but they knew no human language. Sometimes one of them would cry out weakly, like a wounded kitten.

I remember I fell to cursing. I cursed Mr. Cox, who had pretended to know nothing. I cursed the *Unco Stratagem* that had brought me here. I cursed Miss Halshaw for putting me on board her, and Captain Estranguaro for reading about her in the newspaper. I cursed the Rodneys for not preventing my folly, and then I cursed Papa for not guarding me properly, and for drinking his tea like a blockhead when the taste alone should have told him what I was about.

When I ran out of people to curse, I curled up and wept. I didn't mean to weep very much, but once I started I kept on and on, weeping horribly, shaking and sniveling like a mad thing, and that frightened me. I think it frightened the angels too, those of them alert enough to care. I could not stop weeping until the fit was out of me; then I lay on the gritty stone floor and felt very weak and cold and thought what a fool I was.

Fear came and went. Worse was the terrible boredom that set in at once, and outlasted everything you could think of. I had already lost all sense of time, and now space disappeared. I slept in snatches, the hard floor beneath me and the cold iron on my leg waking me every other minute. The only time we saw light was when they brought us our meal—every day, for every virgin, her own clay bowl of stewed roots. We were the chosen ones, and worthy of that special treatment. There was moss in the stew too, I am sure, to keep us sleepy and feed our dreams. I found half a packet of Nitrox lozenges in my breeches pocket, and made myself ration them very carefully.

One—night, I almost said; I suppose I mean I was asleep when it began—one of the angels started to wail and shriek. I don't know where she found the strength. She wailed and wailed until I started to shout at her. She kept on wailing. Every so often some of her sisters would rouse and start sobbing too, or chittering feebly at her. Every so often she would stop. Soon she would start again. After a while of this, and more than a while, there was a clatter at the gate. A man came in with a lighted taper. He moved around looking at bodies, faces. Soon there came a soft thump, and the wailing ceased.

Life on Mars is deathly; and death is a demon with many arms.

In ancient times Mars was the name of a god. I remembered him in my Ovid: a god of war. While I lay I would listen for the sound of him in the lake beneath us, under the water so still and black, feeding. And I knew the Martians were right, and Papa too, for he had said the same thing. If there was a God, Who made everything and was in charge of it, that was what He must be like. A God of destruction and devouring. A God of Death. That was all that went on everywhere. That God ruled everywhere I had yet set foot.

I thought of the garden of death, next to St. Saviour's church, where my mama lay unmarked and unremembered. I had spent an hour crawling in wet grass trying to find a stone with her name on, but I suppose she and her sisters were souls too cheap to deserve a memorial. I had looked into the church for someone to ask, but everybody was on their knees while a parson with a black beard talked loudly to them about sin and sorrow. I came out again quickly and, buying an apple from a fruit-wife in Cheapside, asked her the way to Turkey Passage and the house of my birth.

I knew I should know the house as soon as I came to it. Its very brickwork would be raddled and spotted as any space hulk with the stains of the vile things done within—why, the whole street must be bruised with suffering.

It was not. It was a street, Turkey Passage, like any other, homely and grimed and bare. I walked up to the house, straight up the steps and leaned over to look in the front room window. The glass was thick and dirty, and the room within unlighted, but I could see bare floorboards, no curtains, and no furniture at all.

I knocked on the door, and when no one came, knocked again and tried the handle. The door was locked.

I waited a moment, then came slowly back down the steps and turned on the pavement to look at the house. I thought that the newspaper artist had had it right, for it was nothing but an ordinary house, with seven dark windows two and two and two and one by the narrow front door, the one I had looked in. There was a line of rusting railings and an area full of dirty paper and soot. As I stood there gazing at it people were beginning to look at me from windows

and doorways, and a policeman started to saunter toward me
slowly.

In the dungeon I shifted my numb bones and thought about
Mama. I wondered why she had had me in the first place. She
must have known the remedies. No explanation could I think
of but the simple one. She had had me to look after her in
her old age. Were there not pairs, mother and daughter, both
in the trade? It stood to reason there were. Had Fate not inter-
vened I would have been brought up by my mama to be of
her profession; as sure as geese have feathers. That was why
she had given me no name. A girl without a name might be
any girl that any man wanted.

I had been foolish to go to the house in Turkey Passage.
Mama was not in that house. She was alive, and coming
to find me—I could see her, in the air before me, just as
when she'd had wings and a face; no less now she had neither. There she was, in the dungeon, with the sheet over
her head and the ring in the palm of her hand, held out
to me. "Mama!" I gasped. "You have come at last!" Yet
how could she not have come? Had she and her companions not also been sacrificed to some god: of jealousy, or
vengeance, or righteousness? I was the product of her trade
and should have gone her way, and died beside her. I reached
for her hand—I could not clasp it, yet I could see it so
clear, the flesh gray as lye between the darkening blood-
stains.

"You should have kept me with you, Mama," I told her,
"and not made me wait so long." At last I knew that all my
life I had only been waiting, ripening; food, growing for the
God of Death.

I heard a clank, and lifting my weary head, saw the gate
open and two men come in with torches. One was a Martian,
a priest, the same priest, I thought, who had admitted me to
that select company. The other was a human man in a long
brown robe.

I sat up.

The man in the robe lifted his torch and saw me. I saw he
was a monk, with sandals on his feet and a rope around his
waist, and all the hair shaved off the top of his head.

"Mr. Monk, sir?" I called. "Can you tell me something,
please?" I was shocked and bothered to hear how weak my

voice had begun to sound. "I want to ask you something about God . . ."

The monk said something to the priest in Martian. They both looked at me warily. The priest had his ears laid back, and the monk looked surprised and sorrowful. He stepped forward cautiously, making the sign of a cross in the air.

"Why is God always so *hungry*?" I shouted; or tried to shout.

The monk came close, stooping over me, and said something to me in French, which tongue I did not then understand. He spoke in a low, imploring tone. I supposed he was asking me not to shout at him; but next he said something urgent and reproachful to the priest, in Martian; and sharply the priest said something back to him, but I thought he did not sound very sure of himself. The monk put his hand to my forehead and started to pray, moving his lips but making no sound. Behind him the priest shuffled, fetching out his key. He unlocked my shackle, and the monk picked me up. "Put me down," I said. I wanted to stand on my own feet. The priest wrinkled his temples and made a sign, and the monk let me go.

My legs were weak. I stumbled back and stopped myself from falling with one hand on the wall. All around the room the eyes of the young angels stared at me, understanding nothing. I waved my arm and told my rescuer: "Them too!"

But the monk only said hurriedly, *"Tais-toi, mon enfant,"* and he grabbed me by the hand. He made the cross sign again and blessed the whole assembly in Latin, then led me out of the gate and rapidly away along the corridor.

As we climbed the stairs he asked me in very bad English, who was I and where was I from. I said my name was Sophie Clare, but would tell him nothing else. He said his name was Frère Lambert and he was my friend, and he gave me Nitrox, and some grapes, which were the most delicious things I had ever tasted. Then he put me on his mule and took me straight out of the city, all the way up to the Convent of S. Sébastien, where he abandoned me to Mother Lachrymata and the Sisters of Lamentation.

This was not an arrangement that found favor with me. I argued; I pleaded; I made a loud complaint. They told me in English to be quiet, and to be grateful. Instead I kicked and screamed, and they whipped me and locked me up in a cell.

I wept, and begged and demanded to be sent back to Earth. I told them I was the daughter of a rich man who would give them an enormous reward. I told them my father's soldiers would descend from the yellow sky to shoot them. I might as well have whistled a jig to a milestone, as the Irish say. Nothing would suffice but that I got down on my knees and prayed.

After I had prayed for three days without food they dressed me in a shift of cactus-cloth, took me back to Mother Lachrymata and told me to apologize to her. I apologized. They gave her the ring they had found on a bootlace around my neck and she asked me about it, in English. She called me Sophia. I didn't care. I told her the ring had been my mother's, no more than that. Mother Lachrymata said they would keep my lozenges and dole them out to me, one daily. "When they run out, Sophia, you will learn to breathe the air," she directed. "It is perfectly good for you." Then the sisters took me away and shaved my head, and set me to work with the novices and the other poor orphan girls they had taken in, to study prayer and learn both French and Latin.

Father Matthieu, my confessor, told me to accept my place with a willing heart. He reminded me sternly that the Lord had sent His servant to save me from the jaws of the beast.

"What about all the angels?" I said sulkily. He invited me to remember their souls in my prayers.

I lost my temper. I said I wished the Martians' God had taken me. I said I'd rather have been eaten in that pit than rot in this one. I think I kicked the partition of the confessional box and would not stop until they came and dragged me out. I was punished again, and counseled to beg for mercy from Le Bon Dieu Tout-Puissant—certainly there was none to be found anywhere else in the establishment—I suppose they had no room for it among all their rules and regulations.

At S. Sébastien they knew even more about God than Mrs. Rose. There were three things He could be. None of them was a big gray monster that lived underwater. One of them was a sort of pigeon, disappointingly; and another was a man, a carpenter, which did not surprise me, for I remembered the men in the yards of High Haven, how they threw things about and made foul noises, and cared nothing for women young or old. And when the sisters spoke of Notre Père, I kept seeing Papa,

walking the Eastern Docks with his lamp, mumbling and calling out my name.

Jacob Farthing was still the only father I knew, since my
real father continued to deny himself to me. And like Jacob
Farthing, the Sisters of Lamentation had me toiling from before
dawn to after dusk, in the kitchen, in the greenhouse, at the
laundry, washing the clothes of the sisters and the priests.
I lasted almost another week before I rebelled again. I sat
down at the well with the yoke still on my aching shoulders
and refused to draw another bucket. Sister Martha sent me
to Mother Lachrymata, who told me humility was a lesson I
needed more even than Latin. I told her I had learnt all the
humility there was in housekeeping.

"Then we must find you another study," she said, and rang
her bell.

They led me outside, out of the great iron-studded gate of
S. Sébastien, across the sand to an apron of rock. There was
a pit there, a shaft dug straight down into the ground. There
was a lid over it, a plain slab of pink rock. The sisters lifted
it off and lowered a long ladder into the dark. They told me
to climb down it. When I resisted they overpowered me and
thrust me down with staves. At the bottom I stepped into dry
sand, with hard rock beneath. Sister Dominique shouted down
to me to consider the filthy black sins that were caked about
my soul, and humble my proud spirit. Then they drew up the
ladder. I clung on to it, but they jerked it out of my hands.
I shouted in fury. They slid the lid back over the pit. Loose
sand rained into my open mouth and into my eyes.

Thus was I prisoned again, and this time alone. Once again
there was no light. There was barely room enough to turn
around. Fear clutched my heart. The walls were rocky, but I
could not get a foothold, and I battered and grazed myself with
falling again and again. Then I sat down and cursed. In time
I began to weep. And then I took a deep breath and breathed
in sand and made myself cough; and when I finished coughing I started to curse again. I had a number of new people to
curse now.

So life on Mars to me was nothing but a series of holes
in the ground, just as Papa had warned me. In the black pit
I sat, and thought of the *Unco Stratagem*. I wished with all
my heart to be off this wretched world and back on board

her, journeying ever on—scarcely thinking of my real self from watch to watch—never fearing what might lie at the journey's end. I suppose I had not had time to notice, but I had been happy on that ship. Pinned by my own ridiculous puny weight at the bottom of a dry well, I knew that worlds pull you down into their traps, down into their mud, and set their irons upon you. I pretended that I was in space again, that the blackness in the pit was the void between the worlds. I imagined I was in flight, with the aether wind buffeting my coat. That made me think of the poor angels again, and the sand started to sift down on me, stirred by the sound of my crying.

They drew me out very penitent and meek. I barely spoke a word, except to whisper thank you to them, in a soft, hoarse voice. I would not lift my sore eyes to the sky, but looked at the sand. "*Grâce à Dieu, mes soeurs,*" was all I would say.

Then obediently I washed clothes, I scrubbed floors, I peeled foul Martian vegetables. I said grace over our meager fare. I learned enough Latin to sing psalms and confess my besetting sin, the name of which was pride. I spoke to none who did not first speak to me. For four long Martian months I saw none but my sisters in God, and the wounded French miners in the sanatorium, and the native girls who came to us to learn about Jésus and Marie. Outside the wind stirred the land about and scoured the windowpanes with sand.

In due season came round the feast of S. Sébastien. There was no feasting for us, but Frère Lambert came, and le Père Matthieu, and the bishop, and his curates, together with a number of priests we had never seen before, all splendid in purple and gold, to dine at high table. I decided it was the largest and most powerful audience I was likely to get. I do not remember how I got up there. I remember only standing on the table surrounded by white-faced staring girls with lentil soup in their hair, screaming "*Laissez-moi partir!*" which was the best I could manage. "Let me out of this place!"

Clucking, the sisters swooped on me like starlings on a crust, and hurriedly swept me away and locked me up. I resigned myself to daydreams once again; but my enemies had had enough, and they surrendered. All sorts of folk were coming and going at S. Sébastien at that season. Within the day I was taken out and handed over into the care of a band of pilgrims traveling by mule out across the Gah Sheraa. I was amazed to be out in the world again, and sat on the mule they gave me making faces at the sky.

Mother Lachrymata was furious with me for showing her up. "Since you behave like a wild animal, you are to live as one," she informed me. It was her last word. The bishop was sending me to live out in the desert.

That evening was when I first saw Toussous, that ragged little town at the end of the world, its shabby buildings leaning on one another like shipwrecks in the sand. I saw the moons race, hurtling toward each other. Above the town a lone angel circled, a pink fleck in the thick red sky. The cold air smelt of rust and smoke, and tingled in the back of my throat. I saw how poor the people looked, and how dazed too, as though they were unable to understand why coming here to dig in the sand had not made them rich yet.

The pilgrims stopped to fill their skins and water their mules. While his brethren refreshed themselves at the cistern, one stood on a box to preach. He preached a truth revealed to him and his companions in a vision: that Jésus Christ had indeed risen from the dead, and ascended, yet not to Heaven but to Mars, to continue his mission. I did not understand everything the man said, but the proof was apparently a footprint at an oasis. Where was that oasis? They did not know. Their vision did not tell them. But they would roam the Ulovar until they found it. They would know it by a tabernacle of gold the Martians had built there, centuries ago. "*Les merveilles de Dieu!*" the pilgrims said, continually, smiling and crossing themselves, their eyes like great round lanterns lighting the way to Paradise. I knew they were completely mad.

I was sure of it next day when we came to Canyon de S. Charles and they showed me that we were to go down into it. Only two of them escorted me, one before and one behind. It was a hard path, the ground flaking and splintery, and the mules were quite unhappy. Angels were flying about everywhere, not seeming to take any notice of us. I looked up, watching them swoop and dart, and I caught sight of a low cave like a shelf in the cliff. Within, there was an angel family, squatting on their haunches. Once you saw the caves, you realized they were everywhere, with vines running up to them. There were caves in every nook you passed. Some of them were so large they held buildings inside, wonderful lopsided platforms of wood and tin.

We stopped below a steep tilted slab of rock where half a dozen tiny angel fledglings were clinging to the creeper with their little yellow fingers and toes. No one arrived to protect them, though now there were three or four angels flying over us with great exaggerated displays of chest and wing, calling out in tones of warning. My escort began to shout too—there was some scuffling—and then a human head looked down from a ledge above the slab.

"*Benedicite, fratres, omnes!*" the head cried, and it grew a body that came scrambling nimbly down the creeper past the fledglings, not treading on any of them, though they squealed and bawled in alarm. It was a small man in middle age with thick gray hair and big black eyebrows, lean strong legs and long arms. He wore a brown robe kilted up between his thighs and carried a little ladder on his back.

That was my first sight of Brother Jude. I thought he was a hermit, and I still think so. He thinks he is a missionary. He is one of the Brothers of the Bright Arc, who follow a commandment of Christ's, to shine His Light abroad. I was surprised to find he was expecting me, and he welcomed me in English. He put his hands on my shoulders and beamed in my face. His teeth were nearly all gone. He called me Sophia, as everyone always did.

Brother Jude clasped my hand. He said: "You ask, Sophia, why do I carry this ladder? I tell you why: to climb up to Heaven, when my time comes!" And he smiled his toothless smile. His breath smelt like Mr. Crii's, fearsome.

When the two pilgrims had had his blessing and departed again on their glorious quest, Brother Jude told me he had a visit to pay, on someone called Thérèse. "I'll introduce you," he said. "You stay there, *mam'selle*, I'll bring her down."

"I want to come up," I told him. In truth what I meant was, I did not want to be left alone. I pulled on the creeper. It was strong, and though I was so light, it hurt my hands to hang on to it. But I struggled up that great slab with my weight on my elbows and feet, as Brother Jude instructed me, and when I got within reach he held his ladder down to me. His long arms were tremendously strong.

Thérèse's cave was not far up. In fact the caves Brother Jude visited were few, and easy to climb up or down to. The farther they were from his own, I discovered, the less likely he was to be welcome. They had broken his bones when he first came, knocked him down, picked him up and dropped him. Still he remained among them, smiling at all adversity, not even limping, and continually praising the Lord. I thought of Mrs. Rose, and how much she would have admired Brother Jude.

"Thérèse is one of my trusties," Brother Jude said. With Thérèse we would be quite safe, he wanted me to know. Thérèse did not look very safe. She sat in a bower of dead vines and palm leaves, chewing an antiquated bone. She wore a dress encrusted with ugly, dried black blood. She spread her wings and lifted her sharp, sloping head and rolled her lips at the sight of me climbing up after the missionary.

I think Brother Jude had hoped she would be kind to me. Of course she ignored me, except when he spoke to me and I answered, when she bridled up with jealousy. In her heart Thérèse was still feral, though she knew much French. She knew *estomac* and *vite* and *gosier*. Her conversation was curt and repetitive, and seemed to be all about hunting, about desert rats and the gulley crabs that swarm in the cracks of the dry rock. Because of the way their mouths are made, Thérèse was able to crack a crab shell with her jaw, but quite unable to say her own name. For many others, the case is the same.

I thought she smelled like Mr. Crii, yet different: pungent, but not so sour as he. When you get used to it you can smell there is a sweetness in it. Yet Thérèse's habits were foul. She took no care. She paid no attention to the tiny children clinging outside on the cliff, though Brother Jude said several of them were hers. Sometimes the little ones fall before their wings grow strong, he told me, sorrowfully. "They return to Jésus," he said.

Thérèse preened herself, making a great commotion. The dress she wore was the one the Bright Arc recommends for them. It is like an Indian lady's *sari*, wound around above and below their complicated shoulders. Thérèse would go about in one, first proudly, then carelessly, for three or four days at a time; then she would tear it in a fight and lose it altogether before flying off up the canyons with some hunting

party. Sometimes she wouldn't come back for days. Sometimes when she came back she seemed to have forgotten
everything, and I despaired of her. She would sit there in
the sun reeking of blood and filth, her mouth open and her
mighty throat aquiver, and spread her wings in triumph.

Brother Jude knew her. He knew which hymns to sing to
calm her down; he knew how to stroke her head above the
ear until she would let him comb her tangled hair and dress
her once again. "Thérèse understands," he told me. I saw then
how impossible his task was, and knew I had nothing to fear
from Brother Jude. Dear Reader, I began to pity him.

He would have me read to him in French, magazines and
scriptural tracts, and read the Bible to the classes he tried to
hold. He gave me the brighter ones, Thérèse and Rachel and
Elise and a lanky boy called Gaston, to help them with their
letters. He would hand out little rewards, a slice of fruit or
a licorice toffee, to anyone who actually learnt anything. In
Toussous and all its barren environs, he kept turning up new
things to attract their attention: a bank note with a picture
of a winged Victory; fragments of fossil wood from ancient
days; the pictures in an exporter's catalog with the names and
prices of goods spelt out beneath. Three or four angels would
listen for a while, then get up without warning and fly out.
Sometimes, on the other hand, they would be inspired, and go
about gabbling whatever it was he had told them. They always
got it wrong. Thérèse insisted that Jésus was born from a cow,
because of the story of the stable; and she thought France was
another part of Mars. Of other worlds she was altogether ignorant; they all were.

Brother Jude was sure he was making some mark on them,
"like a drip of water eating a hole in a stone." He dropped
on his knees on the spot, lifted up his arms and prayed like
an enthusiast. "Make me a raindrop in the desert, Lord!" I
laughed at him and ran away to my cave. It was cruel of me
to laugh; but it was a cruel place.

The cave I called mine was near his, up shallow steps across
the cliff face to the right, along from a small one kept closed
and used as a store. I started out sleeping in the store itself,
but the angels who were living next door took one look at me
and flew away, never to return. After a few nights I grew bold
and went in to inspect the abandoned cave. The roof was low

and black with smoke. The rear was packed with palm and milt-moss, making a nest that was surprisingly warm. Inside it was lined with clumps of soft hair and curls of down tucked into every crevice. Every morning I would wake up and think my eiderdown had burst. Then I would smell the stench and smile to think how the Sisters had taught us to pray each night for four angels to watch over our beds—and here was I with all mine arrived at once.

One morning, however, I woke to find hardly anyone around at all. Everyone was keeping under cover. Anyone who came out at all was keeping close to the canyon walls, skimming swiftly from cave to cave and screeching eerily all the way. The sky was clear, no sign of a storm. I crawled out of my cave and looked upwards. I saw sentries, several of them, quartering the area, flying fast and swooping low. One saw me and came dropping down to my ledge. It was Hercule, Elise's mate.

"Sso-o-ophie," he warned. "*Pr'nez ga-arde! Pillards!*"

I looked up where he pointed. Silhouetted against the rim of the canyon above me were three or four men on lizardback. They looked less like bandits than miners, and I could see they were carrying picks and crowbars. I realized the thin screeching sound the angels were making was a call of warning, ready for defiance.

"Who are they, Hercule?"

He gnashed the air, scanning the canyon rim with his tortoise-shell eyes. "*Cherchent escla-aves . . .*"

The companies take wild angels for the mines, when they can catch them. Angels are stronger than any human miner, more docile, once you take their wings off, and they will work steadily and tirelessly. An angel makes a good slave; but not for long. They work themselves to death.

"You should get away, Hercule," I said, "and go into space!"

But Hercule only gave a dismissive backward jerk of his head, his long hair flying out around his noble skull, and went soaring back to his post.

Later, after the raiding party had departed without incident, I was working in the garden with Brother Jude. I said to him, "There was an angel pilot on the ship that brought me here."

He lifted his hands in praise. "The angels of the east," he said. "Ah, Sophie, what a miracle if one of ours could ever reach so high!" He chuckled, leaning a moment on his knees. "What do you think? Look around you. Can you see Elias making his *doctorat*? Or Gaston, learning to fly a ship?"

"Why not?" I said. Gaston knew his name and some fragments of multiplication table. I was convinced they should put him at the helm of a spaceship, to try what he could do.

Brother Jude waved away my fancy. "In the east they are civilized," he said.

It was hard to work out. The tribe caught bats out of the air and ate them on the wing, then loosed their bowels in midflight. Sometimes it would hit someone, then there would be claws and blood, and raucous laughter. Yet some of them, like Gaston and Gabrielle, were happiest when Brother Jude or I were nigh. They took pleasure in showing off to us. Gaston liked to swoop down on me silently from behind and catch me up under the armpits, then fly slowly and determinedly to the top of the canyon holding me tightly to his chest. As I hung suspended beneath his laboriously beating wings, feeling the strength of his arms and the incredible heat of his body against my back, my heart would start to race with an excitement I did not understand at all. I thought it was a thrill of fear, fear of falling. It made Brother Jude fret to see me fly, dangling thus from Gaston's embrace. "Look at her, the little starling!" he would cluck. "Gaston, put her down! Put her down at once!"

Gaston was my friend, and Gabrielle too, and even Thérèse, though most of the flock neither knew nor cared who I was or how I chanced to be living in their midst. Coming upon me unexpectedly in the open, one would glare down at me like a mad policeman, then kick me to the ground suddenly for no reason at all. Yet they would play with me too, now and then, those of them who could forgive my clumsy, earthbound body. Brother Jude did not approve, but kept calling me away on this pretext and that, to water the garden, or boil up the tough leaves of desert herbs and distill their precious liquor. That was the goodness of his heart, to make medicines for the sick and wounded that the flock would leave to die. The dying converted quickly, staring suspiciously up at Brother Jude's crucifix like a conjuror's audience expecting a sudden explosion. They understood his attentions not at all.

"Sophie! *Où est-toi*, Sophie? It's time to strain the potion . . ."

But I pretended not to hear and drew Gaston into my cave.

He snuggled his cheek against my shoulder. "*Cinq fois sept 'rente-cinq!*" he muttered. When he spoke, the sounds made a blur like the words of a letter left out in the rain. "*Cinq* hun'red and twenty pou-ounds!"

"Hush, Gaston, he'll hear us."

Gaston wriggled his head free of my embrace and went to the back of the cave, to tease a coppermoth he found there. Brother Jude was right, he was daft, and quite likely to let me fall one day when we went flying. Thérèse used to insult him. "*Son c'veau . . .*" she would hiss, cuffing him. "His brains— ssssoft." But what if he was a little childish? She was no better. What were they all but children, powerful children with the bodies of supermen, given to sudden squabbles and scraps, in love with the slightest novelty, unable to concentrate for five minutes together.

"*Sept francs le leeevre!*" yowled Gaston, menacing the moth.

I went and took hold of his hand to capture his attention. "Gaston, let's fly to the moon! Which shall we go to, the big one or the little one?" I pointed to them bowling across the sky like giant marbles. "What a noise there would be if they ever bang into each other!"

But here came Brother Jude again, interfering. "Sophie, come down here! You must go into town for me—fetch some barley sugar for the students . . ."

I put my head out of the cave and looked down at him. "Can Gaston come too?"

He frowned. "Not today," he said. "Those miners may still be about." He clapped his hands. "Quick, child, *dépêche-toi*. Take Alexis."

We had a cart, with an aged austrich to pull it. Alexis was her name. I would give her a bag of turnip tops and *kstryf* while I harnessed her up, rubbing all her legs with wax to protect her from the sand. "Good girl, Alexis," I said, patting her wiry plumage. "Are you coming into town with me? Shall we find that water trough?"

Alexis was always thirsty. If you failed to keep tight hold of her on the road, she would lift her head and sniff some waterhole, miles away, and off she would go, away out into the desert to find it. The French pumps confused her, alarming noisy things that smelt so good. She yelped when she spotted the trough outside the grocery and cantered the last hundred yards to it. I hitched her to the rail and went inside.

While I waited to be served I looked out of the window. In the yard behind the canteen there was a gang of miners just come off shift, with the dirt still on their boots. They had drinks. They would drink there, spending half their wages at the company store and losing the rest at *trente-et-un* to lizard herders heading for Svaufvaast—it did not take them long— then they would go back underground again.

Though the men who owned the mines were rich, the men who worked in them were always poor. Yet because the Martians were slaves, paid nothing at all, some of the humans managed to convince themselves they were well-off. They liked to celebrate payday, singing loudly but wearily over their cups. Chained to a stake in the canteen yard they had a desert lion that was dancing, or rather lunging, irritably, at a dead snake shaken in front of its nose by a Martian man, who played a squeaky clay pipe all the while.

At one end of the crowd that had gathered to watch the lion there was a stranger. He was a short young gentleman in a long dusty coat and a knitted cap with a long ponytail hanging out from under it. He carried a knapsack and what looked like a folded wooden clotheshorse on his back. "Who's that?" I asked.

The grocer always knew everyone the instant they set foot in Toussous. "That? That's Signor Pontorbo, the painter."

I heard myself giggle. "What a funny-looking creature," I said.

The grocer shrugged. "He's a great artist, they say." He grinned, exposing a gold tooth. "Perhaps he will ask you to sit for your portrait, Sophie!"

I made no answer. There did seem to be something slightly odd about the young man, apart from his appearance, I mean. Or perhaps it was nothing at all. Perhaps it was just this: that he was the only person in the yard who was not watching the lion. Everyone else in the yard was looking at the lion; but Signor Pontorbo was looking at them.

14

An unpleasant interview

On Io, largest moon of Jupiter, the atmosphere is thick and
green: more like turtle soup, in fact, than air. Within its gluey
embrace the famous volcanoes spit and fume, belching their
tribute of smoke into the brew. Thermals batter one another
ceaselessly, and fierce winds blow up, forcing the sluggish
gases this way and that, spraying red-hot cinders across the
pumice wastes. Is it day or night? On Io, the difference is
insignificant. The sky, when you can see it, is filled with
moons.

Naturally there is no life on Io, none at all. From pole
to pole, the only beasts to be seen are a scattered herd of
capricorns. They do look rather like that specimen of the
astrologer's menagerie, with their serpentine tails and armored
heads. Roving in their clashing herds from moon to moon, the
capricorns wheel down upon Io now and then, to lick up her
salts with their steel-file tongues. It is their six-inch scales
you can hear in the fog below Hunchback Fell, scraping as
the capricorns browse on the encrusted rock.

Sapient life avoids the place completely. Even the Hrad,
who carouse on Callisto and gamble on Ganymede, do not
like it on Io. Since the planting of the Union Jack, there have
been no citics built, no lonely observatories, not even a penal
colony. On the whole moon, there is one building, and one
building only. It is not far from Hunchback Fell. It is white,
and glistens in the murk like a freshly iced wedding cake. It
is a white marble mansion.

It looks considerably like a wedding cake, in fact, with its
fluted pilasters and scrolled cornice work, its curly ramparts
and stucco *putti*. There are many more than the two stories you

can see. It goes down underground quite a long way, through basements and subbasements into a vast galleried cellar without a floor. Beneath that is a pit, a crustal fault of unknown depth and fluctuating temperature. It glows red and orange, sometimes, in the dark.

The mansion was built by an Austrian architect who went mad on the spot, and died before he could leave the planet. Part of the main west corridor collapsed a few years ago, and the statues around the walls have begun to look rather battered, but otherwise his work has stood well. It makes a fine home, for one who appreciates the location.

Who could have ordered such a mansion built here, beyond all prospect of company? Only one who prefers to keep the trappings of civilization but dispense with the annoyance of neighbors. Already we suspect he must be the most confirmed misanthrope. He must be an extremely rich misanthrope, too, to put himself to the cost of importing all his food and water, not to mention the extravagance of having every breath of air washed and altered before it is allowed into the house.

Heat, on the other hand, costs him nothing. There is power enough and more from Io, free, for one who has been audacious enough to reach down into the turgid, fractious earth and open a vein. And, of course, he spends next to nothing on entertaining, for the only visitors he receives are those whose business obliges them to come: postmen, envoys, officials of state, representatives of this government and that. Only officers of the Pilots' Guild land here voluntarily, fearing what might happen if it became known they passed by and neglected to offer their duty. No one ever stays very long. Yesterday, there was a pilot heading out up the Calliope roads, who brought greetings and papers for the Master from his associates on Mars, notes from people he saw at the funeral. Today the pilot has gone off, leaving the master and his aged manservant in sole occupancy.

"Shall I clear away, m'lord?"

"In a minute, Fortescue."

The Earl of Io sits alone in the banqueting hall, his elbows on the table. While the clock ticks, he gazes unseeing across a snowy expanse of Irish linen littered with the remains of his dinner. He has eaten without pleasure, his man can tell; the news the pilot brought was bad. An ugly nuisance has returned to haunt them; returned from the very grave.

Lord Lychworthy, Master of the Most Exalted Hierarchy and Worshipful Guild of Aether Pilots, is a solidly built gentleman in his late fifties. His is a broad, florid face to which the winds of space have not been kind. His nose is rather flat, and quite round; his mouth now as always most inexpressive, habitually set in a motionless straight line from cheek to cheek. His eyes are large, and very dark in color, the iris almost black. Black too is the thick straight hair his lordship wears to his collar, and the splendid set of "Dundreary" whiskers, very fashionable in the inner worlds just now; not that he cares a hang for fashion, or even decency. Everyone is corrupt, every clergyman's cock twitches at the sight of a pretty petticoat.

A large wheel-shaped device is creeping across the floor of the banqueting hall, sucking dirt out of the carpet through a leather tube. It looks like a giant and stately snail. Fortescue moves his foot out of its blind, automatic path. In the dull silence, between the slow ticks of the clock, he listens to it go by with a tiny, wet, nibbling sound.

You might think it is clockwork, but it is not; or if it is, it is clockwork that has hit upon the trick of winding itself up. His lordship has many such advanced machines, some commissioned to his own design, others acquired from unspecified sources. Lord Lychworthy prefers machines to people. Machines go where you tell them to. They do not interrupt or interfere. When his lordship wishes to indulge his fondness for a melodious female voice, he has a machine that will reproduce the sound of a celebrated singer for him, as many times as he cares to turn the handle. When he wishes the singer, or anyone else for that matter, to cease, then he has devices that will do that for him too.

It is only people that let you down, Lord Lychworthy thinks.

Lord Lychworthy never married. Lychworthys have always found women particularly tiresome, or at least women in their domestic aspect, to which even the most handsome inevitably dwindles as the years encroach. The present Earl detests their incessant chatter, the triviality of their minds. Their charms, when younger, he would be the first to acknowledge; yet taken over time they prove emotional, unstable, mentally unfit for anything more taxing than tapestry work.

Fortescue does not like to disturb. But he hems, and says, "Sir—?"

His master speaks, not looking at him. "Clear now, Fortescue." He pushes back his chair. "I shall take a turn in the Portrait Gallery," he announces. "Afterward you may wash up."

When Fortescue has eventually shuffled away the half-eaten meal, Lord Lychworthy goes downstairs. Fortescue follows behind, a skeleton in musty black, holding aloft a three-branched candlestick. No more light than that for Lord Lychworthy, he knows, not in the portrait gallery. The master never wishes to look too clearly on the faces of his ancestors. Their presence, dim and staring, is all he requires.

Master and man pass through the Orrery Room, where the candlelight gleams faintly on balls of gold and silver that run on exquisite jeweled movements and bearings afloat in baths of mercury. Lord Lychworthy ignores them as he ignores the worlds they represent. They cross the floor of the Armory, the flames of the candles reflected in the glass doors of the instrument racks, catching an answering glint from cherry wood and ivory and steel. Many pieces in there are unique, and were surely fabulously expensive. His Lordship has had help from alien associates far outside the register, if the design of some pieces is anything to go by. Only here, on a poisonous moon far off the beaten track, could he keep all these treasures without fear of intrusion and burglary.

They arrive now, the earl and Fortescue, in the Portrait Gallery. Behind them the double doors swing bumpily to and fro, and fall silent. The room is utterly still, the air torpid with the scent of old varnish. The walls are the color of boiled cabbage. Upon them, great black oils loom up in the shadows like the sails of funeral barges. Here and there, a detail leaps to the candlelight: a compass badge; a pendant underlip; a tightly swaddled child.

Lord Lychworthy glances first at a small portrait of his mother. He says nothing. He has been thinking about mothers, and the care some of them apparently take of their offspring. He cannot recall that his own ever cared for anything but gossip and the exercise of malice. When she spoke, it was regardless of who was listening, and always concerning what opinion this one secretly held of that one's dress, and how clever she herself had been to conceal that she had found it out. He remembers her letters to him from the villa at Nice, when he was up at the academy: incoherent with petty spite and innuendo, full of exclamation marks and details of indetectable vengeance she had taken for slights paid her by the other wives in exile there. She was always giving him instructions, too; always intruding with her advice.

His father gave him instruction too, when he saw him; but that was different. That was work, men's work. There was much, public and private, that the boy had to be prepared to inherit.

He had never spent much time in the company of either of his parents. First there was the long succession of schools, and then the requisite postings throughout the regions. He was on the bridge of a star-schooner when they brought him the news of his father's death, and his mother's so soon after: within the month, in fact, while he was yet on his way home for the occasion. They say he took it very well; scarcely seemed surprised, in fact, such coincidences of fate being, after all, not unknown. The new earl was even able to make a casual remark to the archbishop about the convenience of a double funeral.

He had had enough of worlds, with their stupid and troublesome inhabitants, and a hundred times more than enough of space, when he succeeded to the eminence he now commands. The craft of threading the shifting mazes of the flux had never held much interest for him, and he was glad the time had come to quit the practice of it. Now, on the rare occasions when he must leave his fastness, he has no need even to pilot his own vessel.

Lord Lychworthy turns to face his fathers. There is a wall full of them, in two ranks: the previous Masters of the guild.

The present incumbent gives a muttered command. He directs Fortescue to hold the candlestick up to the last canvas in line, the twenty-seventh earl, with his beard like a black escutcheon and those deep green hollows around his eyes that nothing, no joy or conquest, ever seemed to fill.

"Fortescue," says Lord Lychworthy, as if presenting the old gentleman to him. "My father: the twenty-seventh Earl of Io." His Lordship ponders. "He was a great man," he says.

"A great man, sir, he was," mutters Fortescue reverently.

"The first man on Correggio," says the earl. "Others claimed the credit."

"Wicked liars, sir," Fortescue says.

The earl takes another step, and another; and stops in front of the portrait of his father's father, who had been bursar to the guild before he succeeded to the presidency. The artist has pictured him in his gold chain, his stock pinned with a wildcat's claw. There is something in common, one can see, a family resemblance between all the faces: a certain wariness in the eyes; a hint of strong teeth in that weighty jaw.

"Fortescue," Lord Lychworthy says. "My grandfather: the twenty-sixth Earl of Io." He pauses. "He was a great man," he says.

"A great man, sir, yes, he was," Fortescue affirms.

"He took the barquentine the *Tragopan* around the Horn of Cassiopeia before he was twenty-two years old!"

"Great men in those days, sir," Fortescue opines.

The earl rounds on him, vehemently. "Yes, Fortescue!" he says. "Great men! And great servants too. Trusty men."

Fortescue hears the anger in his master's tone, the vast black rage that lives with him always, that hovers on dark wings in him like a crow in a tomb. The candle flames bob and lengthen in his eyes. But his gaze is far away, past Fortescue, back along the gallery, as if he were looking out into the sea of space itself, watching for a vessel coming on a distant tide.

"Yes, sir," says Fortescue; and his voice is hushed.

The earl looks down at him then, focusing on him. The hint of a smile stirs that sober mouth. A forefinger points at Fortescue's waistcoat.

"Trusty as that engine in your chest," he says.

"Sir?" says Fortescue.

"Your loyal heart, Fortescue," Lord Lychworthy says.

"Why thank you, sir," says Fortescue, touching a bony finger to his forehead, "why thank you very much indeed, sir, yes, sir. I hope and pray this loyal heart may beat just so long as your own sir, and always to serve you."

Fortescue is glad to know it is not with him that the master is displeased. He has a good idea who it really is. He sent the signal himself, to call in the emissary.

Lord Lychworthy is looking now at the gaps on the wall of his fathers, the gaps he will never see supplied. The first gap waits for his own portrait, which hangs now in its place of honor at the Aeyrie. Beside is the gap where the portrait of his son should one day go. Lord Lychworthy has no son. And this, Fortescue believes, is the root of all the trouble. He himself has neither wife nor child, though he did have both, formerly, many years ago. Lord Lychworthy has neither, never had; but there is time for a son, Lord Lychworthy's man reminds himself, still plenty of time. After all: it only takes a moment.

When Mr. Cox arrives, some days later, Fortescue asks him to step upstairs directly, where the earl wishes to see him in his study. Mr. Cox puts his gloves in his helmet, and gives that and his stick to the manservant, then makes haste to comply. He has no foreboding, or none that he would dignify with his attention. It is not the first time he has been recalled from space for some more urgent duty.

Lord Lychworthy is at his desk, writing something on a paper. As soon as Mr. Cox is announced he sweeps it aside and seizes on an envelope that lies at hand.

"Cox, good day to you, sir," he growls.

Mr. Cox makes his bow. "Your Lordship. I came as quickly as I could."

Lord Lychworthy waves him to the chair in front of the desk. From the envelope he takes a small item, which he puts in the palm of his hand and holds out for Mr. Cox to see. It is a gold finger ring, set with a crystal, an oval of the fine Martian *suprême* engraved with the eye and arrow, his personal crest, taken from the arms of the guild.

"What would you say this is, Mr. Cox?"

"Your ring, sir."

Mr. Cox does not recognize it at once, not this particular ring, and he wonders if he should. But his master says only, "Exactly."

Mr. Cox watches as he reaches into the envelope and pulls out a large folded sheet of paper written in a precise, assertive female hand. He unfolds it and looks into it as he says: "Perhaps you'd care to tell me how it comes to be returned to me from Mars?"

"From Mars?" echoes Mr. Cox, unsure. A horrid surmise is beginning to frame itself in his mind.

"Aye, Cox; *Mars*, Cox. You do know it? Recollect, Cox: was it not on *Mars* where we last met together?"

Lord Lychworthy is being sarcastic. Mr. Cox looks at him with narrowed, speculative eyes. The Master of the Pilots' Guild thrusts the paper over the desk at him, as if it were a dagger to his breast. "Take it, man. Read it."

Mr. Cox begins to peruse the paper. It is a letter addressed to Lord Lychworthy, Io.

"Aloud, sir!" says that gentleman.

Mr. Cox reads.

"From the Mother Superior, Convent of S. Sébastien, Ulsvar, Mars. Dated the seventh of last month. 'My Lord, I pray this finds you in health in your remote—' "

Lord Lychworthy growls impatiently, hitting the desk with his fist. "Not that part! Come, come: to the meat."

Mr. Cox reads on.

" 'Enclosed with this please receive a ring found by our sisters on the person of a young waif called Sophia Clare, or Sophia Farthing, origins unknown, recently arrived on Mars and given into our charge by our good Friar Lambert. She says she was brought here by your man Mr. Cox; whose ship having already departed this world, we return the ring to you, supposing only that the girl must have stolen it from him.' "

"She's lying, of course," Lord Lychworthy breaks in. " 'Supposing only'! I can imagine her supposings. Pah! *Well?*" he says testily, and motions abruptly with his hand, as if encouraging a dog to jump. "Go on, go on!"

"She says: 'The girl says the ring was her mother's.' "

"And?"

Mr. Cox looks up, raising his eyebrows a fraction. "That's all, sir. She commends you to the Love and Mercy of Our Lord and Sav—"

"How the devil do you account for it?" the earl demands.

"*I* can't account for it at all, sir," replies Mr. Cox, his voice soft, his emphasis barely discernible.

The earl's voice coldly and firmly overrides his impudence. "You knew the girl had that ring."

Mr. Cox squeezes his brow between finger and thumb as though his eyes were bothering him. He had always known the whore would be trouble, from the very first. It is Lychworthy's fault, the whole thing, for indulging his appetites imprudently. "She told me she had pawned it, sir."

"She *told* you she had *paw*—" Lord Lychworthy echoes,

explosively. He reins in his temper, baring his teeth and suck-ing a mouthful of breath. "Contemptible stuff, sir!" he barks.

Mr. Cox stiffens his back and defends his ground. He com-plains, "I disposed of her weeks ago, my lord! I gave her in at the Black Well." He thinks of the Martian priest and makes a little sarcastic snort. "I should have wrung her scrawny neck wi' m'own hands . . ."

Lychworthy sits back, his mouth a hard line. "Was it you brought her to Mars?"

"Aye, sir," Mr. Cox admits.

"On my yacht?"

"Aye, sir."

"Why?"

The syllable is abrupt and short. Mr. Cox breathes, reflect-ing on what he is to say. The matter is a delicate one for the Master; he must not be annoyed more than is unavoidable.

"The lass turned up first at the High Haven, sir. Followed me back to Earth, if you please. When she turned up again trying for a berth on the *Stratagem* just before we sailed, I decided to keep her where I could see her, sir; to see how she was minded." Years ago, his spymaster had taught him: the best way to keep watch on someone is to let them think they're keeping watch on you.

The earl's face is very red. "You took a girl on the *Stratagem*?"

Mr. Cox pulls at the lace on his cuffs, straightening them. "Aye, sir," he says, refusing to be distracted by accusations. He says: "She was in disguise as a boy, sir." He thinks, *And not a man jack of them spotted her. Not even Mr. Crane, who has an eye for young ladies. That should have meant something; yet she never played her hand.* Time after time Mr. Cox let her search his cabin, but she never took a thing. Eventually he had become convinced she had no hand to play.

"The child's soft in the head, sir," he says, looking his employer in the eye. Mildly he says, "She took me for her father." Maybe that will reassure him.

It does not. "And I was to be kept entirely in the dark?"

Mr. Cox does not rise to that. "It'll all be in my report, sir," he says equably. "Which I'm drafting for you now." He plucks the knees of his breeches. "She's safe enough in the hands of the good sisters of Saint Sebastian." He smiles politely, baring his black iron teeth, and reaches into his waistcoat pocket for snuff. "Will ye take a pinch, my lord?"

"Damn your bloody snuffbox!" cries Lord Lychworthy, with a violent glare. "Did it never occur to you, Mr. Cox, that it was your *duty* to hand the child over to the guild proctors and send me a signal at once?"

Mr. Cox puts the snuff away. He is growing irked with the Master's obstinacy. Stuck away out here the man forgets that things can go perfectly well without his direct supervision and control. Mr. Cox says, as placatingly as he can, "She is nothing. A wee chit of a girl who knows nothing, my lord, of rings or any other matter!"

"Was that for you to judge?" demands Lord Lychworthy, implacable.

Mr. Cox wants to say: It was plain for all eyes to see. But he knows the earl would hear only the implied rebuke. When he spotted him there at the funeral, sitting with the dukes and bishops in the distance, he had been obliged to act in haste. *Haste spoils all*, he thinks gloomily. The plan he had made for little Miss Farthing had been less brutal: transportation to a distant colony, somewhere primitive and obscure; a new life, under a new name. Not a cruel life, but a hard one: hard enough to keep her busy, in one place, out of harm's way. Well, she has that now. But damn that stupid priest. And damn the incompetent fools who were supposed to have dispatched her in her cradle.

Mr. Cox feels numb, sweaty in the overheated house. His wig itches. His jaw has begun to ache, as it does when he is uncomfortable. "I do apologize to you, my lord," he says, keeping his voice neutral and pleasant. "I considered you had more important things to occupy you than the fate of a— thieving ragamuffin," he adds, with delicate emphasis.

"Your excuses bore me, Cox," says Lord Lychworthy, loudly and rudely, and he drops the offending ring into his pocket. "But what, confound you," he says, scratching his broad belly, "and confound the child. Let us go into the parlor," he says, standing up and pushing his chair back from the desk, "and talk of more pleasant topics."

Mr. Cox is relieved, but wary. "My report will explain everything, sir," he starts again.

"You mind it does, Cox. Hang the bloody report. Let's have some whiskey."

They go into the parlor and speak of business, the Trinity Races around Venus, the new record for a polar orbit. They drink an excellent malt, in honor of Mr. Cox's ancestors. Lord Lychworthy even toasts them with his tumbler. "May they welcome you as their beloved son," he entreats, obscurely. Mr. Cox supposes he has been let off the hook. He is very tired, and it is getting hard to fathom anything. His eyes are growing heavy, his vision foggy. He supposes it is the fumes from the abyss that come with the warm air up the flue. He blinks and rubs his eyes. Lord Lychworthy seems to be in the middle of an anecdote about a fox and a dowager. Mr. Cox is trying to break in, to excuse himself and leave the room, but it is as if his mouth has rusted shut; he cannot make the words come out. He is aware of the manservant, Fortescue, standing behind his chair. Then everything goes swirling around in a great black vortex, and Mr. Cox is swallowed into the vasty deep, to rise no more.

"Take him down, Fortescue," says Lord Lychworthy, as the aged man heaves the body over his shoulder. He will have Mr. Cox cremated in the cellar, like the Austrian architect and all the others since who have been inconsiderate enough to die on the premises. "Wash the glass up too, when you've done. Then I shall want you to go up to the *Stratagem* and bring me this report and anything else he's put in writing. Check the secret compartments. God damn the man!"

The earl slips the ring out of his pocket and looks at it. Its crystal sparkles in the firelight, clear and pure. There was only ever one ring. Only ever one stupid mistake, in a time of youth and folly. Lord Lychworthy slips the ring back on his own finger, whence he never should have pulled it in the first place, and downs the rest of his whiskey at a draft. He sits there a moment, fingering his whiskers and listening to the moaning winds of Io that toil eternally over and around his home. He thinks he feels the floor quiver, as if from a distant tremor. "*Tutt' é coperto*," he mutters to himself, sourly. "Nothing left to chance."

It is the unofficial motto of the Ancient and Circumspect Order. How long must he go on paying for one stupid, trivial, insignificant mistake?

Fortescue comes back with his tray for the glasses. There is now no more trace of Mr. Cox in the house than if he had never landed. His post is vacant, and no replacement ready— another nuisance. Lord Lychworthy sits in a fug of foul dyspepsia at the gall of the man, and wonders how he thought to use the girl against him: dead or alive? Dead now, convent walls or no. The Earl of Io has sent his hound, who will even now be upon her.

15

Society and the Artist

Sister Dominique told us about the Muhammadans, when I was at S. Sébastien. The followers of the prophet Muhammad believe that everyone alive has his destiny written on the inside of his forehead. It takes a very holy man even to see it; and only the Angel Azrael can read it. I have wondered sometimes if Mr. Crii could read mine. I remember on board the *Unco Stratagem*, how he always seemed to reserve a special expression for me, a look, as I thought it, of mischievous menace. He would arch his eyebrows and open his great mouth, tossing his head at me for all the worlds as though he had horns and was pretending to gore me with them. Naturally I supposed he knew I was not Ben Rodney and thought it a great joke—and I feared he would give me away one day, on purpose or by chance. You can never be sure, with angels.

Ben Rodney had ceased to be—but sometimes in the canyon I saw that same expression on the face of Gabrielle.

You must suppose us now, Dear Reader, sitting in my cave, side by side, looking at the pictures in Brother Jude's book of saints. Gabrielle, if I remember rightly, was wearing a solar topee her sisters had stolen; and I was huddled in my feather blanket. There was one picture Gabrielle liked, of St. Agnes

hovering over her bonfire. She scratched at the page with her
claw. *"So-phie p' voler,"* she said.

She had said that several times, that I could fly; it was her
usual joke. "I'm still fledging," I would tell her, and wriggle
my shoulders, pretending to preen my feathers.

Then Gabrielle blinked slowly like a cat, arched her eyebrows, opened her mouth. Roughly she wrapped me in her
wing, smothering me. She chattered, scolding me. She was
adamant, I could fly.

That was a strange sanctuary I had come to, in S. Charles
Canyon. I would sit there, receiving my callers, passing the
time of day with talk of food and folly, while overhead wild
wings beat in an orange sky. In the gully below my cave
a group of the older women liked to gather, and sit there
for an hour together digging centipedes out of the sand and
feeding them to one another. I remember the muttering sound
they made, the squawks of the infants protesting while they
groomed them. The noise floated up to me echoing and blurred,
like the sound of laughter in a dream.

My school had fallen by the way, or had changed into an
odd kind of nursery. Every day at some hour a gaggle of
youngsters would be bound to chase one another into my
cave, at a romp. They were all over everything, like the cats
that plagued Mr. Crusoe. If I shouted at them, they might sit
down for a moment, like a proper class; but swiftly their mood
would change, without any warning, a new emotion seizing
the whole pack of them at once. In two minutes they would be
poking each other with sharp bits of bone, yodeling, brawling
in and out of my nest, and biting one another's ears.

Gabrielle was a frequent visitor. Some days I would wake to
the sight of her glaring down into my face, half-spread with all
her scars upon her, like the Angel of Death herself. Sometimes
she had come to bring me a titbit, a stolen pear or a tender
young rat she had saved for me. One day I remember, she
seemed particularly agitated. She would not close her wings.
Though I stroked the thick muscles of her back, she would
not settle. *"Qu' est-ce que tu as, Gabrielle?"* I said. "You've
forgotten my breakfast."

"Les hom-m-mes So-phie," she said, humming. *"Revien' . . ."*
And with a great flare of her wing she pointed upwards.

My heart sank. I went out of the cave and climbed up the cliff a little way until I could see where I thought she meant. Gabrielle flew up, keeping behind me, as though she thought I must protect her, rather than the other way around.

"I see him," I said. It was not a raiding party, but one man alone, mounted on an austrich. It was the young painter, Signor Pontorbo. He was off the path, near the edge of the cliff. "Oh, Gabrielle," I said. "Let's go closer."

Unlike her brother Gaston, she wasn't always willing to transport me when I asked, but that time she did, lifting me by the wrists and almost pulling my arms out of their sockets as she hauled me up the cliff. "Put me down, Gabrielle!" I cried, my voice puny beneath the pounding of her wings. *"Dépose-moi!"*

I am glad to say at last she did, and we came to rest on a high shelf of rock. From there I could see the young gentleman in his long coat and his knitted cap with the hair spilling out of it, brown as beer. He was drawing in a little sketchbook he had propped against the bow of his saddle.

"Gabrielle!" I whispered, rubbing my shoulders. "The gentleman is a bird-spotter!"

My own wit dazzling me, I began to giggle. That made Gabrielle start to caw, and I panicked, and flinging my arms around her neck, urged her to fly away again at once before he heard us. Holding me tight she flew, making me giggle again with fussing noises in my ear.

The next time I saw Signor Pontorbo he was accompanying Father Matthieu, Toussous's pillar of rectitude.

Father Matthieu's eyebrows were shaven, his gloves were white, his back was stiff with righteousness. When he spied me in the streets of Toussous, he would put his nose in the air and ride on by. For their part the town had little love for their sour priest. As the grocer would say darkly, "The ones they send up here are always ones who have disgraced themselves at home." Father Matthieu would come only with great reluctance out to S. Charles Canyon usually to hear Brother Jude's confession. After my convent days I refused to make any more confessions, or even to kneel down, so he never spoke to me unless he had to, but glared at me with hatred.

He knew Brother Jude never laid a hand on me, nor felt the slightest tickle of lust for the selfish, scruffy little girl at his

side, any more than he did for the wild beauties of the flock
with their bare breasts and titans' thighs. Brother Jude's mind
was on higher things. Still Father Matthieu suspected me, and
hated me as a daughter of Eve, the first betrayer of all mankind. If he had had his way, he would have sent me back to
S. Sébastien to be starved and beaten into submission; yet the
bishop had spoken, and here I was, living free and mired, no
doubt, in sin.

I own I didn't care tuppence what the good father thought.
He was a visitor, and visitors were rare. They made a change
from gardening and trying to get rid of the little white snakes
that did no harm but kept crawling into my nest. When Father
Matthieu arrived next, at the end of that week, I combed my
hair out of my eyes with my fingers and clambered down to
Brother Jude's, just to see him; him and his companion, the
young gentleman from Sicily.

Father Matthieu was making introductions. "Signor Pontorbo, this is Frère Jude of the Bright Arc—and this is his
ward, Miss Clare."

Signor Pontorbo murmured, "*Signorina*," and gave a little
bow. He made no further move, nor said anything, and hung
back so among the shadows, I could not have said what his
face was like. But when I looked, I caught him looking at me,
and though I smiled meekly, I think he did not.

Brother Jude said, "I beg you both to do me the honor of
taking some tea."

"I'll make it," I said, which made Brother Jude raise his
eyebrows and blink at me in innocent surprise.

Signor Pontorbo spoke then. His voice was rapid and light.
"I have a bottle of wine in my saddlebag," he said, "if it is
acceptable."

Father Matthieu inclined his head, and Brother Jude smiled
and gestured to me. "Sophie, perhaps you would like to climb
down and fetch it?"

"Please, *signorina*, it is not to think of," said the young
man quickly, and with a little general bow around the cave,
he scrambled off down the rocks. I could see he was more
agile than he looked, and perfectly at home in the Martian
gravity.

Father Matthieu gave Brother Jude a thin smile of pious
approval. "An altogether earnest and devout young man," he

announced, quietly. "His donations to our work have been most generous. He particularly asked to be introduced to you, brother."

"Has he shown you his paintings?" Brother Jude asked.

The priest looked a little pained. "They are rather modern, for my taste," he said. "After the new manner of France," he added, his smile restoring itself, "rather than the Old Masters of his own country."

Brother Jude clucked his tongue. What he knew of painting would have covered an outhouse door. He said, "Things do change so, nowadays."

Just then I heard Alexis start up. She had caught sight of Signor Pontorbo, I supposed, at some business with his own mount; and that was enough to set Alexis squawking fit to wake the dead. I went to the edge and shouted down to her, but she took no notice, so I was obliged to go down there to shut her up.

The young man was tugging at the straps of his saddlebag, his back to me. I saw that his head was squarish, his long hair brown and soft and loosely bound with narrow strips of black leather. There was something quiet and contained about the way he stood, as if he held much inside him, like a wise old turtle drawn into his shell. Then he turned around, hearing my step, I presume, and I saw his face in full daylight for the first time. It was very smooth and bland and plump. There was no bridge to his nose, and I thought he seemed quite pale for a Sicilian. Yet his eyes—Dear Reader, how can I make you see them? They were the color of a willow pool in summer, and as deep, I was sure. Many things had sunk without trace into the depths of those eyes. I had noticed already how he was always staring at everything, and I supposed that was how you looked at things if you wanted to remember them, to put them in a picture later. Now we faced each other across the back of a caterwauling austrich; and he was staring at me.

I realized how dusty I was, my hair as red with rust as an Indian's with *henna*, my frock a rag and, in truth, barely decent. I felt a terrible urge to scream with laughter. Instead I scolded Alexis: "A sparrow has more brains!" I told her, and tugged at her tether and patted her neck, looking all the time across her back at him. "What are you so jealous of, you stupid thing? There now."

Then it was only right I should introduce Alexis to our visitor; and I asked did his bird have a name? "Only in Martian," he replied. "I can't say it."

I suddenly realized I had spoken to him in English, and he was answering in the same tongue. When I remarked on it he said: "I travel constantly."

"You speak it very well," I said.

"*Vi ringranzio, signorina*," he said. "That is Italian. Do you know it?"

I had to shake my head.

"It means, my thanks to you, Miss Clare." I decided I liked him then; but I did wish he wouldn't stare at me so, for I feared he would stare me quite out of countenance. He came towards me, lifting his arm. "Will you allow me to help you back up to the cave, *signorina*? The rocks look most, how do you say—treacherous."

I didn't want him to touch me. "I live here," I reminded him, avoiding his arm and starting back up towards the cave. "It's easy, look."

"Such a place!" he exclaimed, and he began to follow me back up the rocks, placing his small feet carefully.

"Signor Pontorbo, you've forgotten the wine!"

"Ah!" he cried, smiting himself on the brow, and he started back down again.

When at last he got back up with his bottle, Signor Pontorbo took out a slim silver knife and cut the lead from the crown, then expertly prized out the cork. The wine was sweet and cold. In a while it warmed your fingers and toes. Father Matthieu and Signor Pontorbo took Nitrox with theirs. Father Matthieu was speaking to Brother Jude about Brother Lambert, who had been missing for a week. Now a traveler had found him, Father Matthieu said, lying face up ten miles out in the desert, staring at the sun with his eyes burned out.

Brother Jude shuddered as though a scorpion was running up his leg. "Dead?" he asked.

Father Matthieu bowed his head. "Quite dead, Christ be thanked."

Brother Jude crossed himself. "He must have crawled out there all alone," he said, "following some holy vision."

I felt I had hated my unhelpful rescuer enough while I was at S. Sébastien, and now I felt peculiar and sad. The last I had heard of Brother Lambert, a woman in the grocer's was telling how he had been speaking out against High Priest Keegheeta and the worship at the Black Well. I had carried that tale to Brother Jude, and Father Matthieu knew it too, I could tell. Now I could see each of these holy men trying to conceal the same doubt in his heart. On Mars, sometimes, you have these understandings—people become suddenly very apparent to you, what they feel, what they intend—and perhaps I was particularly sensitive that morning for some reason, at that gathering.

Understanding nothing, presumably, catching only the word *vision*, Signor Pontorbo interrupted. He praised the Ulsvar and its deceitful light. "The sky is full of angels," he declared, "but the rocks are the rocks of Hell!" He lifted his hand and made as if to snatch the light out of the cave mouth like a moth out of the air. "I shall have it! I shall have Canyon de S. Charles," he said, deferring, though rather grandly, "*con il vostro permesso*, Frère Jude."

Thus he spoke, rapt and sure of himself, as I was to see him thereafter. I noticed, though he addressed his request to Brother Jude, yet he turned his eyes upon me, as if it was my permission he thought he had to ask to paint there. Why, Signor Pontorbo, I wanted to say in mischief, do you think we own the canyon? I swallowed my laugh in a mouthful of wine.

I saw Father Matthieu had noticed too how the young man fixed his gaze on me; and he it was who spoke next. "One thing is certain, Signor," said he to his excitable companion. "Out here it is wise not to trust our eyes too well, lest they lead us to where *le pauvre* Lambert has gone. Where illusions beckon," he pronounced sternly, lifting two fingers together, "there waits Satan."

I had been wondering what the young gentleman had found to draw out there in the desert, unless it was his own noonday dreams. Around the canyon the landscape stretches glaring off in all directions like an endless headache. Nothing there is to relieve the dreariness of the plain, nothing but the silicate reefs with their blades as sharp as knives. No trees grow there, only the gray cactus, spindle cactus growing singly, or in sudden clumps that rise together straight into the air. "Organ cactus," I heard Brother Jude name it. "Would that we could hear those magnificent vegetable anthems!" Sparse dry weed sprouts among the gray-green pipes, and *kstryf* bushes whose roots the very soil will rub away. Then the slightest breath of wind will pluck them up and send them bowling aimlessly across the sand like big ragged dandelion clocks, to fetch up under another cactus, where they will seed themselves again. Truly, Mars does not encourage you to think well of the purpose of Nature, unless you are another such as Brother Jude.

The angels, I must say, fared very well in that expanse of waste. They roamed far and wide in search of fruit and game, and cared not whom they robbed. I was angry with them sometimes for their wickedness, not that any of them took the slightest scrap of notice. How often I had to run back to the vegetable patch to chase away youngsters nibbling the shoots I had just watered, while the adults sat watching from their caves, laughing. I remember on Earth, how people like Mr. Mountjoy, who was perfectly happy for wild angels to go down the mines, used to object passionately to their civilized cousins' guiding our ships through space. "It's not right," he would maintain, leaning on the bar of the Hope and Anchor, "they ought not to give them charge, not of human passengers." Mr. Mountjoy would not have been reassured to see the S. Charles flock, when game was scarce, or sometimes just for fun, fly twenty miles to raid the fields of the desolate villages along the Gah canal.

They are always taunting and bickering with each other, too. They are all so contentious, I think they are in love with discord. I have seen Thérèse and her sisters swoop down and drive off the *kiiri* feeding on a lion carcass, without any intention at all of eating it themselves. Gabrielle and Luc flew away together once, up out of the canyon and into the desert. After a few days Luc returned alone, and had a thunderous fight with Gaston. Gabrielle came back much later, under the racing moons, with a dozen snake-skins tied in a fringe up each arm, and more around her waist, snags of bloody meat still hanging from them all. Gabrielle then had a fight with Luc. They tore at each other with their claws. I did not watch, or try to dissuade them. I had given up with them long before.

Afterward Brother Jude was evasive—his English failed him, and I could not understand his French—and the tribe was unhappy. I asked Thérèse what was wrong, but got no explanation I could understand. She truly did not seem to recognize that the Gabrielle who had returned was the same person who had left. Some people think angels believe anyone who leaves the tribe for more than a few days must become irrecoverably changed. The only change I could detect in Gabrielle when she returned was that she stank even worse than before.

Not long after that visit of Father Matthieu's I thought a cowled woman came to me in my cave, one of the Sisters of Lamentation I could see it was, from S. Sébastien, but I could not make out her face inside the shadow of the cowl. She said she was in danger, and called on me to save her. I was annoyed with her for some reason—still I told her I would, and somehow she was so small that I could pick her up between my thumb and forefinger, like the little people in the *Travels* of Captain Gulliver. I remember I put her in my mouth and swallowed her. I woke up then and laughed at myself, remembering how her voice tickled inside my belly.

That morning I met Gaston, and we went for an outing. A meteor had landed up the canyon and he took me to see it. We did not stay long there—a party of French officials had arrived to inspect the meteor and have their pictures taken dividing it up with measuring tapes and little flags. The sight of the people made Gaston nervous—and I was always in fear of being reclaimed and sent home, or to some other fearsome institution—so he flew me to the top of a pinnacle some miles further on. There we sat, I on his huge knee, with his wings wrapped around me to keep me from the wind, and watched while the ore freighters came lumbering over, heavy in the sky. I tried to get him to talk, but he only made yammering noises and sang a slow lugubrious song, rocking me backward and forward like a human mother rocking her baby to sleep. I laughed and bounced up and down. "*Laisse-moi, Gaston!*" I cried, and pretended I was going to pull his feathers out.

Suddenly we saw someone below, riding on an austrich. It was Signor Pontorbo, and he had seen us. He plucked off his cap and greeted us in Italian. His light voice came spiraling up to us on the wind. Gaston made a rude noise with his mouth and, tipping me sprawling off his lap onto the ground, he jumped off the rock and flew away.

"Gaston! Gaston!" I cried, bending my knees and banging myself on the shins with my fists in exasperation. "Gaston, come back! Come back and get me down!"

But my escort had abandoned me.

I looked down at Signor Pontorbo, suddenly embarrassed to have him come upon me in that predicament.

He lashed the side of his boot with the reins. "That rascal! I shall go after him!" he cried angrily, though Gaston was already vanished from view among the cliffs.

"Don't worry, Signor Pontorbo, I can get down. It's not that steep." It was, in fact, quite, but not impossible, though you would not have wanted to fall off.

"If you can come down, *signorina*, then I can come up," said the young man gallantly. He was already off his bird and jumping up the first part as he spoke.

"Oh please, Signor Pontorbo, don't!"

He said something that obviously meant it was no trouble, and up he came, with his knapsack on his back, while his austrich mooed unhappily after him. He was very strong, I could tell, and not afraid of physical effort. I called down some directions to him as he came, and I wondered suddenly, before he reached the top, why was he trying to impress me.

I was certainly impressed. "Well done, Signor!" I cried, brushing the rock dust from his chest and arms. "What a climb!"

"What a view!" he said, panting in the thin cold air.

He stood right at the edge and looked around, shading his eyes with his hand. I suppose what he saw was that we two were tiny mites inside a great cleft, an old wound of the planet—that we were high up in the air, and everything about us was brown and orange and dusty, the cliffs on all sides craggy and pocked with cracks and caves—where even the vines were brown, and not a leaf glowed green. The silence of the place rang in our ears. There was no one to be seen anywhere.

"Such a view," he said again. "Such raw, forgive me, Miss Clare, such *savage* beauty." Yet ever and again, all the while he was gazing, his eyes would turn from the view to my face. He was still breathing hard. He seemed constrained, I thought, the way he moved, as though something was frustrating him and making him cross. Still his face was empty, nothing there to say what was on his mind, what it was that made him stare at me so.

"Look, you can see the railway from here," I said, and pointed where the cliffs broke, away to the north.

He moved closer to me. "That streak of silver? *O cieli magnanimi*," he muttered, in a preoccupied manner.

"It is fifty miles long," I said. "The trains come bringing truckloads of diamonds down to Coin Brut. Brother Jude says for every yard of rail there is a poor miner dead."

"What mountain is that?" Signor Pontorbo asked suddenly, and took hold of my arm to direct my eyes. He had put himself into a position behind me, with his other hand on my right shoulder, looking over my left. I was surprised at the familiarity of him. "Yes, that one, there. Is that Mont Royal?"

I could hardly speak with him at my back like that, so solid, so close. I did not know that I cared for it. "Oh no, sir," I said. "Mont Royal is over there," and turning to point out where he should look I ducked my head and tried to shrug his hands off me.

There was a strange instant then when I thought he was not going to move; that he was going to stand there and not let me move back from the edge of the rock. Then he yielded, and followed the line of my finger, but impatiently, as though if Mont Royal were not indeed where he thought it was, he had no time for it.

I felt sorry for him. Though the canyon was my home, I had been a stranger here once. I knew it could be difficult to get your bearings. To comfort him I said, "I should very much like to see your drawings, sir. If I may make so bold."

I could see that flattered him, rescuing him from his dilemma, whatever it was. With a tight little smile and a neat little bow he took the horn tablet from his knapsack and gave it to me.

Now I knew nothing at all about drawing, and less about painting, even after lectures from Mr. Cox about the pictures I dusted in his cabin on the *Unco Stratagem*. Even then, as I turned the pages it seemed to me there was something wrong with those drawings of Signor Pontorbo's. They were very energetic and wild, so much so in most cases that you could not make out what they were intended to be. "They are very rough, these, Miss Clare, *naturalmente*," he kept saying.

"Ideas, only." But he said it in such a silky way, with his chin up and his broad chest out, that I understood he was actually quite proud of them. I wondered if perhaps he might be a rather bad artist; or if I could be even more ignorant than I imagined.

"Let me see your ring, Signor, may I?" I said: distracting him by asking him for something else, just as I used with Papa. I had noticed the ring when he opened the wine. Rings interested me; and anything was better than having to talk about his drawings.

He spread his hand to show me. It was a plain gold signet ring, without any engraving. Lovely hands I thought he had, white, and small, and neat. "It was the ring of my father," he was saying, in a high, indifferent voice. "I never think of it at all."

I touched it, and touching it touched his finger too. "Shouldn't it have initials on here, sir?"

He huffed, lightly, through his nose, dismissing the suggestion. "Of his father, and his father," he said. "No, no initials."

"I used to have a ring," I said. "It was my mother's. Mother Lachrymata took it away. I asked for it when I left the convent but she wasn't speaking to me."

I thought the Signor seemed to tighten again suddenly, as though his breathing was constricted, and I remembered once more how new he was to Mars. I looked for a lozenge to give him, but he waved it away. All he said was: "And did it have initials on it, your—mother's ring?"

I recalled it for him. "It was gold, or very like, with a little piece of crystal in it, that was engraved with a little tiny sign. There was a human eye; and under it an arrow, like in a compass."

"Indeed," he said brusquely, looking out at the view again, with his hands clasped behind his back.

"There is something like it in the crest they have in the Pilots' Guild," I said.

"Indeed," he said again. "Indeed."

"Signor, are you all right?" I asked. "Should we go down now, do you think?"

"No!" he barked.

His eyes that were like willow pools had darkened now as if clouds had closed overhead, shadows of distant thunder gathering. I began to feel afraid, and to want very much to go down from that high place.

Then the young gentleman sagged, and looked tired, and seemed to be longing very much for something. I could not imagine what. "Yes," he said. "Yes, soon we must go down. Soon."

I thought he was a very strange man indeed; and I wondered what it was about my ring that always made gentlemen so excited.

He spoke on. "Your face," he said. "In this light." He lifted his hand, as if framing my cheeks in the air. "*Signorina*, will you do me the honor—of allowing me to paint you?"

"Now?" I cried.

"No," said the young gentleman. "Not now. Nothing is possible, now. But you will come here. Tomorrow. At this same hour. Tomorrow is another day." And he smiled, fierce as any lion.

I led him across the top of the rock, trying to usher him down the path ahead of me. It seemed important to keep talking, in case he started to say something I did not want to hear. "In the Bible, sir, I suppose you know, being from Italy as I take it, sir, where the Pope lives, I expect you know the story where it says Satan took Jésus up on a rock like this in the middle of the desert, sir, and said he could have the whole planet if he knelt down."

Perhaps I could have come up with something more suitable. At any rate I had not eased his agitation. His face stirred, strangely, as though some mysterious emotion was working beneath the skin, and his eyes seemed about to start from his head. "You are most amusing, Miss Clare," was all he said.

"Let me lead the way, sir," I offered, starting off the top at once. He followed, saying nothing now. "Don't worry, Signor Pontorbo," I said loudly. "We won't fall, you know. And if we do, why, you know what we say here, Signor?"

"Amusing but not very encouraging, Miss Clare," he said. I heard the rustle as his boot slipped, inches above my head.

I looked up in alarm, but he was safe. I laughed then. "We say, if the winged men don't get you, the *kiiri* will!"

I was thinking that those carrion eaters, those horrible scraggy things with their clutching toes and their wings like scaly mackintosh: they were the angels on Mars, not

Thérèse and Gaston. The *kiiri* are the true messengers of God. And as I thought that, I heard the thumping of huge wings coming through the air, and looked to see which of them it was.

It was Gaston, of course, come back to snatch me away in his arms, which he did, leaving Signor Pontorbo scrabbling there on the rock, while I laughed and protested, hammering his chest and shoulders with my fists. "Gaston, put me down! I'm all right, I don't need any help! Gaston, no! *Aidestu* Signor Pontorbo, *pas moi!*" But the needle of rock with its tiny clinging figure was already receding in the distance. Deafened by the beat of Gaston's wings, I waved and yelled: "Good-bye, Signor Pontorbo! I'll see you tomorrow! At the same hour tomorrow!"

"*Se't sous le boisseau!*" boomed Gaston sternly, scolding me. "*Deux 'res et quart! Deux 'res et qua-a-a-rt!*"

For some reason he did not take me home, but to Thérèse's, where he and she sat down at once to share the remains of what looked as if it might have been a dog. They offered me some, but I was too nervous to eat. Thérèse's latest brood, still yellow and scrawny, were tumbling sleepily over one another, squeaking like untuned violins. I tried to imagine having babies, things inside you, growing. Then they would come out. It sounded horrible. I wondered why Thérèse let it happen so much.

"That was bad of you, Gaston," I said, "to leave the poor Signor dangling. You must go and get him, now. *Vite!*"

Gaston took no notice.

I sat with my feet hanging out over the ledge and watched a star rise. I knew it was not a star but the moon called Deimos. Phobos and Deimos, Fear and Dread, always circling. Thérèse was boasting to Gaston about strangling pelicans. "Thérèse, what do you think of that man?" I asked her, interrupting rudely. "Signor Pontorbo, I mean?"

Thérèse turned to me, hooded her eyes, and broke wind. Then she started quarreling at once with Gaston, who had found a good bit. The subject was closed.

I met him again the next morning, as he had instructed, at the foot of the rock. He looked tired, as if he had not slept in the meanwhile. Still he gave me an elegant bow and said, "Good-morning, *signorina.*"

"Good-morning, Signor," I said, and grew very shy suddenly.

"I hope the angel bore you home safely," he said.

I lied and said he did.

Signor Pontorbo looked into the sky. There was no one there, no one nearby at all. He looked around slowly. Then he said to me, "There is something you must see."

16

In which I cast my fate once again to the winds

I can see him now, him with his fine broad brow and his skin like candle wax, standing there with the yellow rock soaring up into the air behind him. He had his big loose blue knitted cap on, and an old Chinese topcoat with curved swords printed on it; and he had his easel and his knapsack on his back. He looked like a figure out of a pack of cards.

I, too, had dressed heavily, putting on everything I possessed. I'd supposed you had to sit very still to have your picture painted, and there was no shelter on that rock; so I was wearing my trousers under my frock, also my coat that they had given me at S. Sébastien, and a tam-o'-shanter and a long tattered scarf Elise had given me, fetched from who knows where. What a sight I must have looked.

"Show me, then, sir," I said.

He looked away among the rocks. "It is not here," he said.

I supposed it was some painting he meant, back at the inn at Toussous. "Shall we go and see it, then?" I said.

"Yes," he said, mildly enough. "Yes, we shall. Heaven forgive me!"

Dust went swirling past us on the breeze, blown down off

the rock. "Signor Pontorbo," I said, "what are you talking about?"

He turned down the corners of his mouth and shook his head. "*Mi vogliate perdonare.* I cannot tell you, *signorina,*" he said. "Forgive me. *Dunque* . . . if I say something, you will think it so," he continued.

That was not very clear.

"You must see it with your own eyes," he said. "That will be the proof positive." I sensed he was having difficulty with this, as though he would much rather have thrown me in a sack and carried me away, but was struggling to behave like a gentleman. I set my mouth.

He struggled on. "I have thought about it, and this is best," he said stoutly. "My own wishes are—irrelevant," he said.

I had to laugh. "Yours too, Signor?" I said.

I know it was rude, but I couldn't help it. It was happening again. Everyone I met had a plan for me. None of them ever came to anything, but they all involved hurrying me on from wherever I had just sat down. I was a feather on the breeze. "All right," I said, opening my arms and making my latest abductor a little curtsy. "Very well. And where am I off to this time?"

"To Io," he said.

"Io!" I cried. Well, that was the best joke of all. It was the back of beyond—a frozen rock—grimmer even than the Gah Sheraa. I couldn't even remember which world it traveled around. And with him standing there with his manner so earnest and intense, I just laughed and laughed. Then of course he began to protest, and tell me what to do, and I ducked my head and dodged away from him, busying myself with tethering Alexis, who was confused because we were arguing and because I had laughed. She butted me with her bristly bare head, telling me she disapproved. Her, too, I dodged and stepped up on the rock, pointing upward.

"Race you to the top, sir," I said.

He startled me then, how fast he went for it. He darted me a look of pure animal reflex, head drawn in, eyes hooded; and then I heard the soft thump and clatter of his knapsack and easel bouncing in the sand while I was racing upward with him behind me, bounding like a goat. I yelped aloud and scurried and scrambled, and still made it to the top hardly a whisker before him.

I stood on top of the rock and threw my arms in the air, panting, grinning at Signor Pontorbo as he came up. "Here we are, Signor! Now how would you like me to pose? With a smile? Shall I duck my head and say, I'm most obliged to you, sir?"

"You might," said the Sicilian, crossly, gathering his breath. "For so you are." He folded his arms and raised his chin. "You are the most fortunate girl in all the worlds."

"Why, then, thank you a thousand times, sir," I said, boldly. "You would not find a more grateful one this side of the Asteroid Sea, I do assure you. But indeed, sir," I said, not giving him a moment to speak, "I heartily wish my fortune was not such a giddy one," I said, and I sat down. "And I wish you would not stare at me so, Signor."

He was struggling again. With an edge to his voice he said, "Pardon me, I cannot help it when you are near."

I could see no reason for that. "Then let me take my leave, sir," I said, "and go elsewhere."

He lowered himself slowly on one knee, leaning forward on his hands, his other leg stretched out to the side. He brought his face level with mine where I sat. Then he lifted his right hand and showed me his finger and thumb crooked in a circle, their tips almost touching. "And I am close, like so, to saying yes, go, because you ask it. You are a witch!" he said. "You have bewitched me."

"I haven't done a thing!" I objected.

He drew his lips together, reflective still. "Why do I let you toy with me like a puppet?"

That was good, coming from him. "Stop *looking* at me like that, sir!" I said. I turned away from him, contemplating the view. "I was not born to be looked at," I said.

I had never been rosy, and living in London had made my cheeks sallow as dripping. Now the foreign air of Mars had darkened my skin, and my eyes were always red with dust and wind.

Yet the painter was not dissuaded. "The man is a liar who told you so!" he said, brusquely. He held out his hand to me, but I ignored it. "Come with me, Miss Clare! Come to Io. Your future happiness depends on this single journey."

He shut his mouth, as if to say so was too much.

I sat on.

His gaze began to smolder. "Let me beg you, *signorina*. Do not be stubborn. Do not let us contest this." His voice turned dark, but I had had plenty of that in the days of Papa. "Let me not lose my patience," he said.

I had no intention of getting up. I planted my hands firmly on the rock. "Your patience?" I said. "What about mine? What do you want with me, sir?" I demanded. I heard my voice start to grow shrill. "Why will people not leave me alone?"

The young genius closed his eyes. "What I want is not in question," he said, tightly. Then he opened them again. "What I want," he continued, in his congested manner, "may never be." He stepped closer, pointing his finger at me, wagging it. "For you I have failed in my duty!" he told me, as if that was my fault too. "Never before! For you I have shamed myself and my family. All for you!"

"I would very much rather you did not do anything on my account, sir," I said, roundly.

At that he reached out and seized me by the hand. He dragged me to my feet. I came closer than he expected, and stamped on his toe. "Shame indeed!" I shouted, and had the satisfaction of hearing my voice ring from the bald rocks all around.

I did not struggle against his grip. I made no move to get free; but stood there and looked him straight in the eye. Very quietly I said, "If I am to go as far as town with you, Signor, it will be on my own two feet."

Warily, he let go of my hand.

"I'm not going, though," I said.

He grabbed at me again, but I ducked. "There's nothing on Io!" I said. "No one lives there!"

He cursed in a foreign tongue and grabbed at his hair, as though he wished it were mine. "Ignorant girl!"

"I could call *you* a name," I said, which was what Mrs. Rodney always used to say when Gertie was being rude. "You're not a painter at all, are you?"

"I am!" he maintained. "I paint!"

"How can I trust you if you won't tell me the truth?" I said, my voice rising.

He batted at his chest. "*I* show you the truth! On Io, you will see!" he said. He was losing his temper. He was not accustomed to being crossed. And he was clearly not going to back down.

I turned and walked away, almost as far as I could walk across the top of the rock. I was about to start to climb back down to the ground, but somehow I dallied. I bent and broke off a piece of the rock and threw it out over the edge.

"This has to do with my father, hasn't it?" I said.

"I cannot say," he muttered fiercely.

I watched while my missile dropped gently out of sight. I thought of Mama, and felt then as if I might be about to cry, but I made myself not. Mama was at rest, in a quiet place. There was nothing more to seek for her.

"It's all right, Signor," I said, "I don't want to know. I don't care about him any more. I don't need a father."

There were a couple of angels in the distance, circling over the organ cactus, hunting for mice. I watched them for a moment. I said, "They don't mind that I haven't got a father. I'm Sophie Clare: that's who I am. I'm the funny foreign girl. The one who lets the children make a rumpus in her cave. The one who laughs when Brother Jude is preaching. The one who shouts and throws sand at you when you try to nick her food. That's me, you see, sir, Sophie Clare. But you: you won't let me be, now, will you? You have to come and haul me off to Io, for goodness sake, and what for? Because I was supposed to be someone else. Well, I'm not." My voice was growing louder. "I'm not her! I never was her! I was never meant to be *born*!"

There was a pause. He stood there, poised, like a dancer. I hoped his ears were cocked. I hoped he'd taken some of that in.

"Nevertheless," he said, looking down at the rock, and casually drawing a line in the dust with his toe, "you were. And you will come," said he, most affirmatively; and now he lifted his eyes to me, his head still bowed. He lifted his eyes to me, and he smiled. "You know you will. Because it is in you, *alora*, like a worm. It eats away at you. If you do not come, I shall go and you will never see me again. You will look for me, but you will never find me." He held his head up and stood with his legs apart. "Stay here, *signorina*, in your comfortable *hole*, eh?" The word rang with his contempt. "Stay here and dig for your vegetables. Stay here, and

grow into an old woman." He came closer to me, stepping
over his line. "So you may, Sophia Clare," he said, "so you
may; but you will never forget me. And you will never be
satisfied. The worm will eat out your heart until you die."

"You really are the limit," I said. I was disgusted with him,
and with myself. "And I am a fool."

"Ah," said my self-appointed guardian, quite gently, and
with as much relief as triumph. His shoulders relaxed. "You
will come, then?"

"All right," I said, ungraciously.

"Thank you, *signorina*, thank you," he said; and he bent to
kiss my hand. His lips felt cool and moist on my skin, and as
he raised his face I saw his eyes lit from within by pleasure
and pride. I realized some of his pride was pride in me.

I didn't want his pride. "Go away now," I said. "I don't
want to talk about it any more."

He said, "But we leave now."

That took my breath away. I reminded him, "I must go and
say good-bye, sir!"

"There is no time," he said, motioning me to the path. "We
leave this world at once," he said; and as I started down the
rock, going backward, he told me: "Miss Clare, you are in the
gravest danger. There is no saying when it may strike."

"If it wasn't for people like you there wouldn't *be* any danger," I said; but I didn't know what I was saying. I was only
grumbling. It would be better not to say good-bye to Brother
Jude. He would be sure to try to stop me from going. He
would call upon Marie and Jésus and reproach me with the
bishop; and then with Gaston and Thérèse and the little ones,
and that would only make it worse. Already I could picture
his dismay to find I had flown my nest. I would write him
a letter, from our first port of call.

Io. The very thought of it made me despondent. I must
believe there really was some wonderful, mighty thing on Io;
or at least that the young gentleman believed there was, if only
because he had got himself in such a lather about it. As for
his protestations, I thought he would not willingly betray me;
and that was more than I could say for most of my neighbors
and acquaintances. Besides, I had never had the attentions of
a young gentleman of my own species before, and perhaps a
tiny part of me was in awe of him. If he was a rogue, he

was certainly a mysterious and dashing one, like the young
Sinbad. Perhaps he was a rogue spirit, in human form—a
genie!—the Genie of the Ring! Absorbed by these and similar
weighty reflections, my foot slipped on a patch of crumbling
rock and I caught myself up short. Alexis mooed up at me
as I clung, pressing my front to the rock, my heart beating
overtime. At this rate I would not get as far as the port, let
alone Io.

All the while the young gentleman and I were climbing
down the pinnacle Alexis continued to fuss, knowing something was wrong. Along the path she kept turning round, trying
to go home. I had to chivy and coax her all the way up out
of Canyon de S. Charles, and along the line of stones that
mark the desert trail to Coin Brut. "You must keep her quiet," Signor Pontorbo said, and then he stopped talking to me
altogether. When I spoke to him, asking what marvels there
were on Io, and how long he thought our journey would take,
he did not reply.

I thought perhaps he did not speak in case whatever he
said might make me change my mind about coming. Then
I thought perhaps he was cross because I did not trust him
completely, and thank him for taking me along with him like
a spare lizard on a leading rein. There was no knowing what
he thought. All I could see of him was the back of his hat and
his long ponytail, flopping gently up and down as we rode.
Alexis continued to whimper and shake her shoulders from
side to side, and I had to kick her hard. Needless to say,
my companion's mount behaved herself perfectly, swaying
on ahead, ignoring Alexis's nerves in that dogged, stoic way
they have.

In a while we turned off the trail. I had to suppose the
Signor knew where he was going. Over the hard brown dunes
we jolted, under a hard yellow sky. Against the light a line
of failed French pumps stood like crippled austriches, silent,
seized up, choked with dust. We rode all morning and saw no
one, though once I smelled a cooking fire and heard afar off
the murmur of a steam train, high in the hills, and somewhere,
I thought, a goatherd playing his pipes. Already I was beyond
the limits of the world I knew.

Yet this stranger, this newcomer, as he said, led me far up
the Gah canal, directly to a spot along the bank where the

natives come to cut the wax reeds, to bind them in bundles and from the bundles make boats, boats the shape of canoes. The natives hid from us, as from a fearsome sight. Signor Pontorbo gave them no more notice than if they had been mice. He directed me to two finished boats inside a shelter of canes with a canopy over.

He dismounted, with his pack on his back. He looked in my face like a doctor, expressionless, and having seen what he wanted, perhaps, or not seen what he would not have, said stiffly, "Help me here, please, Miss Clare"; and then I had to help him steal one of the boats, dragging it down the bank and into the water. No one shouted or tried to stop us. The place seemed to be deserted, as if all the natives had run away. Signor Pontorbo went back to the shelter for the paddles, and threw a gold piece into the hollow where the boat had lain.

"Get rid of the bird," he told me.

His own mount had run off the minute he slapped it on the back of the neck, not waiting around to ask why. Alexis, scatterbrained Alexis, Alexis who had to be tethered every minute of the day to *stop* her running off—Alexis was suddenly struck with a fit of loyalty. She would not leave. She crowded us while we were launching the boat, and saw us off with clamorous protest. Up and down the canal she scurried, as if looking for a stretch that was not water so she could chase after us. Long after she was out of sight I could hear Alexis, complaining of her desertion to the four corners of Mars.

The canal was brown and tan and cold. Particles of grit blew around in the air, stinging our faces. I pulled my tam down over my forehead and hunched myself up behind Signor Pontorbo's back. I had had little practice at this craft and I grew very hot, paddling hard in so many clothes; and for all my labor the boat kept veering all the time in my direction. We were far from civilization here, and met little traffic coming the other way: a gravel merchant's pram, I think, and a native with a brace of lizards pulling a string of low, closed barges. Once I looked up at the skyline and saw the distant shapes of people standing there, watching us go by. They were men with spears, thin dark men standing motionless, with women crouching around their feet. K'mecki. I said nothing. I was sure Signor Pontorbo could see them, and he did not speak. I wondered who it was that was supposed to be pursuing us, and I was sure it was Mr. Cox, coming to punish me for failing to die at the Black Well.

"Were you ever in London, Signor?" I asked the broad, blue back in front of me. "I wonder if you met my mother there. She lived in Turkey Passage, you know, in the shadow of St. Paul's Cathedral." I could see him, a little boy, determinedly climbing the steps at the front. "I wish you had painted her picture, for there was not a good one of her in the paper; and though I try and try, I cannot recall her face."

Perhaps I did not speak but only dreamed I had spoken. I was very tired, and Mars had wrapped her strange glamor around my brain. I thought the wuffling of the wind was the beat of angry wings, pursuing us, and I spoke at random to distract myself. In any case, I knew my abductor had made up his mind to ignore me, to ignore everything but the urgency of our flight. He thrust his paddle blade into the water as though it were the body of an enemy.

On and on we went. To one side, black pelicans flew, silently skimming the icy water. The stone faces of the banks were caked with orange lichen. We paddled into a region of rocky hills, through a narrow canyon where the walls were very high and every sound we made went bouncing up the rock like an india rubber ball.

The imaginary wings still beat in my head, and my exhausted eyes began to see shadows flicking here and there across the water. Then they were upon us, before I could shout out, Gaston and Hercule, and Gabrielle too, diving down on us out of the brightening air, skimming the tops of our heads as they swerved out of reach, gaining height and turning to do it again. *"Di'-se't fois trois font soixante-qua-a-a-atr'!"* cried Gaston, and I heard the heavy *swoosh* of his wings, and smelt the rank heat of his body as he swooped low over the water. There was a hard thump, and Signor Pontorbo huffed in pain and surprise, while the canoe rocked alarmingly. Gabrielle was there beside me, her bosom bare, her arms open, her wings troubling the water beneath her. "Go back!" I shouted, standing up dangerously with knees bent, wobbling in place. "It's all right! *'Suis en sécurité!* Go home!"

But they took no notice. "Ssophie!" they cawed, grimly. "Sssso-o-ophie!" One by one they tried to snatch me out of the boat, which creaked and shifted sickeningly in the water. Signor Pontorbo turned and brandished his paddle at them,

cursing them in some foreign tongue. He did not seem to
be hurt. The angels evaded him with ease. They risked tipping us into the water, but would not fight hand to hand.
Signor Pontorbo caught Gaston a lucky crack on the hip, and
he screamed like an eagle, thrashing the air in his rage.

"Paddle, *signorina!*" shouted Signor Pontorbo. "Paddle for
your life!"

My legs were wet now with the water we had shipped, and
it soaked through my trousers and chilled me in the breeze of
our passing as we fled. For a mile they chased us, Gaston and
Gabrielle and Hercule, harrying us from all sides. It was me
they wanted. They thought I belonged to them. They took no
notice of my pleas.

"Let me go back, Signor. We can go to Io another day."
He took no notice either.

We came then to the place where the locks begin, the
ones that lift the water into the hills, and the first of them
was against us. We could flee no farther by water. Signor
Pontorbo leapt ashore, hauling his knapsack from his shoulder,
swinging it from one hand while he delved urgently in it with
the other. The angels flew at him from the water with wings
outspread, trying to drive him back from the bank, away from
me. I stayed where I was, shivering as I clung to the stone
side of the canal, trying to draw myself into some corner of
safety.

I saw Signor Pontorbo pull something out and throw the
knapsack from him. My mind was in a whirl. I thought it
was a paintbrush in his hand—I supposed he wanted to get
Gabrielle down on canvas, that he would be shouting enthusiastically about yellow ocher and burnt sienna even while she
dug her claws into his throat. I saw him standing at bay only
for a second, feet braced, holding up the slim black wand; and
then Hercule was upon him, bowling him over on his back. I
think I screamed. I know someone screamed, but perhaps it
was Hercule, for that instant there was a small flash bright as
winter lightning, and a vile smell of burning.

Then Hercule was bouncing backward, head over heels,
spread-eagled—landing with a crash and a high squealing
cry on the stone edge of the lock wall and sliding into the
water alongside with a mighty splash. Drenched, I cried out
in horror and alarm and, dashing the water from my face with

my arm, I jumped ashore and stood on the brink, searching the
brown canal until I saw my angel friend come swirling slowly
up, surging back to the surface, to hang there bobbing with
his spine arched and his eyes and mouth wide open. He was
dead as mutton.

The others cried fiercely in their own tongue, backing
up into the air. Gabrielle raged furiously, treading air as she
cursed us, showing us her buttocks, and they beat up a storm
with their wings.

I heard a high-pitched sound like the buzzing of a wasp,
ʼand saw the dazzling flare again. It was coming from Signor
Pontorbo's hand. Blinking, I saw it was the thing I had taken
for a paintbrush that was burning, brighter than any fire you
have ever seen. It was that which had killed Hercule, Hercule
the biggest of them all, at one fell stroke. Now the young
man was menacing the others with it, bellowing at them to
beware.

Away they flew, shouting bitterly and keening in fear, leaving their dead comrade floating in the water like some vast,
broken swan. Signor Pontorbo came running to me, caught
me up in his arms, crying, "Are you all right, *signorina*, did
they hurt you?"

There was still a blue dazzle like little fish swimming in
front of my eyes. The horrid weapon had gone, I did not see
where. "You didn't have to kill him!" I complained, pulling
myself free, and I said a great deal more, though there was
not much sense in it, and then I burst into tears.

He reached for me again to comfort me, but I lifted my
hand and he halted, arms spread as if I had conjured up a
cage around myself. I turned and looked at poor Hercule, and
sobbed. Thwarted, Signor Pontorbo hustled me back aboard
the sagging craft, and climbed in in front of me. "They would
have drowned us both with their antics," he said, irritably.

We paddled away at once, abandoning Hercule's enormous
golden body. I remember the reek of burnt feathers. I wept,
and paddled, and wept.

My companion was conciliatory but cold. "They are animals, *signorina*, wild animals. You are safe from them now."

"They're not animals!" I protested. I turned on him. "What
do you know about them, anyway, except how noble they look
in the glorious desert light?"

"An angel will always let you down," he said, simply and finally, as though he had known a hundred and been betrayed by every one; and I grew weary and fell silent again. My faith in Signor Pontorbo was perfect at last. I had forgotten that to be a hero and rescue maidens, a young man has to kill everything that gets in his way. I was not afraid of him now, but angry and miserable with myself for betraying my only friends. It was no consolation that they would forget Hercule in a day or two. I shall remember him forever, lounging in Thérèse's bower with her babies crawling over him, offering me the choicest bits of a raw leg of goat.

Where angels fear to tread, the poet tells us, fools rush in. On and on I rushed, foolhardy. That is a good word, foolhardy—I was hardy then in folly. Folly to chase my doom. I had time to wonder what Gabrielle would actually have done to me, if she had got her hands on me, and whether even Gaston would have protected me then if the others had come at me in wrath. And I wondered how close behind Mr. Cox might be, and if he might delay, stopping to look at the dead angel floating in the water.

Signor Pontorbo led me up the canal, among mountains I had never seen, whose names I didn't know. We saw no one, not even a K'mecki, and I began to think no one was chasing us after all. There were so many locks I was glad we did not have to work them, but my arms ached from heaving the boat out and up each time, and from paddling between. It was light enough, the boat, but growing ever heavier as we climbed and my arms grew weaker, and the reeds became sodden with water. We rested, I think, for a spell. From a bag he had, Signor Pontorbo gave me to eat some strips of tough dried cactus. We spoke little, saving our breath for the work, nursing our separate concerns in silence. I, for my part, was imagining what sort of complexion Brother Jude would put upon the calamity. Would he not weep and pray for my soul, and tell the tribe that Satan had taken me?

I shifted my sore limbs on the hard ground. "Where did you get that thing?" I asked, thinking of the device that had laid Hercule low and hoping never to see it again.

"*Alora*, it was my father's," said the champion. He gave me a quick, proud look; then committed himself to contemplative study of the dreary landscape.

We left the boat at last, abandoning it in a lonely reach of the canal where nothing moved or grew, nor looked as if anything had for the last ten thousand years. We went on up on foot, to the top of the mountain. I gave in and let him take my arm, to help me up. Little as I weighed there, I don't know how I would have done it otherwise. I was ready to drop by the time we breasted an upright lip of rock and I saw we had arrived.

We were standing on the rim of an extinct volcano, miles from anywhere. Beyond, no sign of civilization except the gray line of the canal running away into the distance and invisibility. The sky was the color of wet pease porridge. At our feet, tiny brown moths crawled on a low fringe of Martian sage.

Below, nested in the crater, lay a secret dock, large enough perhaps for two small ships. One was there already, winched in tight at the capstans. All her sails were reefed and there were lifting balloons fore and aft, fully inflated.

I stood a moment looking all around in wonder. My bad mood was quite forgotten. "Is she yours, sir?" I asked, as Signor Pontorbo led me down to the ship where she floated four feet off the ground, nudging at her web of lines. She was a smart space cruiser, her hull painted a simple gray, her name, *Gioconda*, written in blue across her stern.

"She is, Miss Clare," he said. "Mine to command." There was a hint of defiance in his tone, as though he half expected someone to dispute his claim.

At some distance along the jetty stood a glowing brazier well stoked with coals. A family of Cæruleans sat around it, warming their hands. There was a mother, a father, and any number of offspring. The tallest of them did not come up to the top of the brazier. I could see how they squatted, upright, balancing on the strong shapely tails that came curling from the hole in the seat of their britches. Behind them there stood a screen, a striped blanket stretched between three poles like a desert windbreak. I knew behind that was where the natives would be, crouching in the sand.

"Whose is this place?" I asked.

"It belongs to a professional fraternity," said Signor Pontorbo rapidly, "of which I am a member."

"Are they all painters?" I asked. I don't know what I was

imagining. A brotherhood of landscape artists flying hither and thither among the worlds.

"You must rest now, Miss Clare," he instructed me. "It may not be an easy passage at this season, through the Shoals of Callisto."

A heavily built man in a peaked cap and an unfamiliar dark gray spacesuit came out on the deck of the *Gioconda*, coiling a rope on his forearm. He had thick black eyebrows and a thick black beard, and an expression as if nothing ever surprised him. I saw Signor Pontorbo make a swift sign to him with his fingers. So he knew the spacers' hand speech. What a very accomplished young man he was, I thought. Either that or a Freemason. I remembered on High Haven, my Papa fulminating against Freemasons. They were even worse than Methodists, if I remember right.

Signor Pontorbo introduced the man to me as Captain Andreas, and started to address him in a foreign language. I did not know if it was Sicilian or Greek or what it was, a kind of Martian even. I heard him say my name, but nothing else could I understand. By now the surprise and delight of the secret harbor had turned to mere confusion. I was tired, aching from my exertions, desperate to lie down.

I looked at the Cæruleans, and saw the father weaving briskly toward us, his head down, scurrying along on his powerful haunches. I do not know if you have ever seen a Cærulean. They are wiry and lithe, in shape like a cross between a squirrel and a monkey, though their face is very like that of a fox; and they are blue as the sunlit seas of Earth. This one seemed very excited and cheerful. He greeted us, yapping in a squeaky voice, bounding around me, and jumping up at Signor Pontorbo like a terrier.

Signor Pontorbo seemed embarrassed by this effusion. He told the little man, in a lordly way, to get down, and his hand tightened on my shoulder. He was steering me toward the boarding ladder that rested against the side of the gently swaying boat. Suddenly he stopped me. His grip was like iron.

I did not see what it was at first. I thought it was a bone, lying at the foot of the ladder. Then it moved, sidling swiftly away as though it sensed its danger, and I saw it was a white desert snake, no doubt drawn from a crack in the rock to the warmth of the fire. There is no harm in them, for they have neither fang nor sting—still Signor Pontorbo stepped back from me and I heard a soft whizzing sound as something flew through the air over my shoulder—and there was a long silver knife fixed most precisely in the planking, with the little beast writhing on its point. All this in an instant; then Signor Pontorbo had his hand on my shoulder again, and was urging me forward. "Miss Clare, *se volete*," he said. "Proceed."

The dying snake shuddered and thrashed. I stepped past it, onto the ladder. I had never felt more desolate in my life. Behind me, my defender stooped to retrieve his knife. It was an ordinary one. In a distant, uncaring way I thought: he had not used the lightning-knife, to spare my feelings. I wondered if his bid to look after me and my interests would lead him to slaughter the entire population of the solar system. I wondered if he might not be happier in the service of the Martian God.

Below decks the cruiser was smaller than the *Halcyon Dorothy* of Miss Halshaw and Captain Estranguaro, and neater too. Between decks was low, with dark wood partitions. I took no notice of anything except the stern cabin, with its well-made bunk.

"This will be yours, *signorina*," Signor Pontorbo told me.

The cabin was small, unfriendly, and bare: Spartan, you might call it. Certainly it could not have been more different from the luxury of Mr. Cox's cabin on the *Unco Stratagem*, with its stately furniture and velvet curtains; still I understood that it was his own cabin the Signor was giving me. Frankly I did not care one way or the other, and sank down on the bunk at once in sheer collapse. He tried to speak to me, offering me food or drink, but I told him to go away; and he did, bidding me as he went to "try to sleep," as though I needed his instruction to do that too.

For himself, Signor Pontorbo had the captain and crew make room for another hammock forward, where they slept. It did occur to me that he had fixed his berth as far away as he could get from me on that ship, unless he was to sleep in the crow's nest. But that was later. The moment he left me and closed the cabin door I curled up to sleep. In the depths of my exhaustion I could hear how overhead he, on the contrary, set himself most energetically to work, as if he had not already today ridden many dusty miles, fought off death from the air, and paddled a boat up a mountain.

I think I did sleep for a little while, and was woken by a piercing whistle. I lay and heard Captain Andreas calling harshly in his foreign tongue to the Cæruleans, who could shin up a mast and out along a spar as fast as any monkey, and hang from the shrouds by their tails. On their home world they live up among the treetops. After a cold night in the shadow of the foliage, they go pattering up the branches to balance at the very end, and stretch their little blue hands out to the rising sun.

We were bumping from side to side, starting to lift. I came properly awake and knelt up on the bunk. I looked out of my portholes and saw the natives had come out to launch us, running us out at the capstans. Men held the lines, jumping, swinging as the ship pulled them easily off their feet. I could see their mouths were open, they seemed to be giving the *heave-ho*, yet with only a horrible whining noise that they were making. Those halyard men could sing no chanteys. Every man jack of them was dumb, his tongue cut out by his masters.

While they disappeared rapidly from view, I could not bear to stay put. I looked in a space-chest and found a helmet and a lightweight suit that was not much too big for me. I put them on and went out through the air lock and stood on deck.

The *Gioconda* was going up without lights, flying silent and dark. The skirtsails were all run out, like fine gauze petticoats around the thick red canvas of the balloons swelling fore and aft, tightening as the pressure of air fell. We were already two thousand feet up, the desert like crumpled brown wrapping paper beneath our hull. I saw the Gah canal, like a shiny streak of green, and wondered where I had been. Where was Canyon de S. Charles, where S. Sébastien? The city of Ys I could see—it had seemed so distant and so huge from our desert solitude, and now, look—it was barely a handsbreadth across. There were the tiny zigzag streets, disappearing, there the narrow peak of the Black Well spire shrank to the size of a pin—and there, beneath us, came the clipper the *Roc of Madagascar* crossing out of the western night, silhouetted against the long threads of the canals like a jewel-tipped spider sliding across a web.

Now there was black sky all around and Mars started to come whole beneath us, round and red as some inexplicable

third balloon fifty times too big. Deimos was on the horizon,
rising into view. I gazed up beyond the mastheads and saw we
were climbing toward Phobos, keeping tight within its shadow. It hung overhead like a gigantic potato, blotting out the
sun. Through the violet helmet, space was indigo and faintly
ashimmer.

I saw the Blue Boys aloft in their miniature suits, scampering
among the crosstrees. Already the rigging glistened with a white
rime spray. They were lowering a spinnaker, casting a broad
net for the aether wind. Captain Andreas was at the winch. The
wheelhouse was empty. I could not see our commander anywhere. "Where is Signor Pontorbo, captain?" I asked, pressing
my helmet to his. He scowled at me with his fierce thick brows
and pushed me firmly but clumsily away, jerking his thumb in
an unhelpful signal. I could only suppose he meant below.

Inboard I could find no one until I tried the galley; and
there he was leaning over a white enamel basin, wiping his
face with a towel. The hank of his hair hung halfway down
his broad back. I opened my helmet to speak to him. "There's
no one on our tail yet, Signor!"

He looked so much like him from behind. He was wearing
Signor Pontorbo's Chinese coat with the pattern of swords,
and he had Signor Pontorbo's ring on his beautiful white
hand. But when he stood up straight and lowered the towel,
I saw the face of a man I didn't know.

17

Ancient history

"Who are you?" I cried. "What have you done with Signor
Pontorbo?"

The man's face was raw and red, grazed here and there with
blood. His forehead was high, his cheekbones too—his nose

small and rather snubbed—his cheeks were not so broad or full. My rescuer had vanished; and left only his eyes behind, in these dark, hollow, unfamiliar sockets. He had no eyebrows.

The man held the towel between his hands. "Miss Clare," he said. It was the voice of Signor Pontorbo, rapid, warm, and full of resolve.

He had been shaving. He had shaved his whole face, that was why it was so red and so bald. His eyebrows were gone. I clung to the doorjamb and wondered what magic razor could have carved beneath the skin and trimmed his bones into a different shape.

He looked at me with Signor Pontorbo's eyes and grimaced. He stepped aside, giving place to me. "*Mi vogliate perdonare*," he said; and he directed me to look into the basin.

With great misgivings, I looked. I know I shall never forget what I saw. The water was pale piss-yellow with little flecks and streaks of pink and white. In it, inside out, and all covered with frothy pink slime, floated the face of Signor Pontorbo.

My stomach heaved in a way that had nothing to do with the motion of the ship. I found myself backing toward the door, arms spread wide. The man made no move to stop me.

I screeched: "*What have you done to him?*"

"Nothing, *signorina*," said the man firmly. "I am he. It is me. Signor Pontorbo does not exist," he said. His was the expression of one who has just pulled off a conjuring trick to his own perfect satisfaction. "See, see," he said, holding out his hand. "My father's ring. It is I, *signorina*, truly!"

My heart was in my mouth. I was ready to flee. But where was there to go?

My voice quavered as I said: "Who *are* you, sir?"

"You must call me Bruno," he said. "Bruno. That is my own right true name. Believe me, Miss Clare, I beg you. Upon your mother's grave I swear. You must believe me now; for now and forever," he declared, in some relief, "I renounce all subterfuge."

I stared into the basin again. Signor Pontorbo's face hung there in the liquid like a dying jellyfish. It was cut in several places where his hand had slipped. On the raw edges and where the slime had come away the flesh of it was white as watered milk, with tiny clear veins running through. You could see the speckle where his hair had grown right through the thing.

"Is it a mask?"

"It is the finest kind," he said. "We take the faces of dead men and bring them back to life!"

He plunged his hand in the basin and took the face out by its forehead. He held it upright, the chin still under the water, folded against the bottom of the basin. "Who was he? Some dead soldier, some executed prisoner, some cutthroat's luckless victim. Under our craftsmen's hands, he lives again! Here, *signorina*, see?"

He turned the face over. Eyeless and gaping, Signor Pontorbo flopped into the foul water. "A slime mold," said the man who now called himself Bruno. "From Uranus. They spread it on the back." He made a movement of the hand, as though he was buttering a piece of toast, then touched his fingers to his cheek. "It feeds," he said apologetically, "*vogliate scusarmi, signorina*—on the perspirations."

Instantly I was goose pimples all over and my head began to spin. I could feel my nerves sparking like squibs. He, meanwhile, dropped the face back in the water with a little light splash. The pink slime seemed to grow even paler, and creep sluggishly together. "It will die now," he said, and he smiled ruefully. "Alas." He wiped some blood off his face and dried his fingers very precisely on the towel.

I was horrified. "You're proud of it!" I said.

He frowned, as if what I had said was not quite true. He indicated the basin again. "*Signorina*, there lies all my pride—my inheritance—my duty. I abhor it. I sacrifice it all, for you."

I couldn't stand any more. "I don't want your sacrifices!" I shouted. "You can't do anything without killing something, can you!" And with that I went barging away to the head, where I wrenched my helmet off and vomited until my insides hurt.

I felt better after that, though weak and shaky. I paused, my eyes closed, seeing whirling lights like Catherine wheels, and I hung there until I realized they were not going to go away. When I pulled myself upright and turned around, though, I saw my champion had followed me. He was leaning against the bulwark, his eyes wretched. His mouth was tight, the corners drawn down, as if he had bitten into something bitter. His own face was much more expressive than the mask had been.

"The man was dead already," he said, his voice like a whisper, and he held something out to me. "Here," he said. It was a dipper of water.

I opened it and swilled the sour taste from my mouth, and spat it away down the head in a great slow roiling plume. "Then you ought to have left him in peace, sir, and not robbed him of the last thing that was his!" I said. "Anyway, what about the thing from Uranus?"

"It feels nothing!" He seemed baffled that anyone should care. "It is a vegetable!" For a moment I was afraid he was going to go and fetch the face from the galley to prove it to me.

I wiped my mouth on the back of my hand, feeling a little stronger now and still angry. I gave him back the dipper. "And what are you, Signor Bruno, that you go around stealing other men's faces?"

"I am no one, *signorina*," he said, looking at me steadily. "No one that I was."

That told me nothing. "Just plain Bruno is it you call yourself now, sir? What kind of name is that?"

"I have had too many names," he said. "They would dishonor your lips. Bruno is enough of names for now." He looked at me in concern. "Are you hungry, *signorina*?"

I looked back at him suspiciously. I thought no man had ever consulted me in such a tone. Men had told me it was dinnertime, meaning I was to put food in front of them.

My head was aching, the way it would every time I set sail. "I could eat something," I said, and heard how grudging I sounded. I wanted to hate him. I did not want him to be kind to me.

"There is fresh bread, and fresh pelican eggs, and olives from Earth. Captain Andreas even found us some tomatoes somewhere, though they are the size of cherries. Will you come and eat, Miss Clare? All too soon we shall be reduced to poorer fare, *vogliate scusarmi*."

"All right," I said. "All right."

"Are you well now? Let me help you."

"No. You go first, please."

He led me back to the galley, where the air pump wheezed like a sighing cow. I saw that someone had already been and emptied the basin he had used, washed it out and dried it. It stood back behind the battens on the wall along with everything else. Most peculiar I felt, looking at it.

"What happened to Signor Pontorbo?" I said.

Bruno frowned at me. "I do not believe I know the gentleman," he said carefully, while he unfolded a seat for me. "Miss Clare. If you will."

When I sat down and buckled myself in, he hung a cloth in the air in a very particular way and began filling me a pan with strips of ham. His fingers moved deftly and precisely, slicing, trimming. Anything that threatened to escape the pan he caught in the cloth. As he looked down at his work the galley lamp shone down gold on his shaven skin. He was quite young, I realized suddenly. In fact he was not that much older than I. I thought how rich he must be, to have his own ship, and go where he would; and how I envied him when I thought that. I wondered if it was his wealth that made life so cheap to him, that he spent it so freely.

Or was he poor? His clothes were old—and the *Gioconda* was a bare little ship; no stained glass or pretty carvings here. Perhaps he had stolen her. Perhaps he was a thief, as well as a liar. Was that why he went about in disguise, like Robin Hood or a bandit in the *Arabian Nights?* I wished then I could see Signor Pontorbo again, only for a minute, only to see if I could truly not tell he was not real, that he had this other face underneath.

Bruno looked up and caught me looking at him. He smiled and held out the pan. "Eat this quickly, while we still have a little gravity."

Captain Andreas came in, nodding to his master, ignoring me. He was in haste, scooping up his own food and a tub of dried shoots for the Cæruleans, Mr. and Mrs. Caspar and their children. They rarely came below decks, preferring to live where they worked, out in the rigging. They have to be stopped from weaving nests for themselves among the futtock shrouds. Ours were friendly creatures, nonetheless, and would eat from your fingers, holding on to a bearing strap with one foot. They speak in a kind of yap or whine, but cannot learn another tongue.

Captain Andreas was Greek, and spoke no English, nor understood any he didn't have to. He had a heavy face with long ears and long cheeks pocked and striped from years under the fierce rays of high space. He was indifferent to the reemergence of his master from his mask; and as to my presence on his boat, to him it seemed no more than if Bruno had decided to bring a kitten aboard. I supposed he had carried many mysterious passengers, captives, runaways. He collected the food for himself and his crew and went back to the wheel.

Bruno was sucking a cup of hot water, flavored with a few berries. I was toying with my food, trying to make it all float at once inside the pan. I realized we had stopped talking when the captain came in, as though we were two members of a conspiracy.

I said, "Is there truly someone chasing us?" Or was that another lie, I meant.

Bruno took the spout from his mouth. "Miss Clare," he said, "you are quite safe with me."

I was, you may imagine, far from persuaded. "What about your lodge, sir, your temple, or whatever you call it—I mean your brotherhood?"

He stared at me. Whatever his name, whatever his face, still he had nothing to do but stare at me.

"The ones that own the dock," I reminded him. Perhaps they were imaginary too. "Where are they?"

His gaze left me for an instant, slipping to the table and back again. "On Deimos," he said.

"Deimos?" I said, pointing down through the hull with my eating tongs still in my hand. "Why don't we hide there?"

"Not there, Miss Clare," he said, with a crooked smile. "There least of all." He sounded amused now, but abashed. I thought he was the least comprehensible and most infuriating person I had ever met. I still think so, very often.

I thought about Io. I remembered the ships from Earth leaving the High Haven on the first leg of the Jupiter run: the *Donna Amanda*, with her crew of blackamoors; and the *Olympianus*, who had the broad face of the planet itself on her colors, crimson spot and all. "What then, will we catch some fast frigate?"

"The *Gioconda* is fast," her master assured me. "Captain Andreas is good. He worked for my father."

"All the way to Io in this?" I said. "Was that part true: we are going to Io?"

"To Io," he confirmed.

I had some more to eat. "What is it on Io, sir?" I said.

"Something you must read," he said.

Something to read, he had not told me that before. At once I pressed him. "What sort of thing?" I said. "Is it a letter?"

Yes: on consideration, he could admit it was a letter.

"Who to? Is it to me?"

But Bruno had conceded enough. "For what you don't know, be grateful," he advised. "Ah, ah, ah," he said, waving away my protests. "Do you not say, ignorance is bliss? Eat, and be blissful. Trust me," he said, smiling with all his teeth.

"Who is chasing us, sir, just tell me that," I said quickly. "It's Mr. Cox, isn't it?"

"You know Mr. Cox?" he said.

Perhaps I had said too much. I put food in my mouth and said no more. Let him know I could keep secrets too.

"I do not know who," he said, briskly. "It could be anyone. Only with me are you safe."

I doubted it. He was merely trying to make me biddable.

"I know you're not doing this for my sake," I told him. "You're doing it for her, aren't you, sir? For the girl I was supposed to be." I hardly needed to ask—the fact that he was not who he was supposed to be either was proof enough.

"You told me not to do anything for you," he said, draining his cup.

Well, he had me there. I swallowed a yawn, then yawned openly, there was no stifling it. I felt cross and tired. "*Why* don't you just tell me?" I complained. But I was only moaning. I had already agreed to it all, there was no point in going on and on.

Bruno thought so too. "Do not torment yourself," he said, "but only have patience."

I turned away from him. Through the porthole I watched Captain Andreas and the Caspars. Captain Andreas hemmed and clicked his tongue, and by waving his arms sent a line of little blue men chasing out along a side-stay. It should have been too much for those tiny creatures running that ship under full sail; I didn't know how they could manage.

I rubbed the glass with my finger, making it squeak. "I want to go to High Haven," I said.

"Miss Clare! There is no time!"

I faced him squarely. "I want to go there," I said. "You set great store by your Papa, Signor. I want to say good-bye to mine."

He lowered his eyelids. Now that the flush of its razing had died down, his new face suited him, I decided. I hoped it was real this time. I hoped there was not going to be another one underneath it. He was talking to me, saying "urgency," and "put into jeopardy," and "allowing me to be the best judge of your interests—"

"Who's chasing us?" I said, pointing out through the glass. "Nobody! We haven't seen another ship all day!"

Oh, how it went against the grain. I could see that, once he set his mind to something, he would never relax, never deviate until it was done. Having failed, as he put it, in his duty, this man Bruno was determined to keep everything else under control. There was nothing to discuss. He set his right hand flat on the table, fingers toward me. "We must keep to this route," he informed me, "or we shall start to attract attention!" He was good at making things sound fatal.

"It's on the route, sir," I told him.

He sighed, lifting his eyes to the deck above. He twisted his buckle, spread his hands on the tabletop and bounced lightly down off his stool to the floor. "Have you enough to eat there, *signorina*?" he asked, aggressively, bobbing as he nodded. "All right, heh?" Then he launched himself away toward the door.

"Signor—"

"I show you," he said, not looking at me. And off he went.

I sat and listened to the pump, and looked out at the deeps of night. Space was so black you could touch it: hard and smooth and solid as ebony. The stars were hard too, still and cold, like chips of diamond. Earth was there, declining on the weather bow: I was sure a glass would show a tiny blue crescent with the night between its horns.

Bruno came back in with a chart and a fat red book. "This book," he said, tapping it with a pencil. "This is your

Rossington's Tables, hm? This is the book the captain uses to
chart our course. All captains use it."

"I know," I said. I took the chart from him. Our position
was marked, but he pointed it out to me. Then he read out the
vectors and coordinates and I found them on the chart. He said
I must be wrong, but I showed him where I'd written them all
down as he said them. I traced them out with my finger, and
put a cross there with the pencil.

"How did you know that?" he said.

I shook my head. "I grew up there, sir," I said.

He shook his head too, as if this was not good enough.
Indeed I hadn't the least idea how I knew which quarter the
High Haven must be in, in all the sweeping paths of all the
worlds. I simply knew it, in my bones. The numbers were just
another way of saying it.

I still had not finished my meal, but I did not want to eat any
more. "My head hurts," I told him. "I want to lie down."

It was the first thing I'd said that coincided with Bruno's
wishes. He swept me back to my cabin and buckled me
into the blankets as if fearing I would rise up in my sleep
and drift away overboard. I slept; and dreamed of poor dead
Hercule, that he came floating to me again, and I tried to pull
him out of the water with my own hands. Though he was
dead, he was trying to speak to me, to tell me some urgent
piece of news: Hercule, who knew ten words, and most of
them foul.

I slept through five bells and six, and woke as we came
jolting into a high tide, every last bit of gravity fled, and
the *Gioconda* creaking in every joint. I thought I could hear
high and hoarse laughter forward, and a ghostly sound of
music. I pulled my head down into the blankets and slept
again.

When I woke, Bruno was at my side with a cup of coffee.
I smiled, thinking foggily of Gabrielle and her breakfast tit-
bits, and sucked at it hard before I knew what it was. It was
the first time I had had strong coffee, as the Italians drink
it. The richness of it swam in my head, and I started talking
at once, asking him a score of questions, none of which he
would answer. He seemed to repent of his earlier candor. He
was in a good humor, and insisted that day on making good
his promise, to get my picture.

I had to wash myself in precious water and sit in the saloon in my frock while he set himself to capture my likeness with his pencil. But I was restless. The coffee was making my teeth buzz. I was going to see Papa, and Kappi! I felt I could hardly wait. I couldn't bear to sit there, strapped into a chair, while there might be something I could do to spur the ship on faster, faster, to my childhood home.

"How are you getting on, sir?" I said. "Let me see." And I started getting out of my seat. He held the paper up, forestalling me. I knew I was no work of art, but still it looked nothing like me, no matter how he did stare. I told him it was very well, but he was not satisfied, so I had to keep sitting. The walls of the little ship were pressing in from all sides—they would collapse and squeeze the air out of the vessel, and the life out of me. I felt a great impatience to get outside, with the Caspars, among the stars.

"For pity's sake, sir," I begged, "let me do something useful. Let me not sit idle here."

"Perhaps . . ." he sighed, looking at his latest effort and shaking his head. " . . . the galley . . ."

I was ready for him there. "Why, yes, sir," I said cheerfully. "I can work in the galley, sir, and not spill anything, and not burn anything either. I'm sure it won't be any different from cooking for Brother Jude."

He looked uncertain. I had seen how fond he was of his food. He rubbed his chin.

I pressed on. "The cleaning, then, sir."

This he would not hear of. "You do not clean aboard my ship," he said grandly.

I smiled a bright smile. "Mrs. Caspar could teach me, sir," I said.

"You are not a servant, Miss Clare," he said.

How pleasant it was to hear that! Now I must try him. "There's plenty of work," I said.

"Where?" he demanded.

I pointed outside.

He laughed. Captain Andreas would never hear of it, he told me. "To Captain Andreas it is bad luck even to have a woman on board." What about Mrs. Caspar and the Caspar daughters, I wanted to know? But he waved me off in scorn. *Human* women, he meant.

So for the time I sat and endured more of the pains of artistic creation, his pains and mine; until the Haven came sliding up on the starboard beam.

He let me break out the signal for one of the little Caspars, permission to take on stores and fresh water. Nothing about me, of course. I thought Captain Andreas was glad of the unplanned stop. He joked with the Cærulean, who was capering excitedly about, the bunting flapping around him like cloaks of many colors.

High Haven lay beneath us like an island of brick and iron. We were coming in high over Hanover Way. Ten thousand panes of glass suddenly glinted in the moonlight! Then the rafts went shelving down away from us under the black lace of their canopies, and I began to see places I knew. "There's Toomey Street, sir, and the market! Look at all the little people!" Bruno and the captain exchanged glances, amused and as if embarrassed by my eagerness, but I was caught up in the geography of my childhood. There was St. George's; the Jericho Viaduct; the reservoir where Kipper Morgan had tried to steal a kiss. Ancient history it seemed already; and the place looked smaller somehow, like a replica of itself, a model village spinning in flight around the Earth.

The *Gioconda* banked, the Haven tilted, the lines went whirring through the blocks as the sails came in, and into the down stream we sailed. There were the docks, the Prince Edward lighthouse gleaming and a big ship in, towering over the hangars. I craned my neck to see the Eastern Dock—it was night here—were the lanterns lit in the watchman's tower? I cried, "Oh captain, please, lend me your glass!" But he shouldered me aside, I had gone too far, and also he was doing five things at once, of course, as Captains do.

My ears popping, I stepped ashore at a pier I didn't know. As a girl I had never been this far from home. The gantries of the unfamiliar dock rose all around me, echoing with the shouts of hawkers and handlers.

Bruno put his arm around my shoulder. I wanted him to take it away. "So, which way is your home, Miss Clare?"

"I don't know," I said. And indeed I didn't. I had come to know Lambeth better than I ever knew this place.

So we took a cab, and I told the driver: "St. Radigund's Wharf, please, next to the timber yard." And off we went, leaving the captain to look after the customs and the chandlers, and in no time we were crossing Half-Moon Street, and there among the passersby was a familiar small mushroom-colored figure, coming round the corner with his cart. "Kappi!" I shouted, and leapt down from the moving cab and ran to meet him.

"Miss Sophie!" he cooed, and he reached up with his big mitts and clasped me by the waist. Forgetting himself altogether in his surprise, he crushed himself to me, pressing his big knob of a head sideways into my midriff. I had forgotten the smell of him—like dusty wool—it was the smell of my childhood, reading fairy stories on the kitchen floor. His skin was hard, his eyes were moist, and he had gone mauve from top to toe, with deep blue blotches.

I was babbling, hugging him, patting him with my hands. "Oh, Kappi," I cried, almost sobbing in my joy. "I didn't mean to run away, truly I didn't! How are you, Kappi? How is Papa?"

My little Ophiq teacher—my first and only friend—you looked up at me then, and turned a drab mustard yellow with sadness. "To die is soon, Sophie . . ."

I almost screamed and tugged my hair. The cab was leaving, pulling away to reveal the young Sicilian gentleman standing there on the other side of the road in his Chinese coat and ponytail, watching this strange reunion with his head drawn back as if he was not at all sure what to make of it.

"To lose Sophie set fair to break the heart of Mr. Farthing," said Kappi, sorrowfully, as Bruno came across.

"Kappi, no, no, no!" I cried. It hurt me keenly. I could not understand why he would not raise his snout and tell me, no, Papa was perfectly well. I wanted him to fumble in his pouch and bring out a coin or a wilted flower for me, to dry my tears, as he always had.

Instead he said, "To die is general, on all worlds. To die is not to know pain more." And that was all his comfort.

I looked at my new guardian, who carried death in his pockets. He took my trembling hand between his firm, gloved ones, and he looked at me with a sad surmise; and then he turned to Kappi and whistled low, like a bird catcher. And Kappi turned pink with surprise and whistled in reply.

I looked from one to the other, at a loss. Bruno could speak

Ophiq! "What are you saying?" I asked them. I could not bear it, that they could speak and I not understand.

Bruno it was who answered me. "To die at last is best," he said, very lightly.

Then from out of his greatcoat he produced a handkerchief, and offered it to me with a small bow. I accepted it, glaring at him through my tears. Was there no end to his accomplishments?

While I composed myself Bruno stood and surveyed that little row of buildings on the edge of nothing. "Next to the timber yard," he said. "This," he said, pointing, as though I should not know my own house. "Have courage, Miss Clare."

"Miss Farthing," objected Kappi, puzzled.

I shook my head at him. "No more, Kappi," I said. "Never was," I said, though seeing Kappi flush lavender at my reproach tugged at my heartstrings and almost set me crying again.

I was being weak and feeble. Instead I went to the door and turned the handle that seemed to know the shape of my hand; and calling out, "Papa? Are you there, Papa?" I set foot again inside the shades of that dark house.

I sensed rather than saw Bruno recoil at the stink. It stank of neglect, and old tobacco, and sickness. Of course, Kappi, you had done what you could to help him keep it clean; but that house was grim, I think, in the very lath and plaster. Despair dwelt in the grain of the bare floorboards and the salvage furniture. All the curtains were closed and no lights burning. Then came Papa's voice, calling out from the kitchen, weak but imperious as ever. "Is that you, Kappi? Why do you keep taking the laudanum away? How many times have I told you to bring it here and leave it here . . ."

Mr. Jacob Farthing sat slumped and shrunken in his old chair pulled right up close to the stove. He was swaddled and wrapped about with blankets. On the table beside him was a candle in a candlestick, which needed snuffing. Ever and anon the flame would dip and leap up, and the light of it fluttered on his old cheek like light from some distant storm. His hair had gone quite white, white as snow on Lambeth Palace. His eyes were sunk in deep black pits and when I took his hand I felt that he was shivering, very little and low, like a tiny animal.

"Hello, Papa," I said. "It's Sophie, Papa." I could not feel any response in him, and I could not bear to hold that clammy, quivering hand; so I went down on my knees beside his chair and turned at once to the cat, who lay curled at the other side of the stove. He raised his head and scanned me warily and dimly. "Hello, Percy," I said, my courage starting to wilt. "It's me, Sophie." I gave him my hand to sniff.

"No," said Papa then. "Not Sophie." His voice was like a distant foghorn calling out across an empty sea. "Sophie's gone."

It clove me in two to find him so much worse, and to think myself the cause of it. I had abandoned him without warning or apology. I had been too selfish and too guilty to write. He was my father, in all but nature. He had brought me up, and I had spurned him. He was sick and infirm, and I had fled his side.

And then I thought, no; he himself had driven me from him, by clutching me to him, and demanding everything of me, and denying me everything but his own wisdom, which grated in me like a rusty saw. It was not I that had done him this damage. Ever since I could remember he had been killing himself, destroying himself with fantasies and tempers and suspicions and the black poppy juice.

I knelt there, stroking Percy, and wondering how I was to say what I had to. I was not to faint or falter, or let him take charge. I had wept already, and I should weep again; but I would not weep now. I must be Sindbad, facing the Old Man of the Sea. One wrong step and he would be upon me again, clinging; though from the look of him I did not think he would be clinging to anyone for much longer.

I began to weaken. These were surely his last days. Who would nurse him if not me? Who knew better how to? Who had nursed me, when I was young and helpless?

"I didn't mean to go," I said.

What a wretched, bad beginning that was!

He said nothing.

I said, "How are you feeling, Papa?"

"Nothing wrong with me," he said. His eyes were focused on empty air, his jaw twitching as though it was chewing something. I wanted to catch his eye, to make him listen, make him pay me some attention for once.

"This is Signor Pontorbo, Papa. He's an artist."

"How do you do, sir," said Bruno, most respectfully.

We might as well have been talking to the wall. Beneath the slack flesh Papa's jaw clenched and clenched again.

"An artist, Mr. Farthing!" chirped Kappi, animatedly.

"No remedy—sir," said Papa, as though Kappi had said "a doctor." "No remedy—for death; and none—for time, nor any for—ingratitude!" His eyes snapped onto mine, glaring like coach lamps. "Who are you, miss? I think I know your face . . ."

"Don't play with me, Papa, I'm not a child!"

Kappi pushed between us, protecting him from me. "Not to mean it," he tooted querulously. "Not to understand you, Miss Sophie, is the reason."

But I thought Jacob Farthing understood well enough.

"I've been to London," I said. "I saw the house where my mother used to live."

"Estelle," moaned Papa, and clutched his arm beneath the blankets.

"No," I said. "No. Molly, her name was. Molly Clare. You remember, Papa," I said. "She came from St. Paul's. Red hair," I said, touching a black tress of my own.

He was shaking his head, his eyes wide with fear. "Demon, begone!" he croaked. "Begone, phantom! Begone, ingratitude!"

I stood up then, and took a step back. "I'll be gone indeed, sir, and that soon enough."

He grew agitated, rocking backward and forward in his chair until its feet started to skip off the floor. "You are not real!" he assured me. "You are a dream! I have—no—daughter!"

"You speak the truth!" I said, but there was no talking to him. He was coughing and wheezing and demanding medicine; and Kappi was there with the bottle and glass, pouring the dose awkwardly with his paws. "Let me," I said; but when I touched the bottle the old man started to cry, "Poison! Poison!" and for two pins I would have thrown it at him.

"To go outside and walk!" pleaded Kappi, rippling violet.

I looked at Bruno. He was already halfway out of the room. "We'll go outside," I told Papa. "We won't go far." He was spluttering, trying to talk and drink at the same time. "We'll

only be here outside," I told Kappi. Then Bruno came and
pulled my arm, and got me out of there at last.

The moment the front door closed I burst into tears. Bruno
put his arms around me and held me firmly. I leaned on his
shoulder and howled. He pestered me with his handkerchief
until he realized I was going to keep on crying, and then he
gave me his permission, indeed encouraged me to cry; but I
took no notice of any of it but the warmth of his chest and
his arms that held me.

As I began to grow calm I heard Papa indoors shouting
angrily again. "Come," said Bruno then, and led me away
down the wharf to where the men were unloading barges,
calling out jokes and insults to one another as they swung
the sacks. I recognized them. I recognized them all, but I did
not know any of their names.

We stopped by the signal mast. I found a fig in my pocket
and offered half to Bruno. He didn't want it, and neither did
I. I ate it anyway.

"Were you planning to stay, *signorina*?" Bruno asked, his
voice low. "What you call, second thoughts?"

I shook my head. I didn't know what I'd been planning. I
was too tired and shocked and miserable to make any sense
of it all. "Now I want to go," I said. "Run away and leave
him to get on with it." I looked back to the front door with
dread. I would not look at the window next door, where
the clerk would be sure to be watching. "I hate this place,"
I said.

Bruno patted my hand, resignedly. "*Dunque*, take your time,"
he said. "I wait here."

"No!" I said. "I need you!"

He looked at me then with a curious, lopsided smile, as
though I were a child and had said something wonderful in
very innocence. "It's good," he declared, warmly, and seeing
me gather my resolve, suggested we go back inside.

I told him to go and knock first and ask Kappi how Papa
was. He started to go. "Bruno?" I called. He turned. I said,
"Where did you learn to speak Ophiq?" He smiled broadly,
but said nothing.

I watched him walk away, the tail of his coat riding gently
up out of the road. The street I knew best in all the worlds
seemed mysterious now, with him there; as though he was

something that had not been thought of before, some alien creature it had not made allowance for. His broad back and long coat blocked the narrow door of the cottage. When it opened I couldn't even see Kappi.

There was a moment of low whistling. Then my ambassador turned and nodded, beckoning me. I went.

Papa was quieter, and there was some color back in his face. Kappi was struggling to stoke the stove, and Bruno went to help him.

"Papa," I said.

"The pain, Sophie . . ." he said pitiably. "Such indescribable pain . . ."

"Yes, Papa," I said. I stooped to him, but did not kneel down. "I have to go away, Papa. I've come to say good-bye. I'm going to Jupiter, with Signor Pontorbo."

Papa grasped my sleeve, pulling himself up a little in the chair and staring glassily at Bruno. He obviously had no memory of seeing him a few minutes before. "Who is this, Sophie? Is this the man, your gadabout with the iron chin?"

"No, Papa, this is Signor Pontorbo," I said, but he ignored me.

"I know you, sir!" he said, his voice slow and dreamy. He drew his hand from under the blankets and pointed a wavering finger at Bruno. "You are the dandy with the barley-sugar boat. You are the scoundrel who carried her off . . ."

"No, Papa," I said. "Papa, *listen.*"

He gazed up at me, his eyelids sliding down, and gave a silly high-pitched laugh. "Jupiter!" he said to me. "There's nothing on Jupiter but battlefields and rain that burns your skin off. What are you going to Jupiter for?"

"The truth," I said. I didn't look at Bruno. I didn't want to let Papa understand how foolish I was, that Bruno was a man no different from him, who refused to tell me anything; yet I was following him to another world.

"Truth!" said Papa, echoing me again, and giving a big shudder. "No escaping that, child, morning, noon, or night!" And he rubbed his eyes, and clawed slowly at the air before him, as though he was trying to sweep away a cobweb that had fallen in his face.

I put my hand on his shoulder. "I'm not your daughter, I know I'm not," I said quickly. "So you won't have to worry

about me, will you? I've got a new name now," I said, "after
my mother. I'm Miss Sophrona Clare. All right?"

He was murmuring. I had to lean closer to hear him properly.
The candle flame danced in the pits of his eyes. "Her name was
Farthing," I heard him say. "Molly Clare Farthing." I shook
my head, and drew away, weary of his worn-out lies. I was
ashamed that Bruno should have to hear them. I wondered if
perhaps in his poppy-stewed confusion he had come to believe
them himself. " . . . mother's sister's name," he mumbled.

"Hush now, Papa," I said. "You go to sleep and don't worry about it. I'll talk to you again when you wake up."

In all honesty, Dear Reader, I don't know if I truly meant
it when I promised it, but he did fall asleep then, trying to
form another sentence even as his jaw hit his breastbone. I
tucked him up and pulled up a stool and sat on beside him
as I had always used to. I looked into Bruno's eyes, knowing
we could afford one delay, one watch for Papa, since it was
the last I would give him.

Bruno besought me to lie down. "Let me watch him,"
he said.

"No," I said, "you go back on board. I'll make something
to eat later. What time is it anyway?"

"Are you hungry? I shall make a meal."

"I'm not hungry," I said. "Go on."

He would not. He sat at the table. "I'll watch the fire," he
said, pointing at it. He was as tired as I.

"Go upstairs and lie down," I told him. "You can have my
bed if you want it. Upstairs on the left."

He gestured. "It is your bed," he said stubbornly. We glared
at each other, both of us determined not to sleep. "It is the
middle of the night!" he said, trying to sound solicitous but
failing.

"It's always the middle of the night here," I said. "Please,
Bruno."

He grimaced, giving in with great reluctance; and upstairs
he went, making a gallant exit of it, leaving me with Kappi.

Kappi asked me to say where I had been, and how I had
come home; so I started to tell him my adventures, that I had
come from Mars, where I had lived with the angels, but I got
that muddled up with the convent, and before that there was
the Black Well with its hungry god—but my little friend was

most uneasy with this tangled tale. He kept interrupting and looking out of the door. He did not seem to understand me very well. Then he told me he had to go to work. "Lamps to light!" He looked relieved to be on the point of departure, but he was an Ophiq, and had to think of something encouraging to say; so what he said was: "To write everything down is a good commemoration."

I tell you now, Kappi, if I had known what labor you were putting me to, I swear I'd never have started.

So I sat there then while Papa snored and muttered, and I thought about it, that I could write it all out in a story one day, this homecoming of mine; and I thought of all the people who would have to be in it, Miss Halshaw and the clerk at the Registry, and the Rodneys, and all the folk at the Hope and Anchor; and thus I fell to thinking of Mrs. Rose, and then of Mama; and I thought Papa had married her after all, but cast her down from the Haven with his own hand to tumble into the gutters of St. Paul's, because he preferred the beautiful Miss Crosby. I thought I could see them, Estelle and Papa, dancing at their wedding, while Betty Pride and Mr. Cox and all the crew of the *Unco Stratagem* rejoiced and threw rice. The rice turned into little colored fish in the air. "No, Betty," I was shouting. "Not her! She never married!" And I tried to pull Betty away, but my hands were like mist, and she turned into Gertie and laughed at me.

Later I came to and found Papa speaking to me. "Sophie," he kept saying, weakly but quite clearly, "you're going to Jupiter to find the crown, aren't you?"

I lit a candle, and asked what crown.

"The Beuritz Crown," he said. "The one that started the Jovian War. You remember, Maximilian von Beuritz gave it to his native bride. She was wearing it when they c-carried her ashore."

I helped him sit up. His forehead was burning, but his hands were icy cold. He talked to me while I stirred up the stove. "We all s-saw her. She opened the curtains of her p-palanquin and called out for water. Roger McMurdry rushed to take her some, in a plain china cup!" He chuckled at the memory. "Three months after," he said, "the crown was lost, the Gräfin was dead, and the whole of the Erevnine basin overrun with Hrad. Were you not there?"

"Count Beuritz died before you were born," I told him. "Would you like some soup?"

He looked cunning. "Ah, you're going to poison me . . ."

"You poison yourself, you stupid old thing," I said.

He laughed, as if it were a good joke. "Your young man," he said.

I pursed my lips. "He's not my *young man*," I said. I went and got some more candles and lit a couple.

"Where is he taking you this time?"

"Jupiter," I said. "To Io, actually." Inside I cursed and stamped my foot because I had not meant to tell him that part.

"What for?"

I filled a kettle and put it on the stove. "To read a letter, he says."

"There's no need," said Papa. "It is here. I have it. Kappi," he said, raising his voice to summon his little drudge, "it's in the tin box, behind the clock, you'll need something to stand on—"

"Kappi went off hours ago," I told him. "What about it: will you have some soup or no?"

He stared at me. "You don't believe me!" he said. "I kept the letter. I always kept it!"

"Yes, Papa," I said. "I'll look after I've made the soup."

Then he started whining on about "ingratitude" again, and saying I had no faith in him, which indeed I did, faith that he would continue to make everything as difficult as possible for everyone else, right up until the last moment. I went to the stairs and called Bruno.

He arrived in haste. I could see he had been to sleep despite his intentions. "Young gentleman!" cried Papa as soon as he came in. "Young gentleman! I have the letter!"

"What is he saying?" Bruno asked. "Is he all right?"

"Here, Papa," I said, "here's Signor Pontorbo," and I realized I had been calling him Bruno, as if it made any difference in this madhouse. "Signor Pontorbo will look for your letter while I make us all a nice bowl of soup."

"Box," said Papa impatiently. "In the box! You all think you can get around me, *I* know where it is . . ."

I opened the food cupboard, to see what there was I could cook. A carton of Colman's mustard powder and a couple of potatoes, sprouting gamely. "Behind the clock," I told Bruno. "He says he hid a box there." I couldn't remember if there was really anything there or not. I suppose I hadn't ever looked.

"Running off to Jupiter . . ." Papa was saying, disparagingly.

"Here is the box," said Bruno. He brought it out. It was a flat black tin box, like a cigarette tin. I didn't remember it.

"Well, then, open it up, open it up," Papa badgered him, leaning out of his chair at an alarming angle.

"Is there a letter in there?" I asked, trying the other cupboard.

"It's, *alora*, a kind of note," said Bruno, while Papa cried: "There you are! There you are, you see? My eyes are gone, but not my wits . . ."

"Let me see," I said to Bruno.

It was a sheet of flimsy paper, torn from a jotter like a shopman's pad. I have it still, it is before me as I write. It is written in pencil in an unsteady schoolbook hand. Some of the writing is quite faint.

"Doesn't it say there," Papa appealed to Bruno, "about her?" pointing to me as though I was cargo on a bill of lading.

The note says: " 'Mrs. Clare begs you will keep Baby & Give her a Home & not tell the Arthoritys. God Bless you for a kind and Christian soul and Do Your Duty. Her Name is Sophrona.' " I read it aloud to them, thinking of Mrs. Rose and her matchbox for rescuing spiders. Tears pricked my eyes. "Was this in the basket?" I said.

"I told you," he said triumphantly, though that was exactly what he never had done.

"And the ring too?" I asked.

He scowled. "I should have sold it," he said. "I always said I should. You were crying, and I brought you indoors and gave you a spoonful of my broth, and you—you ate it! I kept thinking who to give you to, but there—" He groaned. "—there was only the church, and the market women—and the port women, no better than your mother . . ."

"What did you mean about Mama?" I said sharply. "About her name?"

"Clare, she was," he said. "Her middle name. They named her after Mama's sister . . ."

I clung to the table as though I thought the gravity was going. "Your sister! She was your sister!"

"No, no, Sophie, you never listen!" he cried weakly. "After our *mother's* sister, I tell you . . ."

But I had my answer.

Bruno too seemed satisfied. He looked at me as if he was vindicated already. I sat down at the table, and Percy came and sat at my feet, and little by little the story came out of Papa, wandering hither and thither on feet so light the merest thought could carry them astray.

They were born in London, to a tailor in Whitechapel, he and a sister: Molly Clare. He came up to seek his fortune, as young lads always will. When the Venus Fever scoured the city and took their parents off, young Jacob went home and found Molly already taking in gentleman callers. "How else am I to pay the rent?" she demanded; but he was so ashamed of her, and of himself, of his poor position, that he fled back to the Haven, vowing never to leave again, and to put her and her fate forever out of mind. And thus, I supposed, he had rid himself of the entire human race.

I looked at the soft old piece of paper in my fingers. What a horrible shock I must have been to him: a curse; a mockery. "Did you never write to her?" I said.

He glowered and showed me his fist. "A plague on her and all her gentlemen!" he shouted.

But I knew him, and his old pride. What he meant was, he would have had to get Kappi to do the writing; and no one was to know he had come up from London and deserted a sister there.

His face tightened with pain. There was something else he had to say, though it racked him. "I suppose you saw her, Sophie, didn't you," he said, slowly, "in London?"

I said, "No, no, Uncle Jacob, I never did"—thinking this was his memory wandering again—and then in a moment I understood that in the prison of his fearful isolation he had never even heard she was dead. "No," I said, watching the black poppy sleep come once again over his fevered eyes. I whispered: "No, Papa."

I thought then that I had not meant to forgive him, and yet I found I already had, in the only place he was left to forgive, which was in my heart. He never opened his eyes again, and his mouth only to breathe, which he continued to do until a small space after midnight, when he ceased forever.

Sometimes I believe he had been keeping himself only to tell me that, the last story he had for me.

18

Disaster strikes the Gioconda

No one came to the funeral but Kappi and the old women who mend the sails, who make the harbor-side deaths their business. Bruno insisted on laying out Papa with his own hands. I was numb, and most grateful to him. I was glad he seemed to know what to do with a dead body.

We gathered out at the St. George pierhead. The women sang some sort of moaning hymn. I remembered the Emperor of Mars, and kept silent, and wondered why I felt not at all like weeping but rather dry and shrunken. Bruno stood close by me. He tried to take my hand, but I would not let him.

With the stars bristling over our heads and beneath our feet we stood and watched while, sewn in his shroud of worn blanket, Papa was shipped out beyond all the roads of the living and launched on his long slow journey to the Sun. The savants say we all came from the Sun originally, the seeds of life flung outwards by an arm of fire. Thus we return, when we have withered, to be burned to ashes; and our ashes consumed, as everything will be in the end, I suppose, by the appetite of God.

I wished we could have carried Papa with us, but Bruno did not offer and the *Gioconda* was not my boat. From the bridge I watched as we left the High Haven, and said a silent good-bye forever to the yards and alleys of my youth. They looked as usual, dark and narrow and choked, and they folded themselves up behind the eaves and shrank beneath the piers of the town. I was sure I could see Kappi all the while, a lone brown sentry guarding the harbor with his broom.

I slept a long time, then woke feeling exhausted and sad. Outside the stars hung white and cold and glaring. I managed to get dressed, then ran out of life and hooked myself on the edge of the bunk, where I sat staring at the mat on the floor. It was stained. The edges were frayed where it was tacked. It was a color that might once have been light blue, but had long ago faded and grayed to nothing at all.

There was a knock on the cabin door. It was Bruno. He was wearing a tight suit of some shiny black stuff, with a little partlet ruff and leather gloves. He smelt of violets and cloves.

"Ah, you are up; I am glad. Did you sleep well, *signorina*?"

Dully I said yes.

"I come to see you if you are ready for breakfast."

Dully I said yes again. I suppose I looked so forlorn he was emboldened to come in and perch beside me on the bunk. He did not know what to do with his hands. He clasped them together in front of his chest. He said, "How do you feel now, *signorina*?"

"Horrible," I said.

He took my hand then, with a little murmur of pity. I felt soft and floppy, as if all my bones had turned to marzipan, and I let myself drift against him, sideways, my cheek against his shoulder. His arm slid gently around me.

I would not accept his comfort. I opened my hook and flew to the far end of the cabin, where there was a rope stretched from the deck hatch. I snagged it with my foot and turned around to face my visitor, holding the rope with my legs crossed.

He said: "That's a sailor's trick. Where did you learn to do that?"

My hair floated out around my head like black feelers. "On the *Unco Stratagem*," I said.

I had counted on his not knowing that—I had hoped he might be shocked to hear it—oh, and Dear Reader, he was. He hid it well; but in his very stillness I could feel that one strike home. Then he spoke in a voice like the Martian wind. "And what were you doing on the *Unco Stratagem*?"

It was my turn to smile enigmatically and not answer. Instead I said, point-blank: "Who am I, sir?"

Still he shook his head, and taking the long tail of his hair in his fingers he stroked it. "I don't know," he said. "I don't know, I don't say." He gave me a peculiar smile, a smile with pain in it. "*Alora*, I did not think there was anything I did not dare, uh? But I dare not hurt you. Come back, Miss Clare. Sophie. Sit down here."

I ignored his invitation. "Will you tell me who you are, then, sir?" I said.

He laughed a short barking laugh, exasperated. "For one thousand times, I beg you, ask me no more questions! Miss Clare—"

I interrupted. "Miss Farthing," I said. "My mother's name." And I gave him such a frown he frowned too and looked away.

"Well, then, sir," I said, "let me tell you what I know about you. You're a painter, you say. You sail from place to place, painting what you find. You are a member of a secret society with its headquarters on Deimos—" In my mind's eye I saw it, like S. Sébastien, but centuries old: a towering citadel where monks in habits of black leather cut up bodies and painted pictures of what they found inside them. "—and you're very rich," I said, rushing on, "with your own cruiser and crew. Everything you have is from your father; and *he* dealt with worlds far beyond the ones we know."

"Why do you say that?" he asked, suspiciously.

"Your magic knife," I said. "That is no human thing. Not all the engineers of Scotland could make such a knife." Overhead, on deck, we could hear the familiar sound of little feet scampering. "And your wonderful crew," I went on. "Captain Andreas did not train them."

He looked displeased. He did not like having anyone else's fingers rummaging through the coffers of his inheritance. He began to make excuses. "The knife belongs to our patron," he said. "This is our patron's ship," he added, as if he cared nothing for it. "A vessel of his guild."

I frowned again, beginning to lose my way among the official details. "Somebody has paid you to do this?" I said. "To kidnap me?"

He looked directly into my eyes, saying nothing, giving his head a little shake.

"Who?" I said. "Who is it?"

His chin came up. "I had a patron," he said. "I was proud to serve him." He made a neat sideways motion of his hand. "No more."

I puzzled at it. "You mean, you had a commission to go to Mars," I said.

He gave me the most woeful smile I had ever seen. I hardly knew what to make of it.

I tried again. "You mean, it was Signor Pontorbo who had the patron," I said.

Too late I realized I had given the man a sidetrack, and he was off down it like a hound after a hare. "*Signorina*," he said grandly, "there was no Signor Pontorbo." He offered me a suave smile. "Signor Pontorbo was an illusion: a part, yes, that I played? You wish to know who I am? I am no one. I am every man. A sea captain? A scholar? A spy? Well, I am he. You must think of me," he said, "as an actor"; and I know you will not believe me but I swear: he spread his hand upon his chest.

I had to laugh; but it only encouraged him. "An actor is all men," he told me, "just as all men are actors, and all women actresses. Does not your William Shakespeare say, They have their exits and their entrances?"

I hadn't the least idea what William Shakespeare said. My feet were aching from holding on to the rope, but I was damned if I was going to give up now. "You said you were a painter," I objected. "Are you an actor, now?"

"The most promising in the galaxy," he said, and I saw a gleam in his eye. He was teasing me. He wanted to make me laugh again. You could see he was not really so very eager to renounce his glory.

I spread my arms and lay back on the wall. I said, "Indeed you were very good, sir, as Signor Pontorbo. I never would have guessed."

"It is the greatest play in the galaxy," he said. "The only play; the oldest play. Since the dawn of creation it has been running. The audience never tires of it," he said. "Well, no more. I bow out," he said. Yet he clenched his fist, making a flourish with his ring, and his pride simmered in him. He was longing to tell me; bursting to.

"You know, sir, it is as you say: I am a bit of an actor myself, sir, in my own small way," I said. I saw him start to shake his head again and open his mouth, to assure me of his own superiority, I'll be bound. So I quickly said, "I played the part of Ben Rodney, a cabin boy, on the good ship *Unco Stratagem.* At close quarters, watch on, watch off, from Earth to Mars, the long way round. No one there guessed *me*, either. Except," I had to admit, "Mr. Cox."

This did rather take the wind out of Bruno's sails. He raised his eyebrows and pursed his lips, just as if he meant to whistle himself up some more. Instead, he said: "What did he do?"

"He gave me to the priests, to be eaten by the Black God."

Bruno looked startled; then dismayed; then disgusted. "Mr. Cox did that?"

I nodded.

He mused, seeming bewildered. "How crude. Grotesque! And to leave so much to chance! I would not have thought it of him, he is so fastidious. I thank Heaven he did not succeed," he added, soberly. He held out his hand to me, inviting me once more to sit.

"He was in a hurry," I said, taking no notice of the hand. "He seemed to be frightened of something. I suppose he's a member of your brotherhood too," I said.

"Indeed no," he replied pointedly. "He is merely an officer of the guild. But how did you come to sail on the *Unco Stratagem*?"

I shrugged, bouncing lightly as I changed my grip on the rope. I had said enough, it was his turn now. "I was destined," I said, thinking of the Muhammadans, thinking it was the sort of word he would like.

"You were running away from your papa," he said.

"Looking for my mother," I said.

Bruno grimaced, rubbing his hands and muttering something in Italian. He raised the faint brown shoots of his returning eyebrows. "Let us hope we are not chasing the wild goose."

"Let us," I said. I did not like the sound of that.

"*Vedete*," he said, spreading his hands, palms upward. "Miss Farthing: you were in disguise, no? It may be that Mr. Cox took you for a member of the order, with a commission naming our master. The letter may be about some other child. But no, no, it is not possible," he decided, staring at my face and drawing one knuckle down his cheek. "There is no mistake."

Letter about a child, I thought to myself; but out loud I said: "A member of the order, sir? You mean, the order on Deimos," said I, hoping I had the right one.

My renegade looked a little pained. "She goes back long before Deimos," he said. "She is an ancient and subtle craft," he said. "She was the first of the crafts of Man."

I guessed. "Cooking," I said.

"Ah." He shook his head, smiling. "Yes, we will eat, in a moment," he promised. I said nothing.

He mimed throwing a spear. "Before the cook, the hunter," he said.

I smiled too, not kindly. "Butcher, you mean," I said.

He brushed that aside. "Ours is the oldest profession. *Alora*, the prostitutes, you know, they claim that—but we were first."

I objected strongly to that. "My mother was a prostitute!" I said.

"Ah," he said again. "It is as I feared."

"What's wrong with it?" I demanded.

"Ask your mother," he said.

My mouth tasted as if I had been sucking a stone. "Mr. Cox knew me," I said rudely, and made my face hard. "He knew me and he knew my mother. I think he knew her very well, sir." My heart was racing in my bosom. I felt as if any instant I might burst out into peals of laughter, or start to scream.

I swam back over to my bed and came to rest on it at an unsociable angle. I perched at the head and drew my feet up, as far from Bruno as I could. I stared at him blackly over my knees.

Bruno would not talk about Mr. Cox.

"The order itself was founded only in the eleventh century," he said, calmly, from the other end of my bed, "by Hassan i Sabbah."

I stared, hating him. He was no better than Papa.

"You have heard of the Old Man of the Mountains?" he said. "No? Hassan i Sabbah enclosed a valley," he declared, "and set a fortress at the entrance strong enough to resist all the world. Within, he had a garden made, and he called the name of it, Paradise. From there he sent out his young men, saying, Go, and let there be no more news of such a one; and fear not, for if thou shalt die, I shall have thee restored to Paradise. So said the traveler Marco Polo.

"We do not court fame," he went on, with mild dignity. "Obscurity is our watchword. You above all, Miss Farthing, who have been so brutally handled, you who have been thrust into the teeth of the Creature of Ys—you above all might approve our methods. The ideal subject feels no pain, merely—" He snapped his fingers, his full sleeve flopping lightly up and down about his wrist. "He does not know we are there. He would die in any case. A butcher is—" He made a slow, dreamlike mime of a violent action of the arm. "—some bully with a club," he said, in disgust, and he gestured to me with his open hand as though the club were really in it. Then he closed his hand; the invisible club vanished. "We make all neat," he said, complacently. "Professional."

Then his face went dull. He gestured to his mouth. "But listen to me. I defend the Ancient and Circumspect Order who have disgraced and forsaken it. I have broken my oath, and will never go again to that garden. My bloody days are done, and I shall kill no more."

He might be done, but I wasn't. "How many people have you butchered?" I asked.

His mouth twitched with irritation. He said: "Including the angel?"

"Including everybody!" I said.

"Fifty," he hazarded.

"Fifty?" I cried.

"*Naturalmente*, if you are wishing to include servants, bodyguards, policemen—" he said, waving his hands to indicate the great abundance of people not worth the numbering. "Maybe fifty. Maybe more . . ."

"Liar," I said. I had had enough of him. He sickened me to the heart.

I saw he was turning red. The nicks and scars of his razing stood out clear all over his face. Quite crimson he grew, and began to smile a very peculiar smile. Then he reached up the bunk and took me by the arm.

I was sure I had made him angry. And I remembered what he had said about never hurting me. I knew it had been only words, fine words, he was good at them.

I felt myself harden to him completely then, like a rock. I wanted to smash his boat and sink him. I wanted to hurt him. I could not imagine why I had ever liked him.

But he was not angry. He was embarrassed. Surprised, and embarrassed.

"You are right," he said. He shook his head, chagrined. "These old habits. Miss Farthing, I apologize," he said, and he kissed my hand. I let it lie in his clasp, limp as a dead eel. With my limp arm, I tried to tell him how much I loathed him.

"It was only thirty-nine," he said. He searched my face with eyes of wonder. "But how did you know? *O cieli magnanimi!* How did you know I lied? In my life," he said with an awkward laugh, "no one has ever been able to tell this before."

I pulled my hand away at that. "Shame on you!" I cried.

But Bruno became impatient. "It has been my work, my vocation. I say again, *signorina*: I have been a great actor. Those who have seen me have seen not me, but so: they have seen a gambler, a choirboy, a page to a rich widow. Others never knew I was there at all!

"All, all people wish for lies. Lies, we like best. We all think we are immortal, no? So, I have honored that fine illusion. I preserved their innocence. They did not know," he said, with enormous emphasis.

"Only die," I said.

He nodded his big head, snorting like a colt that has run a hard race. "Only die," he echoed.

"And you don't think that's a shame?"

He begged for mercy. "*Signorina*, at the very least, consider any soldier. Why, they *butcher* men by the dozen."

"Shame on them too!"

"Miss Farthing, enough! I am the worst and most loathly poison insect that ever flew, not worthy to be smeared beneath your feet, but please, Miss Farthing, I beg you—tell me how you knew I lied."

"I saw it in your face," I said.

The great actor went as pale as a parsnip. He pinched his cheek, looking foolish. "My face!" he said. "I forget you can see my face."

Abashed, he swam up and gathered me from the bed, muttering, "But come, come, you must eat." I thought, he thinks he can get out of anything by feeding me. But I was hungry, and tired of arguing. I let him lead me away and feed me on soup and a sort of frumenty. In the galley I caught sight of the empty basin on the wall, and I looked away. If I thought of his sloughed face again, I would want to skewer him with one of his own knives.

He saw me look, and look away. I swear he saw every breath I took. All the while he was preparing the meal, and all the while we were eating it, still his brown eyes bathed me with their regard. I confess I began to play with him, knowing he watched every detail—I might eat sliced sausage with gusto—the instant he was about to reach out to serve me more I would spurn it; and look longingly at my cup. Would Miss Farthing care for some wine? I sat sullen, as if displeased: no, Signor, I would not. Come, just a little, perhaps? It would bring the warm sun of Napoli into my sorrowing heart. But no, I would not hear of it. But see: the wine was as beautiful and dark and strong as the *signorina*'s eyes. Startled, I raised those eyes to him, and looked back at once at my pan. "Go on, then," I mumbled, and squirmed crossly in my place. I had been on the point of giving him a smile.

He made himself absurd—as if I could not do a thing for myself, but he must do it for me and I must thank him and be touched. He deplored the bully with the club; but did he indeed not bludgeon me, with his flattery—his airs and graces—his stupidity when I questioned him—but ah, no; stupid he was not. He was quick, and sharp, and clever. I it was that was stupid. I had drunk too much of his attention, and now I was giddy with it. When he was occupied I must fish for him; but when I caught him, and he was easy to catch—oh, he was at once too much. Then I despised myself for an idiot, and drove myself into a sulk. I was like a stubborn icicle, a broken stalk of winter. My papa was newly dead, and I was an ignorant little girl.

The great actor who was also a great painter began to woo me to stay below, to let him finish his picture; but I set my mind that he should not have his way in anything. At once I recalled the great triumphs of my apprenticeship on the deck of the *Stratagem*, and spoke knowledgeably of runners and splices—I tied a Flemish eye without looking at my hands—in short, I pestered him until he ran out of ways to tell me nay. Then Bruno and a grumpy Captain Andreas began to teach me the ropes, and the Caspars helped; though a slow and butterfingered hand was the best they could make of me, when it came to it. The work was hard! In truth I was no better placed out there, in the midst of the frozen storm of stars, than I was inboard. I had no knack for riding around with a bellows between my knees, tugging at cloth that had no weight. How many times did I see Captain Andreas grab his beard and shake his fist, cursing me inaudibly through the glass? How many times was I thrown against the hull by a sudden and invisible wave? I was a mass of bruises by the time we crossed the orbit of Mars.

My final disgrace came when Captain Andreas signed me aloft, bearing a precious tool, and I let it go and lost it overboard. Even the Blue Boys weren't quick enough to catch it. We hung there and watched it tumbling swiftly away, its steel head winking in the starlight as it turned over and over, up into the darkness. Captain Andreas bellowed, and banished me below.

After that they let me stand watch and work the decks but never go aloft. When things were busy I was to keep aft and not get in the way of Mr. and Mrs. Caspar and their family; and to keep me occupied when things were slack, they set me to learn the signals, in semaphore and speech. Thus for a good time we sped keenly and smoothly along through the blank silence, like an ice yacht on a frozen sea at midnight. Sometimes, though, there was something to see. I saw Switzer ships, and ships of Spain. I saw the barquentine the *Archimèdes* under full sail, her bulwarks encrusted with malachite. I saw wreckage drifting, blackened and frozen. One day I saw something huge in flight, far off. It did not look like any ship I had ever seen. It was brown, and long. Through the glass, it seemed to be moving.

"What is it, captain?" I asked.

"Gryphon," he said. It was the same word in Greek, Bruno said. I had never believed in them before. If it was true, that it was such a creature, then it was the most enormous living thing I ever saw, or am likely to. It kept its distance and went out of sight before the end of the watch.

Standing watch on the afterdeck I used to try to hear the *Gioconda* creaking under my boots, and feel her long gray timbers flexing with the swing of the wheel. We were making good headway. The tar was bubbling and bleeding out of the planking, while strange radiances crackled silently in the rigging, like crystallizing fire. I wanted to open my helmet and smell the wild salts of the vacuum, and let them scour my cheeks. I would climb out and polish the glass of the running lights, and feed them, fumbling with their little pellets of oxygen in my thick gloves. Then I might hang over the rail for a while, and look out into the void. If I stared hard enough along the dark side of the ship, with my eyes half-closed— and especially if I watched the space between two sails when they flapped slowly apart—I could see the aether. Like a great endless curtain of ripples it passed across the stars. In a hurtling rush it swept beneath and over and past us, whirling us along. On the starboard bow it was like a million tiny saw blades, yes—while abaft was it not more like glass cracking, like flaws in a windowpane?

No. I am cheating. I could not see all that, not then. I doubt if I could see any of it—but I wanted to so much. Sometimes I strained my eyes so hard looking for it I made myself giddy and confused, and felt as if there was music playing in my head, but all backward and jumbled up.

Once when no one was watching I crawled as far out along the port mainmast as I cared to, and hooked on to a spar. At once three little Cæruleans came boiling out from behind the topgallants, and darted around me with worried writhings, anxious for their territory. While I sat and stroked them, looking aft I watched the Sun hanging in the void, spreading her petticoats of light. That is where we dwell, all of us, in the petticoats of the Sun, afloat in eternal tides of colored dust that spiral around and around, softly, glowing, burning. Pink burned into amber, and amber into green.

I thought of Papa, endlessly falling, falling into light.

Good-bye, Papa.

Time passed. Bells rang. The watches came and went. Sometimes, when the work was done, Captain Andreas would play a battered-looking silver flute, and then Mr. Caspar might dance a jig, capering in midair with merry yaps and squeals. He was not always merry, though. One night, when the stars were quiet and the *Gioconda* was rolling easy with the tide, he suddenly went to earth in the sail locker and would not come out. We left him his pan, filled with sugared water, and drifted back to the saloon. Bruno tried to prevail on the captain to play on, but he would not.

The captain was already drunk. He started to badger Bruno, saying the same thing over and over again. He was trying to get Bruno to do something. No, no, Bruno said, again and again.

I leaned over to him. "What does he want?"

"He wants me to sing," he explained.

"I'd like to hear you sing," I said.

"No, no," he said. He sucked in air and shook his fine white hand as if he had burned himself. He stroked his ponytail. I imagined it felt very soft and sleek. "You sing," he said, "if you want singing."

"Me, sir?" I said. "I can't sing."

"Your little friend on the High Haven said you can."

So he had taken the opportunity to quiz Kappi about me. I hadn't even noticed. The corners of my mouth turned down. It still felt strange, having someone so interested in me. It felt as if he were a detective, and I was his suspect. It felt as if *I* were the one in the mask, in half a dozen of them, and he was after peeling them from me, one by one. "I was a child!" I objected. "I never sang anything properly."

Captain Andreas had lost interest in our conversation. He floated upright, about to depart, taking his flute from where he had hung it. The whole evening seemed poised to slide into misery and boredom.

"Oh, don't go, captain!" I cried; and at once I started to sing, "*Mr. Wisty went to market, bought himself a pound of tripe,*" which I sang until Captain Andreas laughed, and shook his head, and started to follow me with his flute. I swear I sang for an hour or more by the clock. All the old songs I could remember learning at the Hope and Anchor: "Barbara Allen," I sang, and "The Turning of the Tide," and "Cinnamon Mountain." Then Bruno sang "Whither Shall I Follow Thee, Pretty Little Maid?" and followed it with something lewd in Italian, which made him and the captain both laugh. They refused to tell me what it was about, though I plagued them for it.

My hair grew long and Mrs. Caspar plaited it. Even on the *Unco Stratagem*, I'd always had it cut short and never worn a pigtail. Now I waxed it until it was as stiff and black as a cable. I spent so much time on deck that my skin grew darker and my cheekbones started to appear in the round pie of my face. I had breasts too, no doubt of it now. I was seventeen. I wore a kerchief wrapped around my head and knotted behind my ear. Captain Andreas laughed and pulled a comical face. "He says we'll be fitting you for earrings next!" Bruno said, translating. He himself grew a beard, a little fringe around his chin from ear to ear, and he let me trim it for him, along with the ragged ends of his hair. Secretly I stroked it, tucking my fingers under the comb. It felt just as soft as I'd imagined.

I sighted a merchant fleet coming back from the Spice Moons, and read their signal, which told us it was Christmas. We feasted on hard dates and dried sardines, and drank two bottles of thick red wine. The Caspars dined with us, on dried grubs and maggots which they ate out of cocoa tins. It was a night of low gravity, but steady, and after a couple of cups of wine the stars turned into snow falling, if you squinted. In Lambeth Walk, I remembered, they set great store by snow at Christmas.

Captain Andreas played Greek carols on his flute, then turned to his usual queer jigs and hornpipes. The Caspars were whooping and keening along to the music. One of them thrust his muzzle into his tin and start playing it with his hindfeet like a drum. Bruno stood on his tiptoes and bowed to me gallantly, holding out his hand. "Will you dance, *signorina*?"

"Me?" I said. "Dance? Me? I don't know how to dance."

"Then permit me to instruct you," he said. He had the captain play something simple, a children's song like "Oranges and Lemons," while he taught me something he said was a gavotte, though I'm sure it was nothing of the kind. Then the tune changed, and we did it faster. I laughed and gasped. I thought it was a fine feeling, dancing to the music, two moving as one. For once I did not mind that Bruno had his arms about me, guiding me. I wished I had had a long dress swirling around my legs instead of my patched old frock, and more room to leap about in than the *Gioconda*'s forecastle. Why should we not whirl out among the stars, and dance our way to Jupiter?

By that time we had left behind the rainbow zones of burning dust. We were heading into the Asteroid Sea. Rocks of all shapes and sizes drifted by, slower, faster, tumbling like shuttlecocks or hanging still and silent in cloaks of moss. All currents are treacherous there, Bruno told me: apt to change in a second, to sweep the unlucky traveler to a shattering end.

I already knew Captain Andreas did not like to use the pilots' diadem, and he was loath to pull it on even now. He took the wheel—he put a pair of the Caspars to it—he took it again, and left it again—he stood by with his hands in his pockets, hemming and clicking his tongue to tell me what to signal to Bruno, on deck. I felt the *Gioconda* stall and start listing. She pitched, and began piling smack into the trough of every wave that came. Captain Andreas rushed out and hung from the quarterdeck, Rossington's in hand—I swear he was counting minutes and measuring the shifting of the stars by rule. The ship pitched again, heavily, and the men at the wheel squeaked as it pulled them sideways.

Bruno signaled to me, pointing out the famous shapes. There was Carlsberg, which looks like a giant pyramid— and Kwinana, like a long pear with a bite out of it—and Wormwood, where they send the convicts. Then the Fremont Cascades were upon us, and the order was to strike topsails and close-haul her.

Bruno was in the shrouds and Captain Andreas was forward helping Mrs. Caspar brake the winch when a rock came flickering up between the larboard mizzen and main and silently punched a hole in the mainsail. I saw the burst sail wallop out and snap the spar off at the parrel. The stays ran loose, flailing like frozen snakes behind the broken spar as it came free, floating straight up the deck like a branch in a gale and taking Captain Andreas square across the back.

They got him below at once. His faceplate was cracked, but he was alive. Bruno poured rum down his throat and probed with expert fingers. He could feel a broken shoulder: nothing for it but to set it quickly, near as he could, and bind it fast. Captain Andreas panted and clawed his fingers, cursing and crying out like a dog in his pain. Two little Caspars chittered and scolded as they scurried around and around with the bandage.

In this parlous state, all we could do was look for a place to lay over. Repairs would be hard without trained shipwrights on hand. Bruno's Cæruleans were highly skilled, but it was not wise of him to put to space and go sailing about everywhere with a crew that had so little bulk between them. At least there was no shortage of materials. Bare as the little ship seemed beside every other I had known, there was an entire spare suit of sails on board, and plenty of wood.

"Will we manage?" I asked Bruno, looking doubtfully at the captain.

Bruno was in a black mood, and did not reply.

We dropped down out of the main and drifted with the tide, limping along in hope of sighting a haven. Captain Andreas muttered gloomily about Wormwood and about his arm, until Bruno opened a bottle and put it in his hand with a cruel oath. I went back on deck.

While we swept idly around and around with the flotsam, I watched the black deeps and thought about Io, and imagined that in some corner far away from all the volcanoes and at the end of a long road, there would be a castle, and we should see the drawbridge flung down and the doors open wide upon a merry hall, with a great fire going, and the boards groaning with food and drink; and there, silhouetted in front of it, the stout form of our host, with his ermine robe and his jolly red cheeks and his long white beard, and his arms stretched open wide: Father Christmas, the Duke of Cockayne. What a welcome he would bellow, and how he would hug us both to his bosom, Bruno and me.

We grappled to the first sizable rock we could reach, and set a fixed anchor. I cannot tell you the name of the rock, or even if it had one. All I can say is, had anyone truly been chasing us, he would have found us easily. We would have been a sitting duck for him in those days, anchored to our bald lump of basalt with all our yards bare and one limb broken. Nor was there anything there to cheer or succor us, neither goats nor turtles nor any of the other comforts enjoyed by Mr. Crusoe; though I swear the tides thereabouts were as wild as ever his seas of water were.

The damage was not all to the mast and sail. The entire forward balloon mounting and the pump that made all the gas was smashed and swept away. There was nothing that could be done about that; and the new sail was an age in the opening and the rigging, though the Caspars swarmed everywhere with a will. But before that came the carpentry, and that was like a nightmare. You felt you were hammering with a piece of rubber. The captain couldn't do it at all, and he was bad at holding a nail. He made out it hurt him to have to keep his arm still; but I think in truth it was pride.

That Christmas was a hard season for Captain Andreas, what with his injury, and being angry and in pain, and shame too. When it came time for us to leave, he couldn't find the outbound current. We wallowed into space and down again; hung in the void on our rock, stiff as a fish on a stick. Captain Andreas lay inside the glass front of the bridge with the circlet pressed down over his brows and his eyes closed tight. He sweated and cursed and swore. He begged for drink. This time Bruno would not give it to him.

The captain reminded me of Papa needing laudanum. I couldn't bear it. "Let him have it, sir," I said; but Bruno bade me be quiet in his most curt manner. He took the wheel himself and called to me what signs to make. He had them put up the moonsails, which without lift was a complete waste of effort, and crammed the sunward topyards, fishing for the wind, like a drunken man trying to haul himself upright by reaching for the top of a wall. Though he gave the calls with great determination and many a vaunting boast, before long it became clear he had not the first idea what he was about. At last the captain wrenched the golden circlet off his head and sat there above me in his slings, floating all askew, with his hand pressed to his broken shoulder, his head turned that way too. He spoke, resentfully, and I did not understand him.

"What did he say?" I asked Bruno. I had to ask twice before he vouchsafed me a reply.

"The flux is out, he said."

Of course it was no such thing.

I reached up to Captain Andreas. I said: "*Ploíarche*, let me."

Captain Andreas looked down at me distantly, without intelligence, though I stood there holding my hand out. Bruno seemed not to understand me either. "Leave him," he commanded. Outside blue faces peered from the rigging, watching for the next signal. "Tell them to stand down, Miss Farthing. The tides are contrary."

"Let me try," I said.

He huffed, exasperated. "What are you talking about?"

"I can see," I told him.

I truly thought I could. I had stared into the darkness so many times now I knew exactly what was there. I thought it was like an iodine stain, deep *inside* the darkness—and if you looked very hard indeed you could see as if it was made up of thousands of millions of tiny needle scratches, side by side, and every scratch trembling and shaking like a fiddle string, only much too fast to see. It hurt my eyes to look like that— my head started to thump and my skin to prickle all over— and when I closed my eyes it felt as if my head were pulsing in time with the waves.

I reached up and took the diadem out of Captain Andreas's hand.

Bruno swam across and took it out of mine.

"*Signorina*, no," he said in a stern voice, as if he thought I was being ridiculous on purpose to cheer him up, and he was tired of me. "It's not for you." Being a girl, that meant. I suppose it might well have been the first time a woman's hand had touched that headpiece since it was forged.

"He can't use it!" I cried, pointing at the dazed captain. "He's injured."

Bruno swept back to the wheel, all business and urgency. He was angry with me for making a silly nuisance of myself. "She works only for pilots," he shouted, waving the diadem at Captain Andreas. "She don't work for people who don't have the talent: see!"

And he put it on his head.

"See, ha?" he cried. "Nothing!"

"Give it to *me*!" I snapped, and I sprang over and snatched it off his head and pulled it on my own.

There was an instant of horrific, biting sickness, as though someone had thrust a truncheon into my kidneys. Then it went deeper, buzzing through all my bones and making my teeth chatter; and then my body went away and I could see. I couldn't have steered to save my life; but I could see.

He took it off my head. I discovered I was doubled up, clutching my midriff.

"I can do it," I protested, exhilarated by the shock. I waved my arms and legs about wildly. "You don't have to have the talent."

Bruno's face was grim and closed. His eyes seemed very deep in his head. He had witnessed something he did not wish to acknowledge; therefore, he had not seen it. "You are a girl," he said; though I thought he hesitated as he said it. "You do not know what you are doing."

"I can *see*, Bruno," I said, trying to get the thing back from him.

"You see nothing," he said, barring my way with a broad forearm. "Please, Sophie. You make this more difficult than it need be." He gave the diadem back to the captain, who was pleased to put it away in its special box.

Bruno gazed into space. I knew he could not see a tenth of what I saw. How the darkness glistened and the stars shimmered beneath our bow. How they shimmered harder where the flux was squeezed between rocks that flew toward each other—and where the rocks flew apart, how the stars seemed to swirl outward, light and loose as ashes from a fire. The faint glow in the blackness was a treacherous light, drawing the ship on to destruction. He must know this was no safe spot we had chosen; yet we were to wait, wait while the rocks tumbled about our heads: wait for a better tide which would not come.

We stood down. I followed Bruno to the saloon. "It isn't going to get any better," I said.

"We trust Captain Andreas for that," he said. I knew he was really annoyed with Captain Andreas too, but too annoyed with me to let me in on it.

"Sir, he can't do it," I said. "You saw."

"He is the captain. He is the pilot."

"He doesn't know where we are," I said.

"The pilot's word is law. Only a fool would ignore it. I have already killed thirty-nine people, as you remind me," he said, rather stiffly. "I shall not kill any more. Believe me, Sophie, there's nothing you can do."

I said: "If you don't let me try, you'll kill every one of us."

This was fresh air to his grievance, and he bridled up higher. "*Mi vogliate perdonare*, if I hand over the ship to you I certainly shall! What do you know of it? You are a girl," he said again, numbering off my faults with his fingers: "you are too young; you know nothing of ships, heh? What have you been in your life but a drudge to men and animals? How can you pilot a ship? *La mia piccola signori-*

na," he said, pleading, "be sensible. How can we take your orders?"

So that was the heart of it. Then let him keep command of his precious boat and her wounded captain, and let him destroy us all on the next burst of flux. At that moment, I wished he might, and know before he died that he had done it, and I had told him so, and serve him right. Killing people was the only thing he was good for. "Then I wish you good luck, sir," I said aloud, turning on my heel.

For some reason that cut him deep. "Don't wish me luck," he said, slowly, his top lip curling. "Never wish me luck!" He almost seemed to believe it was bad luck to be wished good.

I went to my cabin to wait for the shipwreck, hoping it would hurry up. I wanted to be dead at once, and out of all this. But Bruno could not leave me alone. Within two minutes he was at my door to say: "Sophie, if you knew our danger you could not make so much trouble all the time."

"I!" I said, gaping at him. "Make trouble!"

"You make me confused," he said, while I turned away, one shoulder hunched up as though his voice was a draft of cold air blowing in my ear. "You make me angry and proud of you. Both at once."

"You confuse yourself," I told him, bitterly.

He scrutinized me. "You are angry too," he observed, as one who came down from a great height to say so.

"That's right, sir," I said. "You're right." I felt like applauding. I said: "Tell me something, sir, from all your wide experience—are all men everywhere mules and pigs, or is it only the ones I've met? And are they mules because they are pigs, or are they pigs first and mules as a consequence? Do please tell me, sir, I should so love to know."

Pigs have beautiful eyes, you know. Austriches too. Bruno's eyes are beautiful, and it hurt me then to see them full of pain. It was his own fault—there was no talking to him—I would have left the room that minute if it had not meant going past him, so I slid up to the far side of the cabin, as far as I could get from him. I said: "You're determined to kill us all, why have you come to bother me?"

He said, "I am determined not to kill you, Sophie. Nothing in all the worlds could make me do that," he said, with a low tremor in his voice. "Nor will I let you kill yourself. Nor kill anyone else in your daring. I am pleased and proud you have this daring spirit in you! I admire that in you."

I had stopped listening; but then he said, "I want only to protect you, and bring you to your own."

"My own?" I said. I came closer. "What is there? What's left?"

He grimaced sympathetically, squeezing his forehead between his thumb and fingers. "I know how you miss your father," he said. "I too was a young man at my father's funeral—"

"He wasn't my father," I said. "Who was my father, Signor Bruno Son of Bruno?"

He wiped his cheeks with the palms of his hands. "I have told you everything," he mourned.

"Humbug!" I said, exactly like Miss Halshaw. "You have told me nothing," I said. I said: "And was it your father, then, sir?"

My abductor looked confused again, tired and unhappy and confused. He said: "My father?"

"That killed my mama?" I said.

"Almost certainly," he said. I could tell he had been thinking I had some other meaning and was relieved I had not, even while he was making his apology. "And so it is my life's reason," he vowed, "to protect and keep you safe."

I picked up a boot and tried to hurl it at him. It curled sloppily away from my hand, spinning drunkenly in the air, while I went floating backward again. I grabbed the rope of the hatch and hung on to it with both hands, to stop myself from getting hold of him by the ears and trying to shake him, which would have been even more disastrous.

"How am I to trust you?" I said. I could hear myself; I sounded like a little child whining. Suddenly my anger was disintegrating, falling into grief. "You don't trust me," I pointed out, with tears, hated tears, gathering in my eyes. "Your commission on Mars was me, wasn't it?"

He didn't speak.

"*Wasn't it?*" I screamed. Forward, I heard Captain Andreas shout some drunken insult, and laugh. I raved on. "Why didn't you do it? You think you're such a great performer. Why didn't you do what you were sent to, and save us all this trouble?"

"You know why," he said, wounded, upset.

"You wouldn't tell me," I raged. "If you really cared a brass farthing for me, you'd have told me."

"I tried," he said. "I thought you understood. Then when I saw you didn't, I had no heart."

I suddenly realized he was telling me the truth. He was not bragging, for once, or pretending. He was admitting he had failed, and it hurt him. And somehow then I let him come and put his arms around me. I swallowed. My heart was racing so hard it skipped. "Not telling me, that was protecting me too, I imagine," I said, breathing hard, making myself iron in his embrace. How I resented him; how I resented all of it.

"Yes," he said. His arms were still around me, and I didn't seem to be trying to get away.

"No, sir, if you please, sir," I said. "That was protecting you." I had started to panic, in his arms—I did not know why I wasn't trying to get free—I must try—I did not know what might happen if I didn't try. Instead, I talked. "You drag me off to Io," I said, swallowing, "you talk about protecting me—"

"I could not see," he said. His body was warm against mine. I remembered how I had felt when we were dancing. He said, "I could see no other way. I could not see how I should feel with you in danger. Danger to me is how you would call, second nature. *Dunque*, I jumped like a dog, that has no brain to think," he accused himself, and slapped himself on the forehead. "But I am not as I was," he declared. "You have changed me. Because of you, I shall be a better man."

He was on the point of weeping. He was holding me in his arms, and making promises to me in his soft, light voice, and there were tears coming in his wonderful eyes. Any moment and they would come floating out and burst in my face like tiny bubbles. "And you too," he said. "You too will put your shame behind you."

That did it. "What shame?" I said, and I started to climb out of his arms. "Just because you need forgiving, you needn't expect me to do it for you. You talk to me of shame," I told him grimly. "You don't tell me you were going to kill me. Then when I make you tell me, you expect me to forgive you and you start talking about my shame. You're no better than

Papa! For two pins I'd throw you overboard and tell Captain
Andreas to take the damned ship back to Mars!"

There came the patter of Mr. Caspar outside on the deck.
He appeared at the porthole, bounding around in agitation,
gesticulating at the dark and scrambling in the ratlines. He
too knew we should be going.

Bruno was kneeling in midair, reaching for me. "Let me
be your shield against all the worlds," he said. "For I have a
plan. When the tide turns, let me come to my senses at last
and take you to a place of safety and *bring* this accursed letter *to* you." He smiled, glassily. I felt the boat tremble, long
and low.

I said, "You should have thought of that before. If you
think I'm sitting around somewhere waiting for you, you've
got another think coming."

He looked glad, but sorry for me too. "You have been so
alone . . ." he said.

"Don't you dare pity me!" I said. "It was you killed Hercule
and took me away from Brother Jude and made me betray all
my friends. Take me to Io and let's get this all over with, and
then get out of my sight."

He looked truly miserable. "I have so much to offer you."

"I don't want *anything* from you!" I shrieked.

"Not even a nice cup of tea?" he said.

I couldn't help it, Dear Reader: I had to laugh. I only
laughed a little, and meanly; but then he started to laugh too,
and then I laughed out loud. Then he wanted to hug me again,
and I let him, and this time I let myself like it. We hung there
in each other's arms, laughing weakly and waltzing clumsily
around the cabin.

Feeling somehow as if we had accomplished a great victory,
though a wiser head might have pointed out that the *Gioconda*
was still stranded, and the flux still boiling—and nothing had
been resolved—I followed him to the galley once again. I
wanted to stay near him. I could feel how much it had hurt
him to tell me. I couldn't do that to him and then abandon
him to his own folly. In that hour I had the strange mad con-
viction I could save him from it all; aye, and the strength to
do it. Meanwhile I couldn't stop hurting him, adding to the
hurt between us each time I opened my mouth.

"How would you have killed me?" I asked.

"On Mars?" he said, his voice shaking like a sail being eased into a new wind. "She is the planet of Death," he said, expanding, getting stronger. "A hundred ways. A broken neck; I leave you for the *kiiri*. Take you to a distant ravine and push you in. Tie you up and slip you into the canal. I'm sorry," he said, apologizing for the indelicacy; but I was not offended.

"Why didn't you just poison my cup that first afternoon, with the wine?"

Unbelievably he said, "I did think of it. But you aroused my curiosity."

I traced the grain of the table with my finger. "And now I am letting you make me a cup of tea," I said flatly.

"I know," he said, his voice breaking. "Isn't it wonderful!"

We started laughing again. It was funny! It was very, very funny. It was the funniest thing that had ever happened.

And, you will ask, did part of me not fear, ah, he is acting yet, lying yet? Had he not boasted, how he could foster an illusion, and be whatever I wished to see? What if the only reason he was telling me was that it was already too late?

And I shall tell you, yes, and yes, and three times yes. Yet there I was in his arms again. From which place it was not so hard to believe that at last he had learned to speak true.

I was breathless with it all. "Oh Bruno, what's happening?" I said. "I think I must be going mad."

"You are not going mad, Miss Sophie Farthing. Miss Sophie Farthing," he said, "I love you. I have loved you ever since the first time I saw you, fussing with your foolish bird. I brought you away because I loved you. I betrayed my patron and my order and changed my face to show you. Now everything has changed. Until I met you I did not know what love was. I did not know what life was. Sophie Farthing, I have lost my heart to you!"

I wished he would stop confessing and start making the tea. I looked at him askance. I felt a hundred years old and very wise, though I hadn't the least idea what I was doing. I said, "And I'm supposed to give you mine now, is that it? Oh, Bruno . . ." I said, despairing.

"Say nothing," he said. "Only give me a kiss."

I said nothing. I gave him nothing; but I let him kiss me, on the lips. I was the Sleeping Beauty. I didn't tremble or swoon, it was a kiss like a moth alighting, there and gone. Then he did make us a cup of tea.

He was happy now. His face was so brown and alive and smiling. He told me I had forgiven him after all. I said I thought I had done enough forgiving for one trip. I took a Nitrox lozenge and washed it down with a mouthful of tea. I looked in his eyes and said: "We must leave. Now."

He did not look convinced. But I had the advantage: if I have his heart, I thought, he has no heart to contradict me. Is that not how it works?

Back on the bridge of the *Gioconda* we found Captain Andreas dangling in a stupor with his whiskey flask drifting empty in the air. A pair of Caspars scuttled down the canopy, scurrying in hope of orders from their brother at the semaphore. One rattled his little helmet on the frame in impatience.

I went and got out the circlet of gold again. Bruno said nothing. Even holding it in my hand I knew I could feel the pulse in my fingers, the hard and fickle music of the stars. I took a deep breath and put it on.

At once my whole head was dark, and I felt as if an angel had kicked me in the belly. The ship was gone, and Bruno and the crew, and I was all alone and afloat, gasping, in the midst of a roaring course of invisible light. The light was flowing like water, and flowing through me. For a moment I could not feel the diadem, for I had no head to feel it with, nor a body either. I was nothing but a twist in the aether tow.

Yet—"I can see!" I heard myself cry out once more. I found the flux was pouring through my head, buzzing and hissing in my eyes and nose and mouth like a torrent of iron filings. The flux was what I could see, and nothing else.

Swallowing, struggling, I pointed into the very teeth of the maelstrom. I couldn't see my arm either. I could feel it, though, when I moved it. It felt as if it were being pulled by the flux, torn out at the root. "That way," I heard myself gasp.

It was horrible, like being a pin on a magnet, in a pitch black room full of steam engines. I could see at once why Captain Andreas was not fond of the circlet. I took it off, and everything popped back into view again. "It's stronger over there," I said, panting, still gesturing. "There's a clear passage—like a, a—" I circled my arm in the air. "Like a funnel," I said; and I put the circlet back on and vanished again into that hideous hum. I heard Bruno laughing. "Bring her around," I shouted, "ten points starboard."

I knew the instant we started to swing. I could feel my face turning into the flow. I could feel that, without mistake, in my head and spreading through my body, like creeping pins and needles. I was filled with lightning.

I found my nose and wiped it, and tried to stop my teeth chattering. "Steady the helm," I said.

"Aye-aye, ma'am," said Bruno, in a high cheery voice, while Captain Andreas cursed.

19

Enter Perdita

Pulled by a mighty ox all covered in woolly hair, the carriage jolted us across the tundra. Our lamps were the only illumination in this realm of fog and night. I pressed my cheek to the window, trying to make out the scenery. I saw nothing but blurs and shadows, until we passed between two gigantic ice green pillars of frozen rock that soared upward into the dark like somebody's vast triumphal gate. Beyond, our lights picked out monoliths, enormous slabs of white and viridian, slipping slowly past like the gravestones in a cemetery of giants. Smuts whirled in the air and made black smears on the glass. I thought it must be London Town—"Look, Bruno," said I, "in a minute we'll be in Oxford Street and see the Marble Arch, and drive down to Buckingham Palace."

Bruno patted my hand, smiling slightly but saying nothing. His mood was solemn as the carriage rocked and rattled along.

I had to suppose neither brougham nor beast was local;

and nor was the man I had seen sitting like a statue on the
driver's box. He was thin, though he had huge shoulders, and
he was dressed from head to foot in armored clothes of iron
and leather. You couldn't see his face for a black iron helmet
he had on, and a black cowl pulled up over it. I had said to
Bruno: "I thought this was a secret visit."

"He watches each ship that comes," Bruno answered. "But
you he is not expecting." He took my hand to reassure me, his
eyes glittering in the darkness. "I sent a cipher from Toussous,
the last morning," he said softly, "reporting the success of my
mission." Before he had come out to the canyon, that meant.
I had grown used to him saying things he had not told me at
the time. He had taken me for granted, then. And if he had
not managed to bring me away, what then? Would he perhaps
have decided his cipher must come true? By now he would be
visiting my bones in their secret grave in the Ulsvar, to leave
a single rose, still wet with the dew of another world.

I tucked my hands inside my coat. "Is this one of his men?"
I asked, meaning the stiff-backed coachman.

Bruno gave an odd smile. "It's not a man, this one," he
said. "*Di fatti*, it is a machine. He has many such advanced
machines. He prefers machines to people."

"Who does?" I asked.

I felt him solid and implacable beside me. So he still refused
to tell. I looked out of the window again, into the fog. I
thought we were climbing a ridge onto a high plateau. All
I could see were fissures and potholes, broken rocks and
stones.

Then Bruno said quietly: "His name is Mortimer, twenty-
eighth Earl Lychworthy." And he gave me a sideways look,
as if to see if I would faint now.

I sniffed, and wriggled one shoulder.

"Have you not heard of him?" Bruno pursued.

"No," I said, carelessly.

Bruno touched the forefinger of his left hand, stroking up
and down the seam of his glove. I had disappointed him, and
left him unwilling to say anything more.

"He's the head of the Pilots' Guild, is he?" I said.

Bruno nodded. "He was my patron," he said. He spoke
lightly; but I knew it was no true lightness.

"I suppose he's very rich," I said.

"He owns this moon."

I thought of something Mrs. Rodney often said, that there was no accounting for taste. "I suppose he's very powerful, too," I said.

"We must ensure you do not meet him," said Bruno, in his tone that meant I had had all he would allow me for that time and discussion was closed.

And I kept mum; although I thought, *That's as may be.* Dear Reader, I thought that if I could once meet and talk to the man who was the author of my disastrous existence, then everything would change. The pain would be over and I should understand everything, and everything would somehow be given to me, everything I had never had. There I went, through the world of fire and ice, looking for Father Christmas.

I could feel Bruno's eyes on me then. I turned to face him in the gloom, and knew once again he knew exactly what I was thinking. I looked away, drawing my head into the collar of my coat, feeling disconcerted as I still did whenever I found my thoughts were not altogether my own. Though we had left them far behind, the sands of Mars drift deep into the mind, and you do not soon lose the stain of them.

Beyond the Asteroid Sea I had tried not to be confined with him. I had continued on deck as much as possible, stumbling after Mr. and Mrs. Caspar, left far behind by their nimble hands and flying feet. Along the lines the rime had turned harsh and black; if one of them hung anywhere too long, it could burn the sticky pads of his fingers, even through the gloves. Still I would see the smallest of them tie a buntline hitch with her tail faster than I could do a reef knot with both hands.

There was no end of things I did not know, who had never been to school. Captain Andreas instructed me in a little haphazard practical navigation, grudgingly revealing his small stock of English. If I was to be allowed to knock his ship about, he was damned if he would sit idly by, nursing his shoulder. I flatter myself I did well enough on that first voyage, though not without putting her head through the wind a time or two; and not without making my own head throb from the exertion.

When I was too tired to continue, I let Bruno prevail and sat for him to finish his painting of me. He would puff out his

cheeks in concentration over his labor and pout his lips until
he resembled some overgrown cherub, bearded and bronzed;
for his natural color had returned to him as his blanched skin
recovered, oiled and pampered.

Many were the times my protector declared his love for me.
When he did I would flee to the rigging, where the stars hung
clotted thick as frogspawn in a pond. I didn't know whether it
could be so or not. Never before had anyone cared so much
for me, so much that he took up the hapless zigzag quest of my
existence, even when I had let it fall. I supposed I should be
obliged to him, but that would be as it proved. Mama seemed
very distant in those days. I wished I had her there to ask what
it felt like, to love someone, how you could tell, and what you
were supposed to do if you did. I knew, even if I ever did
manage it, I could not possibly live up to his expectations,
whatever they were. So I confess I thought of Io as little as
possible, and hoped we might sail on forever in that sweet,
safe uncertainty.

Nevertheless, to Jupiter we came at last, at aphelion, and
I saw face to face the huge disk that frowns so with smoke
and storms. Undaunted, Captain Andreas plotted the vector
and let me seek us a clear run. Within the flux I stood, balanced, walked, on tiptoe. It was like dancing, I decided. It
was like dancing with a ship for a partner. Under the vast
belly of the King of Planets we came sailing, into the region
of the moons.

Then for a long time it seemed we hung motionless while
Io came creeping out of the distance, swimming toward us,
rearing up, opening out beneath us like a vast rotting honey-
comb. Through fog and murk the green ice cliffs appeared,
reaching up for us like wraiths, like the towering guards of
some undersea fairyland. Thermals caught the *Gioconda* as
she drifted down gingerly and askew without balloons, and
tossed her one to another. In the shrouds the Caspar family
cowered, subdued. Next to me in the rigging one scrambled,
shaking the tackle with his tiny fists, defying the brooding
face of Jupiter overhead and screaming inside his helmet as
we went creaking down.

The *Gioconda* nested in a natural bay among the mountains, her master and I took lozenges and put on our coats and
helmets. Mr. Caspar opened the hatch and Captain Andreas

sketched a salute and motioned us ashore. As I went bobbing down the gangplank, thunder rolled among the mountains
and the thick, glutinous rain of Io coursed down across my
faceplate. I thought there were no buildings, nor any sign of
civilization. There were half a dozen other moons up: not
one of them could you see. The thunder boomed again, and
I wondered if it was thunder indeed, or the rumble of fire that
belched here deep beneath the ground.

That was when the huge hairy ox came out of the fog,
hauling its ancient coach along behind. Blackened by grime
and night, every trace of paint long scoured away, the coach
still bore on its door a relief of the eye and arrow. Even as I
stared at it, the door swung silently open for me.

The shrouded coachman had made no move, but Bruno nodded, so I got in, and he followed and shut the door. The coach
jolted away, spraying dirt and black water about. Bruno turned
a tap that filled the inside with air, and we took our helmets
off. We spoke then of the man who had bought a moon, while
the coach climbed his mountain in the submarine gloom. At
any moment it seemed the wheels must swing out over nothing and the road run on upon the thick air merely, upon the
ramparts of the fog.

We pitched up into a broad gully as straight and flat as a
railway cutting. The banks at either side were cracked and fis-
sured, big rocks leaning out at precarious angles. Bruno rose
carefully to his feet. *"Mi vogliate perdonare, signorina,"* he
said, formally. "We get out here. It would not do to bring you
to the front door."

So we jumped out and let the carriage roll on without us,
and moving lightly in the low gravity, cloaked and helmeted
and hand in hand we came, up the side of a giant boulder and
onto Hunchback Fell; and soon on a prospect above us saw
a white mansion glowing moistly in the fog like a house of
snow. It was hard to be sure if there was light at any of the
windows, or if they were only reflecting random glimmers that
came and went in the smoke. Everything was crowded with
decoration, pricked and smoothed and curled and furbelowed
and crowded, I saw as we drew nearer, with marble figures,
naked men with spears, naked women with bunches of grapes.
Their blank eyes stared out across the desolate land, rain dripping from their cheeks like tears.

The rough wind at our heels, my escort and I came up at a corner of the mansion where the restless earth had fallen away. Grit and pumice dotted the ground. The wall was shored up with huge balks of timber, worth its weight in food to ship out here: raw timber propping up the wall of a crumbling building on a poisonous moon where nothing lived. I saw that; and I began to understand that Father Christmas did not live here either.

Bruno put his helmet to mine. "*In bocc' al lupo*," I heard him say, which means, Good Luck, to someone stepping into danger. Then he twisted a knife in a keyhole and inside we slipped, through heavy woollen air-curtains into a hallway. The walls were gray stone carved like paneling, and the floor polished black oilcloth. Still there were no guards, not even a clanking porter.

Through the dark house Bruno and I moved on cats' feet. Shapes reared in the shadows: tall doors firmly closed; unlit lamps on iron standards; dried Venusian ferns that towered from black urns. There was a sculpted scene of fat little babies with painfully tiny wings, nothing at all like the real thing, hovering dejectedly over what I supposed was a giant cone of ice cream that had landed upside down. There was another, with an urn on the top and a flag draped over it like a bedspread, and two pale thin women, one either side, bowing their heads and covering their eyes with their hands. Everywhere there were ornamental clocks, polished eggs of semiprecious stone, case after case of glorious-colored butterflies. I thought we were walking into a mist, then realized it was condensation in my helmet. I took it off and hung it on my belt. The air was very hot and stifling, sulfurous and sour for all its laundering. Thick curtains the color of old red wine were drawn across all the windows. Outside the moaning winds of Io threw their rain and muck about.

Clocks ticked us along, marking our passage. Then there came a muffled *boom*, and a tremor. The stone eggs quivered on their shelf. Bruno gathered me to him. *Earthquake*, I mouthed; but he shook his head and stayed me with his hand, leaving me there. Running silently on the balls of his feet, he plunged along the hallway and up a flight of stairs.

I followed, and found him at a window, looking down. There in the drive below was the brougham, all in flames, burning pieces of it still skittering on the ground all around. The ox was bellowing in terror, its long hair singed and smoking.

"Fortescue!" whispered my guide.

The mechanical driver sat stiffly on its box, surrounded by flames. It tipped and tilted, whirling around and around on the pivot of its waist, but could not manage to climb out of its seat. It held one hand to its chest where a rubber bladder pumped continuously inside its ruined coat.

I started for the stairs, meaning to run out and help the poor things, but Bruno held me back. He held me close, his hand over my mouth. "He knows you are here," he murmured.

In that instant the last of the harness traces had caught light, and now they gave to the terrified tugging of the ox. Out of them it burst and away into the fog, as we ran back downstairs, and down again into a basement, and down again. The deeper we ran, the hotter it grew, the heat crawling up the stairs to meet us. Still we had seen no one.

Bruno stopped to pick a lock. I took him by the arm. I said: "Give me a knife."

My assassin did not hesitate. He took from his cloak the silver throwing knife he had pinned the snake with, when we came aboard the *Gioconda*. It was heavy, cored with lead, the hilt inlaid with black lapis.

"Not that one," I said.

He opened the door. "I have only these, and the dirk," he said, showing me the stabbing blade that had suddenly appeared, I know not how, in his left hand.

"And the other," I said, as we passed into a dark room full of obscure furniture. "The one that was your father's." I meant the thing that had killed Hercule. That slew at a touch, I knew, and I supposed it took no skill. I thought I could manage that.

Bruno shook his head, saying nothing. I took the dirk. I hefted it and threw it at the back of the door we had just come through. I threw much too hard. The knife scraped the ceiling, struck the door hilt first, and bounced away out of sight. In a thrill of guilty alarm I leapt after it.

Bruno was incensed. "It's for flesh!" he upbraided me as I picked it up and came back with it. "Wood will ruin it!" But I had already decided. I would not throw it again. Throwing it was throwing it away. I stuck it through my belt, hoping it would not fall out as we ran.

In the dark Bruno got ahead of me. Ahead, around a bend in the hall, I heard a door open, and hurried on. I thought I saw him, beyond a pair of glass doors; but when I pushed through them I found it was only a bust on a pedestal. Bouncing back and forth as they closed, the doors echoed through a large room, completely dark, that smelt of polish and linseed oil. I was alone. I went back out at once, and seeing a light along the hall ran toward it, my footsteps sounding flatly in the dull silence.

The light was coming from three candles. It lit the back of Bruno's head, the long sleek fall of his hair, the broad collar of his cloak. It lit the bald head and the narrow black sleeve of the aged manservant who loomed over him in a doorway holding aloft the three-branched candlestick.

I heard the man say: "You weren't in the coach, sir."

"*Grazie al cielo*, I was not," returned Bruno crisply. I could hear he was glad to be able to speak up, to face another human being at last. "Stand aside, Fortescue," he said, and put his hand to his belt.

Still the man remained at his station. His face was white and whiskery, his cheeks sunken and hollow. How could this ancient scarecrow have created that inferno outside? He was as thin as a man could rightly be, withered with age; yet with the broad shield of his authority in that house he blocked our way.

"This is the master's study, sir," he said. His voice was a dry whisper, reduced of everything but the crushing dignity that heaven bestows on butlers and stewards and majordomos throughout the universe. He was dressed all in black, and smelt musty. Bruno could have picked him up with one hand. I wondered why he did not.

"The master is asleep, sir," the hoarse voice continued, reprovingly. "You must wait until morning."

I thought of the burning coach, and knew I was asleep too, and in a nightmare. "Fortescue," Bruno was saying. "*Se volete di grazia. Signore.* Stand aside," he said. I understood then he was ashamed to use violence against a man old enough to be his grandfather, a man he knew well.

Fortescue's eyes were big and pale and flat, like the eyes of something that lives under the ground. He turned them upon me. "I haven't been introduced to your companion, sir," he said, in the mildest tone.

Unbidden, my hand closed on the hilt of my knife. "Fortescue, this is Miss Farthing, I'm sure you have heard of her," Bruno said grimly. "Sophie, this is Fortescue, who is my master's most loyal man!" He forced heartiness into his voice, though it rang to me with warning. "There is something in that room that concerns Miss Farthing closely," he told the man. "Let us pass, like the good fellow you are."

But Fortescue had ignored all of that save what he had requested, the introduction. "Miss Farthing," he said dutifully, and inclined his head. "A pleasure to make your acquaintance." Leaning down he held the candlestick nearer my face to scrutinize me.

Dazzled, I winced and blinked. Fortescue's front was in deep shadow, bowed over as he was. But surely there was something moving there, beneath his chest?

Smiling an obliging long-toothed grin, the earl's man started to straighten up. Above his belly something was bulging beneath his clothing, like an animal stirring. I thought of the Hrad, with their weasels in their waistcoats. The bulge was bigger than a weasel, and growing purposefully.

It was unbuttoning Fortescue's jacket from the inside.

As I stepped back, shouting and pushing Bruno off-balance, the jacket came open and two extra hands thrust into view, stretching and folding out from Fortescue's chest on horrid arms that opened out like telescopes. His shirt tore with a thin, ripping sound, and the two halves of his chest clapped open like the doors of a monstrous stove, bare yellow ribs racked on a pair of black iron hinges. Inside was too dark to see, but it was wet and pulsed like any man's.

The arms were made of yellow bone. The tips of them were capped with silver metal that glinted in the candlelight. The hands looked like sprung traps of ivory and steel with padding of human flesh. They flexed and slid out of his open chest, rotating purposefully at the wrist. Meanwhile with his natural hands the old man was waving the candlestick from side to side, cloaking himself in the strange violent shadows that waltzed around the hallway.

He wheezed happily. "Will you come in now, young sir?"

"No, *signore*," Bruno cried, sweeping me behind him as he danced backward down the hall, "for I see a large spider, and spiders I cannot abide!"

As I dodged I could feel the knife, useless in my belt. I wanted to be sick; but Bruno was swift and eager, like a dog let off a chain. It was only for my sake he was not already at the creature's throat. Rapidly he scanned the hall, and catching sight of the glass doors, pulled me through them. He took me and thrust me in a corner behind a statue and took a position between me and the doors while they were yet rocking to and fro.

My head rang with shock and I still felt sick and cold, though the house was as hot as an oven. I pressed myself against the base of the statue, trying to make myself as small as I could. The doors fell shut at last, and the room became utterly silent and utterly still. I had a dim sense of tall, dark panels ranged on the walls around us, looking down. They brightened suddenly into color, cactus greens and leathery browns, as down the hall three candle flames came swooping.

I could not bear to hide altogether, but must look out. With a small inarticulate gulp of terror and protest, I drew the silver knife.

The doors bumped open and Fortescue burst in, slashing out to both sides with a pair of short curved swords. "Your favorite, the knife, sir, as I recall," he said, joyously.

I stuck tight; but Bruno was in at once under the long bone arm, driving in with his blade. Fortescue parried with the arm, cutting at Bruno now with both left hands at once, one blade in each, while his other artificial arm came shooting toward me like an errant boom, sliding under the arm of the statue and plucking at my sleeve. Squealing, I stabbed at the artificial fingers, and had the satisfaction of seeing the hand jerked straight back.

Fortescue put the candlestick in the hand, and thrust that at me instead. Even as I ran out from the other side of the statue I felt hot wax splash on my neck. "Here, Miss Farthing," twittered Fortescue, his voice gone all rapid and high—"perhaps you would be so good as to hold the light while I get rid of this naughty puppy!"

I had thrown up my free hand to ward off the fire and found I had grasped the candlestick indeed; while Bruno was thrusting and loudly crying, "This puppy needs no light to bite your leg, Signor Spider!" He tried to draw the man away across the floor, away from me.

I ran and stood the candlestick down by the wall. Somehow the candles were all still aflame. By their malevolent yellow light I could see, as I had supposed, that we were in a great room given over to paintings. A somber audience of grand gentlemen stared disapprovingly at the grotesque ballet of elbows and steel Bruno had brought into their midst. "Ah, yes, look around, Miss Farthing, do!" called Fortescue, who must have had eyes in the back of his head as well as four arms and a belly of iron. "All our visitors admire the splendid array of his Lordship's noble ancestors. Lychworthys have run the Pilots' Guild since the days of King James," he announced, swinging at Bruno's head from two directions at once like a gardener pruning an overweening rose with a pair of giant shears.

Bruno ducked, knocking over a bust and toppling its pedestal into the creature's path. He was nimble as a Cærulean, skilled in this deadly ballet learnt by Mars-light. He spun around behind our clumsy, top-heavy assailant and kicked him smartly in the seat of his breeches. He cried out, jeering in Italian. "And how many of them have you served, old man?"

As Fortescue staggered, knees buckling, Bruno somersaulted furiously underneath the swinging arm and cut hard at his neck, backhand. There was the dismal clang of steel on iron. Fortescue came up under the blow, writhing his body in a great shrug and scissoring both swords close under Bruno's retreating chin.

Bruno kicked out, missing his mark but gaining space. He recoiled, reached for the fallen bust and flung it at the man one-handed. "You are slow!" he shouted with contempt as Fortescue smashed the missile aside with the flat of a blade. "The years are telling on you, *padrone*!" While he spoke he was climbing agilely up on the mantleshelf, which was broad as a road, twisting about and clinging to it with the toes of his boots.

In an instant I knew what he meant to do. There was a chandelier on chains overhead, a great thick spiked cartwheel of black iron covered in dead candles, gobs and strings of cold wax. Fortescue cut with one hand and thrust with the other, but Bruno launched himself out above the creature's head and caught the wheel easily, swinging like an acrobat on a high trapeze. He aimed a swift kick. Fortescue ducked so fast I swear his chin collided with his knees. He flung out all his arms to save himself from falling. I saw him helpless for an instant, and I threw myself at him, coming in from the other side, grabbing hold of one of his mechanical elbows and trying to fend off the other arm while I slashed at his side with my knife.

"Sophie, no! Keep back!" shouted Bruno from above me, seeing me about to be spitted any moment on Fortescue's sword like a winkle on a pin. He swung his body and throwing his feet out set the wheel spinning, whirling himself back around for another kick. Then I fell, hitting my face on the bare boards, lunging away with a strange hand grasping at my heel. I kicked with my other foot, thrusting myself away, frenzied as a goat trying to escape from the grip of an angel; and overhead I heard a clanging, crunching, tearing sound begin. "Lie down and rest, ancient one!" bellowed Bruno, his voice booming from the ceiling; and then the whole chamber shuddered with a mighty crash and I banged my face again and wrenched myself free.

I rolled over and looked behind me. Bruno had torn free the chain that held it and sent the giant chandelier crashing to the floor. In the darkness for a moment I thought he had floored the old man—I thought he must be trapped and crushed beneath the iron weight, impaled on its cruel spikes—but already he was slithering from the wreckage, rising up on all his limbs and rearranging himself like a clockwork scorpion. Bruno, who had jumped free and landed some distance off, seemed to have got the disadvantage of his desperate stratagem. Still he cried to me: "He is mine!"

Ignoring him I hurled myself back into the fray, stabbing wildly at the wide white eyes, the teeth long as a horse's. One arm whizzing like a fishing rod, the old man flung me from him, whipped me away like a tiresome minnow while all the time blocking Bruno's savage thrusts. I remembered savagery was not Bruno's way: how many times had he said so? He was the master of the subtle trap, the knotted handkerchief, the sudden gleam of unexpected steel in a lonely place. I bounced on my bottom, got my legs under me and attacked again, charging in on Fortescue's blind side as he tried to grab Bruno's flaring hank of hair and stab him in the gut. Bruno parried, skipping, danced a mad fandango. He was already cut somewhere, there was blood flying.

I looked at the disgusting silhouette of Lord Lychworthy's man and remembered the thousand-armed Hindoo demon of my childhood; how I had let him plague me, making me creep about the cottage in dread and hide under the sink when the big ships went over our roof—and I wondered what had become of that cowering, creeping little girl—and what would become of the reckless, perspiring, knife-waving little goblin I had grown into. Nothing: that was what I expected. I expected to be snuffed out immediately in a wave of scarlet pain. I feinted and ran aside, and found I had drawn the old man away from Bruno as he had drawn him away from me.

Around I wheeled with a scream, thinking I was playing tag with Johnny and Gertie Rodney, and landed a cut, long and shallow, down the old man's scrawny thigh. I knew I could break his arm, any arm, if I could get hold of one. "A wonder you have any visitors," I cried, running around behind him again, "if this is the welcome you give them!"

Croaking "His Lordship is not at home!" Fortescue whirled, slicing at both of us at once. Bruno had rolled away out of reach. I dodged, circled, trying to come between them. We had come far away from the candles now, our blades slivers of light in the deep green shadow. I was breathing hard, dancing from one foot to the other—I felt a presence behind my shoulder—another flicker of certainty, of knowing Bruno was there and understanding precisely where he would move and how I must bob down and which way we would carry the fight. I feinted straight at Fortescue's open chest where his glistening bare heart pumped, and as his guard arm came up darted back and to the left—but Bruno was not there.

The creature pounced. I scrambled, made another feint, bad, clumsy, and a blade slit the back of my hand across the knuckles. The pain was nothing, then sudden and vile and immense. I kicked at the horrible arm, making it drop its sword, and, just in time, flopped away from the other that came to chop me in two like an axe. "Bruno!" I shouted; but he was gone, I knew not where. Deserted me at last. My hand burned, my blood ran on the floor, I was gasping and panting, tired of the monstrous dance. The room was large and full of shadows, the creature old and unwieldy, but I could not dodge forever. I wanted to go and sit down on a couch and hear the stories of the stern-eyed men with black beards and compass badges that hung above us on the walls.

With his false hand the old man slapped me hard around the head, dizzying me. For an instant my legs forgot to run; and in that instant he had me well. His real hands gripped me by the elbows, while his telescopic arm snatched the knife easily from my hand and drew it back to skewer my vitals.

"Enough, Fortescue!" cried a deep voice from behind him. "What, man! Enough, I say!"

Like a machine unwound, the manservant stopped. His head slid out on his neck like a tortoise's from its shell, and swiveled jerkily to see who called him to heel.

It was Bruno. It was no one but Bruno, calling out in another voice, an elder, tougher, bully voice that Fortescue knew: the voice of his master. Slipping through the lapse of his attention, I kicked Fortescue on the shins; then Bruno was upon him, knocking him down, and me under him. I felt him take the iron-braced body in his arms, wrestling it up off my back. I struggled free and turned, knife up, to see Bruno climb astride Fortescue's back, his knees crushing the artificial arms up hard into his armpits, his right hand pressing the black hilt of his father's knife to the base of the manservant's wrinkled, hairless skull.

"Sir, consider!" said Fortescue. He did not say what it was Bruno should consider, but his arms were squeaking and flapping, his hands scratching at the floor like scuttling crabs, and he started to buck up from the ground, lifting Bruno on his back.

There came a sharp noise like tearing paper, loud in the empty gallery, and a bolt of blue light flashed across the faces of the master space mariners of old. Fortescue shrieked like a wild bird and folded up completely at my feet, arms and legs and swords clattering upon one another like tumbling billiard cues. Little brass wheels and loops of ligament sprang from his open armpit. There was a sudden stink of burnt flesh, hydraulic fluid, and dung.

I fell into Bruno's arms. He held me, hugged me. We panted in each other's arms, exhausted, excited, bleeding, alive. His own wounds were slight; he denied them, but kissed my hand, my blood running down his chin, and wiped another cut I did not know I had, over my eyebrow. He patted my back like a comrade. "You are a tigress," he said, and I burst into tears.

He held me a moment. "Don't weep," he said, rubbing my back. "Especially do not weep for him," he said, turning my face from the dead man on the floor. "Fortescue died long ago," he said, and he kicked a stray pulley away across the room. Then he let go of me and picked up the swords, and the dirk, which he gave back to me, squeezing my shoulders. "Courage!" he whispered. "We have a little time now."

From the polluted picture gallery we raced back up the corridor. I was in an agony of suspense waiting while Bruno picked the lock, but then in a trice we were inside, with the door closed behind us, and he was striking a lucifer for the gas. As the light flared up and steadied I saw we were indeed in the dread master's study, among licorice black furniture upholstered in leather of the deepest burgundy, with the crest of the Lychworthys, the eye and arrow, stamped on everything. There was a tangle of poisonous snakes in a tall glass jar, preserved in spirits, and around the walls a series of engravings of the hunt, as it takes place on the various worlds, and with its various prey. Like the gallery's, the fireplace gave warmth without fire, the heat of Io's molten heart rising up through a vent in the hearth.

And there were books—books in leather, and books in cloth, and books in boards held together by ribbon. There were almanacs, learned journals, Rossington's Tables in every edition, and all the books used to compile them. There were shelves and shelves of books and books and books; and shelves of files and boxes, and rows and rows of drawers. Bruno did not have to search, but went directly to the right drawer. I expected a speech, but he controlled himself, saying nothing absolutely and making no sign as he put a folded paper in my hands.

I unfolded it and saw it was an old sheet of good notepaper, with a short letter written on it. The address was only "St. Paul's," and a date some seventeen years earlier. She had had no formal salutation put to it, so that the scribe would not know who he was writing to. And thus it began, and continued, and concluded, and you shall have the whole of it, and judge for yourself.

"Your Lordship, I did not write until the child was born, thinking never to trouble you if it did not come to term. Now must I risk your wrath, begging your pardon, and call upon you in our need. Not for my sake, nor for the sake of the garden on the Moon, but all for her. And to assure you I will accept any conditions. She is whole and sound in body, but has no name until I know your pleasure. Your humble servant ever."

Thus much in good scribe hand, so I rued how she must have scrimped and starved to have it done, and naming herself hardly more than her child, signing it only "M."

"She didn't mention the ring," I said.

Bruno, whose eyes had been wide with expectation, now opened them wider, and his mouth. He clutched agitatedly at my shoulder.

"M?" he whispered.

"Her name was Molly," I said.

"And my patron?"

I held up the letter. "Was hers too," I said.

Curly red hair, I thought, and tried to picture the rest of her, not as she had been in my nightmares, but as a woman, in her life. Often had I wondered how she spoke, and what her last words to me had been; but Mrs. Rose couldn't describe the one or remember the other. There was no telling from this writing—I remembered how the sailors had liked me to do their letters home, putting formalities everywhere, "the courtesies" they called them, thinking they were obliged to. I wish I could have saved some of those letters I wrote in my office above the pub, to show you, but they are all long gone to their own readers, flown to the twelve corners of the universe, and all I have is Mrs. Rose's letter to Papa, which I have already written out for you, and this of Mama's to my true papa, which now I have written out for you too.

Bruno stood with his feet apart, holding up a fist and grinning fearsomely at the ceiling. "I knew it!" he exulted, though his voice was low with caution. "But Sophie, are you sure?"

"He used to take her to the Moon." I folded the letter carefully back along its creases. I saw I had already smeared blood on it from the cut on my hand. I felt as if I were very cold, hanging in space, somewhere very far away from everywhere else. I unfolded the letter and looked at it again. " 'And to assure you I will accept any conditions,' " I read.

Bruno spoke rapidly. "You see now how I could not tell you, I did not know who was M, and what child, whose, never does she altogether say that she is his, this child: she does not say those words. You see now, I knew nothing. But I knew!"

I remember I pressed the letter to my bosom, as though defending it from him. "How did you know it was there?" I asked.

"It was on his desk one time when I came to see him. It looked so different from all his normal papers, all the Guild proceedings and reports of expeditionary companies—*dunque*, I grew curious. He turned to fetch down a book, I read the letter. Upside down," he added, not without pride.

"You made quite a study of it," I said.

He smiled apologetically, and ran his hand down his pony-tail. "On Deimos, they teach you: the first thing you must find out about your patron is, what one thing does he not wish anyone to know?" Then he pulled a face. "Here it is not one thing, it is everything." He swept his hand up the correspondence cabinet, as if each drawer were crammed with infamy, alphabetically filed and indexed. "But this," he said, gesturing to Mama's letter, "this was different. That is all business," he said. "This is the man himself.

"When he sent me out, I wondered. When I saw your face I was sure," said Bruno. "We are sensitive to faces, we artists," he said, him with the crimson of his painting splashed about his person. He put his arm around me, and bent his face on mine, and his eyes were as dark as a London sky in winter, when night finally loses hold and gives way to the morning—and I wished we were there, in the meanest hovel by the river, or anywhere but here on Io, in my father's study, thousands of miles from any help or rescue.

"Come now," he said, "we have been too long in this house already. Take the letter if you want it." He smiled broadly, without humor. "It is all the inheritance you will get, I think."

I took hold of his hand. I shook it, to make sure he was listening. "Where is he?" I said. "I want to see him."

He held me tighter. He said, "Don't be foolish."

"I want to see him," I said again. "I want to talk to him."

"He has ten ways of killing you without rising from that chair!" expostulated Bruno, pointing at the chair behind the desk.

"Then why isn't he in it?" I said.

"Because he thinks you are dead. He thinks Fortescue is even now disposing of our remains."

I said, "I'm not leaving this room until I've seen him."

My heart was beating like a tilt hammer. He says he could not tell. He says his own was beating too loud for him to hear.

"Then my place is here beside you," said Bruno.

"You're not to kill him," I said. He was about to object. I said, "You're to let me talk to him."

Bruno gave me a bitter look. He said: "You leave me no choice, for we shall certainly not leave this room alive." Then he dropped to one knee and clasped his hand to his heart, saying, "*Carissima*, I do not ask you to take my name. It has been steeped too many generations in the blood of men. But *signorina*, you who have remade me: grant me my heart's desire. Lady Sophrona Lychworthy, say you will be mine."

"Lady Sophrona Lychworthy?" I echoed, appalled. "That sounds horrible!"

From behind me came a soft whirr of hidden wheels, and a loud, lazy voice saying: "Perdita, I have always called you."

I turned and saw a section of the bookcase sliding aside and a portly gentleman in a dressing gown stepping out of a secret passage with a lamp in one hand and a bumper of whiskey in the other. The lamp was like the one in Mr. Cox's theater, that glowed without flame. Lord Lychworthy lifted it to look at me.

"Father," I said. It was all I could say. I was terrified.

He set the lamp down on the desk. He said: "I always knew you were out there somewhere. Little Perdita of St. Paul's. I knew you would turn up one day." His voice was deep, rumbling, brooding with subterranean fire, like the satellite he had made his home. Bruno's impersonation had been a good one.

Bruno had been poised the instant the shelves of books had started to move. He stood with his feet apart, the manservant's swords one in each hand; but the gentleman was in his most relaxed attire and wore no weapon, or none that I could see. It was hard, as he reached behind him and slid the false bookcase shut, to tell his mood.

Bruno lowered his weapons, though he did not move his feet. He stood like a sentry, though his turmoil boiled the aether in the room. "My Lord," he said firmly. "I resign from your employment."

"It's a bit bloody late for that," said the earl testily. He seemed to be moving slowly, as if troubled by aching bones.

The light caught on a gold ring he wore, set with a crystal. "My ring!" I said in surprise.

"*My* ring," he barked. "D'you expect me to believe you didn't know that?" He kept his distance, surveying me with his brutal eyes.

The Right Honorable Mortimer Lychworthy, Earl of Io, was a broad man with a broad face that was red from too much whiskey and port and pork and webbed with the harsh print of the aether wind. As I had guessed in that moment when the candlelight had revealed the faces staring from the walls of the picture gallery, his Lordship's hair was black and straight, and he wore it long, in the way a gentleman will who lives alone and has no care for the opinions of others. He wore no beard, but whiskers curly and full; his mouth was a hard straight line beneath his nose, which was full of fire, and most generously spread between his lowering eyes. They were large eyes, and dark as his hair. I no longer had any idea what my mother might have looked like; for I looked exactly like my father.

My terror flashed like quicksilver instantly to anger. "I was a babe in arms," I said.

Lord Lychworthy drank some of his whiskey. He seemed unimpressed. "What? Did she not leave you one of her famous letters? Did it take him to work it all out for you?" He asked, pointing contemptuously at Bruno, while he spoke at me.

"Have a care, my lord!" said Bruno sharply. "I answer now for the Lady Sophrona."

But the earl waved him down, not looking at him, striking the air between them with his fist. "I was not addressing you," he told him loudly. He took another gulp of whiskey, looking me up and down as if I were a despicable pet, a toy whose ability to amuse him he could only doubt. "Your mother was a whore, child," he declared belligerently. "What have you to say to that?"

"I say my father is a murderer," I said.

This did amuse his Lordship, and he laughed a short laugh.

"Why," he said, "so was mine a murderer, and so was his," he said, waving his finger at Bruno, "and so are all fathers, maybe." He glanced at Bruno then for the first time. "If his father had done his job properly, you would not be here now."

Up spoke Bruno again. "Be warned, sir, if you mean to harm her, you must come past me." He did not raise his voice, yet the tone of it cried: You have talked to him now, Sophie, let me have him!

Lord Lychworthy squinted at me. "Harm her?" he said. "The harm's already done, I'd say. Look at her. She looks like a bloody sailor-boy."

Bruno continued resolute. "I will not hear you insult her, my lord," he said.

"Bruno, no," I said.

The earl had no regard for a chivalrous knight. The corners of his mouth turned down. "She's my daughter," he boomed, "I shall say what I like about her." You could see him smothering his anger like a man who shovels ashes on a bed of coals. "And you, boy, can hold your impertinence!" he said. "And stop playing with those cigar cutters. Now your father," he went rumbling on, "he could have held me to a fight, but times are not what they were, and nor is blood, you can see *that* without spectacles."

Bruno's face set hard as stone. He looked at my father, and then at me, to see how I liked him. I sucked the blood that was clotting on my knuckles. I liked him not at all. He was too like my own papa, hard and black and flinty, his heart crushed in upon itself like a piece of coal.

But he said to me: "Damn your eyes, child, the game's up, and you win. I'll pay your price. What'll it be, to lock up your tongue? Jewels? A house? Shall I buy you an asteroid, you and your valiant boy?"

He slapped Bruno on the back, bruisingly hearty, and took my hand, crushing it between his own. I could smell the whiskey on his breath, the stale reek of his unwashed clothes. "You mustn't mind an old man who has no one to teach him better manners," he said, his harsh voice dropping almost to a whisper as he tried to soften it. "Come into the parlor, both of you, and take a glass of wine."

20

The last of a noble line

Bruno bridled. He was not impressed by this tender of hospitality. "Do you think me a fool, sir, that I would taste your wine, or allow her Ladyship to?"

I took his arm, thinking this opposition would never do. I tried to pacify him as the earl replied, mildly enough, "Your father didn't have a hand in everything in this house, Bruno." He eyed me as he led us from the room. "What about you, eh, Perdy? Spot of wine, will you? Course you will," he said with a grotesque wink, and pinched me on the arm. Then, turning heavily, off he went up the passage like an old badger seeking his lair.

I looked at Bruno. Bruno was watching the earl, every inch of the way.

"Ah, you'll wish you hadn't done old Fortescue in," prophesied the earl as he stumped ahead. "Good men are damned hard to come by out here, y'know." In dismay I understood he was making a joke of it. "Still, new blood, eh? The same all the worlds over. New blood prevails."

I did not know what to say. Bruno, discontented and wary, said nothing.

We stopped at an open door. "Ah," said the earl, as though discovering it himself for the first time, "the parlor. Come in, come in, both of you. Make yourselves at home."

He wound a handle on the wall and dim eternal lights began to glow, hanging in bowls of thick colored glass. I saw the parlor walls were hung with framed maps and rainbow-colored fans made of different birds' wings. There were no windows. The walls were the color of a ripe bruise, the leather chairs quite black in the grudging light. All the cushions were plump and stiff from never being sat on. The air smelled of char and rank Nippurese tobacco.

Determinedly I moved into the room, making for a chair that stood by the hearth, as if I were not already hot as a fresh-baked bun. His Lordship stopped me, calling heavily, "Oh, Lord, wait, wait."

I turned and saw him take up a cushion from a chair by the door and throw it past me into the chair I had been about to sit in. There was a little click, and under the arm of the chair a trap flew open and delivered something onto the cushion, something small and red and spiny that flexed and arched its back in confusion. It was a scorpion. If I had sat in that chair, it would have landed in my lap.

I blenched, while my father laughed hugely, slapping his sides. In the same instant Bruno's curved sword rose and came chopping down, slicing the poor creature in two and raising a puff of feathers from the cushion, which it split. My own knife was in my belt still: there had not been time between shock and stroke even to draw it.

My father laughed louder, and clapped his beefy red hands. Grim, Bruno scooped up the two still-twitching halves of the thing on the flat of his blade and flicked them into the empty grate, where they vanished, falling into the abyss beneath. Bruno's eyes met mine. I faced him stubbornly. My father was protecting me. He had sprung the trap to disarm it, and for no other reason. Would he not have disarmed us too, when we came in, if he yet meant me harm? Would he not have directed Bruno to leave his "cigar-cutters" in the umbrella stand?

"Good stroke, sir," the earl said, in his sport. "Glad to see you can still make yourself useful about the place." He toasted Bruno with his whiskey glass and swigged it off, waving him to take the chair next to mine.

Bruno held back, eyeing the chair. "Have you another little trap here for me?"

"Good God, boy," exclaimed the earl roughly, "we've seen your prowess—now let's sit down and take some refreshment like civilized human beings. Take your damn things off and sit down," he ordered, as he fumbled at the door of a cabinet. "Don't just stand there like a lump of suet. You were quick enough when you scuppered Fortescue." Another joke occurred to him then. Over his shoulder he said: "Sunk him with all hands, eh?" He laughed coarsely and phlegmily, and spat wetly and accurately into the grate. Then he eyed me like a sulky cow and mumbled, "Sorry, m'dear, filthy habit, I apologize."

Bruno looked pointedly at me as I set aside my helmet and began to undo my coat. Bruno unbuttoned his cloak and adjusted his partlet and his cuffs. He, too, that look said, would defer to me, humoring me in this lunatic charade. His guard, those shoulders promised, would never for a second be lowered. The swords he propped carefully against his chair.

Clumsily Lord Lychworthy poured a glass of red wine, and gave it to me. "Your obstinate good health, damn you," he said, returning to his cabinet. "I don't suppose you can sing at all, can you, miss?" he asked. "Your mother could sing, a damned fine voice she had."

I hated him then. I hated him talking about Mama so all the time. I wanted to jump up and say to him, "Why did you slit her throat, then?" Instead I sat tight and said: "I don't feel much like singing at present, if you don't mind, sir."

And all he said was: "Pity."

I thought of the coach, and the manservant, and a wave of fear broke across the back of my neck. "Perhaps later," I said.

He grinned and agreed: "Ah, you'll sing later"; and he poured another glass of wine.

I looked into the glass he had given me, wondering. How could you tell? How could I drink it? My gizzard was closed with mistrust and dread. Yet how could I not drink indeed, now I had finally tracked the beast to his lair and found him peaceable? Could I turn tail and abandon my course?

Father held the second glass out to Bruno, who shook his head, and would not look at it. My heart leapt for him. Why must he provoke the gentleman?

The earl spoke aloud, and sharply. "Oh for God's sake, boy, take the blasted broomstick out of your arse! A glass of wine," he said impatiently, re-presenting it to him, "to toast Perdita's homecoming."

I wondered if I had not set foot in Hell. Which was worse, the prospect of a trick and death in an instant; or having to live here from now on and keep house for this Minotaur? Perhaps Hell was no more than that, to be condemned forever to do over and over again what you have already done.

Bruno accepted his glass of wine. He watched me, his eyes full of lightning.

My father now poured himself a glass, rather larger than mine; and he lifted it, saluting me. "To Lady Perdita of Io," he said; and without waiting for us, he took a drink.

The glasses from the cabinet, I told myself. There was nothing in them, they were upside down. He has poured three glasses from the same bottle, and now he's drinking one. He deliberately saved me from the scorpion-thing. He is not Father Christmas, I told myself, but he is my father, and now he knows who I am and admits it. We've won, he said.

I knew that properly I should wait until Bruno had drunk, because that was how you did it when people toasted you; but it was not fair to make anyone do anything you would not. I had made up my mind to taste the wine, and so I did. It tasted rich and wonderful and strange. I was sure it was the best wine I had ever had. I tried to smile at my father without really looking at him, because I was still afraid, and then at once I looked at Bruno.

"Best French Burgundy," Father told us. "None of your blasted Italian muck."

Bruno lifted his glass and took a sip. He swallowed. I watched his eyes, to see if they relaxed or warmed. I could not see that they did. I could not see that they moved at all. They were fixed on me, as always. They were saluting me.

Then he coughed, and the stem of the wineglass suddenly snapped in his fingers. The bowl of the glass toppled gently into his lap, splashing wine everywhere. "*Porco Dio!*" he said, his voice thick and choked.

I wailed like a cat, sending my own wine flying as I flew to him. "Sit still," barked my father. "Sit down, damn you!" I would not. I flung my arms around Bruno. His jaw spasmed, again and again, like a fish, drowning in air. No other part of him moved. Howling, I shook his shoulders, splashing wine all over my clothes and knocking the glass to the floor.

"Leave that!" My father's meaty hand fell on my shoulder and drew me roughly to my feet. I shouted, trying to hang on to Bruno and grab for a sword at the same time. Brutally he hauled me off and pushed me back into my chair. I think I was keening, sobbing for Bruno. He was rigid, every muscle locked.

"He's not dead," rumbled my father. "I've got a job for him," he said. "He can have Fortescue's old job, once he's fixed up." He drank more wine. "D'ye know, miss, five generations Fortescue served, one way or another. Six, with you. Are you not drinking?"

"I don't want your wine!" I said.

He stared at me, irked. "There's nothing wrong with yours," he said. "You might as well drink it, it's the last you'll get."

I ignored him. I looked at Bruno, and I fear I started sobbing again.

"Leave that, devil take you," said the earl. "He wasn't worth your admiration. What, a flashy boy?" he said, enraging himself anew. He lashed out with his riding boot and kicked Bruno on the leg, though I cried out. "And what were you to him? You're nothing but an infernal nuisance. Two of my best men, now, you've cost me."

I was still gazing at Bruno, whose eyes now looked like glass. It was my fault; I had killed him. And now I was sitting here helplessly, doing nothing about anything. I was transfixed as he, by my father's will, his deadly will. I told my hand to reach for the dirk in my belt. I told it to; but it would not.

The earl was still storming. "My bloody brain must be addled," he declared, smiting his own forehead. "What, send down a lusty young man to deal with a helpless young filly?" he demanded, in a roar. "I think not, sir!" he cried, answering his own question. "Flesh and blood will have their way!" he said, and slapped his knee. "Once before flesh had its way," he said, "and here you are."

Haranguing me, he had turned from Bruno. I wanted to keep him so, that he be not kicked again. The earl seemed inclined to talk: so, I would talk. I wiped my cheeks, and looked around on the floor, pretending to search for my fallen wineglass. I sat to the side, shielding my knife from view. I said: "What was the name you called me, Father?"

"Perdita," he said, sitting down. "She gave you no name, damn her eyes, but I did. Perdita."

I said, "You're too late, Father." My voice was tight in my throat. "I've already got a name," I said. "I'm Sophie Farthing."

"Farthing," he said, reminiscently, taking a large swallow of his wine. "I remember she would say that. *Farthing by name*, she'd say, *though dearer than that to you by a long chalk, Captain!*"

Very well, I thought; let us talk about Mama. "Did she call you Captain?" I said.

"They call all men Captain," he told me. "She had no idea who I was, poor creature, not at first. By the time she knew, she'd become a habit with me. And I was a young fool, as all young men are fools." He reached out from his seat, to kick Bruno again, but he could not reach.

"Let me get you some more wine, Father," I said, and went over and picked up the bottle. "I met someone who knew Mama," I said, trying not to shake as I poured the rest of the wine into his glass. "Mrs. Clare, she called her."

"She was my Molly," he said. "My Molly Clare." He drank wine and grinned his piggish grin again. "*I dropped the Farthing*: that was the other thing she'd say." He laughed a chortling laugh. "*Dropped my farthing in the road*," he said, putting on a high voice like a woman's, "*and it rolled away down a hole. Would you like to see the hole where it went, Captain?*" His voice deepened again and thickened. "God's teeth, she knew how to stir a man—"

I think for a moment he had forgotten he was talking to his own daughter, or did not care. He said: "She had to go, in the end. They all have to go, in the end." He scowled, irritated. "Took it into her thick whore's head to write me a bloody letter."

He glared at me now in bleary disgust, and suddenly reached out and before I could summon up the nerve to smash it over his head, took the wine bottle out of my hands. He looked at it and saw it was empty. He said: "If you're not going to drink any more, then you might as well be off and good riddance to you."

I stared at him in apprehension while Bruno's knife called to my fingers. What did he mean? Was he sending me back to the ship? Was the *Unco Stratagem* waiting to ship me to some further exile, some flying ivory tower?

"Well? What the devil are you waiting for?" my father inquired heavily, waving his hand as if to waft me from the room. "Go on, go on!" he said, getting up himself. He picked up one of the curved swords and ran his broad thumb over the edge. "Lady Sophie Farthing!" he scoffed. "Whore's get! You can walk to yours, save my old bones. I'd call my man to convey you downstairs," he said, with a foul grin, "but damn me if he isn't indisposed . . ."

Downstairs was not away. I did not know what was downstairs. We had come down many stairs already, it seemed to me.

I had no choice. I knew my knife would be useless, even if he turned his back. He would be wearing armor beneath his clothes, secret devices of his own. His mouth would open half a yard and a swarm of Venusian piranha flies would fly out.

"I don't mind walking," I said. "I used to walk all over London."

He took his glass in one hand and the sword in the other, and fierce and careless it looked hanging from his clumsy fist. I walked before him along toward the picture gallery. I thought of the dead manservant lying in there, his unstrung limbs twisted and entangled with the wreck of the chandelier. As we came level with the doors I made up my mind to dash inside again. Then through the glass, by the light of the indefatigable candles, I saw the dim forms of my grandfathers ranked around the room; and I thought of their eyes staring down upon the last of their line as he disemboweled me. Already my feet had moved on past the doors. Helplessly I went on along the hot corridor.

"Through here," my father said. It was a huge dark room filled with the sound of clockwork, and dim shapes hanging in the air, where I thought to run and hide, to lose him at once; but as soon as I moved away I struck a metal bar hanging in midair that gave like a loose gate, swinging away from me; and there was a jangling of wires and a clashing of metal balls around my ears. Something struck me on the head and I stumbled, trying to save myself from falling, while everything I clutched at flew away from me. I knew it was a mechanical trap and now I should truly die, sliced like a piece of cheese: but my father laughed and cursed. "Get on with you!" he growled, and I heard a smash as he threw his empty wineglass at the machine.

I stumbled on to the head of a flight of stairs and was firmly conducted down to the floor below. How deep we had gone I did not know. There was no decoration down here, no statues, no paintings: only the walls crazed by the squeezing of the rock around them. There were no more lights until the earl took down a lantern that hung at the corner of a stair, and lit it with a match. We had just passed an archway closed off by a pair of varnished paper screens. Beyond, the lantern light showed where the floor had collapsed and the walls fallen into it. The stairs were thick with dust and tilted toward the wall, but I hurried on. "Slow down, confound you!" cried my father; and we went on together, down, in silence and dim light, down into the heat.

Nothing was occurring to help me. My hair was wet with sweat and stuck to my head like tow. I tried to make him talk again. If he would talk about Mama, well, so he should. "Was it on the Moon, sir," I asked, "where you gave Mama the ring?"

"No, that was before," he said. "Damn fool I was to give it."

I thought for a moment that was all he was going to say, and began to speak again myself; but he was going on. "I had to go back to Venus, and after to learn the bloody Trans-Solar Vortex. She was in tears. A bloody whore, in tears! I made her a lot of damn fool promises and gave it to her."

"I think it was her dearest possession," I said. While I spoke I quickened my step again, getting farther ahead of him down the sloping stairs.

I could hear his feet stumping down after me. "The devil it was," he said, in assent, "and a dear price she'd have set on it."

The stairway narrowed. "She meant you no harm, I'm sure, sir," I said.

"What do you call that letter?" he returned, cursing. "Black as any mail I've seen."

"She didn't even mention the ring!" I objected. I saw a door and ran for it, and grabbed the iron handle. The door was locked, I could not even shake it.

"I was a bloody fool to give it," said my father again, ignoring my antics, coming inexorably down the stairs behind me, "and she was a bloody fool to try it. If she'd held her peace, I dare say she'd be alive today."

I paused on the landing in the dark. I was hot and tired, and sick of myself, my indecision, my foolish hopes. There was nowhere to run here, nowhere to hide but in the shadows.

"She got her wages," said my father, coming down the last stairs, lantern high. "Payment in full. Ah, but you wriggled away, didn't you, you little grub. You've spent your whole damned verminous life, wriggling away from the skewer."

I thought of Bruno. I stood with my feet apart and drew my knife.

My father looked at me without his sour face changing. "I don't know what you think you can do with that," he pointed out, slowly, almost kindly. He leveled his sword at me, as though to demonstrate my mistake. His rasping voice echoed around the landing. "Your ma made a mistake. She's long gone. Why fill your last minutes with pain?"

"Keep away from me," I said; and though I clutched my knife, I found I still could not do anything with it. My hand shook, my arm was rigid. I found myself still backing away, tears of fury blurring my eyes.

"Shall I tell you something, my dear?" he said, advancing with the light. "You're going the right bloody way!"

The steps went down through rock and along a passage that ended in another heavy door. The end. My lungs heaved in my chest. Frantically I wrestled with the handle, and almost fell over when the door swung open. I jumped and jolted clumsily down a flight of rough-hewn steps, and landed on wood that sprang beneath my feet like the deck of an unsound ship. I could see the edges: it was not two yards wide. Beneath and all around was stifling hot darkness.

There was a narrow handrail on the right that ran off into the dark. I grabbed hold of it and with a lurch of horror felt it give, parting from its joints with a soft crunch of crystallized metal.

I threw myself down and lay flat on the planks, hearing something skid away along the deck behind me. I could smell hot, sour rock and bitter smoke, and there was a faint, low, booming noise going on.

"Here we are," said my father, coming down the stairs with his lantern.

I raised my head, quivering, pressing myself to the deck. I heard the noise, as of a torrent running far beneath me. Hot zephyrs caressed my face. I could see that we were on a kind of upside-down bridge that hung from a rock ceiling high above. Dimly ahead I glimpsed the broad slab face of the great underground cliff beneath the mansion. I supposed the bridge ran to it, and along the side of the gulf. There would be no protection there, but there would be rock to cling to. Beyond the railing here and beneath the boards was nothing. Nothing but darkness, pitch-black, darkness of unknown depth and suffocating heat.

I heard the sound of the lantern being set down; then the boards bounced beneath me as my father came toward me. I tried to get up. Instead I gritted my teeth and whimpered. It was my knife I had dropped, I realized, Bruno's knife. I craned over my shoulder. I could see it, ten feet away, between me and my father. I was on one knee now, pushing myself up. The cliff or the knife? I couldn't decide. Both, I thought wildly, and lunged for the knife, hand outstretched, and saw my father's foot come down and kick it off into space.

My fear bent time, stretching it. The knife was like a falling star, a tiny silver speck curving into the gulf of night, swallowed, gone. I turned to run along the bridge, but my heart failed me after half a dozen steps and I collapsed on the floor again. I heard myself wheeze, my chest seizing up as the fumes of Io filled it. My father came lumbering after me, dividing the darkness with his sword.

He seemed to be moving more slowly than ever. I supposed he rarely moved at all. Besides Fortescue and Mr. Cox and Bruno, he had a whole guild to do his bidding. A ship would take him to his seat in Parliament and another to his office on Venus. Then they would bring him home again.

"You do waste a fellow's time, you women," he growled. "All this time and trouble to do what your ma should have done with a hatpin."

"My mother loves me!" I bellowed. "She is not gone!" Could he not see her standing there, drawn up alongside the bridge, her hair like a red flag of danger? Like Jésus in the chapel at S. Sébastien, pointing to his flaming heart, Mama pointed to the inky hole in her throat. "I was all she had," I charged him, in a voice to split his ears, "but she sent me away, to keep me safe from you!"

"Nowhere," he said, "is safe from me."

Then I said a prayer indeed, not to God, but to a man that danced a high and narrow way across a great black void, with a burning fire below—I thought of Gertie and Abigail, and Mrs. Rodney with her arms around me while we watched him walk—Mr. Spivey! be with me now. No sooner had the silent words flown from my brain than I remembered: Jack Spivey fell. He fell, and died.

So now I faced my true papa. In fury it was all I could do not to fly at him. I sat hunched, my knees drawn up, while he came and stood over me.

"Where will you crawl now, kitten?" he murmured, panting slightly. He waved his blade to left and right beneath my nose, indicating the two edges of the bridge. "Will you oblige me and crawl off?" His chest was heaving with unwonted exertion and bad air. In the sidelong light I could see his face red and sweating, his eyes like gleaming stones.

I had read how murderers were troubled by dreams of their victims, that seemed to rise up still bloody and accuse them of their crimes. "I shall crawl into your sleep and shake your black heart, Father," I cried, "and you will never rest another night upon your bed."

My curse did not impress him. He gestured tiredly. "Will you jump?" he demanded.

"No I won't!"

"Must I kick you over?" Below I could hear the soft booming of the deep and distant fires. "Why must you make this hard for yourself?" he said. Hard for himself, he meant, a stout gentleman with all his servants dead. He drew back his sword to skewer me quite. "Devil take you!"

I dug my fingernails into the wood like little knives and shook my body from side to side. The bridge swayed under us, creaking. Father threw out his free hand to clasp the railing.

Then I it was who kicked, and kicked the mightiest kick I ever did. I kicked at the upright next along with all my strength, and felt it snap, and saw my father fall sideways.

I saw him for an instant in the lantern light, the way you do when something falls, as if he was frozen in the air, his mouth open in a roar, his dressing gown blown upward by the hot draft reaching up to claim him. His left foot was turned under and his right foot lifted, as though he thought to mount upon the air and climb upstairs to bed. Then he was gone, into the gulf, leaving only his roar behind, echoing, and that now dwindling and dying and fading for good and all, as echoes will.

I do not know how long I clung to the bridge and shivered and cried. It seemed like a year, a year of loneliness and grief, without Mama, without Papa, without my foolish and devoted champion. I was stranded on a gangplank over eternity, and not a soul in the universe knew where I was. So then I began to crawl indeed, pushing the lantern along the floor ahead of me, back to the steps with splinters in my hands, and only got to my feet to scramble through the last door. I banged it shut behind me as though something was going to come through it, up out of that abyss, some fiery-headed cousin of the Martian God tempted by that morsel of bait to come and eat up the last of the Lychworthys. Up the stairs I ran, expecting any moment a mantrap under my foot, a huge axe swinging silently out of the dark. Nothing happened. Safe and whole and alive I went back upstairs to the parlor where Bruno sat in his chair as still as death, still holding up the broken spike of the wineglass, and I knelt before him and hugged his knees and wept and wept and wept.

His heart beat slow and he was breathing slow and shallow. I did not know what to do or fetch for him. There was nothing in the house I would trust: no medicine for Bruno but my groans and salt tears. How I wished I had Kappi there, who had always been a better nurse than I to poor Papa, or Mrs. Rodney with her possets and poultices. As I wiped the sweat from Bruno's stiff, hot face I remembered how he had looked as Signor Pontorbo, how real he had seemed, how much he had hidden.

My own cuts and bruises were stinging, and I had begun to shake again. I took the chair that the scorpion-thing had come out of, not trusting any other, and there I sat on the ruined cushion and kept watch. A dozen times I started up, sure he had stopped breathing; a dozen times I sank down in my seat again, seeing how the feather trembled that I held before his lips. "He is dead, Bruno," I told him sternly, "but you must not die. You must live." I posted a lozenge between his unresponsive lips and pressed them a little, with my fingers, like a promise. Then I sat while an hour crawled past, and fell asleep from very exhaustion, dozing in the chair, dreaming that Mrs. Rose and I walked on the tops of grass green hills singing of Molly Malone and ringing handbells until I realized it was all the clocks in the mansion striking together and I woke in confusion and terror. Nothing had stirred. Bruno was unchanged.

The sight of him sitting there before me like a waxwork filled me with a hundred contradictory thoughts. I despised him for tasting the wine—I cursed myself for making him do it—I wept for his impetuous spirit, that my father had set his thumb on like a candle flame. I thought of all the hours Bruno and I had spent sitting like this on the *Gioconda* with easel and canvas between us, and longed to have those hours back. I remembered all the times we would not speak to each other, and could not believe it. How could I have dwelt in such a state and not expired at once from very happiness? And how was it I could not expire now that I wished to, from very misery?

The physicians tell us melancholy is a disease most often contracted in solitude. When a person is shorn of family and friends, her first true swain struck down before her eyes; when she is far from home, hardly knowing what place she should call by that name, or on what world; when all around her is betrayal and death: then she may be lonely and desolate indeed, and feel the *kiiri* coming for her heart. I had saved my own life; but what could a life be if it was alone?

I threw myself from my chair and clung to Bruno tighter than to a swaying mast, tighter than I'd ever clung to Gaston when he swept me up into the Martian sky. Then I slid down and collapsed at his feet, and laid my head in his lap and wept. I told him I loved him, and begged him not to leave me, and I wept. I told him I thought I could now see my way clear to accepting his offer of marriage; and still I wept. Bruno sat unmoved, unmade, extinct. I could not think how there could be tears enough in me to weep it all out.

Then something hit me on the shoulder and bounced off onto the carpet with a soft thud.

It was the base of the broken glass. Bruno's fingers had

opened a fraction, and it had fallen on me. And now his hand fell on me too, clumsily, shakily, like a donkey's first caress.

"Bruno, be careful!" I cried. "You'll knock me out next!"

But his eyes started to shine with the slow intelligence of life dawning on the shores of distant worlds. Two large tears brimmed in them and ran down over his cheeks. He was alive; breath moved between his lips.

Dear Reader, I think you have been mightily patient with me all this while, and a great long while it has been, full of little difficulties and diversions, and infinite details of commonplace things that must have been of no interest to you at all. But I hope you will forgive me if I give myself room here to admit that I did kiss him then; and if that is a shame, then I must blush indeed, for it was such a kiss as threatened to suck out all his returning air—and mine too, very like, for his lips were bitter from the wine; but its poison was spent and no more harm could it do.

"Bruno," I apologized, wiping his face, "I am covered in blood and smoky as a chimney sweep . . ."

But he scrupled not, and leaned forward then and kissed me in turn, and thus so on and so forth, as you perchance may know; and if you do not, in truth you do not need me to tell you, for you may read of kissing in any novel, I think, save only Mr. Crusoe's.

So now I have told the tale as I undertook, of my long and winding journey home; and the rest is little enough to say. We would not eat or drink again in that house, and Bruno could not yet stand or walk unaided. There was a strange coiled creature like a tall thin snail, browsing in the hallway. He knew how to command it, and it rolled along beside us, fitfully, with Bruno leaning on its back while I supported him on the other side. It took another hour and more to creep our slow and painful way back to the surface, where I found the poor burnt ox had come back, looking for water. I coaxed it with a handful of hay and caught it with a rope and somehow, while it was drinking, with the best and strongest knots I knew I tied Bruno behind it, on a broken chair for a litter. Then we left the mansion to the care of the disconsolate snail and I drove the ox, creeping and stumbling through sleet and snow, down the road that leads below Hunchback Fell, until we came in sight of the bay where Captain Andreas was keeping a good watch. They ran to meet us and brought us aboard, and gave us brandy and good air and hot soup and ointments for our hurts; while under full rising sail we lifted up and flew, up through the thick green morning, bound on a course for Venus, to throw ourselves upon the mercy of the guild. I remember how the Sun swung in the rigging like a golden bell, and all the stars strewed themselves in our path like silver lace.

Epilogue

At the Port of Venus, palm trees shade walls of pied brick. The names of the great navigators are picked out in gold mosaic over the gateways. FERRERA, they say. PHILEMON. COOK. Along the colonnades the marble busts of the fathers of flight, sternly bearded, gaze from their niches into nothingness. Applicants to the Most Exalted Hierarchy and Worshipful Guild of Aether Pilots are tested on the names of these, and all the statues that stand around the quads. The steward of the Aeyrie knows them all, every star-browed sylph, every astral deity. Today, he barely gives them a glance.

He takes a shortcut through a gate marked OFFICIALS ONLY, into a cobbled yard. He walks along past a trellis screen, quite new but already half covered in vines. Behind it there are peacocks wandering about, green pheasants from Japan, a mulatto groundsman sweeping up fallen leaves. An elderly captain in a braided cap and visor sits rapt in conversation with an angel. The captain is smoking a cigar in an adapter, nonchalant, despite the atmosphere. He is talking to the angel with his hands, in Vacuumic. He makes the sign for "victuals." The angel, highly civilized, sits with his head forward, his hands on his knees and his wings politely folded. With one hand the captain gestures to the unseen stars. "Andromeda," he signs.

Inside, beneath the dome of the Grand Concourse, things are less sedate. There are always a few people about the port, shellbacks yarning, bystanders, idlers: old men especially, who pass their days in the public rooms, looking up charts and arguing interminably over the so-called "mistakes" in Rossington. Are they printers' errors, as everyone assumes; or do they in fact conceal a code, revealing the names of the True Zodiac and the Path of the Phoenix? Wizened sailing hands debate the merits of the Dutch fivefold set, and compare it with German parallel rig.

Others, more solitary, stroll around the perimeter fence with stick and binoculars and perhaps an old hound for company. They pay no attention to the balloons that rise and fall, taking passengers and crew to the high landings. Only when something winks silver, there, in the west, do they turn smartly and raise their glasses to scan the brilliant air. It is some Callistan caravel, some issuing barque throwing on sail, like a bud opening suddenly in the face of the Sun. The old men's eyes gleam and they mutter enthusiastically in their respirators.

The old women dress all in black and gather on the benches in the Concourse, like a jury of crows along a wall. All week they have been coming by threes and fours to see the dignitaries and foreigners arriving for the ceremony. Today, the day itself, the place is full of sightseers. The orbital heliographs have carried the news, and everyone from a hundred miles around is here. They have been here since five this morning, some of them, drinking bottled ale and eating pomegranates, the children clutching their wilting posies of violets and patriotic ribbons. They have put the harbor master to the trouble of hiring deputies to keep them out of the way.

An excited murmur starts up, and a surge toward the windows. Someone has seen the balloon coming down. Who will it be this time? The constables link hands. It is this arrival that has drawn the steward from his demesne; yet he can see nothing, not even the famous ornamental clock overhead, the one in the shape of the Roc of Madagascar carrying off an elephant: for the steward is not tall, and the crowd does not see him; nor does it let him see anything but knees and stomachs, while poking him with its telescope cases and umbrellas.

Flaring red with urgency, the steward pipes up, calling for the guild marshals. There will be another delay now, before the door of the balloon car opens and the traditional whistle blows, piping All Ashore. If the expected latecomer is not on board, the steward must go back at once to the Aeyrie. There is much still to be seen to. The flowers must be sprayed with fresh water, and the crusts cut off the sandwiches.

These niceties are not simply the result of the wedding. The Aeyrie is not what it was. These days there are cushions at high table and hairpins in the washbasins. An Ophiq, and constitutionally stoical, the steward has taken these feminine innovations in his short but sturdy stride. He has never been heard to complain. He is surprised at the rituals the males of a differentiated species impose on the females, and at the way the females encourage them—the work is no different, after all. But the women are only part of the upheaval.

Since the last president perished so suddenly, with neither a will nor a legitimate heir to be found, the guild has been in the hands of first the council, and now, since the resignation of three-sevenths of that august body, a managerial board. The League must intervene soon in the question of the succession, which is debated constantly. There is no shortage of candidates, but there is a problem of the lack of kin, the surprising number of accidents and misfortunes which have lopped the branches of the Lychworthy family tree. Few candidates claim consanguinity; in fact, not all are human. Hence the resignations, rows, recriminations. Some men in the Junior Commons got up a spoof nomination at the hustings: Beauregard Crii for President. They climbed up the tower and hung a banner, Votes for Roosters, and were pelted with buns by advocates of Montmorency and the Cornishman.

The dark-eyed girl has her adherents too, and not only among the women. There have been more duels over her than any other, yet she still refuses to be nominated and has never shown favor to any man's suit. Only the love of the press and the people she has been unable to reject. They have loved her from the day she landed: how thrilling, how unique, the Navigatrix, the woman who can fly a ship! They love her for her mystery, her fidelity, for the quiet nobility with which she endures her cruel loss. Some call her the Countess, though of course she is no such thing. She can have no claim to the title or estate, though privately the steward knows she has had an income settled on her and enjoys exclusive use of her late cousin's villa in Nice.

Nor is her accomplishment so unique now. Since the dramatic emergence of Miss Sophie Farthing, first a dozen, and then a score of women have appeared with the talent—daughters of the famous lines, to begin with; then the stepdaughters, the sports, the hopefuls, and the frauds and publicity seekers. No doubt there are hundreds of others we shall never hear of, who never venture offworld in all their lives: undiscovered pilots, condemned to steer nothing more exalted than a perambulator.

The cadets will all be there today, of course, men and women alike, in the congregation. Training flights have been canceled and the Celestial Mechanics class will be let out early, in honor of the bride. At this hour, however, she herself is still on duty. She is in the scriptorium with pen and scissors, altering charts to incorporate the latest discoveries by scouts and explorers all over the Western Reaches. While she waits for the paste to dry, there are the digests of theses presented to the Urania Institute to be annotated, in ink, in accordance with reports from Calliope and Carlsberg.

The board and her tutors have thought best to keep her working, during the last days, in this menial capacity. It adds the right note of humility and duty. Such things are to be thought of, in these uncertain times. The more fanciful gentlemen of the press must be discouraged from their irresponsible speculations, the dignity of the guild upheld. Time enough for sentiment and jubilation after the ceremony, when the mob at the harbor will see her depart with her new husband.

Under the wrought iron sign ARRIVALS the doors swing open at last. The curtain parts, and a cheer goes up from the crowd. It is she, in person: the celebrated Miss Evadne Halshaw, Siren of the Aether, resplendent in a high-collared dress of pink tulle, layer upon layer, and a leopard-skin coat. So regal is she one could almost fancy she was one of the allegorical figures: Celestial Harmonia, accompanied by a faun. The onlookers throw flowers, their tributes of admiration outdone by the official wreaths, the bouquets of Cytherian amaranth and gladioli. She raises her visor and acknowledges their applause with a slender hand.

Miss Halshaw's escort is a member of the guild: Captain Tobias Estranguaro from Caraway, her business manager and the pilot of her yacht. He trots forward in his brass-buttoned blazer and caprine spats. His fleece, his whiskers, and mustache are iron gray. He preens and struts, directing the diva's retinue with flourishes of his cane; while the nearest spectators, the true aesthetes and lovers of music, wince and lift their nosegays to their faces.

With much bowing and deference the marshals gather up the unpunctual pair and conduct them to the steward, who welcomes them formally on behalf of the guild. Miss Halshaw, never the most conventional of women, vexes him by picking him up and kissing him on the snout. He turns bright mauve and the crowd squeals with delight.

Flustered, the steward manages to coax and chivy the pair into the coach. The retinue, with trunks and hatboxes and ostrich-feather fans, must follow on, keeping up with the marshals as best they can.

Miss Halshaw waves to the crowd. "Toby, Toby, are you sure we've got the wedding presents?"

Captain Estranguaro opens his mouth, lolling out a pointed tongue, very purple and very wet. "Didn't I see them loaded before everything?" he says thickly.

The pair have been quarreling, but now Miss Halshaw wishes peace. She strokes the hair between the stubs of his horns and cries: "Toby, what should I do without you?" and beams at the steward as the coach jogs and jolts along the forest road to the Aeyrie. The heavy flowers outdo even Miss Halshaw in the vividness of their colors.

They get back just in time. The bells are ringing, and the guests are all assembled. They make a rather peculiar assortment. There are distinguished gentlemen, former officers from the great yacht *Sophrona*, making stilted conversation with the swarthy captain of the cruiser *Gioconda* and the crew of a humble cargo clipper called the *Appleby Bull*. Three French nuns from a Martian order stand looking askance at a contingent from a public house in London—and not a public house merely, but one the wrong side of the river. Merry as they are, this gang of fishwives and market porters seem to be behaving themselves.

The steward looks at his list. Places of honor are occupied

by a Mrs. Rodney, her son John and daughter Gertrude, and Norman, Gertrude's husband. Mrs. Rodney looks uneasy in a full crinoline and keeps saying how happy she is, and crying copiously. Of aliens, there is a Cærulean family chirping and capering about in a way that makes the steward glad that they are not to be allowed into the chapel itself; and a large, fat Lizard, who claims to represent the mayor of High Haven. The steward has also seen one of his own people in an extraordinary hat, in intense conversation with a thin, consumptive starman. The guild itself has made a splendid turnout, though many of the older members are conspicuously absent. The cadets fill the first three rows, the women looking very smart with their pastel corsages pinned to their uniforms.

Triumphantly the organ sounds, and the bride enters on the arm of Mr. Rodney. She looks a little pale and self-conscious, her beautiful large eyes modestly cast down. So much public attention does not agree with her, the steward knows. He likes her; she always has a kind word for him. He is sure she will feel better when it is all over and she and her new husband can be alone. They will spend the first fortnight of the honeymoon in Nice, then go on to Mars to join the imperial grand tour, as the personal guests of the young emperor.

Little, still, is known about the groom. He got in only this morning, returning from guild business in the Centaur. He walks with some difficulty, leaning on a stick. He is a private gentleman from the South of France, and also an accomplished painter, according to the *Times*. His series of Martian landscapes hangs in the Louvre. It is understood that it was he who discovered the long-lost Miss Farthing on Mars and took her to meet, for the first time, her illustrious distant cousin; and that he himself was injured in the tragic great eruption that destroyed the house on Io, master and all.

The steward knows more than that. He knows the order the young man recently resigned from, and how many of his anonymous, sober-suited attendants are his former colleagues. The steward spent some anxious minutes earlier in persuading them to respect the sanctity of the chapel by leaving their more obvious blades in the cloakroom.

Duty is a stern master, and no respecter of sentiment. The steward hears the vows murmured, and sees the ring, and then he is obliged to miss the entire rest of the ceremony in attending to one of the Earthwomen, a Miss Betty Pride, who has fainted from a combination of excitement, altitude, and foreign air. By the time he returns to the reception, he finds that the Cæruleans have spoilt half the canapés with contributions of their own and cannot be stopped from urinating in the plant pots. Meanwhile, carried away by the emotion of the occasion, Miss Halshaw has begun her promised performance ahead of time. She is trying to summon the scowling Captain Andreas of the *Gioconda* up onto the stage to accompany a selection of rousing space chanteys on his bent and battered flute. Meanwhile her companion, Captain Estranguaro, is stalking the waitresses, his scut visibly twitching.

Before he can intervene to calm ruffled tempers the steward is brought up short by an urgent trilling hoot in the Ophiq language, meaning, Hurry, come quickly. The fellow he saw before, the one in the hat, summons him to the roof, where a party of the angel folk has just arrived from Mars. There are half a dozen of them, carrying bizarre wedding gifts: a bag of stones and a wreath of shaggy feathers for the bride and groom. They are the wild desert angels from the south. No one knows how they came here. Several of them are naked or nearly so. The claws on their hands and feet are hard and brown as varnish. They stink to high heaven, grinning like cats, and jostle one another. But how beautifully their wings shine, golden in the sunlight!